THE NORTH BEYOND

PART 3 : HALDUR

P.M. Scrayfield

Pen Press

First published in Great Britain

All paper used in the printing of this book has been made from wood
grown in managed, sustainable forests.

ISBN13: 978-1-78003-491-1

Printed and bound in the UK
Pen Press is an imprint of
Indepenpress Publishing Limited
25 Eastern Place
Brighton
BN2 1GJ

A catalogue record of this book is available from
the British Library

Cover design by Jacqueline Abromeit

CONTENTS

... the story began with:

THE NORTH BEYOND
Part 1 : Numirantoro

THE NORTH BEYOND
Part 2 : Maesrhon

and continues with:

THE NORTH BEYOND
Part 4 : Artorynas

V DREAMS

CHAPTER 33

Farewell to a dream

At the back of the porch, where the first, faint, hint of dawn had not yet touched the darkness, a door opened quietly and a young man stepped out. Treading softly, he came forward and leaned for a moment on a supporting post, and then sat down on the timber boarding of the porch. He was heavily muffled against the chilly air, for today, when the Cunorad would not be riding out, he felt the cold strike him as harshly as it would any other man. Wriggling his toes inside his boots, he pulled his hands up inside the sleeves of his wadded jacket and chafed his fingers. The sky was beginning to brighten as dawn came nearer. Across the valley to his right, the high crags that shut in Rihann y'n Temenellan stood out from the general darkness, cracks and fissures showing up in sharp relief. The young man turned his head the other way, and there above the eastern side of the valley floated soft banks of cloud, aflame with a glory of gold and rose against the clear icy blue of the sky. He could see the gap in the hills where the road climbed through the pass. How many times had he ridden that way in dawns such as this, or up to the head of the valley where the tracks were steep and rocky beside the stream! The resinous scent of the pinewoods reached him on a sweet breath of morning air. Staring away before him, he heard the voice of the river as it rushed down into the valley where shadow still lingered: Lissad y'n Cunorad, river of the hounds, as swift and sure as the Cunorad themselves. The sunlight was creeping further down the mountain-side and now it fell on a curl

1

of smoke rising from the chimney of the house behind him. He heard soft trampling from the stables as the horses, catching the smell of smoke, began to move restlessly in the straw of their stalls, knowing that soon their riders would come to greet them.

The young man got to his feet and walked down the three steps of the porch. Here in the north, even in springtime the temperature often dropped below freezing for a couple of hours before the dawn. He felt the cold nip at his nose, and his breath misted on the air; but already steam was wisping off from the roof of the woodshed and he could see great clouds of it drifting up from the woods across the valley as the sunlight strengthened. He walked down to the gate, and then turning to the left strode briskly around the fence, climbing up the slope at the back of the buildings so that he could look down on Seth y'n Temenellan. Shoving his hands into his pockets, he bit his lip hard. The climb had set his blood moving and banished the chill from his feet and limbs, but he felt that today nothing could warm his heart or lift the shadow upon it. As he stood there he saw the two men who had arrived yesterday to escort him home come out from the guest building and head towards the stables. It was no good moping. After all, he had always known that this day must come. It was just that he had so very much hoped that it would be during his time with the Cunorad that they would find what they sought. Now it would never be, not now that his father had sent men with the message that he must return. With a sigh, he jogged back down the slope, jumping from one boulder to another where they jutted through the thin grass.

All too soon, it was time to leave. They had eaten, and the men of his escort were waiting for him. The four horses they had brought were very different from the horses of the Cunorad, which were light, fast and sure-footed, matched for colour so that even in the stable their bright, golden-chestnut coats gleamed with a burnished glow. Now he looked into the faces of those who had been his companions these last two years. He wondered whether any of them would feel called to make their commitment lifelong. There stood old Cunor y'n

Temennis, the Hound of the Vow: one day someone else would take his place. I would have made that vow, he thought, but the choice of how I spend my life is no longer mine to make. Suddenly, defiance flared within him. No matter that he was dressed now for the journey back to his old life, with the sign of his rank upon him. While he was still within the precincts of Seth y'n Temenellan, he still counted himself a member of the Cunorad, and he would leave them with the farewell they used among themselves before those wild dawn rides. Stepping forward with set and solemn face, he touched each forehead lightly, speaking their names as he did so. 'Cunor y'm Eleth, Cunor y'n Gillan, Cunor y'n Vala, Cunor y'm Ardo,' he greeted them, using the names they had taken when they came to join the Cunorad; but they did not use his in return. Even Esylto, though he looked into her face and named her Cunor y'm Esc, used his given name in reply. Baffled and hurt, he turned finally to the old man, who was gazing past those who stood near, looking out on the dale as it opened to the new day and the mountain heights reaching into the wide morning sky. The faded eyes switched their focus to the face before them and the Hound of the Vow put up his hand to touch the young man's forehead and leave him with words of comfort. 'For you the search is not over, Cunor y'n Tor.'

Almost a week later, the three travellers made camp as evening approached. They saw to the animals, gathered wood for a fire and prepared a meal. As they sat around the embers in the twilight, their talk died away as each man attended to his own thoughts. Eventually one of the escort sat up and stretched, and then lay back comfortably with his arms behind his head.

'Back home in Cotaerdon tomorrow, then,' he said, 'and getting there by roads fit for horses from now on, not these goat-tracks where you've had us risking our necks.' His teeth showed white in the dusk as he grinned across at the young man. 'No wonder those who come out of the Cunorad with their skin still in one piece make the best riders! But mind you remember to tell your father why it's taken us a week to get back. We'd have done it in half the time if we'd gone over the low pass into Two Riversdale.'

An answering grin flashed back from the other side of the fire. 'He'll know I just wanted a few more days of freedom. But don't worry, I'll take the blame and tell him it was my fault. Were you ever in the Cunorad yourself?'

'Me? You must be joking. I was a married man by the time I was eighteen: I had to think about where the meals would come from, not where the Hidden People might be found.'

His companion dug him in the ribs. 'Come on, tell the full story. You were only married because there was a child on the way and your marriage-father was breathing fire and vengeance.' They all laughed, the first man rather sheepishly.

'All right, all right, tell everyone, why don't you! The old boy's calmed down now, anyway. Proud as can be, I reckon: three grandsons and a grand-daughter, and me with a place in the lord's household. He soon stopped ranting about his daughter's dishonour when he saw I could make my way in the world.'

The young man had been enjoying the banter, but now he fell quiet again, twisting the arm-ring he wore – the ring that his companions had brought with them when they arrived in Rihann y'n Temenellan. His brother Heredcar had only worn it for such a short time! He could not ignore how tight it was; he had had to spit on his arm to get it on in the first place. But at least he knew it was not the final one of the set. He looked up from his musings.

'Why has my father sent for me? Why not Vorardynur or Asaldron?'

'Well, Vorardynur's still with the Cunorad, isn't he?'

'So was I, come to that. But they are my cousins, and both older than I am.'

'Must have been what the elders wanted, I suppose. Can't think why they'd choose you, but there's no accounting for taste.'

This was delivered dead-pan and the young man responded to the fellow's teasing with a laugh and a friendly shove: no-one stood on ceremony much in the Nine Dales, where lordship was earned and then worn lightly.

'Yes, but why now?'

'Look, how would I know? I might have a place in Lord Carapethan's household, but that doesn't mean he tells me his private thoughts. All I know is, he called me in and said we'd to come and fetch you back. "Tell Haldur I need him here, it's time for him to come home", that's all he said. But I can tell you one thing,' the man added, rather gruffly. 'I'm glad you're coming back to Cotaerdon. I've missed you about the place and I've not been the only one.'

His words were borne out the following day, as they made their way along the road that wound through the villages and hamlets of Rihann y'm Aldron down towards Cotaerdon, the chief town of Rihannad Ennar, the Nine Dales. People waved and smiled when they saw Haldur, and some of the young folk left their tasks to run up to the roadside and greet him. The valley opened out and there where it joined Rihann y'n Riggan was Cotaerdon, built on the fertile, level land where the valleys met but protected on two sides by the rivers; a few miles beyond the town the Lissa'riggan poured into the Forest River and the doubled waters, broad and deep, refreshed the fields of Rihannad Ennar's most heavily settled valley before flowing away southwards out of sight and knowledge. By late afternoon they were trotting through the smallholdings and gardens that lay on the outskirts of the town, accompanied by quite a crowd who had come out to meet them as word of their approach spread. Haldur spotted friends and acquaintances and his smile widened as he acknowledged the cries of welcome. If he could have had his wish, he would have stayed with the Cunorad y'm As-Geg'rastigan; but his open, generous nature could not help but respond to the people's goodwill. He had always been well-loved, even while Heredcar was still alive, and now that the sorrow and loss that men had felt at his elder brother's death was beginning to fade, he was more popular than ever. Haldur realised, with a pang of regret, that now even he could summon up only a hazy memory of Heredcar's face, although in his mind's eye his brother stood for ever young, tall and good-looking, golden and strong like their father Carapethan.

Family duty

The lord of the Nine Dales came out to greet his son when he heard the little cavalcade arriving outside the hall. As Haldur and his companions dismounted, he stood smiling on the porch, shading his eyes from the level sunlight of early evening. Carapethan typified his people: it was as if all their characteristics met in him but were somehow magnified by his position as their leader. His hair and beard were thick and fair, although now that he was in the second half of his fifth ten years there were ashy streaks of grey at his temples and lips. When he rode out, or took exercise of any kind, he braided his hair; but when, as now, he was at leisure in his hall, he wore it loose. It fell to his shoulders, held back by a circlet of twisted gold wirework. His eyes were bright blue, in a frank, high-complexioned face with ruddy cheeks under a tan that came from many hours in the open air. Middle-age had thickened his waist and put a little weight on his muscular frame, but he was still powerfully-built and strong, a bear of a man. He had the air of someone who enjoys life to the full, especially its good things: food and drink, companionship, mirth and laughter; and his authority fitted him well, sitting easily on his shoulders like a familiar cloak. Yet for all his bluff exterior and hearty manner, there was a shrewdness in the vivid blue eyes, and a lifetime's experience of leadership informed his mind: he was rarely wrong in his judgement of men.

Nor was he a stranger to sorrow. There had been dark hours in his life, sad times that had left their mark in the lines that traced his forehead. Heredcar's death in young manhood, the result of an accident that need never have happened, and the loss of his wife not two years later had been bitter blows. But those who lead cannot surrender to grief as other men may, and Carapethan had forced himself to continue with his duties, upheld by the love and support of his folk. In due time he had married again, to a widow with no children of her own. She was a quiet, serene woman who brought him peace and comfort; and when it became clear that there would be no second family with competing claims for precedence to worry over, his people too were well content. And now his younger son was home again. Carapethan wrapped his arms around Haldur in a tight embrace and then held him off by the shoulders, inspecting him with a smile of welcome.

'A bit taller, I think, but not much wider! Don't they feed you, up there in the clouds? Well, come on in. I hope you're hungry now because they've been working all day in the kitchens in honour of your return. Aldiro's waiting inside to welcome you; I'll be back in a moment after I've just had a word here.'

Carapethan crossed over to the stables for a quick handshake of thanks with the two men who had escorted his son from Seth y'n Temenellan; he never forgot to show his appreciation of service rendered, knowing it was always time and thought well spent.

Haldur took the steps of the high porch two at a time and found his stepmother standing just inside the doors. The two of them could easily have passed for mother and son, but then Aldiro was not unlike Carapethan's first wife Ellaaro, whom Haldur resembled more than he did his father. As Carapethan had already remarked, he had grown a couple of inches during his time with the Cunorad; but even though now he was very slightly the taller of the two, he was still only just over average height. In build he recalled Ellaaro, with a light frame compared with most of his stockier fellow-countrymen. He was certainly much less powerfully-muscled than his father, though as strong as any even if more spare. Like most men in the Nine Dales he was fair rather than dark, but where Carapethan had strong, corn-coloured hair with a lift to it that took it off his face, Haldur's hair was straight and heavy, its weight making it hang in a thick, shining mop which would fall back into place even when the wind blew it awry. It was browner, too, especially in the winter-time; but because this was caused by red, gold and even some black strands among the dark-honey tones, the sun could bleach it to an unusual silvery gleam, rather like the sheen on willow-leaves when they turn in the breeze. Not that Haldur's own mind had any such picture of himself: he would joke that when the springtime tan on his body deepened as his hair lightened, there came a time each year when he was the same colour all over. He had a store of such self-deprecatory quips, an armoury built up from the heightened awareness of early adolescence, when there had seemed such a contrast between what he saw as the dazzling good looks of Heredcar and his own depressing ordinariness.

But it was never in Haldur's nature to be gloomy for long. There had been no strife between the brothers, who both agreed well with their parents, loving their mother and respecting their father's perceptive leadership of men. They had acquitted themselves with credit in all aspects of their schooling and training, Heredcar excelling more with his hands at woodwork and metalwork, Haldur leaning rather towards the written word; and the younger son was a strong swimmer and a leader in the fell-races of summer, whereas Heredcar was the better of the two at wrestling and faster over the short-course races on the flat meadows beside the river. Both were well-versed in the history and legends of their people, and had been instructed in their laws. Carapethan had brought each of them, as soon as they were old enough, to sit quietly by, listening and observing, when he deliberated with his councillors, the Haldan don Vorygwent. Yet there had always been an introspective streak in Haldur that was completely absent in his elder brother; and Carapethan, glancing at Haldur from time to time as they sat at the table in the hall that evening, thought he knew where it came from. I can see it in his eyes, he thought. His mother's eyes. Ellaaro's father had been the most important man away in Rihann y'n Wathan, the smallest, most remote and secret of the

Nine Dales. He came rarely to Cotaerdon except maybe once a year to trade, or for a festival; one summer he had brought his daughter with him and Carapethan and Ellaaro had met. Yet though she had settled happily in his hall and been content to live in his chief town, Carapethan knew there was a part of Ellaaro that stayed as wild as her mountain valley with its rocky river. She had been born and raised among those drifting clouds and sometimes he could see them in her mist-grey eyes.

Next morning, he sent for Haldur early and the two of them set out on foot, strolling through the streets and lanes of Cotaerdon. It was a pleasant town of some six or seven thousand people, snugly situated. The hills to the west were steep and rocky, dividing the vale where Cotaerdon stood from the two smaller valleys where Ellaaro had been born and the other where Seth y'n Temenellan was established; but to the north the slopes were lower and more gentle and the farmsteads here ran sheep on their high pastures and kept the cattle lower down where meadows stretched along the riversides. Lissad nan'Aldron was the swifter of Cotaerdon's two rivers and the mill was situated on its banks on the outskirts of the town, but the Lissa'riggan ran down straight from the mountains that bounded the Nine Dales to the north. Its valley was heavily settled, for though it was short and the snows of the Somllichan na'Haldan towered behind, it faced due south. Within its sheltered arms, open to the sun, stood fruit orchards whose blossom was thick in spring and this was where the most prized apricots were grown. The quieter waters of the Lissa'riggan were led off to feed the market gardens that lay outside Cotaerdon, and within the town they were diverted into several shallow brooks that ran sparkling in stone-built channels crossed by many low bridges. There were no bridges over the rivers themselves, although each was fordable above the town and the wide waters of Two Riversdale could be crossed by ferry further down the valley.

Carapethan and his son walked at a leisurely pace, talking together and acknowledging the greetings of those who passed. Many of the buildings of Cotaerdon were constructed of a stone that glowed grey-gold in the morning sun, but most had wood-framed upper storeys and some were entirely timber-built, with roofs that were a mixture of thatch and slates quarried in the mountains. At first Haldur could hear the distant rush and rumble from the mill-race, but as the streets became busier this was gradually drowned by the noise of many people going about their daily business. The shops were mainly open-fronted and before long the air was filled with the cheerful din of folk crying their wares, hammering and banging in the forge and carpenters' premises, and much clattering and shouting from the market-place where stalls with bright awnings were being erected around the stone-built arcaded structure at its centre under which the sellers of cheeses and other dairy products could keep their produce cool and fresh. As he walked, Carapethan glanced about him keenly and attended to what he heard. He liked to keep a finger on the pulse of the town, get a feeling for the mood of the people, and they in turn liked to see their lord among them. All were free to approach him and speak, and often men did so; many times Carapethan had been able to sort out a grievance, or prevent trouble that was brewing, as a result of this informal mingling with his folk. But this morning, after an hour or so, he headed for the open green at the heart of the town where he could speak privately with his son without being overheard. They walked over a graceful, low-arched bridge, the water babbling serenely below them, and crossed over to a seat that stood under a huge oak tree. One or two other trees studded the wide green space, and nearer to the stream there was a stand of ancient red hawthorns, their pink blossoms now beginning to fade and fall. Several families of ducks followed them hopefully, but soon waddled back to the water when no crusts were forthcoming.

After sitting in silence for a few moments, Carapethan turned to his son. 'I want you to come with me this year, when I ride around the dales.'

'Really?'

Haldur sat up with a delighted grin. He had felt heavy-hearted when he awoke, knowing that the council was meeting that afternoon. He thought he could guess only too well what their purpose was, and what it would mean for himself. But maybe he had been mistaken, perhaps they were only going to ratify his father's wish! Every summer Carapethan took a small group of friends and advisers with him and travelled up and down the Nine Dales, meeting the leaders in every community, showing himself to the people. As soon as the good weather opened the passes he would set off, returning before autumn was too advanced. All his life Haldur had looked forward to his father's return, hanging on his every word of what he had seen, heard and done. Sometimes it seemed to him that Carapethan must know every field and tree in every dale, recognise the face of the smallest child, remember the feats of the most ancient elder: not without reason was Carapethan a leader so well loved and respected. Haldur had longed for the day when he could be included, would know the thrill of looking down into those valleys he had not yet seen, have the excitement of breaking camp with a new horizon to cross.

'Yes, you will be twenty years old when the harvest is gathered this autumn. It's time the people saw you.' Carapethan leaned across and looked at the silver ring above Haldur's left elbow. 'You must have struggled to get that on. It will have to come off soon, whatever may be decided today.'

Haldur's spirits sank again. 'I know, it's too tight.' He battled with himself briefly, but the words burst out. 'Oh, why does it have to be me?'

'You should be proud that they are happy to keep the lordship within our family.'

'I am, it's not that. And so they should be happy, you are a worthy leader of us all.' Haldur flushed slightly, but kept his eyes steadily on his father's face. 'Whoever follows you won't find it easy to live up to the standards you have set, least of all myself. If they must have a member of our family living in the high hall, why don't they examine my cousins also?'

'Possibly they will, if they must, although I think it would be done with reluctance. I know that if Heredcar had lived, the choice would certainly have fallen on him. But he is gone, and it seems to me that they turn to you because you are the nearest to him and also because they believe it would please me.'

Haldur studied his feet. 'And would it please you?'

'Yes, it would. As a father, I'm glad that men seek to honour my son. But I am also the lord of Rihannad Ennar, and I must put its people before my family and the wishes of my own heart. As leader of this land, I look always to guard its wellbeing; and with that in mind, if Haldan don Vorygwent want you to follow me, then it is my judgement that their choice is right.'

The sinking feeling inside Haldur intensified. He sat frowning, lost in his own thoughts. It was still only mid-morning; if he had been allowed to stay with the Cunorad, he might have been high on some lonely moorside by now, or looking down into a hidden glen in the mountains he had never seen before. He wondered if they had felt called to ride out today, whether they would be following their dreams in a wild chase while he in contrast was being examined by the council. At this thought he felt an unexpected twinge of nerves, speculating at what he might be asked to say or do, and then a sharper stab of anger at the idea of the council putting him through his paces like some pedigree horse or prize beast. The ring tightened on his arm as his muscles flexed when he gripped the edge of the seat. Maybe by this evening he would have had to put on instead the torc that the heir to the leadership of the Nine Dales traditionally wore, but if this seemed to him a burden, then how heavily did the circlet lie on his father's head, who had been lord of Rihannad Ennar these many years? He looked up, gazing over towards the bridge into the town, and suddenly shame swept over him to think that he dwelt on his own discontent when Carapethan put his duty first. For two years he had been free to follow his heart's desire, leaving his father to rule the people with no son to stand beside him; but Carapethan would be alone no longer. If he thought his son was good enough to follow him when the time came, then Haldur was determined to be worthy of that trust and to make sure that the council were of like mind. His dark mood lifted and he stood up, pulling his father to his feet.

'Come on, we've sat here long enough. Let's walk round the rest of the town. If I've got to spend the afternoon closeted indoors, I want to see as much as I can of the old place first.'

Tried and chosen

In the event, Haldur was surprised to discover that if he had stayed in Cotaerdon, then the first thing the council would have wanted to see for themselves was his prowess on horseback. When his father brought him in and presented him to Haldan don Vorygwent he realised immediately that the meeting must have been arranged well in advance, timed so that those who lived in the more distant valleys would be able to travel in order to attend. He recognised some members of his mother's family from Rihann y'n Wathan; even the steward who ran the estates set aside for the lord of the Nine Dales in distant Rihann y'n Car was there, along with others whose faces he could not place. However, after the initial formalities, it was one of these unfamiliar men who rose in his place to propose that the test of horsemanship be waived on the grounds that anyone who had lived for two years among the Cunorad y'm As-Geg'rastigan must, by definition, be a rider whose standard need not be questioned. As he looked about him, Haldur saw smiles here and there as others remembered their own days in Rihann y'm Temenellan, and when Morescar seconded the motion, it was passed withour demur. But the stranger was standing again and it seemed he had more to say.

'We do require, however, to see proof of this young man's skill with the bow. Before he left the lord's hall to live among the Cunorad, rumour of his accuracy had already been heard even in the most distant parts of the land. But is his eye still as keen today? And what of his strength to draw, now that two years have passed? We have brought with us the champions of each of the Nine Dales. Let Haldur son of Carapethan tell us now if he is willing to compete with them at the butts.'

All eyes turned to Haldur as he stood before them. So that was it! He had seen the group of nine men sitting talking together beside the well in the courtyard when he came out from the hall, each with a different coloured band tied at the right knee, and had wondered why they were there. Trying not to appear complacent, he indicated his assent to the proposal gravely, but secretly he was full of glee. If there was one thing of which he was fully confident, it was that he could still beat anyone when he stepped up to the mark.

They emerged into the golden light of a serene afternoon to find that a small crowd of admirers was hanging about around the nine champions, hoping to see them in action. After Haldur had collected his own bow and other gear, they made their way down to the butts. By the time they got there, quite a number of onlookers had assembled as word spread of what was about to happen. It was the law in the Nine Dales that all children, girls as well as boys, must begin formal tuition in archery at the age of seven, and regular practice was also compulsory throughout life for men and women alike; each town and large village had its own professional instructor, paid from civic funds. Standards were high and competition keen, and a champion bowman of any valley was a person of note; so to see all nine demonstrate their skill on the same occasion was a rare treat and today's event carried the bonus of watching Haldur too. Before he went off to the Cunorad people had said he was shaping up to become the best of all, so this contest promised to be something remembered and talked about for a very long time. As the nine men and Haldur strapped on their arm-guards and looked over their arrows, Carapethan spoke to the crowd, giving them the customary warning to keep children behind the lines and to make sure that any dogs, whether their own or not, were secured on a leash or tied to a fence post. Then he called on one of the Haldan don Vorygwent to clarify the terms of the contest.

The man who had earlier asked Haldur if he was willing to compete now stood forward, announcing himself as having come to Cotaerdon from Rihann y'n Fram. There would be three separate tests, he said. In the first, each man would have three shots at a static target, which would be moved progressively further away. In the second, they would fire at a moving target; and in the third, each man in turn would rapid-fire to see who could loose the most arrows during a set time. Haldur and the nine shook hands, and the contest began. The onlookers were not disappointed. Gasps and whistles of amazement at the prowess being demonstrated before them rapidly became shouts of appreciation and loud cheering for all the bowmen, but for Haldur most of all. Although the council wanted him to do well, so that no questions could be raised about their choice of Carapethan's successor, there was much muttering among the judges as they put their heads together to examine the shots. They could scarcely believe their eyes: in a contest of champions, he was the best every time. Almost every man was hitting the bull with each shot, but there was no mistaking Haldur's grey-flighted arrows and no matter what the distance or the difficulty, their points were unfailingly lodged in the tiny gold eye at the dead centre of the target.

'We have all the proof we need,' said the council's spokesman to Carapethan. 'It is clear that rumour has not exaggerated your son's skill, and we are more than content.'

But he was prevented from bringing proceedings to an end so tamely: the crowd wanted something more to cheer.

'Hey!' shouted a fellow in the front row, grinning round at his neighbours. 'We could have told you who would win, but who's the best of the rest? Let's see whoever came second in a straight shoot-out with Haldur!'

So much enthusiastic yelling greeted this proposal that Carapethan raised his hand in assent and called the judges to him. They in turn indicated the champion wearing a yellow band at the knee; he came forward and spoke briefly with Haldur. The two of them retreated to the mark while the others moved back behind the barriers. The man who had operated the winch for the moving target paced out the long course and then, moving the straw targets aside, fixed a slender peeled wand in the ground. No more than the width of a spring-grown withy, it showed up white in the sun against the green of the butts behind. Complete silence fell as the man who had taken second place aimed and loosed. His arrow passed so close that the withy trembled in a disturbance of air, but it nevertheless remained intact and the arrow thudded into the earth bank. Now it was Haldur's turn to draw, and a second later his arrow was also lodged deeply in the butts behind the withy, but the wand itself was split cleanly in two. Amid wild cheering, the bowmen smiled in acknowledgement of each other's skill, but then Haldur turned and saw his father and the Haldan don Vorygwent coming towards him. The smile faded from his face as he remembered that the afternoon of testing was not over yet for him. Reluctantly he turned from the merry crowds and the bright sunshine and headed back towards the hall. This time, he was required to sit beside Carapethan in the place reserved for the lord on the cross-bench. The contest with the bow had been all very well, but he was far more worried about the verbal grilling which he expected, and which it seemed was now about to begin.

Sure enough, Ir'rossung was getting to his feet; Haldur braced himself for a searching examination of his knowledge of the law. It went on for what felt to him much longer than the hour it actually took: they put him over ancient rulings to do with land disputes, the customs pertaining to family inheritance, how to apply old precedents to new cases; a man who said he had come all the way from Rihann y'n Cathtor almost caught him out by asking him to name the four tests for granting permission to build a watermill on a river-bank where fishing rights were commonly-held. Eventually the questions ceased and it seemed Haldur had given an acceptable account of himself;

but before he could breathe a sigh of relief the council moved on to other topics. When it came to the history of the Nine Dales, Morescar was the chief of those testing his knowledge; while Poenellald felt it was important that their lord should understand his people's most pressing problems and concerns and consequently wanted to hear what he could tell them on matters of agriculture and craftsmanship. Finally they wanted to satisfy themselves on how well-versed he was in the traditions and lore of Rihannad Ennar: how fluently he could explain the various interpretations of disputed points in their oldest myths, how competently he could recite a story or poem, whether he had the ability to catch and hold the imagination of his listeners. All this would have been easier for Haldur, who had always had an ear for words and been moved by the legends of his homeland, had it not been for Maesmorur of all people coming at him with things like 'Summarise the third part of *Maesell y'm As-Urad*' and 'Give us the beginning of the second-last section of *Stirfellaerdon donn'Ur*'.

But at last it was over and it seemed that he had acquitted himself to the required standard, for Ir'rossung unlocked the ancient wooden chest that had been set before them and lifted its lid. Haldur was beckoned forward and bidden to remove his arm-ring and place it back in the casket. In the few moments while he worked it to and fro, struggling to move it past his elbow, quick thoughts flitted through his mind. He wondered whether he would ever stand, as Carapethan now stood, watching a son of his own take up his inheritance; he looked at the five other rings, four smaller than the one he now replaced and one larger but all worn with use, and felt a strange bond of fellowship with all those others who had borne them in their time; then once more a pang of grief ran through him when he thought how briefly Heredcar had worn the ring he now relinquished. But he himself had scarcely worn it at all, and now as Ir'rossung slid out the lower tray of the casket to reveal a single torc, it struck him how urgently the need to choose Carapethan's heir must have been felt for Haldan don Vorygwent to dispense with the sixth of the set. Unlike the silver arm-rings, which were adorned with carefully-matched pieces of amber, the neck-ring of plain, heavy gold, was dull and without decoration except for a single twist at the back and finials which resembled stylised eyes, one looking inward to the heart of the wearer, one out to the hearts of other men. Carapethan lifted it and fitted it onto his son's neck and the two of them stood side by side. The councillors rose to their feet to speak the traditional words of allegiance, and Haldur in turn pledged himself to the service of his father and to the Nine Dales when his time came; then they opened the doors of the chamber to show their future lord to his people.

The full council ate in the high hall that night, and all the chief men of Cotaerdon were there too, together with the nine champions who were included as honoured guests. As they moved towards their places, Haldur fell into conversation with his rival in the final archery test.

'Which dale are you from?' he asked.

'I'm from the Golden Valley,' said the man. 'My home's on the west side of the river.'

'Rihann nan'Esylt? I've never been there, but I'll see it later in the year. My father's taking me with him when he rides round the Nine Dales this summer. We can have a re-match, if you like!'

'I'll look forward to it, you'll be welcome.' The man smiled with pleasure at this sign of friendship from the lord's heir, then looked at Haldur for a moment. 'You were a worthy winner, Haldur. You must have the eyes of the As-Geg'rastigan!'

The meal that evening was generous and tasty, the pork roasted until crisp on the outside and succulent within, dried apricots pushed under the skin to add sweetness to the meat. There were fresh spring greens to accompany it, served with apple and fried sage leaves, and the loaves had been baked that day. Haldur was enthusiastic about the food, as if this sort of fare might have been something he had missed during his time away, and indeed Carapethan doubted whether provender such as this made many appearances in Trothdale; but though he laughed and talked animatedly with others at the table as they ate, his father noted that he never introduced any word of the Cunorad into his conversation, even though the compliment which the man from the Golden Valley had paid him would have made it natural to do so. Haldur was sitting across from his father and in the bright light his eyes shone as vividly blue as Carapethan's; but when he fell silent, looking aside, his father saw how in the shadow their colour shifted strangely to the mysterious grey he remembered from Ellaaro. One of the marks of Carapethan's leadership was his ability to listen carefully, and he had long ago realised that what men did not say was often equally or more significant than the words they actually spoke. With Haldur, the more important something was to him, the less he would speak about it. His father had noticed this trait in him from early boyhood and he suspected now that, had it not been for his brother's death, Haldur would have wanted to stay longer with the Cunorad y'm As-Geg'rastigan – might even have taken the vow. Well, my son, he thought, I too made a promise and I kept it when you held me to it, reluctant though I was to let you go once Heredcar was lost to me. You have had two years to follow your heart; now you must leave the Hidden People to themselves and learn to lead your own folk.

An inheritance threatened

By late summer, Carapethan felt happier as he saw how Haldur was growing accustomed to his role, taking on the mantle of heir to the lordship with greater assurance. For the past couple of months they had spent much time together, as with half a dozen chosen companions they rode around the Nine Dales. As for Haldur himself, though he might make this journey every year of his life from now on, he knew he would never enjoy any future occasions as much as this first time of all. They had begun by heading up Wealdale but then, turning away from the path he had taken when he came home from

Seth y'n Temenellan, they had followed the summer pass and come down into the apricot orchards of Rihann y'n Riggan from the west and so back to Cotaerdon and on down through the many villages and settlements of Two Riversdale. When they came to the place where the lower of the two ferries plied its trade, they lodged for a few days with the chief man of the district before wending their way through the hills into Rihann y'n Fram, the broadest and most fertile of all the Nine Dales and the one where most of its arable land lay. These were all familiar places that Haldur had visited before, yet somehow he seemed to see them with fresh eyes now that he knew that one day the trust of this land and its folk would be vested in him. At the beginning of the journey, he had been keenly aware of the weight of the torc on his neck: when he noticed it, his stomach would clench at the responsibilities of his new position. But as the days went by he became gradually more used to his new status, touched and somehow deeply humbled when he saw the joy on men's faces as they looked at him. Then he would put his hand to the gold at his throat as if it were a secret talisman, vowing silently to be worthy of the people's hopes and strong enough to carry their fears.

And now as they travelled further east, new horizons opened before Haldur. For the first time he looked on Rihann y'n Cathtor, lying open to the sunrise, and saw why men had named its bright stream Lissad Esylt and its upper course, reaching far back into the mountains, the Golden Valley. Here they were welcomed with special warmth, for the champion of the dale had arrived home full of the tale of events in Cotaerdon; and Haldur's new friend proudly escorted him around all the hamlets of the valley. Then it was time to ride on into Rihann y'n Car, the most north-easterly of the Nine Dales and one of the smallest. As Haldur knew from his history lessons, this had been the first of the dales to be settled, for it was here that the people, after their desperate and dangerous flight from Valward far to the east, had finally struggled over the mountains and seen what would become their new land stretching out before them. As they prospered and increased, they had become too numerous for the valley to support; so gradually they had spread further south and west, taking in more land to till and finding wider dales to dwell in; but because their settlements were scattered, and divided one from another by roads and passes which winter often closed, it had been found that those they took as lord had little time left from the exercise of leadership for ordering their own affairs. Eventually therefore they had decided that Lordsdale should match its old name, and after Cotaerdon had emerged as the chief town of Rihannad Ennar and the seat of its leader, the lands in Rihann y'n Car had been worked on his behalf by a steward. The produce and revenue of the dale maintained an estate village and its workers, and the surplus went to sustain the lord of the moment, his family, household and staff, and to support him in his duties.

By the time Carapethan had concluded his business with his agent in Rihann y'n Car, the summer was far advanced. The rainfall had been lower than usual and one hot day had followed another, so he decided to turn west and make for Rihann y'n Wathan by the mountain route. Above the spring-line on the southward face of the Somllichan na'Haldan there was a high trail only passable during good summer weather and along this they rode as the sun rose behind them each day and swung round the sky to shine low into their eyes as they made camp at evening. Haldur loved the solitude of these high, empty places, the silence broken only by the fall of the horses' hooves and the occasional cry of a raven from the crags above them. Sometimes they passed small *numirasan* where some wayfarer before them had felt the presence of the As-Geg'rastigan; and then they would dismount and stand quietly for a moment, leaving an offering of their own. The further west they went, the more familiar the lie of the land became to Haldur; the green, forested hills and the snowy peaks marching one behind another into the blue distance were well-remembered from his time with the Cunorad. They began to pick their way towards lower slopes, where mist drifted across the rocks and the ground became mossy and damp; then one day towards noon they saw Cloudsdale below them and as they dropped down beside the foaming falls of its leaping stream, there was the lord and his men climbing on foot to welcome them.

After a few days, Carapethan took two companions only and rode off to consult with Cunor y'n Temennis, leaving Haldur to stay on a little longer in the house of his mother's family; but when they met again as arranged, taking the low pass back into Rihann y'n Devo Lissadan, he had nothing to say of his speech with the Hound of the Vow, and Haldur asked no questions. As they climbed to the pass out of Trothdale, he had looked on enough of its lower course to realise that his heart was still sore at leaving it; he was glad not to have had to see Seth y'n Temenellan. But when Cotaerdon came in sight once more, he put his regrets firmly behind him. His father had spoken to him privately, praising his words and bearing; his mind was teeming with vivid memories that could be enjoyed whenever he chose, right through the winter months; he was home again, to the comfort that Aldiro provided; his people had found him worthy; the future was as shining and bright as the cloudless blue sky above. They came to a halt in front of the high hall and Haldur felt a huge grin spread across his face in spite of all his efforts to look suitably dignified. But Maesmorur came out to greet them, and there was no answering smile from him. He wasted no time coming to the point.

'Carapethan, your return is welcome indeed: we have an urgent matter to consider. Men have arrived here, fugitives begging for sanctuary by right of old ties of kinship. They claim to have come from Gwent y'm Aryframan, which they say has been attacked and its people enslaved.'

Chapter 34

The wanderer

The same summer morning which saw Haldur ride out with his father, going to meet his people whose lord he would one day be, shone down as well on another young man, not so much older than himself, who also had a journey to make. Unlike Haldur, this traveller was on foot, and alone; but both of them went forth into lands unknown, and faced the new day with eagerness and apprehension mingled in their hearts. Maeshron felt time nipping at his heels, harrying him to begin his quest once more. The season was far advanced: he dared wait no longer to attempt the mountain crossing that lay before him. All morning he climbed steadily, glancing up frequently to check his direction, trying always to keep moving towards the east and to seek the signs in the lie of the land that would lead him to a pass low enough to be accessible. Eventually he stopped to rest briefly, drinking from one of the many streams that rushed down, and then turning to look back over the way he had come. The air was hazy with the misty blue of summer, but he was almost sure that further north the mountains continued to bend away more toward the west; snow-clad heights lifted above the heat-shimmer, one beyond another, as far as his eye could see. If he was right in his calculation of how far north he had travelled up this further side of the Somllichan Asan, then once he crossed to their eastward slopes he should be near the place where long ago Geraswic had seen Arymaldur emerging from the wilderness. What an old, cold trail that would be to follow; and it led into Na Caarst, thought Maesrhon with a shiver of dread.

Days passed and he was deep in the heart of the silent, empty mountains. He travelled steadily, methodically, carefully, always remembering old Torald's lessons in the wisdom of the wild places. Each morning he rose early and ate as well as his rations allowed. Soon after dawn he would be walking, allowing himself a short rest in the heat of mid-day, trying to find a path on the high slopes below the snow where the ground was bare and stony. By late afternoon he would drop lower, below the tree-line, looking for a camping-place with water, fuel and shelter. He would halt while the sun still gave warmth, wash off the sweat of the day, eat and rest while checking over all his gear. If there was a suitable stream it would hold a fish trap in the hope of a trout by morning, and every three or four days he would stop earlier to allow time for laying snares or an evening walk with his sling. But long before sunset brought on the deep, bone-chilling cold of the mountain night he would be ready for sleep, wriggled snugly within the tiny shelter into which his pack unfolded, his fire banked to last through the darkness. Rest, food and warmth were vital if he was to succeed: he could not afford to take risks where one mistake might mean death. He slept lightly, his habit of vigilance causing him to wake frequently; and often, as his way took him deeper into the mountains, he would wake with the feeling that some vision of the Starborn had visited him, to retreat tantalisingly ever further out of reach the more he tried to recall it.

But the day came when, even though some hours were spent in weary climbing, Maesrhon's way led mostly down. When he settled himself for sleep, he could feel that he had used different muscles as the gradient changed; his legs ached and cramped, and the night hours were restless. He awoke with a start, thinking he heard Arval's voice. Peering from his shelter, he saw that dawn was yet some time away, although the eastern sky was already changing from black to deepest blue. Drawing his head back into the warmth, Maesrhon tried to sleep again, but without success. The feeling that Arval's presence was close to him was so vivid, he wondered whether Arval too was awake and thinking of him: maybe beyond the hidden door in Tellgard, far away he too looked up at the morning stars. To think it was two years now since they had parted, two years of wandering for him, two years of … well, two years of what for Arval? Maesrhon frowned in the faintly-growing light. The lines were more deeply etched between his brows now, after so many months of staring into the distance against wind and weather; his face and limbs were lean and spare from countless miles of walking. At last with a sigh he gave in to necessity, waked his fire and set water to heat. As he sat wrapped against the cold, waiting for the sun to rise, his mind drifted back to that final evening in Caradriggan. Once more he was slamming the doors of the hall behind him, striding across the compound at Seth y'n Carad, walking quickly back to Tellgard. He remembered the extraordinary awareness of power, of strength, that had possessed him; the sensation almost of weightlessness, as if his feet left no print on the earth; the feeling that he was unassailable, invulnerable, that no man could touch him. He had swept into Tellgard, and before one word had been spoken, Arval had known that the time had come at last …

Escape from Caradriggan

Through the dark streets Maesrhon went, swiftly, silently. His heart beat with a wild elation to be away at last, all doubt cast aside, all waiting over. He felt as if at one and the same time he was invisible, yet clothed in light. Towards the southern wall of the city he hurried, through alleys and narrow ways that were all but deserted. This was the poorer quarter of Caradriggan and any revellers here were long abed, faced with the necessity of rising before dawn to the next day's toil; but any who looked out, or whose business brought them home late, hastened to put their doors between themselves and the night, sensing something uncanny in the air, some presence that moved abroad, though hidden from their eyes. Maesrhon heard the small sounds of fear: here a bolt being slid home as quietly as hands that trembled could manage, there a scuffle of feet as a lone walker doubled back around a corner and ran for home in panic, and smiled to himself as he thought of the warning he had flung in their faces, back in the hall. Yes, he thought, by morning this city will be alive with rumours, each wilder than the last: see how you like it, Vorynaas, when rather than talk about your triumph men swear that Arymaldur sat beside the fountain unscathed, that an unseen power roamed the streets scattering a fire whose flames froze rather than burned, that this one or that one said they had it from those who had seen with their own eyes that a stranger who must have been Artorynas passed by their window, walked across a deserted square, was free of the city gates and the swords of the guards could not touch him. At this he almost laughed aloud, but told himself immediately: be wary! He was not out of the city yet, and after that, he must reach the forest within two days at most, or all would be lost.

Arval had not been so far off the mark when he wondered how long Maesrhon had been preparing himself for his journey. If he had been there to see, he would have remembered their shared laughter on a night, long ago, when he had eaten supper with an overawed small boy unhappy at the prospect of five years in Salfgard. Arriving in a dingy lane near the south wall of Caradriggan, Maesrhon looked carefully about him. Detecting no hint that he had been followed, or that he was watched by any hidden observer, he quickly strapped on the climbing spikes he had once demonstrated to Isteddar. Taking a long coil of rope from his shoulder, he trebled it, twisted it, and working his hands into the loops wrapped it around the stout wooden upright of the huge balance that had once been used to weigh sacks of grain and meal in the days before Vorynaas and his cronies began to tighten their grip on such commodities. The grainstore still stood, but it was empty and abandoned, redundant now that there were huge undercrofts at Seth y'n Carad fully stocked and guarded by armed men. Maesrhon swarmed up the post and then leapt from the cross-beam into the open doorway high above the ground where once the sacks had been hoisted by pulley; clouds of dust rose about him as he landed and he heard squeaking and scampering as the rats and mice fled. He removed his spikes and stowed them in his pack, then made his way carefully across the dilapidated floor to the far side of the building, where a small window hung crookedly from its hinges. Wrenching it from the rotting wood of the frame, he squeezed through and dropped onto the roof of the small house adjoining the granary where its owner had once lived.

Maesrhon edged along, feeling small stones beneath his feet and occasionally the crunch of bones. The house stood empty like the store, and the city wall passed right by it; bored guards had whiled away their hours of duty by picking off the pigeons that dozed on the tiles. Now Maesrhon was at the corner of the roof nearest to the wall; this section was about half way between the south and east gates. He breathed deeply, collecting himself, measuring the distance, and then leapt across the gap, landing on the wall walk. His momentum carried him hard against the breastwork and he stumbled, feeling winded and slightly sick. For a moment or two he sat, forcing himself to be calm before reaching for his rope once more. This time he used it singly, at its full length, but tied it securely so that it formed a single loop. Making sure that the knot was at the lowest point, he passed it around a battlement and cushioned it with a thick wad of rough leather; then sitting in the gap he pulled both down-strands towards him, twisted each into a loop around his feet, and gripping tightly with his hands swung himself to the outer face of the wall and slowly lowered himself down. At ground level, he quickly undid the knot and re-coiled the rope, stowing it once more across his shoulders; the leather fell at his feet with a soft thud and he stuffed it into his pack. Again a wild elation flared within him, but again he quelled it sternly. It must be already well past the mid-point of the night and he had twenty miles at least to cover before day came. Gloomy and dim though dawn was in Caradward, he knew it would bring pursuit. He moved off, setting a pace he was certain of keeping up indefinitely. They would put the dogs on to him, he felt sure, but he thought he knew a way to throw them off the scent.

By the time the first hints of grey had begun to show in the deep darkness, he had arrived at the western bank of the first of four or five small rivers that flowed out of the Lowanmorad and down into the wider waters of the Lissad na'Stirfell. This was country familiar to Maesrhon from his time with Atranaar's scouting units and his plan was clear in his mind. At each watercourse he turned either right or left, laying a false trail, before retracing his steps and fording the streams, wading or jumping from rock to rock; with luck that should delay those who hunted him, even if they were using dogs. He forced himself to keep going as far as possible before he stopped to rest; it was his guess that Vorynaas would order his men to search west and north towards the border first, but this was no more than a surmise and it would be foolish to assume too much. While the day was broad he lay hidden, taking cat-naps and keeping a keen watch all around, and at evening he moved on again. Only when black night had fallen did he permit himself a few hours of real sleep, knowing that success the following day was likely to mean the difference between escape and capture; and the second dawn after he fled from Caradriggan saw him drawing near to the river. Wide, dark and daunting it flowed before him, but he had crossed it before without being detected and he was going to cross it again. The large, flat stone at the water's edge that he had used before was still there. He tested it thoroughly, making sure it was firmly bedded and stable.

Turning downstream, he hurried along for a couple of miles, planting a footprint here and there in the muddy ground where the banks were softer. Eventually he stopped and slithered down to the very edge of the water, breaking off the sedges and turning over a tussock or two, leaving plenty of traces. Then as carefully as ever he could he climbed up again and set off back to the point at which he had turned, following his outward steps but treading this time as lightly as he knew how. Finally, some twenty paces short of the spot, he paused, looking out over the rolling water. The river here was divided into two channels by a low, scrubby island, lying nearer to the bank where Maesrhon stood. He took the stave from its holder at his back, hefting it in his hands. How many times had he been ridiculed in Caradward for his prowess with the stave, a pursuit only fit for Gwentaran peasants! But he had found uses for it other than sparring, and now it was going to help him get away. He sprinted forward, planted its end on the flat stone and leapt, using the stave as a lever to increase his distance. His dark hair lifted as he flew over the water, landing with a crunch of gravel on the island. So far so good! He hurried across to the far side, checking that here too all was as he remembered. Yes, there was the patch of rocky ground. He paced out his run, knowing he would need the whole length of the island in order to attempt the further, wider channel. Over he went, not making the full distance this time but landing in shallow water. He floundered up onto dry land and then as the breeze freshened a little with the new day, he heard it. Faint, distant but unmistakeable it drifted down the wind to him: the cry of dogs on his trail. Ramming his stave back into its holder, he sped up the bank towards the forest. It loomed before him, no more than a mile away now, but it seemed further as he ran, heart hammering, desperate to reach the cover of the trees.

Once within the forest, he concentrated on finding a suitable tree for his purpose, rather than trying to penetrate deeper within them. He was gambling on his pursuers not following him into Maesaldron, for if they did, then there would not be enough time for him to outdistance them; but he must be able to see what happened when they checked at the river. Now he could hear nothing except the branches sighing as they swayed in the moving air; all other noises were blocked by the thick leaves. He made himself move carefully and quietly, fighting down the urge to blunder along in panic, forcing a way through the tangle. At last he saw what he wanted, a tree whose trunk rose up straight far above his head with no lateral branches until it topped the lower canopy of shrubby growth. This was where his climbing spikes came into their own again and soon he was emerging through the twiggy understorey to scramble into the first branches of his own tree. It was even better than he had realised from ground level, for the trunk divided into three and between them were several smaller offshoots all entwined with ivy that had formed a thick mat. He could hide here in relative comfort and safety if only their inborn fear of the forest kept the chasing pack at bay. Cautiously parting the leaves, Maesrhon peered out.

At first he saw nothing, then clearer and nearer he heard yelping and excited barking and within moments his ears picked up the sound of men shouting and the muffled thunder of hooves. Suddenly he saw them, about a dozen hounds streaming down to the water's edge followed by a similar number of riders. With a shock of recognition Maesrhon identified the leaders as Valahald and Heranar; they were urging their men to follow as the dogs turned immediately on to the trail he had laid. They came to the place where he had deliberately broken part of the bank and paused, the horses and dogs milling about. Some of the men dismounted and seemed to be staring into the river, but the brothers drew their horses a little apart and spoke together separately. Eventually they rode back to the others and there was much talking, punctuated with pointing and vehement gesticulation from Valahald. Maesrhon could guess what it was all about easily enough. The brothers had been with him in Salfgard and knew he could swim; but the others, eyeing the river, were not persuaded that a man could live in its waters. They were reluctant to continue the chase, while Valahald wanted to cross the river and pick up the trail again beyond it. Well, to do that they would have to double back and use the bridge; and in the end, after more angry shouting, they all mounted again and rode off, straight past the place where he had actually crossed.

Maesrhon did a quick mental calculation of the distance to the bridge and back, plus time to find out whether anyone had seen anything suspicious there; then more time to pick up his trail on this side of the river. One day, not more. He turned his attention to making his temporary hiding place more comfortable, fixing the bracing-rods from his pack into the wood of the tree and stretching the folded-out fabric between them over the springy mat of ivy. The following morning he was on the watch early, but the hours crawled by without alarm. As the day crept on, Maesrhon felt the tension within him increase. Surely it was too much to hope that the chase had been called off? Then suddenly once more his straining ears picked up hound noises. Here they came again, cantering along the near bank of the river this time, heading swiftly for the place where Valahald thought he might have swum ashore. Maesrhon watched, knowing what was going to happen well before they reached the spot. Sure enough, opposite the small island the leading hound checked and the others began to quarter the ground, noses working. Then they all turned and raced towards the forest. Their handler galloped after them, calling them back, and at the edge of the trees he dismounted and slipped on their leashes. Up rode Valahald and Heranar and the others. They were so close, now. What wind there was blew from them to Maesrhon, but the hounds whimpered and fretted: they knew the trail led into the forest. Maesrhon fitted an arrow to the string. If they overcame their fears and followed him into the trees, he would be trapped, but he would make a fight of it first.

What was happening now? More argument had broken out: the dog handler was walking away, shaking his head as Heranar walked beside him, leading his horse; the man jerked a thumb at the animal and then pointed back towards the trees with a dismissive gesture. It seemed he was indicating the impossibility of taking horses into the pathless tangle of the forest. Valahald was shouting at his men, clearly trying to insist that they continue the chase. But it was late afternoon now; the louring evening of Caradward was not far off, and they felt the menace of the forest about which so many sinister stories had been told. Maesrhon looked up at the darkling sky and hope began to grow in his heart. He knew the kind of fears that were waking in his pursuers' minds; like them, he had been brought up on tales of the nameless terrors that lurked in Maesaldron. The horses, unsettled by the shouting and their riders' unease, began to plunge and circle nervously. Valahald was on foot now, remonstrating angrily with another man who stood his ground stubbornly and then, when Valahald struck him across the face, seized his arm and shoved him towards the trees. It was so obvious that Valahald was being told to lead from the front: show us the way, captain, if there's nothing to fear, you go first. But Valahald didn't trust them to follow, and he was afraid too: no braver than his men when faced by the silent threat of the forest. He argued for a moment or two longer, then throwing up his hands in furious exasperation he spat savagely towards the trees, climbed back on his horse and gave the order to withdraw. Hidden in his lair, Maesrhon smiled as he noticed how fast they rode away.

Friends in the Outlands

Almost a month later, he was far away in the south, in fact further south than he had ever been before. He had waited a few days, safe in the forest, to be sure that his pursuers would not return, and then had emerged to begin a long and weary trek, circling around the eastern fringes of Caradward, beyond Staran y'n Forgarad, down towards the Outlands. He had journeyed swiftly by daring to use the roads at night when other travellers were few and easy to avoid; when a village drew near, he would hide while familiarising himself with its buildings and features and then proceed warily around it by day when there was less risk of raising an alarm or disturbing unseen dogs. But though he had made haste, time was speeding faster. Within two months at most he must reach his intended over-wintering place before the season closed in on him, and this was not going to be possible while he travelled alone and on foot. It seemed it had been worth using up precious days in laying a false trail to the forest, daring the danger of luring the chase so close after him; now he must take another calculated risk. He pressed on until the last permanent settlements of the *sigitsaran* were well behind him and then, choosing a camping spot part-way up a low escarpment, he waited. On the second day, a few hours after dawn, he heard what he was hoping for approaching from the east.

Standing up, Maesrhon shielded his eyes and stared into the distance. It was not so dark, down here in the far south; but the sun was obscured nonetheless in a heat haze through which gritty sand blew constantly. Peering into the distorting mirage of wavering dust-devils, he saw that a large group of people was drawing near accompanied by many animals. Goats were bleating and he heard the shouts of children and the barking of dogs. Lifting his pack onto his shoulders, he walked down the slope towards them, stopping at fifty paces or so. A man dismounted and walked to meet him, his head and face muffled like Maesrhon's against the harsh environment. Maesrhon pulled down the cloth covering his mouth, and held up empty hands.

'Good day and good fortune to you, Lord Sigitsar of the *gradstannad.*'

The man's dark eyes moved swiftly over Maesrhon, noting his arms and equipment. He too revealed his face; like his eyes, it gave nothing away, but when he spoke Maesrhon could hear he had been pleased by his courtesy. 'Good health and good journey to you, fellow-traveller.'

'I would ask something of Lord Sigitsar. Will he permit me to journey onwards in his company? I will take my share of work, in payment.'

The Outlander stood for a moment in silence, then turned and called out to a youngster who led up a tough-looking little riding mule and threw a blanket over it. The older man handed the reins to Maesrhon. 'Ride with us today and eat with us tonight as our guest. After that we will talk about tomorrow.'

Steadily they travelled westwards. Sometimes their progress seemed slow to Maesrhon, but even so it was faster than walking and a day came when he was almost sure that he had caught a distant glimpse of the Red Mountains over the noon-tide shimmer. He worked hard to help with the tasks of the journey: herding, milking, gathering fuel, trying to reinforce the ties and obligations of hospitality, because he suspected uneasily that they knew who he was. On the first evening, in the comfort of a tent jewel-bright with colour and pattern, he had eaten chicken steamed in grains and flavoured with preserved lemons; afterwards he and his host had sat sipping at a herbal infusion, Maesrhon grateful to be resting on soft cushions, his backside sore from the mule's bony rump. The man had told him his name, and laughed at his attempt to pronounce it, telling him he would settle for plain Sigitsar; and then had asked in turn for the name of his guest. Maesrhon had named himself Istorar, using Arval's boyhood diminutive, and though the man had accepted it without question, the hooded eyes in his inscrutable face had flicked briefly to the white lock at Maesrhon's temple.

And now they were beyond the low foothills where the Somllichan Ghent ranged to their southern end, moving at the day's end into a wide, shallow valley dotted with thorny scrub and bushes whose leaves were leathery and tough, well adapted to the arid climate. The goats and sheep were driven into a series of pens whose wooden fences were bleached silvery-grey: clearly this was a semi-permanent encampment or halting place. Maesrhon helped to gather brush and dried dung for fuel, which was piled into a large stack while men slaughtered half a dozen goats and hung their carcases from a frame to bleed. It seemed that a celebration of some sort was planned, although there must be a month yet before the time of the harvest-home feasts that were more familiar to him. But the next day he saw dust drifting in the distance, and a new caravan of travellers wound its way into the camp from the west and spread out into the space left for its tents and animals. These were from the marshes, Maesrhon learnt, folk who dwelt in the Haarnoutan but who met now with their kin and friends for trade, mirth and the exchange of news and marriage contracts. That evening their leader and chief men ate with Sigitsar and his entourage, and the women served goat meat seethed tenderly in milk with almonds and spices. Afterwards they drank a thin curd flavoured with mint, cooling the palate and calming the digestion.

'What news from Caradward?' asked the leader of the marsh folk.

He had been introduced as Tirassigits, but this was really only a nickname given for his eyes, which were a strange greenish-blue. They glittered palely in his swarthy face, so unlike the usual black, impassive gaze of most Outlanders. Maesrhon was reminded of the friend he had made during his military service, Sigitsinen of Heranwark.

'Dark times, to match the dark days,' replied Sigitsar, 'and likely to darken further. Valafoss has pushed his sons forward into Vorynaas' favour. Valestron is angry at their preferment; there may be strife eventually between him and the elder son.'

'They are two of a kind,' said Tirassigits. 'Men say it was Valestron who ordered that all the folk of Salfgard should be killed, and Valahald who laid it waste, out of fury that he found it empty and its people fled.'

Another man spoke up. 'My grandfather knew a man who was marriage-cousin to Sigitsar Metal-Master; when I was a boy I heard them speak of Ardeth of Salfgard. If the tales they told were true, I am glad to hear that he escaped.'

'Only in a manner of speaking.' This was another of Tirassigits' party, a man whose voice was heavy with bitterness. 'Ardeth did not live to see his work destroyed. They say it was the shock of Caradward's betrayal that killed him.'

Horror, sudden hope and crushing despair had torn through Maesrhon's heart as he listened to all this. He did not doubt that what he had just heard was accurate: the *sigitsaran* might hold themselves aloof, down here in the south, and keep to their Outland customs, but he knew they had their own ways of gathering news. The conversation rumbled on as he hid as best he could the desolation he felt. He sat silent, dwelling sadly on memories of happier days, but suddenly he snapped to attention, realising that he himself was now the subject of their talk. Out of courtesy to the guest among them, they had refrained from speaking in the *sigitsaran* tongue; but now Tirassigits switched to his own language. He leaned closer to Sigitsar, dropping his voice low.

'Do you realise who this stranger is?'

Watching from the side of his eye, Maesrhon saw his host nod slightly. 'I do.'

'There is a price on his head,' said Tirassigits.

'So I have heard, but to me he is a guest. Will you betray him, if he looks to travel onwards with you when we turn back?'

Tirassigits showed his teeth and his voice hardened. 'He who takes a blood price will one day pay that price in blood himself.' His strange, pale eyes flicked towards Maesrhon and then roved around the other faces in the tent before coming to rest once more on Sigitsar. 'But not all here are bound by the ties you mention.'

Sigitsar's dark brows drew down. 'We are all cousins. There is no man here who would soil his hands with gold from those who rule in Caradriggan.'

'Yes: when they have ruined all, let them eat their gold and see how it sustains them.' Tirassigits laughed harshly and then turned to Maesrhon. 'We must beg your pardon, Istorar; it is not good to have to listen to words one does not understand. Let us talk together in a tongue we all know, so that you are not excluded.'

Maesrhon smiled, careful not to let his face show he had understood them, and joined in the conversation once more: learning now that there would be two days of trading in livestock and other commodities, two more of arranging betrothals and family matters followed by a great feast; and then Sigitsar and his people would turn back eastward while Tirassigits and his folk made their way back west into the marshes that lay south of Gwent y'm Aryframan. At the end of the second day of bargaining, haggling and arguing over goats, sheep, mules, metalware, fabric bales, dried fruits and other items, he sought out Sigitsar and requested a meeting with himself and Tirassigits that evening.

'I have two questions to put to you, gentlemen,' he said as they sat around a small fire in the dusk. 'Firstly, I would like to know whether Tirassigits will permit me to travel onwards with his folk. I have a westward journey to make and I ask for help in passing through the Haarnoutan swiftly. Secondly…' and switching now to the tongue of which he had picked up a smattering in Staran y'n Forgarad he continued, '…secondly, I ask you to tell me more of this price which Vorynaas has put on Maesrhon's head.'

The two Outlanders sat silent, gaping in embarrassed astonishment. 'We are ashamed,' said Sigitsar eventually.

'But why? There is no need: did you not both say you would never take such a reward?' They looked at each other, unsure of what direction Maesrhon's questions would take. After a few moments, he spoke again. 'Though I am able to understand more of it than I can speak, I would not call myself fluent in your language; therefore with your permission we will not use it further now. Will you help me to pass the marshes, Tirassigits?'

'I would be honoured, my lord, I…'

Maesrhon put his finger to his lips. 'I am no lord, I am Istorar, a traveller. I look forward to being your guest; please accept my thanks. Now, will you tell me more of the news from Caradriggan?'

Sigitsar cleared his throat and swallowed. 'Vorynaas has sent out word that he will pay one hundred gold *morasan* to any man who delivers Maesrhon to him, and half that much again if he is brought in alive.'

'It would seem that condemnation has increased his value somewhat in Vorynaas' eyes,' said Maesrhon with a lift of his eyebrow. 'And do men think it likely that he will be captured?'

Beginning to relax a little now, Tirassigits and Sigitsar exchanged glances and laughed. 'Some say one thing, others another,' said the man from the marshes. 'Heranar maintains he is dead already, swallowed by the darkness of Maesaldron; but though the brothers tracked him to the forest, Valahald is so wild with rage that Maesrhon has eluded his grasp three times now, he has persuaded himself that he lives still and has sworn to take him.'

Sigitsar took up the tale. 'Caradriggan is generating rumours faster than a pond spawns frogs in spring. Men say Maesrhon put a spell on the guests in Seth y'n Carad so that they were unable to move from their seats to pursue him. They say he bewitched the gate guards, and so escaped the city. They say Arymaldur came back from the dead to help him, that the Starborn trod the streets in the darkness and men were afraid to leave their homes. They say Maesrhon himself is *as-ur* and walks unseen; that he wields fire without suffering hurt and used it to dry up the river on his way to the forest.'

A wry smile touched Maesrhon's lips, the old scar showing white in the firelight. He sat, savouring these wild stories whose seeds he had himself sown.

'What is said in reply to all this?'

'The brothers curse and say there is no need to speak of mysteries, that Maesrhon learnt to swim when they were all boys together in Salfgard,' responded Tirassigits, 'but they cannot stop the talk: it runs like a fire with the wind behind it and springs up tenfold the more they try to stop it. Men say that when Maesrhon was with the patrols, he went into the forest and came out again alive; so Valestron has ordered extra vigilance in case he tries to cross into Gwent y'm Aryframan by moving through Maesaldron until he reaches the northern border, and has sent messengers throughout the occupied lands to spread word of the reward for his capture.'

'Thaltor's agents have ridden through Caradward also,' added Sigitsar, 'and they ask everywhere they go for information about one Artorynas. None know who he may be, but all have heard of him. Maesrhon taunted those at the victory feast with the name, bidding them remember it, and they are afraid.'

'If men come to question you, what will you say?' asked Maesrhon.

'We have seen no soldiers, this far south. But if we do…' Sigitsar spread his hands wide, his face blank, and when he continued,

Maesrhon noticed that he had deliberately intensified the Outland intonation in his speech.

'If the lords Valahald and Heranar tracked him to the forest, surely Maesrhon must be dead by now. How could any man live who took refuge there? As for ourselves, we keep to our own paths and our own people, we have seen no Artorynas.'

Tirassigits now leaned forward, speaking in his own tongue and then quickly breaking off with a little gesture of apology. 'Your pardon, captain, I speak to strangers so seldom…' He too was affecting an exaggerated accent. 'I have never been to Caradriggan, I wish to see no evil spirits from the forest.' Then he looked up at Maesrhon with a laugh, speaking normally again. 'But no patrol has ever been seen near the Haarnoutan in my lifetime. I doubt that many in Caradward even know that there are *sigitsaran* in the marshes.'

Maesrhon stirred the outer embers of the small fire with his foot and their light woke an amber glow in his golden eyes. From the pouch at his belt he took a small flask of the fierce, peppery drink the Outlanders distilled from the leaves of one of their thorny shrubs. He uncorked it and offered it to his companions.

'Gentlemen, I am in your debt for hospitality, aid and discretion. If Tirassigits will help me with the loan of a punt or coracle and give me safe conduct, I will be gone from here, through the Haarnoutan and away into the empty west. Let us seal our friendship.'

They drank in turn and then Sigitsar took his hand. 'Istorar is my cousin now.'

'Mine also,' said Tirassigits, 'and numbered among the marsh folk.'

'Istorar is honoured,' said Maesrhon formally. Then he lowered his voice and switched to the *sigitsaran* tongue. 'Maesrhon was taken by the forest, he will not be seen again in Caradward; but Artorynas will return.'

The long road north

So it was that with the aid of Sigitsar, Maesrhon escaped from Caradward and entered the Grey Marshes; and here Tirassigits and his folk helped him to slip secretly through a maze of quiet meres and slow-moving waters where word ran ahead of him so that there was a welcome on each low island and in every reed-thatched village. The marsh-dwellers ate well on the wild fowl and fish with which their watery world teemed, and they sent Maesrhon on his way generously-provisioned with no questions asked. Travelling by boat he made good speed and within a week of the equinox was leaving the marshes behind, climbing westward up the valley of a small river that flowed down into them. Soon he saw above him the pass he had been promised would lead him through the mountains by an easy route. The Somllichan Asan were lower here at the southerly end of the range, but even so he had no wish to use up time and energy on climbing where he could avoid it. The nights were turning chilly and he must reach a place to over-winter while some warmth still lingered in the soil.

He found what he sought in a small, south-facing valley. Several streams ran down its eastern side and joined into a little river that meandered to and fro across the dale before flowing away out of sight; there were patches of woodland here and there: taller trees in the valley-bottom, with ash, hawthorn and hazel coppice further up the hillsides. Maesrhon chose a spot near a water supply, open to the south and out of the wind. Sleeping at first in his tiny travelling shelter he made haste to strip the turf from an area of level ground, stacking it for use. He worked the soil, opening it up and loosening it, and then set it with beans from his store. As autumn advanced he used all the shortening hours of daylight, cutting withies and hazel rods, making hurdles and screens, building up a stock of firewood, gathering fruits and berries. He constructed a simple but robust hut, low and wind-proof, the walls packed with sod for insulation, turves laid on the roof;

inside was a small firepit, a raised platform for sleeping, racks and pegs for storage. In spite of the solitude his heart rejoiced to see the sunlight once more. Though low in the sky it flooded into his lonely valley, filling it with mellow gold. One morning he saw the first of his beans poking through the soil and smiled, wondering what Torald would have to say if he could see his ideas being put into practice. Carefully he protected the tender shoots with low wattle panels, built a bigger, outdoor fireplace with a ground oven, smoked and dried as much fish and meat as he could catch against the harsh weather to come.

When his preparations for the winter season were as complete as he could make them, he began to explore more of the surrounding area; climbing higher, ranging into other valleys, wandering down west where the lands faded into the distance. Always he carried his bow and sling with him, and if he had set snares he would walk the line to check them; but his eyes and ears were constantly alert for any sign that the fulfilment of his quest might be near at hand. While he had lived in Salfgard, like his mother before him he had gazed on the snowy peaks of the Somllichan Asan, drinking in their beauty, wondering whether their name was a hint that the Starborn had ever dwelt in their high places, whether they lingered yet in Ilmar Inenad beyond. When he had laid his plans for escape from Caradward, deciding to take the long route and go south before turning north, he had been partly influenced by these memories and partly too by what Arval had revealed to him of his own young days. But now in the clear blue light of frosty dawns, all he saw was the mountains sweeping endlessly north; and when the sun sank at evening into the red, hazy west, there was nothing to see but emptiness with no sign that either the Earthborn or the As-Geg'rastigan had ever trodden there. The first snows of winter began to fall, and there were days when the weather kept Maesrhon penned indoors; he would sit beside his fire, savouring the warmth and shelter, conserving his strength, fighting the disappointment that lurked in his heart. He told himself sternly that his true way lay northward; had Geraswic not told him that

Arymaldur came out of the north, had he himself not always felt its call? And he had warned Arval that his journey might take years. He must be patient: he would trust that Torald had told him the truth, that his plants were hardy enough to survive with the protection he had made for them; he would wait for spring, harvest a new supply of food, and with summer he would set off again. Maybe it would not be until the second year of his wandering that he found what he sought.

Or the third, thought Maesrhon grimly, returning out of his musing to the present and finding that the sun was now well risen, shining into his eyes and stealing light from his small fire so that its glowing heart looked ashy and dead. He had swallowed down his morning food without even noticing what he ate, as his mind ranged over the memories of his journey. Jumping to his feet, he prepared to go on once more, dousing the fire and removing all other traces of his camp, lifting his pack to his shoulders. If he was honest with himself, he had found it easier to move on again that first spring; leaving his second wintering-place had been much harder to do. When his face was turned northwards in earnest at last, he had gone on his way eagerly. But the days had turned into months, and still the Somllichan Asan rose up towering into the sky at his right hand, as silent and empty as the vastness of Ilmar Inenad that stretched away into the sunset; and eventually he had been forced to leave the real quest for a more urgent search: the need to find another lair in which to wait out another winter season. Maesrhon's features softened as his thought dwelt upon the beauty of the place he had found. When he first saw its small blue lake and untouched freshness it had reminded him a little of the upland vale from which Geraswic had pursued him, long ago; but this new valley was gentler and less wild. There was fertile soil and level land, enough to make fields and pastures for two or three families to live from. As the days lengthened into the second spring of his journey, he had had to wrench himself away, suppress thoughts he had never had before: pictures that formed in his mind of living there in peace, of contentment stretching out into a serene old age.

What is this, he asked himself. Will you falter in your quest in the hope of Earthborn happiness? But maybe, he answered, maybe when the time comes, I will choose in the end to be numbered among the Ur-Geg'rastigan. Perhaps, came the reply, but the choice is not before you yet; do not be deluded by these dreams. You cannot live here: here there is neither friend to love nor neighbour to know nor family to cherish. You are alone and your search is still before you, your promise to Arval is not yet fulfilled. You must go on. And so he had turned away from his winter home beside the lake, where the birds were already busy with their nestlings, and set his feet to seek a way over the mountains. Now here he was, descending their eastern slopes, beginning a third weary year of wandering. One afternoon he rounded a rocky outcrop to find the ground dropping away before him, grey and barren where the mountains met the wilderness. Maesrhon stood staring, forcing down his fears. Somewhere, somehow, Arymaldur had come out of Na Caarst near here, had gone south to Caradriggan, had walked with the Earthborn, had drawn Numirantoro from among them into the life of the As-Geg'rastigan. Somewhere, it was for him now to find the trail that led down to his own strange begetting into the world of men; somehow, it was for him to tread back along that path towards the hope of light returning: towards the Starborn. Now the time had come when he must turn north again.

CHAPTER 35

Desperate measures

Maesrhon dropped to the ground and leaned wearily against the twisted hawthorn trunk. After a few moments he opened his eyes and looked up at the bright new green of its young leaves, almost hidden in a foam of blossom. He'd been right, then: the tree was real, not an illusion born of his exhausted body and labouring mind. He pulled himself into a more comfortable position, feeling the rough bark under his hand. The effort of reaching this tree had almost spent his strength, but he would not, must not, give in to weakness. There was no stream or spring, so his first task was to provide himself with water. Here in the wilderness, where the sun warmed the ground by day but the temperature dropped sharply during the harsh nights, he could use one of Torald's tricks and dig a still that would yield moisture from condensation. After that it was time to turn his attention to shelter and food. The thorn tree was clinging to a rocky bank, its roots holding to crevices among the boulders. Below it was a meagre quantity of dead wood, no more than an armful of twigs fallen in the storms of winters past. Slowly Maesrhon began to gather them together, building a small firepit from loose stones. He dismantled his pack, converting it into his tiny, tube-like tent, spreading out inside it all the spare garments he carried, together with a roll of pelts cured with the fur left on. It was vital that he warmed himself as much as he could before he settled to rest and then wrapped himself up well, for it was obvious that his fire would not last through the night.

With his preparations complete, he put water and meal to heat, crouching over the embers, nursing them with a couple of blocks of dried turf carried from a previous camping-site. He drank the water first, sipping it slowly with his hands wrapped around the horn cup for warmth. The meal was all he had left now, a dwindling supply only sufficient to make a thin gruel; but tonight he did at least have something to go with it. While gathering up his firewood, he had come upon a patch of nettles springing up with the new season, thrusting through the stones at the bottom of the bank. Desperate to bolster his diet with greenstuff, and knowing their food value, he had gratefully nipped out their tender growing shoots and added them to the pot. Firmly he resisted the temptation to eat more than this. His stomach was pinched and shrunken, it would be foolish to overload it and waste what he had eaten by vomiting. If he could hold down tonight's food, tomorrow morning he would add some fresh hawthorn leaves to what he had set aside; and there were a couple of thistles flourishing vigorously just beyond the tree's shade. Maesrhon's mouth watered as he anticipated the crisp sweetness of their peeled stems. At last, with his hands and feet warmed and his hunger partly stayed with hot nourishment, he crept into his shelter, rolling himself into the extra coverings. He made sure his knife was to hand, but felt secure enough to loosen his boots. By now he was inclined to dismiss the old stories of monsters and demons prowling in Na Caarst: the wilderness was more than hostile enough in itself, no place for men.

And yet, and yet… He had been familiar from childhood with the old folk-saying that nettles grew where men had once dwelt and disturbed the ground. Could it be that he was drawing near to the Nine Dales at last? How had a hawthorn come to take root here, here where no other tree was to be seen, here where he had not passed so much as a bush for days upon end? A waft of scent from the flowers on the tree reached him on a shift of air. He was travelling earlier in the season, on this third spring of his journey; usually May-tide was well over before he set out. But he had had no option this year.

After descending the mountains the previous summer his progress had been slow and difficult. Needing to keep the wilderness in sight, yet unwilling to walk within it, he had tried to keep to the higher ground in the foothills of the Somllichan Asan as he made his way north; but climbing in and out of one valley after another had been time-consuming and energy-sapping, and he had seen neither sight nor sound of either the Starborn or the Earthborn. Food had been scarcer and more difficult to gather on this eastern side of the great range and the only place he had managed to find to sit out the winter had been bleak and comfortless. He had endured cold and privation, made harder to bear by the knowledge that his plight was likely to get worse before it got better. Autumn had come early, with none of its usual bounty: earth's harvest of fruits and seeds had been scanty, his traps and snares empty, game almost impossible to find. And worst of all, his cherished beans had failed to germinate. The plants are hardy, Torald had told him long ago, and his advice had eased Maesrhon's journey so far; but it seemed that he had now passed their northern growing limit. When winter turned towards spring, there was no need to wait until it was time to pick and dry them; but equally he now had neither a stored nor a fresh supply.

So Maesrhon had set out again, with little except hope to sustain him. Yet carefully though he husbanded his strength and his stores, he knew he was getting weaker: every day cost him a greater effort. And then one evening the wind had shifted around and blown towards him from the north-east, bringing a faint smell of smoke. He paused, startled, sniffing the air. Just when he thought he must have been mistaken, there it came again. He emptied his lungs and then breathed in slowly, deliberately, letting the air pass through his mouth as well as his nose, warming it, tasting it. Once more his thoughts turned to days spent with Torald. In his mind he heard him speaking. *If you get grease in the fire from meat or fish, you'd be surprised how far down the wind the smell of that can drift.* Faint and far away though it was, what he could smell was the smoke of a cooking fire – or fires. It spoke to him of people, of settlement, of safety. Here was a dilemma calling for more of Torald's wisdom. To reach the source of the smoke, he must turn to his right and strike out across the wilderness. This was a risk at any time, but in his present state, would it be tantamount to throwing his life away? He recalled his promise to Arval, his vow to return whether or not his quest succeeded. Dead men do not return, thought Maesrhon; and I am going to die, if I cannot find help quickly. He savoured that tantalising hint of smoke again, tested the wind against his cheekbone, took a bearing of a distant rock that lay in the right direction. His mind made up, he set off into Na Caarst.

That had been two days ago, and it was in the afternoon of the second day, faint and thirsty, that he thought he saw a lone tree breaking the grey monotony of the landscape. He forced himself to aim for it; somehow it seemed to hold a promise of hope. Refusing to entertain the possibility that he was chasing a mirage, he stumbled on until the tree lifted itself clear from the mist of fatigue in his mind and revealed itself as a gnarled and ancient hawthorn. Maesrhon lay in his tent under the tree that night, his stomach griping. He had held to the direction from which the wind had blown, but had not seen or heard or even smelt anything to show him that he had made the right choice. Yet the berry that grew into this flowering thorn had been carried to this spot somehow, and then there were those nettles... Dare he hope that these were signs that the homes of men could not be far away? His food was almost all gone, now. If he could not get more, he had barely enough for another couple of days, and after that only his strength of will would keep him walking on until the moment when he was unable to go any further. The night passed restlessly as he woke often; and once he was surprised to find that his sleep had been broken by the sound of rain. For a few moments he listened to the drops falling on the fabric of his shelter, close above his face. The wilderness was so withered and arid, he guessed that rain seldom fell there and indeed by dawn it had petered out. But as the rising sun drew mist up from the refreshed earth, and with it the hint of sleeping life that the moisture had wakened in the ground, suddenly Maesrhon caught that breath of woodsmoke again. He stood up and stared around, noticing now that the lie of the land tilted gently up before him so that the horizon was quite close. What might he see if he could only keep going beyond that point? Quickly he assembled his gear and hoisted his pack once more, setting out at a steady pace with renewed determination.

Haldur alone

'There, be good – don't bark now, you'll wake everyone. There's a good lad,' murmured Haldur, dropping to one knee to reassure the dog which had jumped up, a growl in its throat, as he came out of the guest-hall door. He fondled the animal's ears, scratching its neck fur and talking to it quietly.

'There, that's better. You know me, don't you? See, it's only me, it's Haldur. No need to make such a fuss, was there?'

The dog licked his hands, wagging its tail now, leaning against him. Haldur glanced about him at the main hall and other buildings, but it was still so early that no-one was stirring even in the kitchens. He walked over to the wash-house, the dog following him closely, let himself in and shut the door behind him. Stripping off his clothes, he stepped under the pump, shivering and gasping as the chilly water hit his warm skin. A moment or two of that was more than enough, but he stuck his head back under and worked the handle so that a further icy torrent fell briefly onto his face. Grimacing, he wrung the water from his hair and dried himself off with one of the rough towels that hung on the wall, feeling a glow of warmth spreading through his body as he dressed once more. His head felt a bit better, too. As he emerged from the wash-house, the sweet smell of new bread met him. Going across to the kitchen he found that in there the day's work had now begun: the cooks had opened the ovens where bread had been baking overnight.

'Good day and good health to you. May I take one of these?' He pointed to a tray of small round loaves.

'Of course. You help yourself to whatever you want.'

'I just want a bite for myself, that's all,' said Haldur, putting the bread into the bag at his belt and crossing to the barrel against the wall to draw wine from it into a small bottle. 'That was quite an evening, last night! You served a feast I'll remember for a long time. Look, no-one seems to be up and about yet apart from yourselves. Will you take a message for me?'

Smiling with pleasure at the compliment he had paid them, they nodded in agreement. 'Surely we will, Haldur.'

'Well, I don't want to wait, the sun will be rising soon,' said Haldur. 'I must have a few hours to myself. There has been so much noise and talk, so many people, so much going on. If you would tell them at the hall I've gone out for a while, but I'll be back by this afternoon, I'd be obliged to you.'

'We'll do that. Let the Hidden People walk with you.'

Telling the dog to stay, Haldur strode off through the village and down the road through the first fields. It was a still, misty morning but the exercise and the cool dawn air were clearing his head with every step. It was true that he'd enjoyed himself, the previous evening, but this was better: he was glad he'd decided to get away for a few hours. He was the guest of honour at a wedding, representing his father Carapethan. The groom was an old friend of Haldur's, a couple of years older than himself, the eldest son of the chief man in the settlement that had grown up in Two Riversdale where the lower ferry crossed the Lissad nan'Ethan. Haldur passed the entrance of the lane that led down to its wide, slow waters. He could see the feathery tops of reeds poking through the mist lying on the water-meadows, touched by the new sunlight's level rays; but after another bend or two of the road he turned aside in the opposite direction, heading uphill towards the woods that clothed the slopes above the fields. It would not be so long, now, until a year had passed since he had last visited this part of the Nine Dales, when he had travelled round with Carapethan as his newly-ratified heir. How heavily his new status had sat upon him then! He was easier with his place in the world now; but, he thought with a frown, he would still exchange the deference he had been paid earlier that morning for the chance to ride again with the Cunorad y'm As-Geg'rastigan. The winding track he was following climbed to a field gate; he went through it, walked up beside the wall to the stile at the top, and stopped to sit for a moment on its wooden bar. Gazing back down the slope over the way he had come, Haldur found himself looking at the village. Smoke was rising from its chimneys now as folk began to go about their business and his thoughts turned to newly-married Sallic. He too had once numbered himself among the Cunorad, had dwelt for a time in Seth y'n Temenellan; yet it seemed that he had found it easy enough, returning to the life into which he had been born. He had found himself a wife, had turned back to the family home and the ancestral fields.

Haldur jumped down from the stile and within a few strides had disappeared from view into the woods beyond the intake wall. Without really thinking about it, he wandered upwards, pushing through the hazels, his face brushed by catkins. Once, during his time with the Cunorad, they had come this way, taking the low pass out of Trothdale before it was light and feeling drawn to ride on into a second day. The new dawn had found them high on the fells, looking down on Rihann y'n Devo Lissadan, following their hearts towards the fringes of the forest. And there, where the last few trees gave way to the bare hillside, they had dismounted at the place where the call seemed strongest: a tiny hollow, where a mountain stream swirled into a pool and then poured down into the woods. Blossoms floated on its peaty waters from the crab apple at the forest's edge, and on the other side it was open to the empty slopes and the high blue sky. Now Haldur climbed to the spot again, and again he felt the presence that lingered, as if the feet of the As-Geg'rastigan surely had walked there. And it seemed that others had felt it too: the small heap of pebbles that he and his companions had left, rounded from the water and glistening with veins of mineral, lay there still, intact and untouched; but some other wayfarer had acknowledged a *numiras* by offering a small posy of spring flowers, setting their stems in a pool among the rocks. For a moment Haldur stood with bowed head, savouring the peace and silence, wondering if he did indeed stand at a threshold between two worlds. Then, glancing up at the sky, he saw that the morning was half-spent. He would go on to the *numiras* in the trees that he had found a few days previously before eating his food and then returning to the hall to rejoin the wedding party.

He walked slowly, treading softly and looking about him. As the sun rose higher in the sky its light filtered down to the forest floor in an ever-moving pattern of gold and green. The air was loud with birdsong and filled with an earthy smell of leaf-mould and wild garlic; the ground at his feet was carpeted with a haze of bluebells and a few late primroses lingered here and there. Haldur's mind moved to the question that had been much debated over the last year: the problem of what, if anything, to do about the news that had arrived with the fugitives from Gwent y'm Aryframan. They had been welcomed, and places made for them; in fact one was now living here in the village where the ferry plied. There had been widespread anger at the tale they brought; some of Sallic's friends had been vociferous, the other evening, in supporting the idea of action. Yet what could they do? Carapethan, though wrathful himself, had counselled caution. Haldur frowned as he walked, trying to think things through from his father's perspective. Was Carapethan exercising a leader's responsibility, or was it simply a generational clash between young hotheads and those who were older and wiser? Dropping down towards another beck that splashed noisily through the woods, Haldur decided he could think about the problem again later. He gave it up for the present, and reaching the mossy banks of the stream, turned to follow it uphill. The special place he sought was not far away, where the stream cast its arms about a grassy island on which a single rowan tree had taken root. On the near side, the bank dropped sheer to the water and was white with the snowy petals of anemones; on the other, there was a small shingly beach backed by rocks and lapped by shallow ripples. Above this far bank there were wild roses growing. How sweet the air would be when high summer came in and their flowers opened! But for now, catching the heady perfume of hidden violets blooming in some damp cranny, Haldur halted briefly to compose himself, sensing once more the strange blend of awe and joy that had struck him so strongly the first time he had come this way.

Hints and signs

Gritting his teeth against the pain, Maesrhon plunged his bare foot into a pool where the water swirled in eddies at the bottom of a steep, rushing fall. It was so cold that he could not tell whether the hurt of his twisted ankle was eased, or merely replaced by a gnawing, icy chill. He rummaged in his pack and took out a bundle of soft rabbit skins, soaking a couple of them in the water and using them to strap up his foot and ankle before replacing his boot. Using his stave to take some of his weight he winced with every step as he went on down through the woods, cursing himself for the careless moment that had brought an injury when speed was so essential. Indeed it was urgency that had caused him to slip, putting haste before caution in his eagerness to reach safety. Climbing wearily to the crest of a ridge, he had realised with a surge of new hope that the wilderness was coming to an end at last. Before him the ground sloped away until it was no more hostile than bare fellside which then dropped steeply into thick woodland; but away beyond, he had seen a pattern of fields where the far side of a wide dale rose up once more; and curling up into the air between, smoke which must surely come from a village or settlement hidden from him in the valley bottom. He was following the water now, as the most certain way down where direction was difficult to gauge among the trees.

Here and there he had seen indications of human activity: the marks of coppicing, and chippings from axe-strokes lying among the leaf-litter; the suggestion of a track winding among the trees, a level clearing where maybe charcoal had been burned. And there had been other, more mysterious hints. In secret dells he had seen small cairns, topped with a piece of sparkling quartz, or maybe half a dozen matched and coloured pebbles; there had been garlands, some obviously recently renewed, tied on to shrubs that overhung springs or pools; and once he had even found a tiny carving of a mouse placed carefully within a clump of primroses growing at the foot of a ferny bank. Were these offerings, or signs, and if so, what did they mean? Each time, Maesrhon had felt a mysterious sense of standing on some invisible threshold. Dare he hope that the As-Geg'rastigan still lingered here, or at least that the Earthborn still honoured them? Could it be that after wandering for so long, he had found the Nine Dales? But not once did he hear a voice or a footfall, nowhere did the trees thin out to reveal a hamlet or cottage; he walked on and on, stumbling along beside the stream, and still he walked alone.

He had hurt his ankle soon after eating the very last of his food, making help now doubly imperative; but as he struggled on through the day he heard only the woodland birds calling from their hidden nests, saw nothing but boughs swaying in a light breeze. When the light began to fail he stopped, light-headed with hunger and pain. Somehow he scrambled down a low, rocky bank to a place where the stream had carved out a level beach. He drank deeply and soaked the bandages around his foot once more; then, too weary to care much about protection from the night, he simply chocked up his firescreen to keep it from the damp ground and lay down upon it. The night was warm and he was sheltered by the bank behind him; there was water readily available. He drifted in and out of fitful sleep, waking frequently. As the dusk deepened, he thought he saw lights moving before him, then realised it was blossom opening on a young rowan tree, the only one that grew on a small island in the stream. The flowers floated before him against the darkness, confections of lace like foam on cream, luminescent in the gloaming. Maesrhon rested his tired eyes upon them; and as the soothing, never-ending babble of the stream lulled his mind, so he felt a peace and serenity steal into his heart. This is a hallowed place, like those others I have found, he thought dimly; I must find some way to honour it myself. I will do it tomorrow, before I go on... yes, tomorrow... and then exhaustion overtook him. Maesrhon slept long and deeply, but in his rest a dream came to him: stranger, clearer and more vivid than any he had ever known before.

The golden riders

It was one of those rare visions whose impact was so strong that he never forgot any part of it: for the rest of his life, he was able to recapture every detail. Perhaps this was because, again unusually, even while sleeping he seemed to know that he dreamt. Scenes passed before Maesrhon's eyes like pictures in a book, but it felt to him that he was actually present: really there himself as events unfolded, and yet at the same time also somehow aware of this. But if he observed himself looking on, it seemed that none noticed him; for the folk in his dream gave no sign either that they saw him among them or realised that an invisible presence watched what they did. It was as if he stood in the shadows at the side of a darkened room where the only light came from a small flame. A door opened and closed again and he caught a dim glimpse of a tall figure, stooping over the flame. Then the brightness increased, for two lamps had been lit now and were set on high shelves. Maesrhon saw that the person who had entered was an old man, dressed in dark blue robes; he was reminded, somehow, of Arval. This man had a similar air of calm authority, but he was taller and clean-shaven although his face was deeply lined and he had the look of someone who was accustomed to spend many hours in the open air. Having attended to the lamps, he lifted a pitcher from the floor and poured from it into a plain earthenware bowl; this he placed in front of the flame. Then he stepped back as if waiting, hands clasped before him.

Glancing around, Maesrhon noticed several things about the room in which he stood. Its furnishings were bare to the point of austerity. At right angles to the table where the flame burned were two long wooden benches, and on each were six bowls containing some substance unrecognisable to him. Behind them on the walls were pegs on which hung clothes of some kind; a flat leather bag on a long strap and a pair of high boots stood below each peg. The floor was stone-flagged and on two levels, so that the table with the fire was higher than the benches. There were four doors: three in the back wall, in the centre and at each side; and a larger one facing these. Overhead Maesrhon could see wooden rafters rising into darkness where a thin smoke from the lamps drifted, but no smoke came from the fire on the table. This burned bright and clear in an apparently empty bowl, seeming to need no fuel upon which to feed. Somehow Maesrhon knew that the room was cold, chilled by the freezing hour before even earliest dawn was in the sky, and absolutely silent. Then the two side doors at the top of the room opened and twelve people came in, six at either side. They filed to their places at the benches and turned to face the old man for a moment, then moved across to the pegs, never breaking the deep silence.

Maesrhon saw that the newcomers were young, no older than himself. There were six men and six women, their faces stern yet preoccupied, as if they concentrated upon some inner vision. When they shrugged off the cloaks they wore, Maesrhon gaped in astonishment within his dream, for he saw that, men and women alike, they wore nothing except a small loin-guard. Taking down the garments that hung on the wall, they dressed quickly, the women in breeches but the men in short kilts, both of soft leather dark fawn in colour. All pulled on the close-fitting boots that reached to the knee, but remained stripped to the waist as they turned once more to the benches. Without a word being spoken, they began to anoint each other with the strange stuff in the bowls. It was obviously soft and smooth, and spread easily, blending with the warmth of their exposed skin into an extraordinary, bright gold that seemed to glow slightly. Maesrhon had never imagined such a scene; even within his dream he was amazed and could not help wondering what such as Ghentar would have made of it. But maybe even he would have been abashed to see the solemnity with which these young people conducted themselves, their minds clearly freed from any thoughts except those appropriate to their rites. When all was done, they moved forward to the table and the old man handed up to each of them what looked like a small package of food and a leather water-bottle. These they placed in the bags, which they slung over their shoulders cross-wise; then each in turn drank from the earthenware bowl that the robed man had filled earlier.

Having looked intently for some moments at the twelve young faces ranged before him, as if he sought some sign, the old man smiled slightly and stepping forward, placed his hand on the shoulder of one of the girls. Her companions inclined their heads towards her and then left the room through the large door. Maesrhon caught a brief glimpse of the sky, which was still black and studded with brightly burning stars; his dream-self shivered with numbing cold but the eleven seemed impervious to it as they went forth silently with exalted faces. He looked back at the girl who waited. All his life he had heard it said that his mother was as beautiful as the Starborn, and now he realised what people had meant. He knew that Numirantoro had been dark, but this girl was fair: she stood before the dancing fire like another flame of gold, tall, straight and strong; her hair was braided, but he could see how every colour from corn-silver to honey-flaxen was mingled in the tresses. Surely, she would have been golden, even without the mysterious unguent with which she had been covered! How could any young man have touched her naked body in that strange rite and not been moved by temptation to caress her, to put his hands upon her with desire? But when she turned to the door and he saw her face, rapt and intense with an inner dedication, he understood how this would not be so.

Now the outer door opened once more and it seemed to him that he followed the girl as she went out, and leaned invisible against the wall, watching. Her companions stood there, with horses beside them: small, light horses with golden, matching coats; they moved restively as if impatient to be away, their breath smoking in the freezing air. The girl took the reins of her own horse from the young man who led it forward for her; they all seemed to be looking past Maesrhon, back into the building. After a moment, the elderly, blue-robed man emerged. Standing before them, he lightly touched each rider in turn on the forehead and spoke some brief phrase, although, his ears still stopped by the dream-silence, Maesrhon did not hear the words. He felt chilled to the bone, but the young people stood there quietly as if they noticed nothing and it came to him to wonder whether the golden salve they used protected them. Suddenly they leapt into the saddle; the horses circled and plunged in a whirl of golden movement, and then as if at a signal they raced away at a furious gallop, following the girl's lead. For the first time, sound broke in on Maesrhon's dream. He heard high, wild cries and a thunder of hooves that shook the ground; but swiftly the clamour faded until deep silence returned. The old man turned away and closed the door behind him and Maesrhon was left alone, looking up into a sky just turning from black to darkest, deepest blue.

He awoke, shaken, half expecting to see the golden horses plunging around him; but there was nothing except a thin ground-mist curling among the trees in the grey light of dawn. Maesrhon was shivering with cold. He struggled to his feet, leaning on his stave, and forced himself to move about at the stream-side, berating himself for not taking more care over shelter for the night. When he inspected his foot, he saw that it was blackened with bruising and his ankle was swollen and inflamed. Suddenly Maesrhon's head swam and he hurriedly sat down, chafing his fingers and the toes of his uninjured foot against the chill that numbed them. He must reach help today. Surely it could not be much further down through the woods to the settlement whose smoke he had seen rising from the valley bottom. Leaning back on his elbow, Maesrhon considered his options. He realised that exhaustion itself was endangering him by confusing his thoughts and making him clumsy. If he tried to move on too early in the day, he might hurt himself again or come to the end of his endurance before any of those who lived hereabouts were abroad to find him or hear his cries. Another day without food, another night without shelter, might be one too many. He would rest for a while longer, gathering what was left of his strength until the sun was up and the day opened out, and then make one last effort to reach safety. But for now, he was so tired, so weary… he would rest for just another few hours…. Maesrhon's head dropped, his hands relaxed and he slept again.

Earthborn or Starborn?

The next time his eyes opened, birds were singing in the woods all around him and the sunlight was slanting down through the leaves. He heaved himself into a kneeling position, drank from the stream and filled his water bottle. As he sat back onto his sleeping platform, the beauty of his surroundings struck him and he remembered his resolve of the previous evening: that he would honour what he felt to be a hallowed place before he left it. How, though? The only flowers he could see were inaccessible on the far bank or swaying high overhead and he had nothing of his own to give. Finally, he knelt again at the stream's edge, plunging his hands into the swift, shallow current. Drawing up water, he let it flow out again through his fingers and then touched the cool moisture to his forehead. Silently he recited the words of the *Temennis* in his heart, and then drew out the knife that Ardeth had made for him. He cut off a small lock of his dark hair, and set it gently on the surface of the stream. For a moment it twirled in a dancing eddy, and then the bright waters bore it off. Maesrhon watched it go, vowing with renewed determination not to fail in his quest. Then as his eyes followed the stream as it sparkled and flashed in the sunbeams falling through a stand of young ash trees, he realised with a shock that someone was approaching him on the further bank. How had this man got so close before he had seen him?

But as Maesrhon watched warily, he quickly realised that the newcomer had also failed to notice him and clearly thought he was alone. A young man of roughly his own age, he moved silently with the practised ease of one well-versed in woodcraft. He had thick, straight hair, heavy and silvery-fair when the breeze lifted it, and a pleasant, rather homely face. Plainly dressed in tunic, breeches and boots, he carried only a small bag and appeared unarmed. Maesrhon saw now how he blended in with the woodland around him. His clothes were by no means new, and their close-woven cloth was worn almost to a smooth sheen; the leather of his belt, bag and boots was dull brown and unornamented. With his light hair, his tanned face and hands and his grey-brown garments he was all but invisible as he moved through the dappled light and shade of the ash trees, passing among their slender grey trunks. He was walking more slowly now, and as he came out of the trees at the top of the bank he stopped, standing above the place where the wood anemones spread out in a carpet of white. What would he do now? His eyes roved over the little glade, the island with its rowan tree, the babbling stream, and still it seemed he failed to see the stranger who silently watched him. Maesrhon noticed the inward, solemn expression on the young man's face as he raised his hands and began to speak quietly. His accent was new to Maesrhon, but he understood what he heard and his heart began to pound at the words.

'May the Starborn return and walk in this world once more. May the As-Geg'rastigan renew their pledge, as the earth renews herself. May the Hidden People show themselves, here where one of the Earthborn has felt their presence.'

Renewed hope surged through Maesrhon so strongly that he could not stop the exclamation of relief that escaped his lips and suddenly the young man across the stream seemed to see him at last. Maesrhon saw his eyes widen in shock, heard the gasp as he breathed sharply and his hand began to make the sign, then drop back to his side as a strange joy lit his face. But as he took in the stranger's gaunt and wayworn air, the joy faded and doubt took its place. He raised his hand once more, this time giving the ancient threefold sign.

'In the name of the As-Geg'rastigan, I greet you. Do you seek the Starborn here?'

Now it was Maesrhon's turn to stare in amazement. 'Why do you ask that?' It was so long since he had spoken to anyone, the words came out in a croak that sounded strange even to his own ears. The young man across the stream was frowning, puzzled. Now he shrugged.

'Why else would a man rest in a *numiras*?'

'A what? I seek Rihannad Ennar: I have been travelling for almost three years.'

'Three years! You are within the Nine Dales now, but… Oh, you're not well! Just a moment, I'll come across.'

As the young man was speaking, faintness swept over Maesrhon again. He had been on his feet, supported by his stave, but now he felt the ground tilt under him. His legs folded and he dropped down to sit again on his sleeping platform, trembling slightly.

Haldur turned away to his left, downstream, away from the high bank where he had been standing, and splashed across the stream. His mind was in turmoil, caught between that moment of wild exhilaration when at last, after so many years of hoping, he had come to a *numiras* and not found it empty, and the desolation which had followed when he realised that this was no lord of the Starborn returned to earth. But now, as he hastened back to the sick man's side, he found himself not so sure. His glance took in the white lock at Maesrhon's temple and the scar on his upper lip, the pack and equipment he carried, the tattered pelts wrapped around his injured ankle, and he told himself that all he had on his hands was a mysterious wayfarer. Then he looked again at the lines of the face before him, the extraordinary golden eyes that met his own, and doubt began to creep over him. Who could this man be?

'Lie quiet now, everything will be all right,' said Haldur. 'I see you have hurt your foot. Do you have any other injuries?'

'No, it's only my ankle, I fell heavily yesterday and twisted it. I have torn the sinews and made it worse by walking on it, following the stream down through the woods. I had to go on, I have no food left…' Maesrhon's voice, rusty with lack of use, tailed off.

'I have bread here with me; we'll share it. When did your food run out?'

'Two days ago… But I have crossed Na Caarst, I have eaten almost nothing for many days now.'

'The Wilderness!' Haldur's brain seethed with questions, but he forced them down. Seeing Maesrhon's horn cup lying beside his pack, he opened his own bag and took out the loaf and little crock of wine he had brought with him. Breaking off a small piece of bread, he sopped it in a drop or two of wine in the cup and then fetched water from the stream.

'Here. Eat this very slowly, and sip the water with it.'

Gradually Haldur fed Maesrhon about a quarter of the loaf, using the middle of it where the bread was fresh and soft. When it seemed that he was going to be able to hold it down, he gave him half a cup of well-watered wine.

'Now, let's have a look at this foot.' He peeled off the sodden rabbit skins and surveyed the bruised swelling. 'Hm. Well, we're going to have to get you down to the village somehow, so I think the best thing to do is to strap it up as best I can for now, and get you some proper attention back at the hall.'

Maesrhon was barely listening. The drop of wine had spread warmth through his body, and now he need worry no longer about food and help he could feel waves of weariness sweeping over him.

Haldur stood up and pulled his tunic and shirt over his head. Throwing his tunic back on and belting it, he set about the shirt, tearing it into long strips. He laughed as Maesrhon's wavering attention was caught by this.

'It's all right, it's an old one.'

Maesrhon smiled in turn. 'Use this, it'll be easier.'

He took one of his throwing-knives from the holder at the side of his boot and handed it over. Haldur whistled as he took the weapon, admiring its balance and elegance and noting its razor-sharp double-edged blade. Mysterious was the word for this wanderer, no doubt at any rate about that! Saving his questions for later, he strapped Maesrhon's ankle with the makeshift bandages and then propped his foot up on his pack.

'Now, we'll stay here for a while longer. I think you'll be able to get your boot on over the bandages, if we lace it together afterwards. That's an ingenious idea, those removable soles. Then you can use your stave, and lean on me, and we should be able to get down the hill together. But we'll give it till this afternoon, and before then you can eat some more bread and rest up a bit. So, now I should introduce myself and tell you something about where you are. My name is Haldur, I'm the son of Carapethan. My father's the lord of the Nine Dales. He's at home in Cotaerdon at the moment, but I'm on a visit here to Rihann y'n Devo Lissadan because a friend of mine has just got married. You say you've been travelling for three years, looking for Rihannad Ennar. What is your errand? Where are your companions?'

The waters of the little stream gurgled past them, leaves sighed overhead in the breeze, birds sang hidden in the branches. Suddenly Maesrhon realised he had been sitting in silence, brooding on how much to tell Haldur. He turned to the other man.

'I'm sorry, please forgive my discourtesy. Three years is a long time to be alone; I have almost forgotten what it's like to speak with other men.'

'You've been travelling *alone*? Why? Where have you come from?'

'From Caradriggan, chief city of Caradward, but my journey began far south of that land.'

'Caradward!' Haldur bit his lip. 'There are fugitives from Gwent y'm Aryframan in the Nine Dales who say that men of Caradward have enslaved their land.'

'They speak the truth,' said Maesrhon grimly. 'There is a price on my head in Caradward. I have been called a traitor, because I refused to march with their army. But my purpose is very different. I look for the Starborn, and on the advice of Arval na Tell-Ur I seek Rihannad Ennar in the hope of help in my quest.' Maesrhon smiled slightly. 'Now I have a question of my own for you. What is a *numiras*?'

'It's a place where we feel the presence of the As-Geg'rastigan. You'll see *numirasan* here and there throughout Rihannad Ennar. They're all different: they could be beside a stream, like this, or up on the mountainside; anywhere, where someone has sensed that maybe the Hidden People have trod. Then usually that person will leave a sign, so that anyone else finding the place can honour it too. All such *numirasan* are revered as hallowed ground.'

'I see. I have noticed such places here and there within the woods, and felt a power that lingered within them. I felt it here, last evening, although I saw no sign. I slept here in peace and this morning, because I had nothing else to give, I offered a lock of my hair to the waters of the stream.'

Haldur looked sidelong at his companion. 'If you also felt the spirit of the place, then surely it is doubly hallowed. There was no sign, because it is only a few days since it came to me that this is a *numiras* and I hadn't yet marked it as such. I returned today for that purpose, and when I saw you…' Haldur smiled rather sheepishly. 'When I first saw you, I thought for one moment that at last I saw one of the Starborn. My two years with the Cunorad are long over now, but for me the search still goes on.'

'The Cunorad?'

'The Cunorad y'm As-Geg'rastigan. I wanted to stay longer in Rihann y'n Temenellan; sometimes I think I would have taken the vow for life. But my brother is dead and I am my father's only son now. The council sent for me, and since this past year I have had to take up the duties of the lord's heir.' Haldur put his hand to his collar and pulled it aside to show Maesrhon the gold torc he wore.

'The Hounds of the Starborn,' repeated Maesrhon slowly, almost to himself. He turned to Haldur, taking his arm. 'Golden riders, on golden horses?'

With a cry of astonishment, Haldur twisted round onto one knee, staring into Maesrhon's amber eyes. Hope, fear, confusion were in his face and voice.

'Who are you? Are you *as-geg'rastig*?'

Maesrhon shook his head. 'The Starborn do not show the marks of hunger and hurt as I do. Their limbs do not shake with weariness, for they are tireless and their voices are clear, not hoarse from lack of use as mine is. But I dreamed last night, and it seems that the dream was of these Cunorad: I saw golden riders, galloping wildly out into the dark before dawn. I was close to giving up hope of ever reaching the Nine Dales, but today is a happy day for me, after all.'

Haldur sat back on his heels and smiled uncertainly. He scarcely knew whether he felt downcast, foolish, relieved, curious, or a bewildering mixture of all at once. But as the shadows shifted with the sun's decline from noon, the two young men sat and talked and gradually a companionship began to grow between them. They shared the rest of Haldur's slender provisions while he explained to Maesrhon how it was that he had left the wedding party to wander in the woods, craving a few hours of solitude; then he went on to outline his plan for the next few days.

'We'll stay here for a while until your ankle is mended and your strength returns,' he said. 'The hospitality of Sallic's father is famous, there's plenty of space in his guest-hall. Then when you feel up to it, we'll travel back up the valley, home to Cotaerdon. My father Carapethan and the council may be able to help you. And you should speak also with old Cunor nan Haarval, the Hound of the Vow: we can ride together over to Rihann y'n Temenellan.'

Listening to all this, Maesrhon felt the weight that he had carried on his heart for so long lift a little as new hope began to grow in him. He forced down a shudder of apprehension at the thought of having to set out again; after all, maybe he would find what he sought here in Rihannad Ennar!

'Come on,' he said to Haldur, 'let's have a go at getting down to the village. You must be absolutely ravenous.'

'Well, I have to admit I'm pretty hungry,' said Haldur with a grin. 'I'll take your pack, and you hang on to my shoulder. Here's your stave. But you've still not told me your name.'

Maesrhon looked up at Haldur as he helped him scramble to his feet. 'My name is Artorynas,' he said, smiling with the sudden realisation that here, at last, he could openly use his true name and leave behind the badge of contempt which Vorynaas had forced him to wear since his birth.

'Artorynas.' Haldur smiled back. 'Well, before we go…' He poured the last few drops of wine into the stream. 'Surely it's an omen, that we should meet in a *numiras*. Maybe it means that Haldur and Artorynas will seek the As-Geg'rastigan together.'

Chapter 36

The Cunorad

Some five days or so later, Maesrhon and Haldur were sitting together one afternoon on a bench against the wall of Sallic's guest-hall. Haldur kept blowing at his hair, where it stuck to his forehead in the hot sun, but its weight just made it fall back to settle once more. They had spent much time together, while the injury to Maesrhon's ankle prevented him from walking; they had talked for hours, often late into the night, and Maesrhon found that his chief difficulty, as their friendship grew, lay in not simply opening his heart and pouring out the whole story of his life. He began to sense what it might mean to have someone his own age to whom he could talk almost as he would to Arval, a companion who shared what the day brought not with deference like Isteddar but as an equal. If only it had been like this with Ghentar, how glad he would have been to have Haldur as his brother! And it seemed as though the same thought had occurred also to Haldur, who when he heard that Maesrhon too was motherless and had lost an elder brother, had smiled and said it was as if the two of them were brothers by fate, if not by blood. Looking around him as they sat there, Maesrhon's gaze fell idly on the wash-house and kitchen across from the guest-hall. All was quiet in the sleepy afternoon; here and there a dog snoozed in the sunshine, and occasionally someone going by on business would greet them briefly in passing. He realised how much he had already begun to enjoy the Nine Dales: he liked the way the valley slopes rose above the house-tops with their drifting haze of smoke, he liked the air of sturdy contentment among the folk, the practical way he had been welcomed and helped, left alone to talk to Haldur without being pestered by prying questions. But tomorrow, he and Haldur would be riding together up the road towards Cotaerdon, and for the present the most urgent decision that Maesrhon had to make was how much to reveal of his background and errand to the lord of Rihannad Ennar and his councillors. Finally he resolved to give as full an account as he could, without telling all. He held a slight advantage in that the first person he had met was the son of the lord, and thus he had not only discovered immediately that fugitives from Gwent y'm Aryframan would have spread a part at least of his tale, but had also learnt a great deal about the land where he now found himself. It would be well to hear as much more as he could while the chance was still available. He turned to his companion.

'Will you tell me now about the Cunorad y'm As-Geg'rastigan?'

'I spent two years among them,' said Haldur, 'and if I could have had my wish, I would have stayed longer. But I have my father to thank for those two years, that he honoured his promise and let me go, even after Heredcar died… but I'm starting my answer in the middle. There's a small valley to the north-west of here, Rihann y'n Temenellan, the eighth of the Nine Dales. Its name comes from the vows that all the members of the Cunorad are bound by, vows to seek for the As-Geg'rastigan. There are always twelve of them, six men and six women, plus Cunor y'n Temennis. It's not a calling that everyone feels. It can be dangerous: there have been riding accidents, some fatal; and the life is austere and not to the taste of all young people. And not all who feel called are able to serve.

'But for those twelve, they go to Trothdale and they live there together in Seth y'n Temenellan, taking new names to use only in the Cunorad. I was Cunor y'n Tor, and my cousin Vorardynur, who still rides with them, is Cunor y'm Ardo, the Hound of Fire. And all are the Hounds of the Starborn, because their whole purpose is to seek the Hidden People. They study lore and legend in Seth y'n Temenellan with the Hound of the Vow, and while they are among the Cunorad they have no contact with the daily life of the other Nine Dales. Their horses are bred specially for the Cunorad and sent to Rihann y'n Temenellan as necessary. And what horses! Always colour-matched, golden and gleaming, and matched for stamina and speed also; lightly-built and rather small, because they have to be able to range far and fast over steep and broken country.

'The Hounds must renounce more than their names. They leave behind their old lives, their status, their identity as men or women. While they dwell in Seth y'n Temenellan, they are the Cunorad only, and bound by solemn vows. Seeking for the As-Geg'rastigan takes precedence over all else, but they must also serve each other and obey Cunor y'n Temennis; they must tend their own horses and produce their own food; they must follow rules of conduct by day and night including times of silence or fasting. And whatever task they perform, they must meditate upon the Starborn while doing it.

'From time to time it will happen that the Hound of the Vow will sense that it is propitious for the Cunorad to ride out. Then they go to their rest in silence, and rise in the dark before dawn, also without speech. Standing before him they anoint each other and dress for the chase, their minds so set upon the As-Geg'rastigan that they feel neither hunger nor cold, fear nor pain. Cunor y'n Temennis looks into their eyes, and after he has read their hearts he chooses a leader who stands alone with him in the presence of the fire while the others make the horses ready. Then in the earliest dawn he breaks the silence by using their vow-taken names; the leader rides swiftly away, following wherever the call of the Starborn seems strongest, and the others hasten behind. Every ride is different: some last only until the sun is up, others can go on into a second day. Sometimes it will happen that the trail goes cold and the Hounds return thwarted to Seth y'n Temenellan; but usually the hunt will lead to a *numiras*, either new or old. Then the Cunorad will dismount and honour the presence of the Hidden People, and only then will they eat their bread. They ride out fasting and take nothing but water until the search is over, but they carry food which Cunor y'n Temennis has hallowed. On the day we met, before I came to the *numiras* in the woods where I found you, I'd been up to the edge of the fells to visit another that we found when I rode with the Cunorad. That was a wild chase! From darkness into light and on into the night once more until the second dawn broke.'

As Haldur spoke, Maesrhon heard his voice change subtly as its tones filled with love and yearning. He glanced sideways at his friend's face and saw Haldur's plain features lit up with an inner life, his eyes resting upon bright memories. For a few moments they sat in silence and then when it seemed that Haldur had finished his tale, Maesrhon had questions to ask.

'Must those who join the Cunorad always be young?'

Haldur returned to the present, blowing at his sticky hair again. 'Well, yes, only young people could tackle that sort of riding. But you have to be at least of full age, though without ties of obligation. If you're married or promised, or you're responsible for a family or other dependants, then you can't offer yourself. And even if there is nothing else to stop you, your parents or whoever are the senior members of your family must agree, in case anything happens to you. That's why I'm so grateful to my own father. All my life I looked forward to the time when I could go to Rihann y'n Temenellan, and the way was clear because everyone could see that my brother would be chosen as heir to the lordship when his time came. But after Heredcar died, even though the councillors might not have chosen me, I was afraid that I would have to stay in Cotaerdon now that I was the only son. But my father said he too had made a promise and would hold himself bound by it, and he let me go, although just for two years.' Haldur gave a rather shy little laugh. 'I did so hope that the Hidden People would show themselves before I had to come home, but it wasn't to be.'

'So there is no set limit to the time one might spend among the Cunorad?'

'No, although in practice three or four years is usually the longest, and many stay only for one year or less before they return to their old lives. Sallic here at whose wedding I have been a guest, he spent just a year in Seth y'n Temenellan and there are many others among the Nine Dales who have done the same.'

'I saw an old man in my dream,' said Maesrhon, 'and from what you tell me now, I think he is Cunor y'n Temennis? Does the name imply some further vow?'

'Yes, that's right. I told you how those who join the Cunorad take new names. These are not chosen for them, they reveal themselves to each person during a night vigil at the beginning of their service. But there is only ever one Hound of the Vow, a member of the Cunorad who has felt called to make the vow lifelong. He or she spends the rest of their days in Rihann y'n Temenellan as guardian of the lore of the As-Geg'rastigan and guide of the Hounds of the Starborn.' After a short pause, Haldur spoke softly.

'If my life had still been mine to live as I wished, I would have made that vow. I've never spoken of this before, but my father is a shrewd man and I can see he knows. He wears the lordship of this land lightly, but it's a burden he had to carry alone while he honoured his promise and let me ride with the Cunorad. Now I too have made a pledge, to serve my people after him. For a year now I have tried to be worthy of carrying their hopes and fears, and I must keep my word; yet I would gladly have dwelt in Seth y'n Temenellan until death.'

An unaccustomed warmth touched Maesrhon's heart, a warmth of gladness and gratitude that he was the recipient of this confidence from Haldur, a glow of happiness at this further hint of what true friendship could mean. He wanted to give Haldur something in return, to share some of his own untold secrets; but the caution of a lifetime, and the knowledge of what was at stake if he made an error of judgement, caused him to hesitate and ask another question instead.

'From what you've told me, it would seem that sleep brought me a true dream. Tell me then, who was she who led the riders out? Tall, and golden: golden even before the rites, and fearless as she galloped out under the morning stars.'

To Maesrhon's surprise, Haldur laughed at this.

'That could only be Esylto. Isn't she well-named? She even hails from the Golden Valley. When I passed through Rihann nan'Esylt last summer, I met her parents: strikingly handsome, her father and mother alike, but the child of their union is as beautiful as the Starborn. There's not a man in the Nine Dales, even old grandfathers and those happily married, who's not more than a little in love with Esylto; and plenty of young fellows who're counting the days until she leaves the Hidden People to themselves and walks among them once more.' More quietly now, Haldur went on. 'But I myself would not be surprised, if I heard that Esylto had made the vow for life. Among the Cunorad, she is Cunor y'm Esc.'

The Hound of the Sea, thought Maesrhon with a slight shiver.

'Tell me one more thing,' he said, turning to Haldur. 'Why do you call the Starborn the Hidden People?'

This time it was Haldur's turn to seem surprised. He hesitated for a moment and Maesrhon could see that he was groping for the right words to express his meaning.

'Because… because now that… it's because, although we hope that the As-Geg'rastigan have returned, they do not reveal themselves. We feel their presence, yet even where we sense their feet have trod, no man has seen their faces. You'll often hear them called the Hidden People, here in Rihannad Ennar. I think folk take comfort from the name; it isn't so daunting as the Starborn. Sometimes it has happened that one of the Cunorad has been killed in a fall while riding out. Then it will be whispered in consolation that while the rest of us must toil on, the lost one has been taken by the Hidden People to become one of their own. Do you have no such tradition in Caradward?'

Maesrhon's face darkened. 'In Caradward today, not only are there many who openly deride the As-Geg'rastigan, but also many more who deny that they ever walked this earth.'

'But you said, you told me when we met that you sought the Starborn!'

'I said many in Caradward, Haldur, not all. You heard me also speak of Arval na Tell-Ur. I have sworn an oath to him to seek for the As-Geg'rastigan, and I came to the Nine Dales on his advice. You have already told me enough for me to understand how wise his counsel was; but then I know,' Maesrhon smiled to himself, 'I know, better than any other man, always to trust his wisdom. Arval too teaches that the Starborn may walk unseen.'

Maesrhon's story

Maesrhon turned this conversation over in his mind as he rode towards Cotaerdon with Haldur the following day. The signs seemed hopeful, so far as they went; but clearly Arymaldur's name was not known in Rihannad Ennar – or if he had ever dwelt there or passed through the land, he had not been recognised for what he was. Maybe it would be possible for himself and Haldur to ride over to this other valley he spoke of, so that he could consult Cunor y'n Temennis. It seemed likely that he would be best-versed in lore: he might have help to give or advice to impart. But before that, he would have to satisfy Carapethan and his councillors; and when the lord of the Nine Dales came out to greet his son before the doors of the high hall in Cotaerdon, Maesrhon saw immediately that he was a man of keen mind who well merited the name of lord. The bright blue eyes searched Maesrhon's face as Haldur greeted his father and introduced his companion. At the bottom of his pack Maesrhon had carried a small quantity of silver coin, almost the last of what Arythalt had given him long ago. He had used some of it while his ankle mended, buying garments more suitable than his wayfaring gear, and was now wearing new clothes; yet he was plainly dressed compared with Haldur, riding a borrowed horse, and still bore the marks of his long journey in his spare frame and gaunt features. But Carapethan, surveying the stranger as he stood tall before him, hearing the affection and even admiration in his son's voice, felt some kind of foreboding. He was a shrewd reader of men, and all his instincts told him that this newcomer was not to be taken at face value.

'This is Artorynas of Caradriggan,' said Haldur. 'He has travelled far to reach our land, hoping for aid in his quest. He was hurt when he fell in the woods above Rihann y'n Devo Lissadan, and I have waited with him until he was fit to ride so that I could bring him to you myself. Artorynas, this is my father Carapethan, the lord of Rihannad Ennar.'

'Lord Carapethan, I am already in your debt. I was not far from death when Haldur found me: your son has saved my life.'

The forthright gaze swept Maesrhon for some moments more of frank appraisal. When he came to look back on it later, Maesrhon saw that from this first meeting, he and Carapethan had been somewhat wary of each other. It was as if each watched and waited, sensing a weak spot in the other's defences, a secret withheld, knowledge concealed; and in time, both had come to realise that their instincts were true. But now, the older man was speaking; his voice was deep and strong, well-matched to his burly frame, and Maesrhon noted in it the same accent he heard in Haldur's speech.

'You come from Caradward and you ask for aid?'

'Not aid for Caradward, lord. I am exiled from that land, a hunted man. The help I seek is of a different kind and doubtless you will wish to hear all my tale before you decide whether to give it or no. But I should warn you that my story will take some time to tell.'

Carapethan smiled at this. 'Best leave it until tomorrow, then. You are welcome, Artorynas; later we will eat together. Haldur will show you where to go; for tonight, you are a guest in my hall.'

The next morning the two young men were eating their porridge with Aldiro in the private parlour off the main hall when Carapethan came in. Waving Maesrhon back to his seat, he addressed himself to the thick slice of grilled meat and flagon of dark, sweetish beer that was brought through for him from the kitchen. Privately Maesrhon was amazed to see such fare served so early in the day; but in due course he discovered that Carapethan's morning routine never varied: he rose before dawn and after breakfasting briefly on bread and warmed water he would walk out through the streets of Cotaerdon, or wherever his duties as lord had brought him, and mingle with his people as the day broadened. On his return some hours later he took the much more substantial, although still simple, food that had surprised Maesrhon, and then he would not eat again until the main meal of the day at evening. There were many customs in Rihannad Ennar that were very different from what Maesrhon was more used to, but in general they tended to increase the esteem in which he held the lord of the Nine Dales, a respect which began that first day when the council met. He had expected that Carapethan would want to hear him out privately, first; but instead it seemed that he was to speak before any members of Haldan don Vorygwent who lived close enough to be present. As Maesrhon was brought before them and introduced, he was struck by their air of self-reliant steadiness. Until he got to know them better, they seemed alike to him: with only one or two exceptions they were all fair like Carapethan, and had the same direct gaze; even the elders among them were sturdy and strong. They sat under the wide eaves that ran down the long sides of the hall, supported by carved wooden posts, where their meeting was open to the view of passers-by who would occasionally stop to listen: something else that was a new experience for Maesrhon. But for now, he sat waiting while Carapethan spoke first and then it was time to tell his tale. He rose to his feet, acutely conscious of the many pairs of eyes upon him.

'I greet you all and I am grateful to lord Carapethan for allowing me to come before Haldan don Vorygwent. For almost three years I have travelled in search of Rihannad Ennar; it was high summer when I left Caradriggan, chief city of Caradward. When I reached the Nine Dales I was near to death, but Haldur here found me and helped me; from him I have learnt that there are fugitives from Gwent y'm Aryframan among you. What you have heard from them is true.

Their country has been overrun, its riches seized, its people slain or enslaved. Caradward has betrayed ties of kin and friendship which go back centuries.

'In Caradward we have a saying, *"The worth of the heart is laid bare in the work of the hands when the will has its way unchecked."* It brings me shame and sorrow to admit that we have proved the truth of these words by our deeds. But there are still some in Caradward who have stood firm against evil and refused to join in it and the chief among them is Arval na Tell-Ur. He is venerable and wise beyond my telling, and I am under oath to him.

'Arval has never flinched from warning the council in Caradward that their feet were straying down a path to ruin; but gradually as the years have passed, more and more members of Tell'Ethronad have been drawn to the influence of another man. Little by little, this Vorynaas built up his faction; and stealthily he began to drive a wedge between us and our neighbours in Gwent y'm Aryframan. In the old days, travellers came and went freely and it was always a tradition that the young folk of each land would be fostered in the other country. But the custom began to die out, and our estrangement grew. Caradward closed its borders and imposed tolls and checks; there was unrest and civil strife.

'Meanwhile, above us the skies darkened until no stars or moon were seen by night and not even the sun could penetrate the louring clouds. Crops began to fail, food became more scarce and more expensive. Vorynaas and those he had seduced to his side were rich men. They could buy what they needed, and buy also the support of poorer folk by filling their bellies. Gwent y'm Aryframan played into their hands by putting up the corn price. Vorynaas paid it, stockpiling corn under armed guard, doling it out to his dependents; his will had its way unchecked, for by now the gold mine in the forest that his slaves had toiled to open had succeeded. The gold flowed, and it flowed into Vorynaas' hands.

'When he moved for war, those who opposed him were too few to prevent him. Now he need pay no more for grain, because he has seized the lands where it still grows in the sunshine of Gwent y'm Aryframan. But his triumph will be bitter and his success all too brief. His life is empty, and despite his wealth and power, he has nothing to look forward to but fear. His stolen fields will fail, for the darkness gathers everywhere the hand of Caradward falls. He will have no answer then for his people; and though many wrongs may be set to his account, it is for the evil he did long ago that he will pay in the end. But Arval's wisdom and compassion is my hope: may they guide me to the fulfilment of my quest. I have little more than four years left now, in which to achieve it or to return empty-handed to Caradriggan. Even if I fail, I have promised that I will not leave Arval to stand alone.'

Maesrhon paused for a moment. He was still not used to speaking for so long and his throat felt dry and slightly sore. He was unsure whether to say more immediately, but then one of his listeners leaned forward with a question.

'Why has it taken you so long to get here from Caradward?'

'There are several reasons. I could not openly travel north, because there is a price on my head both in Caradward and also in Gwent y'm Aryframan; so first I turned south, slipping the net with the aid of the *sigitsaran*, the Outlanders of the south. And being alone, without knowledge of how many miles I might have to tread, it was necessary to husband both my strength and my supplies. I have had to lie up for three winters on my way.'

Carapethan watched as his councillors exchanged glances; then Morescar spoke. 'This Arval, you say he is renowned for his knowledge. Could he not guide your steps?'

'He has been my guide all my life,' said Maesrhon, fixing Morescar with a wide, golden gaze, 'but there is no man now in Caradward who knows where the Nine Dales lie. Nor indeed in Gwent y'm Aryframan: I was fostered there for five years with Ardeth of Salfgard, and even he could tell me no more of Rihannad Ennar except that it was far to the north and the first home of his people. When I asked him once where the road thence might be found, he said it had been long forgotten.

But since fugitives have reached you here, it seems there must be a path to follow. If you will permit me to speak with these men, then perhaps I may learn from them whether it is a trail I could use when I return.'

'Must you return? Why go back, where the hunt is up for you?' This was Haldur; Carapethan's eyes flicked to his son.

'I have bound myself with an oath to Arval that I will return and it is a promise I will not break. If I return having failed, my own fate will be a small thing. But no man in either Gwent y'm Aryframan or Caradward will be able to touch me again, if I do not fail.'

Haldur frowned, remembering how when they met in the forest, Artorynas had told him he sought the Starborn. Did his friend truly believe he could succeed in such a quest, when for time out of mind no man, not even the Cunorad, had ever looked upon the As-Geg'rastigan? And if this could be, dared he hope that for him, too, it might be possible? For the moment he sat lost in thought, not seeing how his father noted the look of yearning that stole onto his face. Carapethan had questions of his own, but he was biding his time, waiting to hear what concerns and queries his colleagues might think fit to raise.

Poenellald had been chewing at his lip, obviously perplexed, and now he spoke up. 'You talk of gathering darkness, but you surely must use this as a figure of speech? No? But you say the sun fails only where, how did you put it, "where the hand of Caradward falls". How can this be, how could such a thing happen?'

Maesrhon shook his head. 'I do not know. Older men than I have told me it began before I was born, and it has spread and deepened. There are those in Caradriggan who insist that it is nothing more than a strangeness of the weather or the climate which will pass in time, but Arval says not, and I stand with him. If it was a natural thing, it would not settle only upon us.'

'And how do you know that it does?' The quiet voice belonged to a man sitting to one side of the group; Maesrhon discovered later that this was Maesmorur.

'I have seen it, sir. You have heard already how far out of my direct way I travelled to reach Rihannad Ennar. Far to the south of Caradward are the Outlands, where those we call the Sigitsaran roam; and beyond the Somllichan Ghent their cousins dwell in the Haarnoutan, the Grey Marshes south of Gwent y'm Aryframan. I journeyed with them both, and though their lands range from dusty to humid, and all are hot, yet they are not dark. I came north on the westward side of the Somllichan Asan, and the sun rises and sets daily over the huge emptiness of Ilmar Inenad beyond. When I was a child, I lived for five years in Salfgard; on the downward road from Framstock one may see the pall of gloom over Caradward from afar as the border gets nearer. And within Caradward itself, I have travelled widely both on business and during my year of military service, which I spent with the specialist mobile units. Like all my countrymen, I was brought up in the fear of Maesaldron and Na Caarst, the forest to the north of Caradward and the wilderness beyond. But I have been into the forest, and I have crossed Na Caarst on my way to the Nine Dales. Maesaldron is dark only within the valley where the slave-worked gold mine lies; elsewhere it is as green and wholesome as the woods above Rihann y'n Devo Lissadan; and even the wilderness lies open to the sun, pitilessly though it looks down upon the barren land below where all is hostile to men.'

A silence that spoke volumes greeted this, a silence in which some of those present looked askance at Maesrhon while others stared at each other with raised eyebrows. The tension was broken by Ir'rossung.

'How old are you, young man?'

Haldur grinned, and one or two others laughed quietly, relaxing once more. Maesrhon too smiled a little as he answered. 'I am in my twenty-fourth year, as of the Spring Feast not long past.'

Unable to wait any longer before asking the questions that burned in his own mind, Haldur took advantage of this lighter moment. 'Tell us the reason for your errand, Artorynas! What is it that you seek? Why does your quest bring you to Rihannad Ennar?'

But before Maesrhon had even begun to form his reply, Ir'rossung intervened.

'We'll come to that in time, Haldur. That's young folk for you, always putting the cart before the horse. There's other things we need to know first.'

Maesrhon noted in some surprise that no-one reacted adversely to this brusqueness and neither Haldur nor even Carapethan seemed annoyed. Clearly in the Nine Dales their lord was first among equals, and men did not hesitate to speak their minds before him. With the others, Maesrhon turned his attention back to Ir'rossung.

'Now, talking of young folk. If it's taken you three years to get here, then by my reckoning of your own account, you were barely into your third ten years when you left Caradriggan. Military service, fostering in Salfgard, business travel – all this, and you scarcely turned twenty years old? And the ear of this old sage, this Arval, as well?' A pair of bright blue eyes bored into Maesrhon. 'This is a lot to take on trust. You seem an honest young fellow, but convince me now that we can believe you.'

Maesrhon sensed rather than saw that the focus of Carapethan's concentration had intensified. He took a deep breath and began. 'These days, a man may be a professional soldier in Caradward, if he will. But all second sons must serve for one year whether they will or no. They are sent for initial training to Heranwark, to headquarters within the fort at Rigg'ymvala, and most hope to be posted to the city garrison in Caradriggan, or to the border patrols. Only the auxiliary units are open to voluntary enlistment, because the training and conditions are thought too severe for conscripts. Just two of my intake volunteered: myself and another man. He wanted to make a career of the army, but in my case I wanted to take advantage of the skills and instruction available.' He paused, and when he resumed, unaccustomed though his Caradwardan accent was to their ears, they heard a new note in his voice. 'The teaching was indeed good, whatever one may think of its application. I learnt well. But it was before this, that I lived in Salfgard.

'I told you how, in days gone by, an exchange of foster-children was traditional between families in Caradward and Gwent y'm Aryframan. It was usual then for girls to go between the ages of thirteen and eighteen, and boys from fifteen to twenty. Some years after the old way fell into general disuse, our council voted to restore the custom. Youths whose fathers had been most opposed to it were specifically selected, including my brother. I was packed off with him, although I was well under the traditional age, just a child of ten.'

'You were sent away from home, sent far away to another country when you were only ten years old?' Poenellald was clearly caught between astonishment and disapproval.

'Yes; but we were sent to my mother's kin, where even though I was not expected, I was made welcome. As for home, my place with Ardeth and Fosseiro at Salfgard was the nearest to a home I have ever known, and I was sad to leave them. But returning to Caradriggan when I was only fifteen, I had two years to fill before my military service. There were tasks waiting for me then, and other duties when I left the auxiliaries, and so it has been that I have visited the mines in the Red Mountains, had dealings with the commerce and industry of Staran y'n Forgarad and travelled through the Ellanwic.

'But if it is true that bidding farewell to Salfgard was hard to do, I can say that the day of my leaving Caradriggan was more bitter to me, for it parted me from Arval the Earth-wise. In the heart of the city lies Tellgard, our ancient courts of learning. Arts and science, poetry and crafts, all are taught there: both the mind and the body are exercised. Medicine, metalwork, history, swordsmanship, old lore, archery: silversmithing or the sparring-stave, excellence in both is pursued alike. However, on Tellgard too the darkness of our time has fallen. It has always been open to all, and free to all, whether to youngsters simply learning their letters, or to skilled artisans who sought time with the masters of their craft; and the members of Tell'Ethronad were glad to uphold its work from the city coffers. But now, though gold pours daily into Caradriggan down the northward road, none finds its way to Tellgard, which these days must be supported from what can be spared by those who have remained uncorrupted by Vorynaas.

'And yet, those who dwell there still hold the lamp of wisdom aloft, and Arval is their chief. From my earliest years, my happiest hours have been spent in Tellgard, and Arval is dearer to me than all others. He is the wisest man known to me, and the most fearless. He has never hesitated to speak out in council, never shifted from the integrity of his position, never failed those who stand with him. He has always been my guide and teacher; my loyalty lies with him. If I have anything of knowledge or wisdom myself, I owe it to Arval.'

As Maesrhon finished speaking, Haldur stared at him in amazement. There was little between them in age, but it felt to Haldur as if he was still almost a child when he heard of all that had been crammed into his friend's short life. Ir'rossung, Poenellald and Maesmorur were muttering together, but fell silent when Carapethan leaned forward, clearing his throat.

'Ir'rossung must surely declare himself satisfied with your answer, Artorynas. You speak with feeling and I think well of your fidelity to Arval. And yet, there is a thing about your story that I find very strange. You say this Arval is the first among those who oppose the leaders of Caradward; but it is upon your head, not theirs, that a price is laid. They remain in Caradriggan and it would seem they are not in immediate danger, however uneasily they may sleep at night, while you are exiled, a hunted man. What have you done, to incur this blood price?'

'I refused to go with war into Gwent y'm Aryframan and for this I was condemned as a traitor.'

'Were there no others who refused?'

For the first time, it occurred to Maesrhon that he had never asked this question himself. Belatedly, he wondered if any other young man had paid the ultimate penalty in the Open Hall after he had fled. He met Carapethan's penetrating gaze. 'My lord, I do not know.'

'Hm.' The deep voice rumbled in Carapethan's chest, and his brows came down. 'Why is it not enough for your accusers that you are gone from the land? Why this thirst for vengeance? It seems to me that you have been singled out to be made an example of: why?'

'Possibly because it was in the council hall, before a full meeting of Tell'Ethronad, that I defied Vorynaas.'

'So you were a member of the council in Caradriggan, even so young as you were then? Did neither Arval nor his other followers support you? Was your father not present, to speak in your defence?'

Carapethan saw how Maesrhon's mouth tightened, his lip twisting slightly under the old scar; he saw his glance briefly meet Haldur's.

'Indeed sir, Arval and many others addressed the assembly most eloquently before I myself spoke. They were unable to influence the outcome of the vote. But then Vorynaas challenged me, deliberately provoking my response so that he would have reason for what he had long wanted to do.' For an instant Maesrhon paused. 'I was raised as Vorynaas' second son,' he said quietly, 'and he called on me to prove myself true to him or face the consequences.'

In the shocked silence that followed this, Maesrhon shrugged. 'He has always hated me. My mother died on the day of my birth, but she lived long enough to give me my true name of Artorynas and to entrust me to Arval's care. Vorynaas put the name of Maesrhon on me then, but I will use it no longer.'

'And yet he allowed you to escape?' This was Carapethan: still on the scent, thought Maesrhon with wry respect.

'He called me coward and traitor, but he knew in his heart I would not run from him. I had preparations of my own to make, while he wreaked havoc in Gwent y'm Aryframan. Nor would I put others at risk. I waited until he returned so that all could see no man had helped me. But though he thought he sat secure at the centre of a web from which I could not break free, I spoiled his victory feast to prove him wrong. They sat gaping in their seats, unable to move for the fear I put on them.' Maesrhon smiled, remembering the scene in the hall of Seth y'n Carad, and Carapethan, catching the look in those strange golden eyes, thought to himself that he could well imagine this quietly-spoken young man raising terrors unknown if he chose to.

'Vorynaas did indeed send pursuers after me, but I had gained the time I needed. Though they came with horses and dogs, they started too late and had nothing to follow but the false trail I had laid for them.'

'But if I follow your story correctly,' said Morescar slowly, 'it seems that although you were forced out from your homeland, you had already intended to leave Caradward? Maybe now is the moment to ask what Haldur wanted to know some time ago. What do you look for, and what aid do you seek in Rihannad Ennar?'

'I come to the Nine Dales, because it is the most northerly land of which I know,' replied Maesrhon. 'My way leads me north, because I seek Arymaldur, who walked in Caradriggan many years ago. It is known that he came to us out of the north. Has any man here heard this name?'

They shook their heads, exchanging doubtful looks.

'Do you mean he is no longer in Caradward?' asked Haldur. 'What happened to him? Did he return to the north? Why do you look for him? Who is this man Arymaldur?'

'Not even Arval can say where he may be. He is gone from Caradward, taking with him something he bade us find, if we would have hope once more. But Arymaldur is not numbered among the Earthborn: he is a lord of the As-Geg'rastigan.'

Several of those present breathed in sharply; Haldur's eyes widened and the colour came up in his face. Then the man with the quiet voice spoke up from his place at the back.

'You told us that a worse deed than the rape of Gwent y'm Aryframan may be laid to Vorynaas' account. Tell us now Artorynas: what was the evil that he did long ago for which you say he will pay in the end?'

'He incited others to follow his lead, and raised his hand against the Starborn in an attempt to take his life.'

In turning to answer Maesmorur, Maesrhon noticed that Carapethan was staring hard at his son; but at these words his hand too was raised with all the others in the old threefold sign that men had used from time out of mind to ward off evil.

Chapter 37

Carapethan's burden

'Turn round now, and look up the valley towards the mountains.'

Haldur was watching his friend, smiling, anticipating his reaction. Behind him, the sun was high enough now to shake free from the early-morning mists; he could feel its hot summer strength on his back. As Artorynas turned, he too now looked away to where the land began to rise, ever higher towards the peaks of the Somllichan na'Haldan towering above all, and saw the sunlight flooding up the valley that wound into the heart of the hills: Rihann nan' Esylt, its river flashing and glinting here and there where the sun shone on the water, its sides rich and green in the new day, lying open to the summer dawn in radiant contrast to the dark shoulders that sloped above.

'The Golden Valley! Isn't it beautiful? Its name is well given.'

'Yes, that's just what I thought when I first saw it. We'll be going that way, in a day or two, when my father's business is finished here in Rihann y'n Cathtor. I've a friend there I want you to meet: he's the champion archer of the dale – at least, he was last year. I told you about the time they all came to Cotaerdon when the council wanted to see me compete…'

The two young men began to stroll back towards the village, heading for the buildings where Carapethan and his party were quartered. Haldur remembered last year's travelling, his eagerness for unknown roads and fresh horizons slightly tempered by the burden of his new status. He was more confident now; and even better, instead of having to settle for the pleasure of familiar scenes, he had the unexpected delight of showing the valleys of his homeland to Artorynas, seeing them afresh through his friend's eyes.

Carapethan had other matters to think of as the days and the miles went by. He had spent many hours mulling over Artorynas' tale, both in discussion with his councillors and in solitary contemplation; and the more he thought about it, the more uneasy he became. Had these arrogant southerners learnt nothing from the lessons of the past? But while a part of his mind said let them do what they will and take the consequences, the Nine Dales are far away and safe in their isolation, each time his thought reached this point another voice spoke up in his head. Far away, yes, said this second voice; but not so distant as to prevent a few strays from Gwent y'm Aryframan reaching us. And now Artorynas tells us of the Caradwardan army and its ruthless skills and training. Will we be far enough away if they turn their eyes and their weapons on us? Then he would hear again in his mind those who had called for action: more of them now, after the news that Artorynas had brought. No, thought Carapethan. We have the means to defend ourselves, down to the last man and woman if necessary. We will not depart from the course we have held to for so long, not while I am lord in Rihannad Ennar. At this he sat up straighter on his horse, shaking off his preoccupied air and looking about him. They were taking a slightly different route this year, unlike that of the previous summer, but Carapethan again intended to arrive at Rihann y'n Temenellan at the end of his progress. He wanted to consult with the Hound of the Vow about the newcomer before Artorynas sought the old fellow out. He knew that the Caradwardan was anxious to spend time at Seth y'n Temenellan; well, he could stay on there once the rest of the party left to return to Cotaerdon, if Cunor nan Haarval would have him.

His eye fell now on Artorynas. Carapethan had invited him to join his progress around the Nine Dales, thinking this an excellent opportunity to observe how his people reacted to the stranger, to form his own opinion of the man, and not least, to come to an assessment of the friendship which was growing between Artorynas and his son. There was something about the stranger that eluded Carapethan. Although he did not dislike him, yet he was unable to warm to him as he saw others did. Instinctively he knew that although Artorynas had told them the truth, there was some matter of importance he had not revealed. What could it be? Maesrhon, thought Carapethan; maybe there is significance in his old name after all, maybe misfortune dogs him in some way. Yet everywhere they went, with the lord's agreement Artorynas mingled with the folk as he sought for anyone who could tell him tidings of Arymaldur, and all seemed to welcome him, to speak with him eagerly. And now Carapethan wondered what Artorynas and Haldur talked about when they were alone. There they were, riding together as usual. It was almost as though Heredcar was alive again, and Haldur had his elder brother back; yet where Heredcar had been the more outgoing of the two, now it was Haldur who seemed the extrovert in comparison with the quiet, rather reserved Caradwardan. Carapethan had been as aghast as the others when Artorynas told of Vorynaas' assault on Arymaldur, nor did he ever fail to honour any wayside *numiras* as they passed; yet when he saw how Haldur looked up to Artorynas and hung on his words he could not help hoping that the newcomer was not filling his son's head with wild dreams of the Hidden People.

Scarcely had this thought crossed his mind when Haldur, laughing at some exchange with Artorynas, turned his head and met his father's eyes as Carapethan watched him. The smile on his honest, open face widened and he grinned at his father happily. Carapethan smiled back, and his thoughts turned yet again. Perhaps he was too hard on Haldur, who after all had never expected to find himself burdened with a leader's cares. He himself had followed his uncle, who was childless, into the lordship of the Dales: a man who had come into the position late in life after his own father had lived to an advanced age. Carapethan's uncle, being already elderly when he took up his duties, had looked to his nephew for support almost from the beginning, and so from early youth Carapethan had been accustomed to the responsibility of putting his people first. Unlike others from his family, and several of his contemporaries, he had never ridden with the Cunorad; but this had been no hardship to him for he had not felt called to offer himself. As a child and a young man he had applied himself diligently to his lessons and the specific training that was necessary for one in his position. He had learnt well and remembered the history and lore he had been taught, and on the subject of the As-Geg'rastigan his position was the standard orthodoxy of the Nine Dales. He felt as confident as a man could that their pledge with the earth had been renewed, but he was all for letting them be. Surely the old story of *Maesell y'm As-Urad* was warning enough to the Earthborn. Why seek out the Hidden People; if now they wished to walk unseen, who could blame them, after all?

It would be interesting to hear what Cunor y'n Temennis had to say. It was Carapethan's intention to relate the Caradwardan's story himself, before the old fellow had the chance to meet Artorynas. He particularly wanted an opinion, from the person most steeped in lore of all in Rihannad Ennar, on the question of the arrow Artorynas had described. Looking for the Hidden People was one thing, or seeking word of this Arymaldur if he was truly of the As-Geg'rastigan; but how could light be contained within an arrow? Nothing had been said openly, but Carapethan knew that this part of Artorynas' tale had been greeted with some scepticism by those members of Haldan don Vorygwent who had heard it. He wrestled mentally for the right words to express his doubt. Light was such a mighty force, a power immeasurable. An arrow, however beautiful, was only a thing of craft even if made by the hands of the Starborn. And even if the one could be held within the other, how was it to be released? If Artorynas ever found the arrow he sought, what was he to do with it? Carapethan sighed, exasperated at having to grapple with these mystical concepts. He was unused to such problems, finding them surprisingly tiring. Give me a day's hard physical work or even a vigorously-contested argument in council for preference, he thought wryly. It occurred to him that by the time they were all back in Cotaerdon, autumn would be approaching. Artorynas would hardly be setting out again at that season, so it seemed that hospitality would have to be extended to him at least until winter was over. Carapethan sighed once more; but then, seeing smoke rising in the distance, realised they were approaching the village where they would pass that night and began to look forward to his supper.

For some reason, the memory of that lifting of his heart as the end of the day's journey drew near, that simple anticipation of food and ease and a night's rest, stuck in Carapethan's mind so that years afterwards a hint of woodsmoke on the air or a chance word could still recall how he had felt on that day, at that hour. When he looked back, it seemed to him that this was the last moment of his old, uncomplicated life. He knew it was not so in reality: rarely in this world were causes and effects straightforward; a man who tried to unravel one thread from the pattern usually ended up with an impossible tangle that could never be re-woven. Deeds that could not be undone, words that could not be taken back, all these had long before set in motion events that would now inevitably run their course; he knew this, and yet sometimes, years hence in the quiet of an evening, Carapethan would grow nostalgic for the time when the Nine Dales went their own way without needing to trouble about affairs in the wider world. Then Aldiro, sensing his mood of regret, would try to cheer him in her quiet way and Carapethan, seeing her grey hair and lined old face and the knotted veins crawling under the age-spots on his own hands would acknowledge to himself the truth in an ancient proverb of Rihannad Ennar: happy the man who arrives at death without ever having said *would that I could turn back time.*

But all joys and sorrows unguessed lay hidden in a future that was yet unknown and for now the business of each day unfolded until Carapethan, leaving Haldur and Artorynas with the rest of his party in Rihann y'n Wathan, arrived in Trothdale to be greeted by Cunor y'n Temennis. As always, he was struck by the profound quiet of the valley. Here and there he could see figures working in the gardens or beyond in the fields, but the only sounds, apart from birds and the sigh of the air itself, were the small noises of hoe on stone, latch on sneb, scythe through grass. Clearly, the Cunorad were not riding out today; but Carapethan, knowing that their other duties were also part of the service they were sworn to follow, joined the two men who had ridden with him in attending to their own horses. The following day, he sent them back to Rihann y'n Wathan with instructions that Haldur was to lead the main party back to Cotaerdon while they returned as escort to Artorynas over the pass to Rihann y'n Temenellan. Carapethan knew Haldur would be disappointed at not being with his new friend when he sought the Hound of the Vow, but instinctively he felt he must keep his son away from the Cunorad for the while. There would be another time, he told himself, and it would do the boy no harm to have the responsibility of deputising for him, nor to have others see him take that place. In the meantime, he settled to his talks with Cunor y'n Temennis, hoping that whatever the old man had to say would clear his mind.

Advice from the Hound of the Vow

The two of them were sitting together now on the deep porch of the house. Carapethan gazed down the valley, waiting patiently for his host to break the silence. His eyes ranged over the scene before him, as many times his son's had done, both of them in their different ways lost in love for what they saw. Eventually Cunor y'n Temennis turned in his chair, rearranging the deep blue folds of his robe, and spoke to Carapethan.

'I have meditated during the night hours on the tale you told me yesterday evening, the account you have been brought of events in Caradward. How strange it seems that one of the As-Geg'rastigan should show himself in that land and not here, where he would have been received with honour.'

'You have no doubt then that this Arymaldur was one of the Starborn?'

'None at all.' The Hound of the Vow was not fair and sturdy like most of the folk of the Nine Dales, but tall, thin and rather sallow. His faded brown eyes were filmed with age, but Carapethan felt a new peace and serenity begin to steal into his heart as their calm and steady regard met his own bright blue glance.

'Nor do I doubt that we should do all we can to help Artorynas. You have done the right thing in making him welcome, in giving him leave to follow his quest in Rihannad Ennar, in bringing him to me. I look forward most eagerly to meeting him.'

'Well, he should be here within a couple of days or so. As far as I can see, no-one he's met so far has been able to tell him anything about this Arymaldur. If it's right that he was seen coming out of the north to Gwent y'm Aryframan, he can't have come from Rihannad Ennar or even passed through the dales. It's not so long ago, someone surely would remember.'

'Yes, even if he used a different name, it seems likely that any stranger would have been remembered. But we should not forget that the As-Geg'rastigan may walk unseen.'

Carapethan sat back in his chair, lifting his hand and letting it drop again with a sound of renewed exasperation. 'Ah yes, the Hidden People! Even the Cunorad, with all their devotion, have not persuaded them to show themselves. How is Artorynas to succeed where they have failed? Will you let him ride with them even though he is not bound by their vows?'

'Possibly, if that is his wish. Please don't think I am being deliberately obscure, but it's difficult to be more helpful when I've not yet even seen the young man. No doubt I shall be able to give you clearer answers to all your questions after I have spoken with Artorynas himself.'

'I know, I know. But I needed to talk to you myself, first, to try to clear my thoughts.' Carapethan sighed, noticed himself and was annoyed: it came to him that he'd been doing rather a lot of sighing, lately, and this was not his usual style. He banged his fist down on the arm of his chair as he turned to the old man. 'My mind is full of fog, I cannot identify what it is that most unsettles me. When I try to pin it down, it eludes me like some will o' the wisp. I tell you, a man might as well try to clear frogspawn from a pond with a hayfork.'

Cunor y'n Temennis smiled at this. He was old enough to remember Carapethan being born and had always been fond of him; he understood how irksome such a leader must find it to be so baffled by abstractions.

'Listen *gerast-is*. Try to put aside all such concerns as whether Artorynas will find Arymaldur or any other of the Starborn, whether he will recover the arrow he seeks, what its potency may be, how it may be used. These questions will burn in your mind to no purpose. Let us wait, and see first whether he can find this marvellous thing he has described to you. Remember that by his own account it vanished with Arymaldur before he was born. It seems to me that when, if, we look upon it, many mysteries may be made plain. But I think there is something closer to home and nearer to your heart that gnaws at you. Will you share your burden with me?'

Now it was Carapethan's turn to smile. 'You are as keen on the scent as you ever were, Hound of the Vow. I do indeed hope that you can dispel a vague misgiving that troubles me. The year is turning towards autumn already; even if Artorynas resolves to travel further in his quest, it will be six months at the least before he can set out once more. Half a year of companionship with my son, and they are close in friendship already. They are almost of an age, but Artorynas seems older. If his own account is to be believed, then it's true to say that more than an average lifetime's experience has already been his, and yet I sense some secret that he has concealed. What this could be I don't know, but I'm certain that he is hiding something from us, or has not told all. And there is something else.' Carapethan hesitated, unsure how to frame what he wanted to say without causing offence.

'*Tell-avar* , you know that Haldur's heart has always been with the Hidden People; because of this, I let him ride with the Cunorad, but now it is time for him to take his brother's place. Yet Haldur looks up to Artorynas, as once he did to Heredcar, and I am uneasy about the influence this stranger from Caradward may have on my son.'

Stealing a quick glance at Cunor y'n Temennis, Carapethan saw that the old man was gazing down the valley again, apparently lost in thought, his fingertips together; he seemed quite unperturbed by what had been said. A few moments of silence went by before he spoke.

'Haldur found it hard to do, to leave this house and return to Cotaerdon, yet when the message came from you he obeyed it and made no complaint. I revealed to him then that his search is not over and this brought him comfort.' Carapethan made a slight movement and the Hound of the Vow raised an eyebrow.

'I see you didn't know this, that Haldur said nothing and drew solace from my words in silence. But do not doubt your son. There will be other difficult moments in his life, when he will have to make decisions that cause him pain, but his choices will bring credit to you as well as to himself. After I have spent time with Artorynas, I will send word to you of my speech with him; but before that, I will send your nephew to you. Vorardynur's days with the Cunorad are complete, he is ready to take his place among your lords and counsellors. And Carapethan, there is no need for you to fear for Haldur. His life will be long and renowned in Rihannad Ennar, and his name will be remembered with honour far beyond the Nine Dales.'

Though less reassured than he would have liked by this reply, Carapethan still felt easier in mind than he had for some time. He reflected that visionaries like the old man before him rarely dealt in plain speaking, and brightened further at the news that Vorardynur would be coming back to Cotaerdon. He had always got on well with his nephew, although they were unlike in many ways, Vorardynur being much more impetuous and inclined to follow his heart rather than his head.

Well, well, he was young still, thought Carapethan. He may be a good counterbalance for Artorynas with Haldur: someone their own age who has served with the Cunorad but who now returns to take his place in everyday life. Why wait for Cunor y'n Temennis to send him on later? He can ride with me tomorrow. So it was that the next day, Carapethan and Vorardynur set out together. As they paused to take their leave of the Hound of the Vow, Carapethan smiled at the old man.

'I am grateful for our words together, *tell-avar*. My mind is easier now.' He swung into the saddle. 'When they arrive, you can tell the two fellows with Artorynas that I've gone on ahead, so they can come straight on after me. If our guest managed to journey alone from Caradward, I'm sure he'll get back to Cotaerdon with no difficulty.'

With a grin and a lift of the hand in farewell, he set off at an easy pace down the valley with Vorardynur. The Hound of the Vow stood on the porch of Seth y'n Temenellan for some time, watching as they dwindled from sight. He had noticed how this morning the tense set of Carapethan's shoulders was more relaxed, the furrows smoothed from his brow, and as his mind turned now to the imminent arrival of Artorynas he was glad that he had decided not to share with the lord of the Nine Dales his instinct that the essential question to ask was this: why it was Artorynas, rather than any other, who had been sent on this strange search; what was it about him that made him particularly suited to the quest?

Two days later, before he had exchanged even one word with Artorynas, he had his answer. He was surprised to find that in spite of there being temporarily only eleven riders in the Cunorad, his heart felt prompted to send them out. The sense of urgency intensified until it could not be ignored, so on the day following Carapethan's departure, he called them together and began the rite. Under the stars of the next dawn they galloped away, led once more by Cunor y'm Esc. Long after the thunder of hooves had faded from hearing, the Hound of the Vow stood unmoving in the early morning chill, and not until the sky began to brighten in the sunrise did he rouse himself and return indoors. In spite of his sleepless vigil and fast, he could neither rest nor eat, and work or study seemed equally impossible. Instead, poised in a kind of trance of anticipation, he stood in contemplation before the flame as the hours went by.

A summer's day

Meanwhile after Carapethan left the main party behind in Rihann y'n Wathan, Haldur and Artorynas spent several happy days roaming through the fields and woods of this remotest of all the Nine Dales. It was enclosed by steep slopes, behind which the mountains towered, clouds drifting across their rocky faces. Small and secluded, it supported only three or four settlements, snug villages of mostly wood-framed houses, with here and there a large single farmstead tucked into a south-facing glen of its own. The local lord's home-place was about half way down the dale. He dwelt at the centre of the village in a fine hall whose steep roof was supported by huge rafters and cross-beams carefully braced and fitted together; some of the timbers were carved into the shapes of strange birds and winged beasts that seemed poised to take flight through the smoky darkness high above men's heads. Artorynas gazed up at these in wonder when they first arrived, but his surprise was soon lost in the welter of introductions to which he was subjected by Haldur. The travelling party was accommodated here and there, Haldur and Artorynas and half a dozen others at the high hall and the rest by ones and twos enjoying hospitality at the homes of the lord's chief men; but it seemed that almost everyone in Rihann y'n Wathan was related in some way and in consequence all were cousins of Haldur to a greater or lesser degree since his mother had been a member of the leading family of the dale.

It all reminded Artorynas of Salfgard; he remembered his first evening there and how he had been sure he would never be able to remember the names of all the new people he had met. But there was one significant difference. He had been Maesrhon then, disdained younger brother of Ghentar. Those who were friendly with Ghentar, or who wanted his good will, took good care to show their contempt for himself; while those who chose to stand with him knew well that this would put them out of favour. Here, Haldur was loved by all, and all wanted to be close to him. If Artorynas was one of his chosen companions, then that was good enough for them: he too was welcomed and made much of and folk sought his friendship also. Everywhere they went there would be some lad who wanted to show Haldur his skill with the bow, or a young woman with a new baby for him to admire; boys tagged along after them, girls made eyes at them, everyone had a smile and a friendly word. Old greybeards dozing in the sun would wave them over to exchange the latest news, stout motherly women swept them indoors as they passed and plied them with treats from the new day's baking. If Artorynas asked, Haldur would say, 'Oh, he's the middle son of my mother's marriage-brother's sister,' or 'He would be second cousin to my uncle's wife,' or 'She's the daughter of my grandmother's cousin;' and then he would laugh and add, 'At least, I think that's right! But they're all family, anyway.'

One day the two of them wandered off towards the head of the valley. Here there were no more cultivated fields, just the drystone walls snaking up the fells where the short grass shimmered in the heat. Down from the heights rushed countless streams, flung back in silver spray here and there where the water dashed against rocks in its steep descent through the narrow ghylls. The late summer sun burned down in a drowsy, silent noon. Haldur turned to Artorynas.

'Can you swim?' he asked.

'Oh yes, I learnt at Salfgard. There was a place where the river broadened out beside the meadows, and above that there was a place where the boys used to dare each other to dive into it over the falls.'

'Come on, then.'

Haldur led the way down the slope to the valley bottom where the main river of the dale, the Lissa'gillan, flowed noisily. It was only a few yards across here, but the water, peaty and cold from the moors above, ran swiftly. To their left it cascaded over a series of short falls, bending and twisting as it followed faults in the rock, until finally with a drop of about twice a man's height it fell into a round pool. On the near side there were several shelves of flat rock, and the water found its way out and down again to a lower level through a smooth, powerful race between two huge boulders worn smooth by the force of the current.

'This pool's much deeper than it looks,' said Haldur, 'and it's the only place this high up the dale where there's enough space for swimming – not much, I know, but just about enough to float around in, and if we climb up to the top of the fall, we can dive into it.'

They scrambled up, climbing with the help of the young ash saplings growing in crevices beside the stream, then jumping from rock to rock over the eddies at the edge of the drop. One after the other, they plunged into the dark water, splashing and laughing as they surfaced, catching their breath at the sudden cold. They swam back to where the water fell, letting it push them under and bear them back to the surface in the middle of the pool, floating with the current until the surge brought them up against the rocks of the outlet. Again and again they hauled themselves out and dived or jumped again until hunger drove them to turn their attention to the food they had brought with them; then dangling their feet in the water they sat on the shelf of flat stone and let the sun dry them off as they ate.

'I remember an early morning with my great-uncle Ardeth in a place not unlike this,' said Artorynas. 'How long ago it seems, now.'

Haldur, who thought he had seen a fish in the water and had been tossing crumbs on to the surface in an attempt to make it show itself, now stopped doing this, feeling a little awkward in view of what Artorynas had told the council and his father about events in Gwent y'm Aryframan. After a moment he spoke a little hesitantly.

'Do you worry about what might have happened to them all, away in Salfgard there?'

'There is no need to fret about Ardeth: he's dead. No, not killed; not slain, that is, although there is little difference. The *sigitsaran* I journeyed with had heard that he collapsed and died when the news of the sack of Framstock reached him. But they said also that though Salfgard too was laid waste, its people were already fled. I can only hope that somehow they escaped, that somewhere they may be clinging to freedom and safety; but I grieve for Fosseiro, who is too old to be hiding in the hills bereft, with her life in ruins.' Artorynas' voice had hardened, but now he spoke more softly. 'She gave me the only taste of home I ever had, at least until I was made welcome here.'

'Yes, more than welcome! But from what you've told me, you must have wanted to stay at Salfgard, when you were a boy.'

'Well, it was a wrench to leave, but I had Arval's teaching still to finish. And while my brother and I lived with Ardeth, he was parted from his heir, which was hard on them both.'

'But I thought you said he and Fosseiro had no children?'

'Yes, but this was the son of his heart, if not of his body. That's how Ardeth used to put it, when he spoke of Geraswic who was his steward in Framstock. He wouldn't come to Salfgard while we were there,' Artorynas explained, seeing Haldur's puzzled expression, 'because he was unwilling to meet my mother's sons. He had wanted to wed her, but when she was lost to him thanks to Vorynaas, he would have no other. And yet he and I did speak together, in the end. He was taken in slavery to the gold mine in the forest, but somehow he got himself to Caradriggan in search of vengeance; although this too was denied him, for when he would have taken Vorynaas' life, he was tricked and murdered Ghentar in his place. And now Geraswic is dead too, put to death in payment for the unlawful killing. I think I have never met a man so crushed with bitterness and despair.'

'Oh, that's terrible.' Haldur sat biting his lip, unsure what to say, shocked at how much unhappiness seemed to lie hidden in the story of his friend's life. 'I'm really sorry about all that.'

'Yes, it's not pleasant to hear, is it. I always find it amazing, how much pain the human heart is able to endure. A man can carry a burden of sorrow within him that would be too heavy to lift if it were a load for his shoulders, yet still drag himself somehow from day to day. And they call it living.'

Artorynas gave a short laugh, so mirthless that Haldur shivered in spite of the hot sun. He scooped water from the pool and traced patterns with his finger, watching as they dried off from the warm stone almost before he could form them. Artorynas lay back with his hands behind his head and eventually Haldur broke the awkward little silence.

'Do you think... You know how you said that you and your father never really got on... and he gave you that other name when your mother died... Well, I was wondering, do you think all the problems with him were because of that?'

'Vorynaas? Well, you could say it's partly because of my mother that he hates me.'

The silence had lasted just long enough, before Artorynas answered, for Haldur to turn and look down at him where he lay stretched out on the flat shelf of rock; and suddenly he noticed with a start of surprise that though his friend was gazing straight up at the sun, his golden eyes were wide open and bright, without a trace of discomfort. But at that moment Artorynas sat up and spoke again.

'You're lucky to be close to your father. Carapethan is a man who well deserves his lordship, which I think doesn't necessarily pass from father to son in the Nine Dales?'

'That's right, though it's been within our family for a few generations now: folk don't like too much change in Rihannad Ennar! But you've seen already, they also like to speak their minds; and if they're unhappy with their lord, or don't think much of his son, well you can be sure that Haldan don Vorygwent wouldn't hesitate to bring in a new man. A lord isn't just a leader, he must put the wellbeing of his people first and be strong enough to bear their hopes and fears. My father is more than equal to the task.'

'So will you be, when your time comes.'

Haldur lit up with pleasure at these words of praise and the two friends grinned happily at each other, the dark mood dispelled. They lazed by the river for a few hours more and then Haldur said he should head back to the village so that he would be in time to take part in the evening's archery practice.

'Right, I'll come too.' Artorynas began pulling his shirt over his head. 'I don't see why you need to be there, though. I've never seen anyone more accurate than you with the bow.'

'Well, practice makes perfect they say. But it's our law, so there's no more to be said, it's as simple as that. I've got to be there with the others.' They set off downstream, following the course of the river. 'You're not so bad yourself, I think you could give the champion of Rihann y'n Wathan a close match. But there's something I've been meaning to ask you. There was no sword among all your gear when you arrived. Why was that?'

'Better to trust to the weapons of long distance, as you do in the Nine Dales, on a journey such as I made, and not let an adversary get so near me as to be within reach of a blade. But I know how to use a sword.'

They walked along for a while in silence, Haldur reflecting that he could well imagine Artorynas was more than skilled at sword-play. He had that look about him, and the build for it, too. Suddenly Artorynas laughed.

'I'll tell you what, though. I can take on a swordsman, and beat him, armed only with a sparring-stave. Do you believe me?'

'Of course, although I can think of plenty who probably wouldn't without seeing it. You can show us, over the winter months. You'll have to stay in Cotaerdon until the spring, won't you, whatever happens in the meantime?'

Artorynas heard the eagerness in Haldur's voice and felt once more the glow of happiness that his new-found companionship brought.

'I expect so, if your father will allow it, although much might depend on what the Hound of the Vow can tell me. I may learn from him; I hope it won't be long before word comes that he's ready to speak with me.'

'Yes, I hope so too. I'm so much looking forward to riding over with you. It will be good to be in Seth y'n Temenellan once more, to see the old fellow again and be among the Cunorad.'

But later that evening, as they sat talking after the main meal, word came to Haldur that men had arrived with messages for him. When he returned after speaking with them, he was downcast.

'They say my father isn't returning here himself before setting off for home. He wants me to lead everyone straight back to Cotaerdon tomorrow, and the two riders are to guide you to Rihann y'n Temenellan.' He brooded on this for a moment, then looked up. 'I know what we'll do. We'll all ride together, we'll go down the valley and over the low pass, then all of us will go up to Seth y'n Temenellan with you. Then if the Hound of the Vow says you're to stay, the rest of us will go on from there to Cotaerdon.'

Not wanting to seem too abrupt, Artorynas waited for a moment before he spoke. 'No, I don't think you should do that. It goes against the spirit, if not the letter, of your father's message, and he may be angry.'

Haldur sat frowning. 'Well, I don't care. I'm angry too, I wanted to go with you to Rihan y'n Temenellan.'

'I know, but perhaps there'll be an opportunity later. Don't make your father displeased with you on my account.'

On the high trail

And eventually Haldur, mindful of their earlier conversation on the qualities of leadership, gave in to necessity with a good grace and set off fairly cheerfully next morning at the head of the cavalcade. Artorynas stood among the crowd of family and friends who turned out to see them on their way from the village and then joined his two new fellow-travellers as they made ready for their own journey.

They introduced themselves as Cureleth and Aestrontor, the one a local man but the other from far away in Rihann nan'Esylt, although both were now quartered in Cotaerdon as members of Carapethan's permanent household. While Aestrontor went off to requisition a third horse, Artorynas gathered from conversation with Cureleth that his companion had ridden with the Cunorad as a younger man, and this gave him an idea. When he had thought that he would be travelling with Haldur to meet Cunor y'n Temennis, they had planned to take the summer pass through the high country at the head of the dale. At first, when he heard of the changed arrangements he had assumed that he would have to forego this idea, but maybe this would not now be necessary after all. He decided to speak.

'I have a request to make. Would you agree to taking the mountain paths, rather than going by the low road? I thought this would be impossible, now that Haldur has had to return directly to Cotaerdon, but I think that both of you must be familiar with the more difficult way. But the choice is yours, since you are my guides.'

The other two exchanged looks for a moment and then Cureleth threw back his head and laughed, causing the two horses that Aestrontor was holding to bump and barge together with flattened ears.

'I might have known it,' said Cureleth. 'I was in the escort that brought Haldur home from Seth y'n Temenellan, and he had us risking our necks on goat-tracks then, too. You're two of a kind, you are.'

'Please, don't feel you must go that way if you'd rather not,' said Artorynas quickly. He turned to the other man, who had now quietened the horses. 'What do you say, Aestrontor?'

'There's no problem for Cureleth and myself, but he's right that it's a risky road for those that don't know it. It depends if you're a good enough rider, and you do need to be very good. You must be honest with yourself, and with us, because if we take you that way and we find you're not up to it, well, it'll be us to blame if anything goes wrong.'

Artorynas smiled at this piece of typical Nine Dales directness. 'I appreciate your plain speaking and I understand your concern. I'm confident that I won't cause you any problems and can say in support of my claim that Haldur had no qualms about riding with me over that route.'

'Come on, then, we'd best get started.' They set off towards the head of the dale, their horses' hooves clattering on the cobbles of the village street. Aestrontor nodded at Cureleth with a brief grin. 'Two of a kind, I reckon you were right.'

All day they picked their way along ever more steep and narrow paths, climbing up until the trees became thinner and the way more rocky. They mostly rode without speaking, since full concentration was needed to avoid any mishap on the dangerous trail they followed; but when Artorynas could spare attention for anything but his riding, he became increasingly aware of the vast quietness through which they moved, a huge, still silence that draped itself around them, seeming imbued with a sense almost of watchfulness. As the shadows lengthened towards evening, they dropped lower in search of a place in which to pass the night, improvising a rough shelter for themselves and the horses from fallen wood and green boughs, and then settling to food and rest around a fire. Night deepened round them as they sat; pale wood-moths fluttered erratically through the glow of firelight and then vanished into the darkness on silent wings. His companions had heard third-hand accounts of Artorynas' long journey to reach Rihannad Ennar, and though Aestrontor had little to say, Cureleth plied him with questions.

'Why was it that you journeyed on foot?'

'Well, I had no means of knowing how long it would take: it was difficult enough to keep myself alive, I couldn't afford to use up effort and resources in caring for a horse as well.'

Suddenly a log collapsed with a soft sigh, its embers sending up a glittering flight of tiny sparks. Aestrontor cleared his throat and sat up as if he had come to some kind of decision. When he spoke, his voice was gruff and awkward.

'I should apologise for doubting your horsemanship, earlier.'

'There's no need,' Artorynas assured him. 'You were right to put your loyalty to Carapethan first, he'd be pleased to know that he can trust your sense of responsibility.'

Aestrontor grunted something in reply, digging at the earth with the toe of his boot, but did not speak again, and soon they all lay down to sleep; but Artorynas found himself wakeful. The summer stars wheeled overhead as he gazed up at them, the faint earthy smell of the forest reached his nose through the tickle of woodsmoke, his ears caught the far cry of some hunting bird or other creature of the night. His thoughts turned to what Haldur had told him of the Cunorad and he wondered whether they too kept a night vigil. Eventually he slept, but woke with a start, convinced for a moment of confusion that he heard someone call his name. It was earliest dawn; he could just see the treetops against the first brightening of the sky and faint drifts of mist curled across the chilly ground. Again he thought of the Cunorad. Maybe even now they were preparing to ride out, rapt in a golden silence as he had seen them in his dream. He shivered, partly from the cold, partly from the anticipation of knowing that he would see them in reality very soon, possibly that very day.

Not long after sunrise they were packed up and ready to move on again, climbing to pick up the trail they had left the previous evening. Then in single file they followed the track as it wound round rocky outcrops, crossed many icy streams splashing down into the woods, and passed through thickets and darker stands of trees. Twice their way took them past *numirasan*, and they dismounted to stand for a moment in recognition of a hallowed place. Soon after their rest and food at noon, Artorynas noticed that they had begun to descend. The path twisted and turned as it followed the most level ground, but its general trend was steadily downwards; and when he asked, his companions confirmed that they had now crossed the watershed between the two dales and were heading down towards the upper reaches of Rihann y'n Temenellan. The forest began to change from the evergreens of the heights to broadleaved woodland where bright shafts of sunlight slanted into the glades until by mid-afternoon they pushed their way through the hazel-scrub and emerged from the last of the trees. Artorynas drew rein and stopped for a moment at the woodshore and the others, seeing him pause, halted also and waited.

Below them lay Trothdale, filled with golden light, silent and empty except for Seth y'n Temenellan which lay at the upper end of the dale about two miles below them. Artorynas could see a thin smoke rising above the main roof, but there was no sign of activity in the fields about, or in the gardens and courts next to the buildings. His heart beat wildly, and yet he felt touched by some solemn exaltation, as though the whole valley was itself some great *numiras*. For a few moments he gazed, noting the lie of the track as it wound down towards the dwelling-place of the Cunorad, feeling almost as if he could take wing through the gulf of warm blue air below him, follow his thoughts as they swooped unerringly, swallow-like, to rest in that serene haven. Returning to himself out of his musing, he turned to his companions. He saw something of what he felt himself written in their own faces as they sat their horses quietly, and was encouraged by this to speak what was in his mind.

'Gentlemen, I have another favour to beg. You were kind enough to indulge my first request, but now I would ask whether you'll permit me to go on from here without escort. You've fulfilled the duty Carapethan gave you, and guided me well. There's no reason why you should go further out of your way than you need: you could return directly to Cotaerdon now. I see my own path clear before me and if I may, I would approach Cunor y'n Temennis alone.'

Being more used to a blunter approach they looked at each other, slightly unsettled by this deference and scrupulous courtesy. But, though they had almost forgotten it in the comradeship of wayfaring, Artorynas was from far away and might be expected to show strange foreign customs at times. They shrugged assent.

'Of course, no need to ask. No problem, you do what you want and we'll tell Carapethan we saw you within sight of Seth y'n Temenellan.

We can go over the pass into Rihann y'm Aldron. Let the Hidden People keep you.'

Artorynas smiled. 'And you. My thanks to you, and we'll see each other before long in Carapethan's halls.'

He set his horse to the downward path, and the other two turned back into the trees. Within moments, all sound of their going was muffled by the leaves overhead and the mould underfoot, and he was alone again at last, with hope rising in him once more of help in achieving his quest.

The chase concluded

Cureleth and Aestrontor climbed up through the dappled sunlight and shade of the woods. It was cooler here in the trees, but there was a long steep ascent ahead of them and they took it slowly. With no need for haste, they let their horses pick their own way where they could, while bearing away towards their right as they climbed, turning away from the path they had followed on the way down so as to strike the track that led over into the valley of the Forest River. They were going in single file, but the gradient eased where a side glen leaned back into the mountainous wall of the dale and the trail broadened as it passed across the slope. Aestrontor moved up alongside Cureleth and for a while they rode abreast, exchanging a word of conversation now and then. Suddenly Cureleth interrupted his companion with a raised hand as a strange sound reached his ears.

'What's that? Can you hear it?'

Faintly, surging and ebbing on the fitful breeze, but growing rapidly nearer and louder, came a noise almost of hounds at full tilt. High, wild cries floated across to them, and now they heard the beat of many hooves in a muted thunder underfoot. Aestrontor's head turned sharply.

'It must be the Cunorad,' he muttered.

'The Hounds of the Starborn! Come on, I want to see!'

'No, leave them!'

But Cureleth ignored the shout and dug his heels in, urging his horse past Aestrontor, brushing aside the hand that tried to grab his bridle in restraint. The horse slithered and slipped down the slope, Cureleth doing his best to control it one-handed as he held his other arm up to fend off the twigs that whipped at his face. Aestrontor hesitated and then plunged down in pursuit, cursing Cureleth under his breath and hoping fervently that there would be no broken legs or necks, either of horses or men, to deal with as a result of his recklessness. In a tangled mess of bruised undergrowth and broken saplings they came to a trampling stop at the edge of the trees, staring. Across to their left the Cunorad came pouring over the skyline and down the fellside. Cureleth gazed open-mouthed at their headlong gallop, hair and manes streaming in their speed, horses and riders alike gleaming golden in the early evening sun. They seemed uncanny to him, beautiful but unearthly in their untamed fervour. To think that Aestrontor had once been numbered among them! He turned to his comrade, but was immediately silenced by what he saw in his face. He looked back, and now he saw what held Aestrontor wide-eyed. It seemed that the Cunorad had sighted their quarry at last. There was another rider down there below them in the valley. Artorynas was approaching the outer wall of Seth y'n Temenellan's precinct, and he too had seen the golden riders when they crested the rise. Cureleth and Aestrontor watched him stop and turn his horse, waiting without moving as the hunters hurtled towards him. Right up to him they swept without any slackening of pace; but then, halting in a swirl of gold, they dismounted and knelt.

There was a breathless moment of silence. Then abruptly, with a jerk of his head at Cureleth, Aestrontor wheeled his horse. They brushed back into the trees, Cureleth still craning over his shoulder, and climbed back onto the track, riding more quickly now. Though Cureleth was burning with questions, Aestrontor was tight-lipped.

'Don't say anything about it. We shouldn't have watched. Come on now, come away.'

Within Seth y'n Temenellan, the Hound of the Vow had also heard the approaching murmur of hooves as he stood in contemplation before the flame. Although there had been times without number over the years when he had witnessed the Cunorad return, today there was a reckless abandon in the riding, an untamed ecstasy in the voices, that made him tremble. He hurried as quickly as fatigue, age and a long unmoving vigil would let him towards the outer door, but turned as a nearer sound reached him. He heard a faint jingle of harness, the sharp noise of a hoof striking a stone, and realised that a single rider was nearing the house on the track that wound up behind it towards the head of the dale. Cunor y'n Temennis hastened to the window. Somehow he knew immediately that the young man who drew rein, looking away to his left, was Artorynas. Then into his field of vision the Hounds of the Starborn came streaming, Cunor y'm Esc in the lead. He saw the expression in their eyes as they knelt, their faces upturned; he saw the golden eyes gaze down on them as Artorynas sat silent on his horse; and realised, as he gripped the cool stone of the sill with unsteady hands, that his own were misted with tears.

Chapter 38

A message for Carapethan

The grain had long been gathered, the fruit picked, the harvest of the season stored and secured against harsh winter weather, but Artorynas had not returned to Cotaerdon. The evenings began to draw in, nights were frosty and mornings foggy, and when still there was no sign of him, Haldur started to worry that perhaps the Hound of the Vow would keep him at Seth y'n Temenellan right through the winter. He plied his cousin Vorardynur with questions, but was not much the wiser as a result.

'No, I can't tell you anything about it. I set out for home before he arrived, and the only thing I remember your father saying on the journey to Cotaerdon was that Cunor y'n Temennis had told him he might let this Artorynas ride with the Cunorad if he wanted to.'

'What, without taking the vows?'

'I suppose so. Maybe he'll take them now and bring the Cunorad up to strength, there's a space needs filling now that I've left. Or maybe the old man reckoned he was already bound by similar vows, given what you've told me about the quest he's following.'

Haldur chewed this over privately. If Artorynas was riding with the Cunorad, who knew how long it might be before they saw each other again. He remembered winters of his own in Rihann y'n Temenellan. Was Artorynas a good enough horseman for the kind of riding he would have to face? What if he had a fall? Would word come over the passes to them, when he had no family in the Nine Dales who would need to know? Then an even more unpalatable thought occurred to him. What if Artorynas, in his speech with the Hound of the Vow, discovered the clue he needed to help him on his way and continued on his search without ever coming back to Cotaerdon at all? This brought home to Haldur with a most unwelcome immediacy a thought that so far he had managed to push away whenever it arose in his mind: he in any case would not be able to go with Artorynas, if it should turn out that his quest were to take him away from the Nine Dales. And this in turn reminded him that Artorynas had told them all of his promise to return to Caradriggan whatever happened, out of loyalty to Arval. Haldur began to fret, feeling the gold torc sit heavily on his neck once more, reminding him that he too was bound by ties he could not break.

In an attempt to prevent thoughts such as these occupying his mind, Haldur filled his days with a round of ceaseless activity. He was always in demand at the butts and happy not just to demonstrate his skill but also to pass on his expertise; now he went up and down the nearer towns and villages helping the instructors, encouraging the youngsters. His own arrows were always flighted with grey feathers, and the fletchers vied with each other for his custom. Carapethan was pleased to note from his son's conversation that Haldur had not favoured one craftsman over another, that he deferred to the champion of whatever community he visited, that he had a good ear for the mood of time and place. All will be well when the day comes for my son to follow me, he thought proudly. Haldur had a wide circle of friends, but now that Vorardynur was home the two of them often went about together, and this too Carapethan was glad to see.

One morning a hunting party was arranged, and Carapethan, along with Morescar and Poenellald and one or two others of his contemporaries, joined the younger men as they set out in the frosty dawn. The day opened out above them, fresh and blue. The chase was successful and by noon they were resting at ease on the hillside where a little dell caught the last warmth of the fading year. Carapethan looked down over the valley, at ease among his folk, enjoying the food and companionship, happy at the popularity of his son. A perfect day, he thought: a day I will remember. Soon the short autumn afternoon began to close in, and by the time they were making their way home the returning frost was already crisping the leaves and grasses underfoot. The sun sank, huge and red, and as they arrived back in Cotaerdon stars were trembling overhead in the freezing, windless air. Later there were roaring fires in the hall, with mirth and good cheer. At the high table Carapethan relaxed with his guests after the meal: Maesmorur and his wife were there too now, as well as Aldiro and Vorardynur. They were all laughing at some joke or other, but Haldur, although smiling, was staring absently down the hall. Just at the moment when Carapethan noted with some exasperation that the familiar misty grey was stealing into his son's eyes, Haldur suddenly started upright in his chair, his face lighting up with pleasure. Carapethan's own gaze flew to the hall door, to see Artorynas emerging from the night outside, shrugging off his cloak as he entered.

He was now making his way up towards them, holding something in his hand. After greeting the lord of the Nine Dales and acknowledging the others around the table, he gave a sealed package to Carapethan.

'I bring you this message from Cunor y'n Temennis,' he said.

As Haldur welcomed his friend, making room beside him and introducing Vorardynur, Carapethan broke the seal and unfolded what the Hound of the Vow had sent him. The message was brief, and memorably to the point. Carapethan read it in an instant and looked up again. His attention was caught now not by his son, but by Vorardynur, who was looking at the newcomer with a most peculiar expression on his face. Suddenly he noticed something else. At one of the side tables nearby some men of his household were sitting. One of them, a young fellow by the name of Cureleth, was staring as if he had seen a ghost, while his companion muttered with some vehemence into his ear. Aestrontor, thought Carapethan automatically, catching a glimpse of the man's agitated face as he glanced repeatedly over his shoulder towards them. Carapethan dropped his eyes to the parchment again, then he crumpled it up and threw it into the fire. There was no need to keep it; he would certainly not forget the message it contained.

I send this word to reassure you, wrote Cunor y'n Temennis, *having remembered our speech together. You were right to sense something secret in this stranger, but there is no need to fear. Put aside your unease, Lord Carapethan. Artorynas is concealing nothing from you but the joy which is newly-come to him in Rihannad Ennar, and has hidden nothing but his parentage. He is* as-ur.

Reassure me! Carapethan's mind raced. If Cunor nan Haarval thinks this is reassurance, then he walks in a different world from the one that I must deal with. Pulling himself together with an effort, Carapethan refilled his goblet and applied himself to picking up the threads of conversation once more. It was no good trying to consider the implications of what he had just read here in the noise of the hall; that would have to wait until tomorrow. He pushed his thick fair hair back under the gold circlet he wore, and wiped his brow. Joining in a burst of laughter he reflected wryly that while his companions greeted some pleasantry, his own mirth was directed at himself in acknowledgement of an earlier certainty. Yes, he would indeed remember this day.

Hard words in the market-place

But by the following afternoon Carapethan felt happier, having decided what to do. Being by nature a man of action he went now in search of Artorynas, wanting answers to several questions. He found him standing in a group of friends, watching Haldur demonstrate his skill with the bow. Carapethan joined them for a few moments and then with a word in Artorynas' ear, drew him away for private conversation. They began to stroll through Cotaerdon, eventually settling on a stone seat in a corner of the market place where the walls behind them concentrated the warmth of the low autumn sun.

'We had begun to think you would not return to us from Rihann y'n Temenellan before the spring, young man,' said Carapethan. 'Did the Hound of the Vow permit you to ride with the Cunorad?'

'He said I might do so, but there was no need. I went with them in fellowship to honour many *numirasan*, but not as a companion of their oath-bound searches. It seems my path does not run with theirs.'

'Oh? Did Cunor y'n Temennis have knowledge of what you seek, then?'

'Well, not directly.' Artorynas sat in thought for a moment and then smiled to himself. 'He is a kindly and learned man with whom I would gladly have spent longer; he reminded me of Arval na Tell-Ur, and I can pay him no greater tribute than that. I explained to him how it was that I came to Rihannad Ennar; that all my life I have felt the north call to me without knowing why until Arval revealed my quest to me; how we hoped that in the Nine Dales I might pick up a fresh trail. And the Hound of the Vow tells me that, though the Cunorad may yet find the As-Geg'rastigan here in Rihannad Ennar, I myself must journey further.'

'Beyond the Nine Dales?'

'Yes, I must continue northwards to seek Asward donn'Ur.'

Asward donn'Ur! Surely this fabled land must now lie beyond the reach of men, if indeed it had ever existed except in legend. Carapethan frowned, caught in two minds. On the one hand he was relieved: his instinct told him that having one of the As-Urad living among them would destabilise the society whose welfare was so near to his heart, and he was glad to hear that the newcomer would be leaving them in due course; but on the other, he felt it was his duty to sound a warning note. After all, Artorynas could not help what he was, nor change it; and he had brought no harm to the Nine Dales, at any rate not so far. It was only right to alert him of the dangers that awaited.

'North of Rihannad Ennar there is nothing but the wilderness and the sea. I know you have endured much hardship on your journey to us, but remember that though you walked in Na Caarst, you only had to cross it once. If you travel north from here, you must pass through the wilderness twice, because there will be no safety for you unless you return to us.'

'Have you journeyed there yourself, and looked on the sea?' asked Artorynas, taken by surprise at these words of Carapethan.

'No, not for myself, but my ancestors did so. We do not forget our past, here in Rihannad Ennar. All our children are taught our history, as I myself learnt it when I was young. Long ago we set out from our old home at Valward, far away on the grim coastlands to the north-east. Many centuries have passed since then, but we have remembered.'

During his years in Salfgard, Artorynas had heard that the people of Gwent y'm Aryframan had arrived in that land as colonists from the Nine Dales, but it had never occurred to him before that they in turn had come from elsewhere.

'Why did you leave Valward?' he asked.

Carapethan stared hard at Artorynas before he answered. Evidently the Caradwardans, in spite of having this seat of learning, this Tellgard, within their city and the old sage Arval to instruct them, had curious gaps in their knowledge.

'The choice was between a slow death or a swift one. The one was certain, the other a risk. It seemed a chance worth taking. But eventually we found our course thwarted by huge, black cliffs rising from a treacherous swell that heaved and surged around the rocks at their feet. That murderous coast stretched beyond the horizon, without haven or strand. The northern sea is grey, pitiless and empty. We had braved its dangers so far, but now we could go no further. We turned to land once more and burned our ships before daring the long struggle south through Na Caarst until we looked on Rihann y'n Car and knew we had found our new home.'

Artorynas was silent for a moment; then something about Carapethan's tale struck him. 'Rihann y'n Car was where you first reached the Nine Dales?'

'Yes, it was the first of the dales to be settled. Small though it is, many years passed before we became too numerous to be contained there. The toil of our journey reaped a bitter harvest of lives among our people.'

'But Rihann y'n Car is more east than north from here, therefore in that direction also the wilderness and the sea that you speak of must lie. Since Cunor y'n Temennis has named Asward donn'Ur as my goal, to find it I will surely need to cross the mountains. My way leads me not north-east, but north.'

While they talked, the sun had slipped below the rooftops; the market square was all in shadow now. Lights shone out here and there as lamps were lit for the evening. A man who had closed the shutters on his shop hurried past, heading for his home, but stopped suddenly when he noticed them sitting there.

'Lord Carapethan, excuse me for interrupting, but could you spare me a moment? I am in dispute with my neighbour over repairs to a storehouse we share; Haldur has helped me with advice, but says I should speak to you. I will wait, if your business here is not finished yet.'

'No, we are done now. It is too cold to be sitting about here any longer.'

As Carapethan spoke, his breath misted on the chilly air, but he was more conscious of the cold touch on his heart when his son was named. He turned back to Artorynas.

'Cross the mountains? Listen: beyond the Somllichan na'Haldan stand the pathless peaks of the Somllichan nan'Esylt; and beyond them the vast dread of Aestron na Caarst awaits. If you are determined to go, I will aid you in whatever way I can with stores and equipment, but I will not permit any of my people to risk their lives by going with you.'

'I do not look for companions. I arrived alone, and I will go on alone.'

Carapethan noticed how even though Artorynas' face was in shadow, his eyes still held that strange, amber light. *Maesell y'm As-*

Urad, thought the lord of the Nine Dales with a suppressed shiver, there is more than a grain of truth in that old tale. He got to his feet, but just at that moment Artorynas spoke again.

'Why did you burn your ships?' he asked.

'We fired the ships to put a flame of courage in our hearts for the ordeal that lay before us. One may imagine the desperate leaders telling their weary people that it meant there would be no turning back, but their gesture of defiance was surely symbolic.' With a rather grim little smile, Carapethan stood looking down at Artorynas. 'What was there to return to, after all?'

Lifting his hand in a brief leave-taking, he moved across to where the fellow who had hailed him was waiting in a doorway and walked off with him, leaving Artorynas at a loss for an answer to this question.

Cotaerdon in winter

Now the year turned towards midwinter, and snow closed all the passes so that for those in Cotaerdon the world contracted until it consisted of little more than the town itself and the other communities which were either near enough, or further down Rihann y'n Devo Lissadan, for the roads to be kept open. As he took part in the work and the leisure of the season, once more Artorynas was reminded of his years in Gwent y'm Aryframan, and once more his heart warmed with happiness as he savoured the crucial difference, here where he had found friendship and companions who made him welcome. But there were two shadows across his path, nonetheless. One was cast by what awaited him next spring, and the other by Carapethan. Somehow, although the lord of Rihannad Ennar was friendly and generous in manner, there was a coolness in their relationship, and Artorynas could not put his finger on the cause. Although he felt that, since his return to Cotaerdon, in some ways Carapethan had become more comfortable with him, yet still there was some barrier between them that he could not cross. As for continuing his journey when the weather made it possible again, he could not hide from himself how daunting he found this prospect. With each year that passed, setting out once more had become more difficult. When he left Caradriggan, he had been buoyed up by a fierce exaltation, a certainty that he would succeed, a burning desire to return in triumph for Arval's sake; but now he felt older, wearied, more disillusioned; and leaving Rihannad Ennar, after what he had heard from Carapethan and the Hound of the Vow, was an ordeal from which he shrank.

It was true that Carapethan, after the initial shock, had found Artorynas easier to deal with now that he knew what he was. He reasoned that a man could hardly go about claiming to one and all that he was *as-ur*, although he wondered why Artorynas still kept silent as the months passed. He was almost sure that Vorardynur had drawn his own conclusions; and seeing his man Aestrontor make a small, self-conscious deference to the stranger as he passed him in the street one day, he remembered that he too had ridden with the Cunorad in his time. He knows, thought Carapethan, wondering as he did so about Haldur, who seemed unaware of what the others had noticed. One would have thought that Haldur, of all people... but maybe it was simply that his friendship with Artorynas over-rode any notions of reverence. And if Carapethan watched Artorynas, speculating as to why he hid his true identity, so Artorynas could not quite put from his mind his conversation with the lord of the Nine Dales. Gradually the conviction grew in him too that Carapethan was concealing some knowledge, that he possessed some vital clue that for some reason he withheld. But meanwhile his circle of friends grew to include those close to Haldur: Vorardynur, and his other cousin Asaldron; Sallic, the young man at whose wedding Haldur had been guest of honour; Morescar's son Tellapur and his daughter Torello; Cathasar and Arellan, the champions of Rihann y'm Aldron and of Rihann y'n Riggan; Ardig, the instructor in Cotaerdon; and Lethesco who was niece to Carapethan's wife Aldiro. Artorynas liked Aldiro; she was about the age Numirantoro would have been, had her path not crossed Arymaldur's and led her away from the world of the Earthborn, and she in turn offered him something of the motherly affection he remembered so fondly in Fosseiro. Maesmorur too, although an older man, he would seek out for his wisdom and quiet speech. With Haldur though, his bond of friendship grew until they seemed closer than brothers.

One day when the driving sleet and bitter winds of late winter kept most people indoors, Artorynas sat with writing materials, trying to build up a map of the world as he knew it, or knew of it. He was drawing on his recollection of the maps he had studied in his youth, both as a boy with other boys in Tellgard and privately later with Arval alone, attempting to add to them what he had seen since then on his journeys and what he had learnt in the Nine Dales. The most difficult part was estimating the scale of areas where there were no settlements or roads to aid his efforts in establishing distances. He frowned in concentration, thinking back over sunsets and dawns he remembered, testing these recollections against memories of Gwent y'm Aryframan as a way of setting up a means of comparison. In spite of his best endeavours, there were still many blank areas on the page before him, and many more where the lines were lightly drawn to reflect the unreliable nature of what he had set down. Sitting back with a sigh, he looked at the far north of his map. He had added what he could, showing the Nine Dales accurately and then indicating what lay beyond on the basis of what Carapethan had told him, but there was much that was simply guesswork. It was all very well for Carapethan to say that men did not forget, in Rihannad Ennar, but who could say what tricks the passage of so many years had played with the accuracy of their memory? He had marked the wilderness beyond Rihann y'n Car, and a sketchy line showed an idea of the coast with the black cliffs marching away out of sight as Carapethan had described them, but there was no way of knowing whether he had estimated the distances correctly. As for the Somllichan nan'Esylt, their height and extent was another unknown, hidden behind the nearer range of mountains. Somllichan na'Haldan towered behind the Nine Dales, sheltering them from the north but blocking from sight whatever lay beyond. Just as Artorynas began to feel the familiar dread creeping over him when he contemplated this area of his map, the door of the room opened and Haldur came in.

Standing over the fire for a moment to warm himself, Haldur chafed his hands together. 'What a filthy day! I'm not going out again in this if I can avoid it. My feet are absolutely frozen solid.' He turned with his back to the fire, and held up the soles of his feet one at a time to the heat. 'Ah, that's better. What's that you've got there?'

'It's just a map I'm trying to make.'

'Oh, let me see it.' Haldur crossed the room to look over his friend's shoulder, but Artorynas began to roll up the map.

'It's nothing, just a rough sketch.'

But Haldur had been too quick for him: the smile left his face as he saw what Artorynas had been working on. He sat down and leaned forward, his elbows on the table.

'Artorynas, don't go.'

'You know I've got to go on. Believe me, I wish I didn't have to.'

'Well, don't then! This is different, it's not like heading for Rihannad Ennar. There's nothing beyond here, if you're in danger or get hurt, there will be no help.'

'Yes, your father has already pointed that out to me.' Artorynas paused, thinking he heard a sound from outside the room, but no-one else came in and he continued. 'I've got this far, I can't turn back now.' He stood up and began to move restlessly about the room. 'I must go on. When I falter, I remind myself that I am under oath to Arval, far away in the dark of Caradriggan. I will never fail him, not while there is still life in me. But there are other reasons that drive me on. I must not turn aside. And I will succeed! There is always hope, if men know where to find it.'

The two friends stared at each other. Why don't I tell Haldur the whole story, thought Artorynas. Into his mind sprang the memory of a day when he had sat, silent and sad, in the market at Framstock, wishing desperately for a kindred spirit with whom he could share his inmost thoughts. His yearned to speak, and yet the words remained unsaid.

Haldur's eyes searched his face; he waited, hoping in vain that Artorynas would say more. 'I'll go with you.' He spoke quietly, knowing it was pointless to say it; they had had this exchange many times before.

'Haldur.' Artorynas sat down again and smiled. 'Your father has warned me that he will allow no-one to go with me, but there was no need. If I could take a companion, we would go together, but you are not free to go, as I am not free to stay. When the time comes to go, I will be alone, as I was when you found me last year. But anyway, I won't be going anywhere for a while yet.' He glanced over his shoulder as a particularly wild gust hurled sleet and hail against the window. 'Not before the passes are open again, at least. Come on, let's go and see who else is around.'

'Vorardynur was in the hall talking to Ardig as I came through, and Torello is here to see Lethesco. A raid on the kitchens first, then,' said Haldur with a grin, brightening up as they left the room together. Artorynas glanced around him as he closed the door, having once more thought he heard someone, but the corridor was empty.

Spring was slow in coming, that year; but all seasons arrive in their own time, however late. In spite of thick cloud that spilled upon the mountains, sending the rivers churning down in spate, the evenings began to open out a little. The winds blew strong and searching from the heights, but the first lambs were born nevertheless and the shepherds struggled to keep them alive in fields where snow still lay drifted against the walls. There was frost at dawn and nightfall, but every noon was a little warmer and the first blackthorn flowers appeared in thickets where no leaf had as yet burst from the bud. Yet though each day the sun rose higher in the sky, each day on Haldur gloom settled more heavily as the time when Artorynas must journey on again drew nearer. Carapethan had his eye on them both; surely soon, now, the Caradwardan would begin his preparations. But Artorynas, ever more silent and withdrawn, had little to say. Time passed, and still he waited; inwardly, he tried to force himself into action, but somehow could not summon the resolve that would set his feet once more on a northward path. Daily he told himself, tomorrow I will prepare to leave; yet when the morrow came, he would find another reason to delay. In the end, matters were taken out of his hands.

Since arriving among them, Artorynas had impressed the folk of the Nine Dales with the wide range of his skills and his readiness to impart them to others. Though unable, like all others, to beat Haldur with the bow, he was more than accurate with his shooting, and had introduced his friends to the sparring-stave and the Salfgard speciality of decoy-shooting with the sling. This, with its potential for generating much noise and mess, had of course been especially popular with the children; although Ardig, the archery instructor for Cotaerdon, had taken it up with surprising enthusiasm and showed a talent for it. When Artorynas proved his assertion that a man wielding only a stave could hold off an opponent armed with a sword if he knew how to go about it, Vorardynur and Asaldron were particularly impressed and went off deep in talk with their heads together, and shortly after that some of the girls, led by Torello, approached Artorynas and asked him to teach them. He had got used by then to what had surprised him when he first arrived, the fact that the womenfolk of Rihannad Ennar were required to learn how to use the bow, and to keep up their skill by regular practice like the men; so this request did not seem so strange as it might once have done. But he had helped, too, with the gentler arts of teacher and doctor, and pulled his weight with the seasonal round of tasks on the land. When the lambs began to arrive in pastures scoured by icy gales, he laboured alongside the shepherds repairing walls and building pens to provide some shelter for the tiny creatures. One evening as he sat over his meal, the far corners of the hall seemed dim to his tired eyes and he felt a dryness in his throat, a burning in his chest; next morning his limbs ached, and he had begun to cough, but he toiled up the hillside again. By nightfall he was exhausted, soaked through and chilled from the stinging gusts of hail, and before the next dawn came he was racked with fever, unable to move from his bed.

Aldiro took charge of his nursing, and Haldur hovered anxiously, for there were five or six days when Artorynas seemed so ill that he began to be afraid for his friend. They propped him up on pillows and watched through the nights when sweat poured from him and he fought for air, coughing convulsively as the infection clogged his lungs. Sleep seemed to bring him no ease; his limbs moved restlessly and he muttered and moaned, occasionally mumbling what seemed to be names. Haldur heard him cry out for Arval, at any rate, more than once.

'How can he be so ill, just from a cough and a sore throat?' he appealed to his stepmother. Aldiro shook her head.

'That's how it started, but he has made it worse by trying to ignore it and carry on. He should never have gone up to the lambing that last day. He must have been forcing himself to take each step; goodness knows what drove him to do it.'

Haldur fell silent, thinking. He had seen how Artorynas tried to hide any sign of what he saw as weakness and knew he had been struggling to make the break and go on. Maybe fighting sickness to do another day's hard work at the lambing was his way of trying to win the other battle also.

'He meant to leave again, soon, you know,' he said, 'to go on with his northward journey. But if he doesn't get well again quickly, it's going to be very late in the year for crossing the mountains.'

He had tried to keep all expression out of his voice, but Aldiro knew what Haldur was thinking. She smiled at him.

'Artorynas won't be going anywhere outside the Nine Dales this year, never mind this spring. By the time we get him on his feet again he'll be as weak as a kitten and in no state to be setting off north alone, late or not.'

Brothers of the heart

The cuckoos were calling and blossom lay like snow on the orchards of Rihann y'n Riggan before Artorynas was well enough to be out and about once more. One day as Carapethan and his son were standing talking together on the steps of the high hall in Cotaerdon, they heard a horse approaching and Artorynas came riding round the corner. For a few days he had been away, the guest of Cathasar, the champion of Rihann y'm Aldron. He dismounted with a wave of greeting and began to lead the horse towards the stables. Excusing himself from further talk with his father, Haldur hurried off after him. In the pungent gloom of the stable, he dealt with the harness and other tack as Artorynas saw to the horse.

'Did you find out anything?'

'Well, not enough to make a definite decision. I still think I should go again to the Golden Valley, first. Do you think your father will allow me to ride with him again this year, when he travels round the dales?'

'I can't see any reason why not; but anyway, I'll ask him tonight for you if you like. What's the matter?'

Artorynas had sunk down to sit on a bale of straw at the side of the stall, leaning his head back against the timber of the partition with his eyes closed.

'A day's ride and I can hardly stand, my legs are shaking under me. What's the matter with me? Why am I so weak? How can I think of going on again on foot, when even sitting on a horse seems too much for me?'

Haldur looked at his friend in concern. In the dim light the white lock of hair at his temple stood out like a feather; he had lost a lot of weight while he lay sick and even now his face and hands were thin. He opened his eyes and Haldur was suddenly strongly reminded of their first meeting as Artorynas lay weak and hurt in the woods.

'Listen, it's not that long since you were bed-ridden. You haven't allowed enough time to build up your strength again.'

Artorynas exclaimed impatiently. 'It was nothing: just a bit of a chill, a spring ague. I should be well over it by now.'

'A bit of a chill! You don't seem to realise how bad it was. You were delirious, running a galloping fever, gasping for every breath. You should have seen the muck you coughed up. Some spring ague!' Haldur had been half laughing, half angry, as Artorynas shook his head unconvinced. Now a new thought struck him. 'You've never been ill before, have you? Really ill, I mean.'

'I've been injured… But no, I suppose I've not been ill, not like that, anyway.'

'There you are, then. And I'll tell you something else,' added Haldur in a flash of insight. 'You had no resistance to the sickness when it came, because you'd been worrying for weeks about leaving; and you're not getting better as fast as you should because now you're blaming yourself for being ill in the first place so you can't leave! Don't be so hard on yourself, Artorynas. There's no point in fighting what you can't help. You'll have to wait until next spring, now, so make the best of it and concentrate on being really ready when the day comes, and meanwhile we'll have time to find out if we can get more information that will help you.'

Artorynas was silent for a few moments, gazing at the floor before his feet. 'Yes, you're right,' he said eventually. He stood up. 'Yes, I'll see what they say in Rihann nan'Esylt at any rate. Come on, let's get finished in here.'

'Just a minute.' Belatedly, Haldur had latched on to what had been said earlier. 'When were you injured? What happened?'

'A few years ago.' Artorynas put his hand up to the pale lock of hair. 'My brother did this.'

Haldur stared, his eyes moving to the white line where the scar ran into Artorynas' lip. 'He did that too, didn't he?'

'Yes, long ago in Salfgard. A foul move in a fight to settle a point of honour; it was nothing, Fosseiro did a good job on it. The other was an attempt to kill, which would have succeeded without Arval's skill. He saved my life.'

'Your own brother!'

Artorynas shrugged. 'He was under orders, but who knows what demons drove him. When I look back, I think he knew very little happiness in life, and now he's dead.' He smiled a little, the old scar pulling slightly at his lip, as he realised he was about to say words unlike any he had ever said before, something it was important that Haldur should know. 'Ardeth used to say that Geraswic was the son of his heart, and now I know what he meant. Ghentar may have been my brother in blood, but you are the brother of my heart.'

For a moment Haldur dropped his eyes to the bridle he was still holding. Then he looked up again. 'Yes. I've been more fortunate: Heredcar was my brother in both blood and friendship, I'll always grieve for him. But now it is different. For me also, you are the brother of my heart.'

Unaccustomed discord

After the meal that evening, Haldur spoke to Carapethan as he had promised.

'Father, there's something I want to ask you. Will it be possible for Artorynas to go with you again this summer, when you ride round the dales? Or at least, as far as Rihann nan'Esylt.'

'Has he put you up to this?' asked Carapethan after a reflective pause.

'No, of course not. We were talking today, after he came back from Rihann y'm Aldron, and he said he thought he couldn't make a final decision about the best way to tackle the passage of the mountains until he'd been again to the Golden Valley. He wondered if you would let him ride with you and I said I would find out for him.'

Now that they were speaking in private, Carapethan had put aside the gold circlet he wore in the hall. He twisted a lock of thick, fair hair in his fingers as he eyed his son. 'This is just another reason you have thought up to delay him from setting out again.'

Wondering at his father's strange mood, Haldur moved to reassure him. 'No, no, I'm just passing on what he said. I know he's got to go on.'

The blue eyes bored into him. 'You're not telling me the truth. Don't think I don't know you've been trying to persuade him to stay, I've heard you.'

Haldur flushed with anger and surprise. 'Father, I don't tell lies to anyone, least of all to you. It's true I've urged him not to travel further, but I was speaking as a friend who fears for his safety. You must know that he's determined to go; he'd be gone already, if he hadn't been ill. Surely Aldiro has told you how sick he was? When I talked to him earlier today, he was even finding fault with himself for this, blaming what he sees as weakness for preventing his departure. You can be certain that he'll be away as soon as he can. And there was no need for you to tell him he must go alone. I know I can't go with him, that my place is here with you.'

Carapethan recognised the hurt in his son's voice, heard the wounded tones as Haldur defended himself against the accusation of duplicity. This is exactly the kind of thing I am afraid of, if one of the As-Urad stays among us for too long, he thought. He put his arm around Haldur's shoulders.

'I'm sorry. You're caught between friendship and duty and you've been loyal to both. I shouldn't have said what I did.'

'That's all right.' Haldur smiled again, his anger forgotten. 'Rihann y'm Aldron runs the furthest due north into the mountains, but the Golden Valley winds into the hills for a longer distance where the range is lower. Artorynas wonders whether he might have a better chance of success if he took that longer route. He wants to go back to Rihann nan'Esylt this summer so that he can climb right up to the head of the dale and look at the lie of the land; but he wants to travel with you, so that men will see he has your support for his exploration and questions.'

'Yes, yes. You can tell him I've agreed, he can come with me.' Carapethan had sat down again, but now suddenly he got to his feet and began to pace up and down restlessly. 'Almost another full year of this stranger living among us,' he muttered to himself.

'Father, why do you dislike him? Is it because he's from Caradward? Surely you can't blame him for that – look what happened to him after he refused to be part of what they did in Gwent y'm Aryframan. Do you know that his own brother tried to kill him, on his father's orders? But he says the Nine Dales feel like home to him, and he's been generous in sharing his skills and knowledge with us in gratitude for our hospitality. He told me he would gladly stay here, if it wasn't for his unfinished search and the promises he has made to the old man Arval. No-one has a bad word for him, and if you think I'm the only one who wishes he could stay, you should ask Torello! Yet you seem, I don't know, suspicious, or mistrustful. What is it that you doubt?'

'It's got nothing to do with likes or dislikes.' Carapethan turned to look down at Haldur. 'When you are lord of Rihannad Ennar in your turn, you may find out how painful it can be, when you have to put the Nine Dales and its people first in your heart, even before your own son. But since we speak of fathers and sons, let us consider Artorynas' parentage. The message that Cunor y'n Temennis sent told me that he is *as-ur.*'

Haldur sat speechless, staring at his father. Images and memories flashed through his mind: Artorynas, hurt and exhausted in the *numiras* beside the stream; the form of words he had used in speaking to the council, when he said *I was raised as the second son of Vorynaas*; Vorynaas, who hated Artorynas because of his mother and put the name of Maesrhon on him; Artorynas, who saw the Cunorad in his dreams, who came to Rihannad Ennar in search of Arymaldur... He dragged his attention back to the present: Carapethan was speaking again.

'Haldur, though I never rode with the Hounds of the Starborn, I honour the As-Geg'rastigan and I look to see their pledge with the earth renewed. But my own pledge is with Rihannad Ennar. I want no word or deed to trouble the Nine Dales, no sadness or regret to disturb the order of their days or the peace of their nights. I am mindful of the warning that lies within the old tale of *Maesell y'm As-Urad* and I am uneasy at the presence of one of them among my folk. Why has Artorynas concealed his true nature from us? I see from your face that he has said no word even to you.'

Now Haldur stood up in his turn and began moving about rather absently in the room as he tried to come to terms with what he had just been told. Carapethan could almost see the thoughts chasing each other across his son's face, the cloud that sat on his brow, the bewildered look in his eyes, and again unease nagged at him, a resentment that any riddle should confuse the counsels of Rihannad Ennar, any shadow fall across the brightness of Haldur's inheritance. Then to his surprise he saw Haldur begin to smile, and his son turned a cheerful grin on him.

'Don't you think you might have put your finger on the answer yourself, father? You say you are concerned about the possible effect, if this secret became widely known, so don't you think Artorynas will have been wary too, and said nothing for just that reason? And it is true that he has said no word to me, you're right; although how in any case could a man go about claiming to be *as-ur*?'

At this, Carapethan laughed aloud to hear one of his own thoughts from his son's lips. The boy is a chip off the old block after all, he said to himself; I can see myself in him as well as his mother.

'Maybe you've got a point. To tell you the truth, that had occurred to me too, that's what made me laugh. Great minds and all that, eh? But listen now, Haldur,' he went on more seriously, 'listen to me, now. This is not to become general knowledge. No whisper has come to my ears so far, and that's how I want it to stay. Artorynas may live among us for a while, but he must leave when next spring comes. He must say no word, and neither will you; and while I think of it, you must find some way to discourage Torello: I've seen the way her eyes follow him. Better her wings clipped than her heart broken.'

But by the time Carapethan and his companions reached the Golden Valley that summer the rumours were already beginning to run. Among the escort was Cureleth, with time on his hands as the miles went by to stare at Artorynas and remember what he had seen in Rihann y'n Temennis; and with no Aestrontor riding alongside this time to bid him keep silent when men sat at ease in the evenings. Carapethan gritted his teeth, trying not to waste his energy on wondering where the whispers had started but rather to decide what his answer would be the first time anyone spoke to him directly, uncomfortably aware of the old proverb that said *he who blocks a chimney only sends the smoke through the house*. He was relieved to discover that Artorynas was not proposing to travel onwards with the company; his business done in Rihann nan'Esylt, he intended to return to Cotaerdon.

Haldur was to go on with the rest of the party as they continued their progress and on their last day together, he and Artorynas took part in a contest to which Ennarvorad, the champion of the dale, had challenged them. As usual, the outcome could have been predicted.

'It's hopeless!' said the young man with good-humoured resignation as they examined the target.

'You've run me pretty close, though,' said Haldur, pulling the arrows out.

'Close, yes. But I've been practising all year, I was so sure I would beat you this time. Oh well, it's what they all say, isn't it? You must have the eyes of the Starborn.' Ennarvorad laughed. 'What can you do? At least I'm still champion of Rihann nan'Esylt. I'll see you two at supper later, then.'

Their host strolled off as Haldur and Artorynas vied with one another for another two or three shots. Artorynas still marvelled at Haldur's uncanny accuracy, every arrow flying true to the gold.

'I know I've said this before, but I've never seen anyone with your skill. That young fellow is right: it must be true what they say about you!'

He had been stooping to look at their shots but as he spoke he straightened and turned and the evening sun shone into his face, waking the gold of his eyes. Haldur remembered his father's words, but could not help himself: they were alone, there were none to hear.

'No, it's not me,' he said, 'not me, it's you. You're the one who has the eyes of the As-Geg'rastigan.'

CHAPTER 39

The shadows spread

It had been a long, hot day as they made their way down through the settlements of Rihann y'n Fram and it was already almost dark when they reached their stopping-place for the night where the local lord, eager to impress with his hospitality, had offered a meal that was generous but rather heavy for a late, sticky evening. Carapethan was expecting another long day on the morrow, but at least now it was time to prepare for rest. He arranged his formal clothes on the stand and threw on his nightshirt. Lifting the golden circlet from his head, he set it down and then for a moment stood looking at it, seeming lost in thought. Artorynas had apparently begun planning in earnest for his departure, he was glad to see. He had decided to take the longer route out of the Nine Dales by Rihann nan'Esylt when the time came, and for now had even turned his horse in, deciding to make his way back to Cotaerdon on foot as a means of starting to build up his endurance once more. Carapethan laid himself down on the bed and closed his eyes gratefully, feeling sleep beginning to steal upon him as his mind and body relaxed; no inkling of the morrow's unexpected events disturbed his rest.

Towards the end of the following afternoon, a rapidly-approaching dustcloud resolved itself into three men on horseback riding swiftly towards them. They turned out to be the leading man and two companions from the village for which they were making; and Carapethan halted to greet them, surprised at what he took to be their desire to hurry forth in welcome on such a warm and sultry day. When he heard what they had to say his mood changed.

'There are men waiting to speak with you,' said the village elder, 'more fugitives from Gwent y'm Aryframan. They were found in Two Riversdale some two or three weeks ago and are not yet completely recovered from their ordeal, but when they told their story, the lord of that dale felt you should have their news as soon as possible. He had them tended and fed, and as soon as they were fit to travel, he sent them over to me by wagon, knowing that you were on your way down Rihann y'n Fram. Carapethan, they bring black tidings. It seems the Caradwardans have brought more than slavery to our kinsfolk in the south. The darkness that lies over their land is now creeping over Gwent y'm Aryframan as well.'

Carapethan's heart sank at these words as if a shadow had fallen upon him also. He looked at the man who had spoken: he was well-dressed and riding a good horse, and had spent a lifetime as a respected leader of his community. He was older than Carapethan, a man to whom other men looked for guidance and counsel, but now in turn he too hungered for reassurance; there was fear lurking behind the eyes that sought Carapethan's. The lord of the Nine Dales reached out and gripped his arm, drawing him alongside so that they could talk further as they rode. He saw how the man was comforted as they spoke together, how his burden lightened as he shifted it from his own shoulders on to his lord's; and when he heard the full tale later at first hand, the full weight of the hopes and fears that his people trusted him to carry for them weighed more heavily than usual upon his strength.

A plea for help

'We are from the far north of Gwent y'm Aryframan, lord,' said the spokesman for the refugees. There were five of them, although Carapethan had been told that another was lost on the way, together with his horse: drowned as they forded a river. He had been warned, too, about the youngest of the five, who sat blank-eyed and silent. It was his brother who had died; he had refused to travel further until they had searched downstream for the body and buried it. Then leaving the dead man to lie in his lonely grave in the wilderness they had struggled on.

'It's only from the north that anyone could hope to get here,' the man continued, 'because if you tried from further south, you'd be stopped and picked off within two days at most by the Caradwardans, curse them. But in the uplands beyond us, in Gillan nan'Eleth, they say men still live free in some secret glen. I've heard tell that it's Ardeth's folk from Salfgard; that they got away in time when the news came that the Caradwardans were upon us. They say Ardeth looks down on Salfgard from where he sleeps on the hill, that if we've got the stomach for the fight, he'll return to us and help us throw off the yoke. Well, who knows? Whatever, tales like that make a winter's night seem warmer, when they're whispered around the fire. Anyway, word came that if we could only slip away to a certain place, there'd be help for us; so we took what we could and sure enough, when we got up to the head of the pass there were three horses hidden in a ruined byre with food and other stuff in packs beside them.

'We divided up what we'd brought with us and were just about to get moving when we found we weren't alone. There was a fellow who must have been watching for us from among the boulders back from the path, and he stood up and hailed us. We thought it was all up for a moment, I can tell you, but I reckon he must have been one of them from out of Gillan nan'Eleth. Obviously, he didn't say, and we didn't ask. His face was covered, but from his voice I'd say he was still young. Anyway, he said to take the horses and set our course north-east as straight as we could go. Well, we looked at each other. Head right into Na Caarst? We weren't as tired of life as that, surely. "Listen," this young fellow says to us, "if you want to make it to Rihannad Ennar, you've enough provisions to do it, if you keep going like I tell you, as fast as you can. In about a month you should arrive at a ravine where a great river plunges underground. Follow that and the valley opens out, it'll bring you into one of the Nine Dales." We asked him how he knew about all this, whether he'd been there himself, but he wouldn't say. So then we said why not come away with us, what was there to stay for? "I've got my own reasons," he says. "I've asked you no questions, so don't you be asking me any. Good luck to you now, may the As-Geg'rastigan go with you." Then he disappeared into the night without another word.

'Well, we mounted up, three of us anyway because it would have to be turn and turn about with the horses, and we went down from the pass. But before we got to the bottom we stopped to take stock. We'd decided before we set out that anything we did, wherever we went, we'd all have to agree on it first; and this idea of striking out into the middle of the wilderness was something we hadn't bargained for at all. We argued it out, but it was clear some of us would never be happy about it, and we'd taken our oath; so in the end we compromised. We reckoned to stick to our original plan, and go north along the foothills of the mountains. Then we thought, if we find no sign of the Nine Dales after two months, we'll risk turning across in the hope of finding the river we'd been told about.'

The man paused, glancing across at the youngest of his companions.

'I suppose we'll never know whether we did the right thing or not. There should be six of us here tonight, but maybe the five who are left can speak the louder to make up for him that's gone. Lord, we have risked everything to find you: one of us has paid with his life. We ask you to remember your kin in the south, to send help to us from Rihannad Ennar. Night is falling now, but here the stars of summer shine in the sky and tomorrow the sun will rise. When dawn comes you will be able to look out over this rich valley where your people live in peace and plenty, where the fields are ripening to harvest. In Gwent y'm Aryframan our darkness is unrelieved.'

A long silence fell, in which Carapethan sat brooding, chin on hand, thinking over what he had heard.

'I will be mindful of the ties of kin you invoke,' he said at last, 'but as lord of the Nine Dales, I must put my own people first. For yourselves, I offer you sanctuary and homes among us. You may stay here if you will and need not fear for your lives again. But lordship in Rihannad Ennar is given and held by consent: any decisions I make are informed by the general will, therefore I shall listen to the opinions of my advisors and the voice of my folk before I answer your plea. I will send messages back to the dales I have already visited, so that my counsellors know to gather before me in Cotaerdon at the summer's end; and I bid you be there also. Meantime, you are my guests here in Rihann y'n Fram. Walk in the fields where the Lissa'mor flows and regain your health and strength. In Cotaerdon we will speak again.'

Carapethan held to his promise: even before he continued his progress riders were despatched to take his summons up and down the dales, spreading the news of the meeting he proposed to hold.

Anxious days

In due time the lord of Rihannad Ennar returned to his hall in Cotaerdon. Not long after the last of the grain was cut and stored against the winter, and Harvest-home was celebrated, delegates from the other valleys began to arrive in Cotaerdon for the meeting that Carapethan had called. While they waited for everyone to gather, the inns and guest-halls where they were quartered buzzed with rumour and speculation as men talked over the bad news which had reached them from the south and argued about what measures Carapethan might take. Meanwhile Haldur lost no time in telling Artorynas all about the fugitives who had appealed to his father for help. Artorynas sat silent as the tale unfolded. He thought of Gwent y'm Aryframan plunged in gloom, but found it almost impossible to imagine Salfgard without its radiant dawns and glowing sunsets. Thank the Starborn that Ardeth had never lived to see his world despoiled and his work all reduced to nothing. Yet maybe all was not quite lost, if it was true what the refugees had heard, that some at least of Ardeth's folk had remained free. Artorynas remembered how the *sigitsaran* who had helped him had also spoken of this, and he wondered now how many of those from Salfgard were still alive: whether Fosseiro was among them, who it was that had helped the fugitives on their way. A young man, they had thought him. He ran through some well-remembered names in his mind, but quickly gave this up as pointless. More significant was the information he had given them about how to get across Na Caarst: how had he found this out? Maybe I will be able to use this route when I return south, thought Artorynas. It sounds to me as though if I travel down Rihann y'n Devo Lissadan far enough, it will prove to be the Lissad nan'Ethan that flows through the ravine he spoke of and plunges underground. As his mind ran on, he shifted restlessly in his seat and then became conscious that Haldur was no longer speaking. He looked up to see his friend watching him somewhat quizzically: evidently the silence had lasted some time.

'Sorry, I was listening,' said Artorynas. 'I was, really; but it's just that I was thinking ahead. So, what's your father going to do?'

'Well, I can't say for sure, obviously. He's already told these latest arrivals that they're welcome to stay, and he's called this meeting so that they get a general hearing. I expect he'll make sure they get any help they need to establish themselves.'

'But they'll want help for those left behind in Gwent y'm Aryframan, won't they?'

'Oh yes, they've already asked him for that. He wouldn't go that far before though, when the first fugitives came to us.' Haldur looked down at his hands, seeming rather bothered. 'Some of the younger members of Haldan don Vorygwent wanted to do more that time, I think. There was some fairly wild talk. It was the year before you got here; I'd only just been confirmed as heir. I remember how I used to wonder whether my father was being wise or not, whether the differences of opinion were just youth and age typically disagreeing. I worried about what I'd have done if I'd been lord when it all happened.'

The full tale of what the refugees had to say did indeed provoke widespread anger and sorrow when it was told at the council. They described a land lying as if blighted, its harvests failing as the light dimmed, its people fading into a sickness of despair. They told how the Caradwardan overlords had begun by refusing to acknowledge any problem, then made proud claims that their skills would overcome it; but their failure was starkly clear as the scale of the crisis grew to disastrous proportions. Gwentarans forced to labour in their increasingly desperate schemes often wasted away as if they no longer had the will to live; bolder spirits who tried to slip away in search of freedom were rounded up and ruthlessly dealt with. Save us, Lord Carapethan, begged the fugitives; do not leave us to die as slaves in the darkness. Come down from your hills and valleys by the path your ancestors trod, sweep all before you and we will rise from our bondage to fight beside you!

Unsurprisingly, this emotional appeal caused feelings to run high. Once the Gwentarans, reassured that their request would be fully discussed, were escorted from Haldan don Vorygwent, its members furiously disagreed about what to do. Again the broad division of opinion was by generation, with younger men urging Carapethan to heed the call to arms and their elders arguing against this; but there were exceptions. Vorardynur spoke passionately in favour of falling upon the Caradwardans, while Asaldron was against this; and though Ir'rossung refused to budge from his opposition to any idea of an expedition, Poenellald and even Maesmorur apparently thought it worth considering further. This was interesting, and rather unexpected, thought Artorynas, wondering what reasons they had. As a stranger, he had not been present, but Haldur had described the scene to him afterwards.

'What do you think should be done?' he asked Haldur.

'Well, I can't help feeling that we should do *something*, after what I heard at the meeting and all that you've told me. But could we succeed? We know little of the route down to Gwent y'm Aryframan, and the information we do have is more than daunting. Even if we reached our journey's end in safety, we'd still be far from home with no hope of reinforcements, fighting what you've told us is a professional army. Before setting out on such an enterprise we'd need to be convinced of our cause and sure of victory. As things stand, while we're not of one mind we can't fulfil the first condition; and for myself, I would not be confident that we could achieve the second.' He spread his hands in a small, rather apologetic gesture. 'I suppose that all sounds hopelessly indecisive.'

'No, it seems to me you've thought things out well. A man who proposes to lead others into danger must evaluate the risks very carefully before he hazards the lives he holds in trust. Have other courses been suggested or discussed? What has your father advised?'

'He has pointed out that the season is turning already towards autumn and that it's too late in the year to make any move. He says this is fortunate, that it gives us the winter of enforced inactivity when we can take the time we need to weigh up all the options and be sure that whatever decision is taken in the end is the right one. I thought of sending out secret observers, to find out for ourselves how things stand … but of course, I realise that if any such scout was intercepted, it would prejudice the success of more direct action.' Haldur sighed. 'I know my father will keep the promise he has made to the suppliants, that he will consider their request for intervention very carefully; but I'm also sure he will make no move if he feels this would endanger the Nine Dales. He is not called the father of his people without reason. But I think he was taken aback and displeased that Maesmorur and Poenellald were equivocal in their support.'

'Yes, I'm surprised by that too,' said Artorynas. 'Do you have any idea of their reasons?'

'Poenellald said … he wondered … Actually, your name came into things. Remember when I brought you here, and you spoke before the members of Haldan don Vorygwent who were in Cotaerdon at the time? Poenellald reminded everyone that you said it's the Caradwardans who bring the darkness; so his point was, shift the Caradwardans and we dispel the darkness, because if we let them be, who's to say they won't bring it upon us eventually. But against this Ir'rossung said Rihannad Ennar is far enough away to be safe, and my father backed him up on that.'

'And what about Maesmorur?'

'Well, Maesmorur's a man who doesn't say a lot, but… He's obviously been turning over in his mind what you told us that day, too, and you've become quite friendly with him since, haven't you? And I think he, well…' Haldur hesitated and then blurted out, '…I think he knows you're *as-ur*. You probably don't need me to tell you that whispers are beginning to circulate, but even without them, Maesmorur very likely drew his own conclusions. He said something along the lines of how maybe a small group of specially-chosen companions might sow enough dread and wonder to succeed where force would fail, and I'm sure he was thinking of you at the head of an oath-bound fellowship like the Cunorad.'

A shiver ran over Artorynas. 'Perhaps he sees Esylto in his mind's eye. When the power is upon her, her beauty is so full of danger that it might well stop a man's heart in his body before ever he had time to think of battle.'

Haldur turned, hearing the strange note in his friend's voice. Artorynas and Esylto, of course! Who else could there be for either of them but the other? But Artorynas was shaking his head, smiling slightly.

'No, don't run away with that idea. As soon as I saw her I was put in mind of what men said about my mother, that she was as lovely as the Starborn; but I think that like her, Esylto too will never be satisfied with the things of this world.'

Haldur was not sure he had fully understood what Artorynas meant by this, but was partly reassured. 'Oh? Well… Torello can breathe again, then!'

'I have spoken with Torello as one friend to another,' said Artorynas, the line deepening between his brows, 'and she knows I will not be staying in Rihannad Ennar. She told me herself that she knows I must go on.'

A rather awkward silence fell between the friends. Haldur, recalling his father's instruction to discourage Torello's affection for Artorynas, felt a little guilty at not having done more, but suspected that he would have had no success in any case. Artorynas meanwhile was thinking about an occasion after he had arrived back in Cotaerdon, following a long tramp from the Golden Valley. With Haldur and many of his other friends still away, and the late summer hush lying over all, the town seemed unusually quiet and he had found himself with time on his hands. One afternoon he had wandered over a footbridge onto the central green space, sat under a tree and let his thoughts drift. Sometimes in the silence of night he had done this, and succeeded in emptying his mind so completely that images had appeared unbidden in his heart. These scenes and people were not dreamlike: they moved and spoke before him as if in reality, though seeming far away beyond guessing. He had seen Arval and many others known to him, and wondered whether what he saw was truth. Could it possibly be that he could call up visions of events and places distant from him, and if so could he train himself to do this at will? Or was what he saw an illusion, born of his secret hopes and fears? But this time nothing new had come to him; for quiet though the afternoon was, he could still hear the distant laughter of children playing, still see the sunlight dancing through the branches above his head even through closed eyelids. As he scuffled a few withered oak leaves with his foot, crumbling them into brown fragments, a few more leaves drifted down. The summer was nearly over. When the sound of footsteps broke his reverie, he looked up to see Torello standing near; he waved her over with a smile and for a while they sat talking together. And if Haldur, though in no doubt that the subject was now closed, was not so sure that Artorynas had correctly gauged Torello's feelings concerning his departure, Artorynas also had cause to feel less than comfortable when he remembered how their conversation had ended that day.

A leader's burdens

But whatever the private concerns of these three young people, there was no avoiding the more serious matter of what action, if any, should be taken when the spring came. This was a constant topic for debate and it seemed to Artorynas that those who favoured intervention were gradually becoming a majority; yet still Carapethan appeared reluctant or even, he sometimes thought, unwilling to commit himself to a policy of war. The lord of Rihannad Ennar had not, so far at any rate, sought his opinion, for which he was rather glad. After all, he himself would be gone once more on his own lonely errand whatever Carapethan decided in the end, and it was this that prompted him to speak one morning.

'Sir, it will not be long now before I must leave the Nine Dales and travel north again. I will always be grateful for the welcome I have been given in your land, for the help and friendship I have found here. If there is anything at all I can do to repay my debt before I go, you have only to say the word. But winter will be upon us soon, and while the weather still holds I would appreciate the chance to ready myself for the journey to come. I need to build my endurance and resilience up to the staying point once more, to train myself anew for the road that lies ahead. May I have your leave to walk and climb in your hills and dales in the weeks before snow closes the passes? I will return to Cotaerdon after each venture in case you need me for some task or duty here.'

Carapethan sat for a moment contemplating Artorynas. He was sure in his own mind that the younger man was going to his death if he insisted upon the course he had chosen, *as-ur* or not; but was not so sure whether he admired or feared his apparent calm resolve. Yes, it would be better for all concerned when his disconcerting presence was gone from among them, when he was no longer there to unsettle Rihannad Ennar.

'You are still determined to attempt the mountain crossing, then?' he said.

'Yes, my road leads me up through the Golden Valley and over the Somllichan na'Haldan to the Somllichan nan'Esylt beyond – and further, if I can find the way. Lord, let me say that the Nine Dales have felt like home to me, as no other place has ever done; but my quest still calls me north.'

'Well, well,' said Carapethan rather gruffly, feeling a little ashamed of his earlier thoughts in the face of this admission. 'Of course, feel free to come and go as you please.'

So Artorynas looked out his travelling gear and pack and ranged out into the wild country above the fields and pastures, roaming further each time, setting himself stern tests of fitness and strength. He walked alone, as part of his preparations for the ordeal he must face; and his comings and goings became the subject of some curiosity. Mellow autumn sun gave way to raw days of rain, driving into his face on a chill wind; frost turned the leaves and the snowline crept lower down the mountains and still he was gone for days on end. Haldur watched the weather anxiously and men turned from talk about affairs away south to debate the stranger in their midst: the whispers about him began to run ever more widely, to Carapethan's increasing exasperation. Finally, on a day of wild gales that howled down the valley, tearing the very last leaves from the woods, at evening Artorynas came back to Cotaerdon to wait out the winter and Carapethan sent for his son.

'You hear it everywhere,' he said, determined to have things out between them, 'and I want to know why you have spoken of this, when I specifically told you to say nothing.'

'Father, I promise you, it has nothing to do with me.' Haldur was uncomfortable at this exchange on the subject of Artorynas, being well aware of the rumours that were circulating freely now but denying vehemently that he had had any part in spreading them. 'I know what people are saying, but as far as I can make out, it started with a tale from some traveller who claimed to have seen the Cunorad acknowledge him.'

'What?' Gradually putting two and two together, Carapethan spoke slowly. 'It must be those fellows I sent back to escort him, Cureleth and Aestrontor. They left him to make his own way down Rihann y'n Temenellan, so they said, but maybe they saw more than they reported.' He sat frowning, twisting a lock of hair around his fingers; Haldur hovered uncertainly. 'I tell you,' said Carapethan, suddenly fixing his son with a piercing blue gaze, 'I tell you, next spring cannot come quickly enough for me.'

But in the time after midwinter, when the mirth of the feast was over but the days were still short and gloomy, with no hint yet of the year turning once more, Carapethan found that he was not so much looking forward to Artorynas' departure as worrying about the decision he himself would have to take. Could he bring himself to put the peace of the Nine Dales in jeopardy when his whole life had been devoted to the welfare of his land and people? But there again, would his sense of justice allow him to ignore the suffering of his distant kinsfolk, could he rest at night if he ignored their plea for help? What if danger was creeping upon Rihannad Ennar whether or not he stood firm against those who clamoured for action? And if the majority were against him, but he denied their wishes, would this cripple his authority? If he no longer ruled by consent, what effect would this have on the wellbeing of the land that was so dear to his heart? These questions beat about his mind as Vorardynur strode from the room where they had been arguing, slamming the door behind him. A moment or two later, Carapethan heard the latch lift and the door opened once more, but quietly; he looked up in surprise to see Artorynas peering cautiously over the threshold.

'I'm sorry, I didn't mean to disturb you; it was just that I thought I heard raised voices, and I wondered what…'

'No, that's all right. Come in.'

Sleccenal

Carapethan motioned Artorynas to a seat but stood himself, moving to the window and staring out without speaking. Suddenly he turned round again.

'Vorardynur grows impatient with me. He speaks for those who want military action; they are pressing me to give the order.'

Artorynas was taken aback at this sudden confidence and assumed that Carapethan would say more; but the silence stretched out until Carapethan addressed him again. 'What is your advice?'

Now even more astonished, Artorynas cast about for an appropriate answer. 'Sir, I feel it is not for me to say. As a stranger here, surely my opinion…'

'Look, if I didn't want your opinion, I wouldn't have asked for it.' The fierce glare swept over Artorynas for a moment or two. 'You've spent time in Gwent y'm Aryframan, you've been raised at the centre of power in Caradward, you've served in its forces; and now you've lived here for, what, over a year anyway. If we go in force down the southward road, can we succeed? I want to know what you think. Whether I act upon what you say is up to me.'

'No,' said Artorynas quietly. 'No, I believe such a move would be doomed to failure, although there are other courses which might be tried. Haldur has an excellent grasp of the choices open to you and their various implications; my advice to all your counsellors would be to listen to what he has to say.'

'Hm.' Carapethan turned back to the window and stared blankly out once more. The silence lengthened, and after waiting for a while Artorynas spoke again.

'Am I correct in assuming that you yourself are not in favour of intervention by force?'

'Quite correct.' Abruptly Carapethan crossed the room. 'Look at this.'

He opened the lid of a heavy chest that stood against the wall, took out a sword and passed it to Artorynas. The blade was rather short, incised on both sides with a flowing, interlocking pattern in an abstract design of curving lines; the grip was decorated with gold wire and a large, polished piece of amber formed the pommel. It was well balanced but curiously light in weight. Artorynas looked more closely. Who would make such a thing? Baffled, he handed the weapon back to Carapethan.

'Surely, this is bronze?' he said.

'Yes. Beautiful, isn't it? Look at the craftsmanship that went into its making: see how the pattern matches, how each strand of the gold is twisted back on itself so the design seems to flow? It must have taken hours, days, to make; to have exercised all the skills of those who worked on it. After striving so hard for perfection, they must have been well pleased when they looked on their finished masterpiece. All that skill and art, all that effort and craft, all that beauty, lavished on a thing that has but a single purpose.' Carapethan paused. 'This is Sleccenal.'

'The Releaser?'

'Yes: the Releaser, the Freedom-Giver. That by which death is unloosed and freedom from life delivered: a destroyer. How much blood do you think has run down this blade, how many lives would you say it has it devoured?'

Artorynas had no answer, watching as the lord of Rihannad Ennar turned the sword over in his hands; this was a side of Carapethan he had not seen before. Suddenly he noticed that when Carapethan wrapped his fingers around the grip, the whole hilt, pommel and all, disappeared within his fist, and it occurred to him how undersized the sword was: it had evidently been intended for a much smaller hand than Carapethan's.

'Was it made for you when you were a boy?' he asked.

Carapethan looked up with a lift of his eyebrows, seeming surprised. 'Oh no. Though I wore it on the day when I became the lord of Rihannad Ennar, as did all my predecessors before me in their turn, it was not made by a swordsmith of the Nine Dales. It comes down from the far past, like the silver arm-rings and golden torc that denote the lord's successor. But we took them for our marks of rank when we found them, as a way of reaching out across the ages to the people who went before us.'

'I don't understand what you mean. How did you find them?'

'They were turned up by the plough, so the story goes; no doubt they'd been hidden for safe-keeping. But when none came to claim them again, they rested where they lay as the ages passed and time heaped ever more earth over them.'

From the moment when he had realised that the sword's blade was forged from bronze, Artorynas had been conscious of a vague unease, which at these words deepened further.

'But... I thought the Nine Dales were empty of folk when you came to them? You mean there were people here after all?'

'Of course not, they were long gone by then. I'm talking about time beyond mind, long before the wars that brought sorrow and ruin to the world. There were people here then all right, and for many generations too if the arm-rings are anything to go by: a growing child only wears each one for a short time, yet all are thin with use. You should ask Haldur to show them to you some time. But anyway, I'm getting off the point.'

Artorynas had felt the hairs rising on his neck as he listened, but before he could speak again, the bright blue eyes were fixed upon him once more as Carapethan put a completely unexpected question to him.

'Have you ever killed a man?'

'No.'

Carapethan stood up and walked forwards holding the sword, until only the length of the blade was between him and Artorynas, never breaking eye contact.

'*Could* you kill a man? Could you give Sleccenal the food he craves?' Watching Artorynas intently, he smiled a little at what he saw in the younger man's face.

'I see you follow my thought. It is not so easy to take a man's life, especially when you are close enough to look into his eyes while you do it. But an arrow will slay at long range: killing seems different if you are far enough away not to smell the fear, not to hear the pain, not to see the light go out in the face of your enemy. An archer delivers death from distance and may delude himself that his hands are clean of blood. Himself – or herself. Every man and woman in Rihannad Ennar is sufficiently accurate to kill with the bow, if I give the word; yes, the women too.'

Carapethan lowered the sword and turned away again to replace it in the chest.

'Rihannad Ennar could field an army of archers second to none,' said Artorynas. 'Why then do your laws insist upon such skill and readiness with the bow, when it seems you are not willing to give that word?'

'For defence. If the Nine Dales were to be attacked, we are ready to fight to the last. Yet even arming in defence can provoke exactly the kind of aggression one hopes to guard against. Didn't you discover the truth of that, as distrust bred anger, and anger led to fear, and fear in turn spawned hate between Caradward and Gwent y'm Aryframan? Perhaps we have been fortunate, in that the lands around us are empty of other folk and it seems unlikely that we will be assailed; certainly it has never happened since we took Rihannad Ennar for our own. But we went through so much before we found the Nine Dales, we paid such a high price in toil and hardship and loss: maybe that is why we have always loved our homeland so dearly. From the earliest days of its settlement, we were determined to take certain measures to ensure its safety, and we have kept that resolve. We maintain no troops under arms, but we are all trained and in readiness. If we must ever face an invader, then we will resist to the last man and woman, to the last youngster able to draw a bow, to the last arrow. But I will not give the word to mete out violence against another people unless we are confronted by a threat that cannot otherwise be turned aside. I will not go down in memory as the leader who forgot the lessons of the past, who ignored the words of *Vala na Naasan*. No, while I am lord in Cotaerdon, it will not be Rihannad Ennar that lets the fires of death loose upon earth again.'

Artorynas sat silent. The habit of a lifetime hid the emotion he felt, but his heart raced as the uneasy apprehension he had felt crystallised into something more defined. Carapethan, glancing at him, saw that the premature frown lines had deepened a little between his eyes, but could not guess at what passed in his mind. He knows! Carapethan knows, thought Artorynas. In memory he flew across the miles and years to Caradriggan: once more he was a small lonely boy, thirsty for knowledge, hanging on Arval's every word. *The bad thing, the bad time.* He could hear the childish phrases spoken in the child's tones which had once been his. *Something bad happened to the world, long ago.* That was as far as most of his teachers would go in explanation; he could see in his mind's eye the furtive, slightly ashamed looks that went with the words. What was it Arval had said to him? *It was some deed of men that drove the Starborn from the earth… I should have asked Arymaldur; but it was a thing so great and solemn, to have a lord of the Starborn among us… I gave in to weakness, I could not find the strength of purpose to hear what he could have told me because I sense some ancient shame, a truth too unpalatable for remembrance… My resolve failed at the last… I failed, I should have asked, but I failed…* Difficult though it was to accept, it seemed that even Arval was ignorant of what Carapethan knew; and if Carapethan had this knowledge, then others in Rihannad Ennar must have it also. All this time, I have suspected him of hiding something from me, thought Artorynas, but I have been mistaken. It is simply that because everyone here knows, he has assumed that I know. But I do not, as Arval did not. And now I am going to have to ask Carapethan, because I must hear the truth of what deed men did to drive the As-Geg'rastigan from the world.

'What is the matter?' asked Carapethan.

Artorynas looked at him, the last words he had heard coming back into his mind. '*Vala na Naasan*,' he said slowly. 'The accursed battle? Fires of death on earth… What lesson from the past do you speak of?'

'*Stirfellaerdon donn' Ur*? Surely you must know this tale? No? Well, like *Vala na Naasan*, it tells of how this world was all but destroyed by men, how in their folly they ruined themselves and wasted the very earth that gave them life.'

'In Caradward these things are not remembered as it seems they should be.' Artorynas had lowered his head to stare down at the floor, but when he looked up, Carapethan saw how the old scar pulled at his lip as his mouth set into bitter lines. 'Nor indeed in Gwent y'm Aryframan; so I am without knowledge of the events you speak of, and I do not know the words of *Vala na Naasan*. I am ashamed of my ignorance, but at least the remedy for it is to hand. Is it possible for you to tell me the full tale?'

Carapethan's hand came up in the ancient sign. 'I could, but I will not. If such horrors must be given voice, better that you hear them from one trained in the telling. I will send the keeper of our lore to you now, if you wish; and we will speak together later.'

Dark secrets revealed

He left the room and after a short while the door opened once more to admit Astell, the senior storyteller of the Nine Dales. During the time Artorynas had been living in Cotaerdon, this man had rarely stood forth to speak; usually it was his less eminent colleagues who entertained at feasts and gatherings, but he always led the rites and Artorynas had been impressed by his dignity and bearing. He was of late middle age, thin in the face with deep-set eyes and a rather large, prominent nose. After greeting Artorynas, he sat down on a high chair with a straight wooden back, looking gravely at the young man.

'Lord Carapethan tells me you wish to hear of the ancient ruin of the world. Would you have me recite *Vala na Naasan*, or *Stirfellaerdon donn' Ur*, or both?' His voice was surprisingly resonant for a man with such a spare frame; its deep tones seemed to ring out, even in the small room where the two of them sat.

'I must be guided by you, sir,' replied Artorynas. 'But you should be aware that I know nothing of the events you are about to reveal, therefore I ask that you tell me the full tale and spare me nothing. I have already heard enough from Lord Carapethan to realise that this will be a matter that is easy to learn, but hard to know.'

The man inclined his head slightly, his trained ear picking up Artorynas' use of a phrase which had a particular significance for him alone. 'Very well. In that case, I think we will agree on *Stirfellaerdon donn' Ur*.'

He paused, letting a silence develop in the way those of his calling liked to do before they spoke, and then began his recitation. But this was no tale such as Artorynas had ever heard before, no narrative of heroes and their mighty feats, no tender story of lovers' dreams, no hallowed legend of the As-Geg'rastigan. He sat aghast as the terrible chronicle unfolded: nations of whom he had never heard devouring the world's resources with a reckless disregard, warring against each other with arms equally unknown to him, weapons so potent and appalling that they destroyed the very earth along with all who walked upon it. The tale wound on to its close, an end in which great civilisations were reduced to rubble, all their achievements now worthless, their beauty nothing but a bitter memory blowing on a wind of death, their hopes gone for ever, their people wiped out. Artorynas was desperate for this history to end, for relief from listening to horrors that seemed to poison his ears and brain, but it seemed there was still more to say. His instructor was telling now of an aftermath in which the few survivors clung on, scratching a miserable existence from fields their own folly had laid waste, holding tenaciously to a life that was now brutish, disease-wracked, devoid of all the comforts they had once taken for granted. Generation upon generation had passed, and in time the earth had begun to renew herself; little by little, men had multiplied once more and started to move away from the devastation they had caused, seeking new lands in which to begin again.

'The Earthborn lived on, doomed to toil and die as they had ever done; but by their deeds they had driven the Starborn away, who now walked in this world no longer. Yet in their loss men found wisdom, late though it came to them. In sorrow they called upon the Starborn: they promised to remember their misdeeds and never to repeat them, if only the As-Geg'rastigan would renew their pledge with the earth.'

The rolling cadences came to an end at last, but the bard had something more to add. While he recited, his eyes had been fixed on time long gone by; but now they rested rather thoughtfully on Artorynas.

'And so it is, in the Nine Dales,' he said, 'we hope that if we hold to our resolve never to forget and never to repeat our fault, the Hidden People my show themselves once more.'

Artorynas said nothing. Dumbfounded to realise the depth of his ignorance about the past, he scarcely knew which question to ask first of the dozens that clamoured for attention in his mind.

'When I was a child,' he said eventually, 'I was taught that Caradward had been established for some five hundred years, and that men had lived in Gwent y'm Aryframan for a similar time before that. And I was told, when I was fostered there, that the Gwentarans in their turn had come originally from the Nine Dales; but today from Carapethan I have learnt that there were people here in Rihannad Ennar before you: so long before, he says, that they had already flourished and gone before you came. And now, what I have heard from you has made me realise that there have been many more ages of this world than those I knew of. Can you tell me how long ago the events of which you speak occurred?'

His instructor smiled slightly. 'Certainly. As it seems you already know, a thousand years have passed since folk set out from the Nine

Dales to found the new homeland that they named Gwent y'm Aryframan. It was more than half as long again before that, when we left Valward and dared the northern seas to come here; and over a thousand more bitter years of hardship and wretchedness lie between then and the days when *Vala na Naasan* ended all that had gone before. But there had been a long, slow story of thousands of years again before that, a story of age upon age during which gradually men increased in knowledge and power until in pride they forsook their learning, acquired so hardly and with such effort, falling from their glory as they destroyed themselves and all they had achieved.'

Turning away to the window, Artorynas thought vaguely what a long time it seemed since he had sat watching Carapethan do the same thing. Their earlier conversation seemed a lifetime away, after what he had learnt since. His brain was still reeling as he struggled to adjust to this new timescale, tried to understand that both sleepy, peaceful Framstock and Caradriggan with her elegant walls and towers, though he had thought them so old and steeped in tradition, were just upstart newcomers in the wider scheme of things, mere imitations of the strength and wisdom that once had been enjoyed on earth.

'Age upon age,' he said in the end. 'How could thousands of years of civilisation take so long before it was able to flourish once more?'

At this the storyteller permitted himself a somewhat sardonic laugh. 'When smoking ashes are all that is left of every seat of learning, and those who debated within their walls must compete like beast with beast to scavenge for each day's food, how long do you think it takes before the erudition of centuries is lost for ever? Within two generations at most such skills and knowledge would be gone beyond recall. Injury and illness would be without remedy, shelter cold and without ease, mere daily survival the only achievement worth striving for. Were those who lived or those who died the most fortunate? But stubbornly those who did live refused to die, doggedly they clawed their way upwards once more from the abyss they had wilfully created. Though the scars of their folly still mar the world today, in the waste at its heart and in the wilderness that surrounds this, their three thousand years of toil have brought us back to such comfort and wellbeing as are ours today. And though our own attainments and standards fall far short of what was enjoyed before *Stirfellaerdon donn' Ur* wasted all, we should be grateful for their efforts, do you not agree? But you will see now how it is that we must never forget the deeds that caused their sorrow and hardship, and never repeat their mistakes.'

Again the man's eyes roved slowly over Artorynas, his beaky features giving his gaze a rather hungry look.

'Yes. Yes, I do see.' Artorynas, already ashamed of his own ignorance, was now acutely conscious of a further burden of general shame. More than anything, he wanted solitude to reflect on what he had learnt, to come to terms with the way the old, familiar world had shifted under his feet. He held out his hand. 'I am most grateful to you for your instruction, sir, and obliged to you for the time and trouble you have taken with me.'

Astell bowed a gracious acknowledgement, but failed to take his hand, or to stand aside so that Artorynas could leave the room. 'Forgive me, I realise you are unused to our ways, here in the Nine Dales. Though all here learn *Stirfellaerdon donn' Ur* as soon as they are old enough to understand it, it is considered inappropriate for use as entertainment in open hall. However, should it be necessary for it to be recited, it is usual for a token payment to be made.' He spread his hands in a slightly deprecatory way. 'No doubt the custom originated as a means of deflecting possible bad luck, by implying that the reciter had only spoken under a duress which must be acknowledged by a fee.'

'Oh, I see. Of course, yes, I'm sorry. In Gwent y'm Aryframan, they exchange a coin for a knife, so that any blade must be seen as a purchase rather than a gift. I expect that's a similar kind of idea.'

Burning with embarrassment, Artorynas was digging in his pouch as he spoke. At the bottom was a small wallet with all that was left of

Arythalt's silver. Suddenly he was overwhelmed with a feeling that he must do something, anything, to lessen the weight of guilt, dishonour, uncleanness that sat upon him now that he had heard the bard's tale. Pulling the wallet open, he tipped its contents into his palm and held it out.

'Please take this. Take all of it.'

'No, that's not necessary, only a token payment is required.' Astell picked out the smallest coin, a tiny silver piece that in Caradriggan would scarcely have paid for a cup of milk. 'There is no need to blame yourself like this. Learning may be the one thing a man can never regret, but ignorance which one cannot help is not a crime, whether it be of a tradition of Rihannad Ennar, or of the wider history of the world.'

The golden eyes opened wide at the well-loved phrase; for a moment the two of them looked at each other in silence and then the older man smiled with more warmth than he had shown up till then. He pushed Artorynas' hand aside.

'Keep the rest of your silver. You may need to buy provisions or other gear before you set out again.'

CHAPTER 40

Father of his people

One day as late winter yielded to the very first signs of spring, Carapethan left the hall after his mid-morning meal; but instead of going back into the streets of Cotaerdon, he had a horse made ready for him and rode off up the valley of the Lissa'Riggan. The sky was bright and open, with high clouds sailing swiftly overhead on a strong, gusting wind. The air blew keen from the snows above, cold but with a hint of new growth in its scent. Carapethan was dressed much the same as any yeoman of the Nine Dales, in leather breeches, double-thickness woollen jacket, wadded jerkin and a sheepskin hat with the fleece left on, coming down over his ears and neck in protective flaps; he was glad of his warm clothing and although he did not press his horse, he was careful to keep the animal moving. As he rode, folk called out to him in greeting and he raised his hand in answer, trotting along the lanes and byways among the orchards that filled much of Rihann y'n Riggan. Passing at length beyond the cultivated area, he reached a place where a dense patch of woodland broke the force of the wind and slowed the horse to a walk in its lee. Letting the reins drop, he sat for a few moments in the shelter of the coppice, looking back over the way he had come and thinking over the debate at the previous day's meeting of Haldan don Vorygwent. Somehow his mind seemed clearer, now that he was alone out here with the spring gale whistling down the valley.

There was one thing about which he was sure beyond any doubt: his first duty was to Rihannad Ennar. The safety of the Nine Dales and their people was his responsibility and this took precedence over any competing claims; but it could not be denied that something far wrong was afoot, away there in the south. Three times now, the tale had been brought to them: by those fleeing from oppression, and by Artorynas. Carapethan mused on the young man's other name, as he had done on more than one previous occasion. Maesrhon. The name had been given in scorn, meant to mark and maim, but there might be more than a grain of truth in it. He did not doubt his courage, but there was something about him, such a bleakness, almost as if misfortune would be drawn to him, or he to it. Carapethan wondered why no-one but himself seemed to sense this. By the Starborn, he thought suddenly, you'd think at least folk would remember the words of *Maesell y'm As-Urad* when they look at him! The horse, responding to Carapethan's involuntary movement, danced sideways under him for a few paces before quieting to a touch on the reins. Carapethan walked the animal up and down for a moment or two. Well, Artorynas would be gone within a few weeks; and anyway, the events he had described to them had happened over four years ago now. More important was the tale the recent fugitives had brought. Again Carapethan drew the horse to a stop. He was calmer now, feeling his mind moving to a decision. Those in Gwent y'm Aryframan were our own people, once, but the ties that bind us to them are no longer strong. Though I will shelter them, if they come to me, I will not endanger Rihannad Ennar by intervening on their behalf. But I must find out whether the Nine Dales themselves are at risk, and for that I must have information: knowledge is power. The only way I can get that knowledge is by sending someone to see at first-hand what is happening in the south. And there is only one whom I would trust completely with such an errand. I will send my son.

Carapethan turned his horse as if to ride on once more, but something on the ground just within the first of the trees caught his eye. He dismounted to look more closely. There in a protected hollow between two gnarled roots, hugging the ground out of reach of the wind, dark green, glossy leaves had pushed through the deep mould of the woodland floor: celandines, the first of the new season's flowers to return. Four blooms had already opened. Bright and brave their yellow petals reached up, shining in the sun more intensely than polished gold. Carapethan felt unexpected tears flood his eyes, and pulled off a glove to wipe them away. You old fool, he said to himself, half laughing. Yet as he stood, one hand holding the reins, he looked out over Rihann y'n Riggan and saw in his mind's eye the orchards all in blossom, and the ripe apricots glowing against the snowy peaks that rose above; and his heart filled almost painfully with love for the Nine Dales. To be the lord of Rihannad Ennar was a sacred trust: he must pay whatever price it asked of him. Grief and longing for Heredcar, and fear for Haldur, suddenly stung him, but he squared his shoulders as he set off back to Cotaerdon. Haldur loves the Nine Dales as I do, he thought. Though it hurts me to send him into danger, though it will hurt him to leave his homeland and go, he will not hesitate when I ask him, because like me he will put Rihannad Ennar and its people before any hopes and fears of his own.

Carapethan's decision

Once back in Cotaerdon with the horse returned to its stable, Carapethan sought out Maesmorur. He lived in a quiet lane leading to one of the footbridges and ushered Carapethan into a room on the upper storey overlooking the sparkling water and the green space beyond. Writing materials and several books lay on a table near the fireplace.

'You've come to a decision, then,' said Maesmorur.

Carapethan glanced at him. 'How did you guess?'

Maesmorur laughed. 'It wasn't difficult. You don't often call on the old badger in his own den, and when you do, it's usually to try out some tough choice on me quietly, in private, so you can take the rough edges off it before you present it to Haldan don Vorygwent.'

'True enough.' Carapethan smiled back, the two old friends taking each other's measure. Maesmorur's eyes were a paler blue than Carapethan's, and he was more reserved in manner with something of a reputation as a scholar: there were many more books on shelves behind him, as well as those upon the table; but both were shrewd men. They were of similar age and had had plenty of opportunities to value one another's worth. Carapethan held his hands out to the fire for a moment.

'The wind's cold today, especially further up the valley there. But the spring's coming, and with it the time to act. You're right, it's a hard choice I've made. I'm going to send an embassy south, just a small party under Haldur's leadership. I must know whether what's happening away there is a threat to the Nine Dales, and this is the most reliable way I can think of to find out.'

'You'll send Haldur? I'd have thought you would prefer to keep him beside you here, maybe send Vorardynur instead.'

'I don't want to send him, but Vorardynur's too inclined to put his heart before his head. It would only take one incautious word, in a reckless moment if his blood is up, and our true purpose would be revealed. I'll have him by me here at home; he'll learn from the experience and mature into the man upon whom one day, no doubt, Haldur will need to rely. One has to think of these things.'

Maesmorur heard the change in Carapethan's voice. He knew well enough that whether or not his leader bore the golden circlet, its weight always pressed upon his head.

'What of Haldur, though? If his errand is to succeed, he will have to dissemble at best, and tell lies at worst. Do you think he will be able to preserve a false front, when his whole nature is to be true and open?'

'I don't doubt he won't find it easy, but he knows he must face hard tasks in life. If he believes it's for the good of Rihannad Ennar, he will do it. But you're right, that's the weak point in the plan. I've got to be sure all those who go can be relied upon to play their part. I thought of sending six envoys only, enough to help each other if they run into difficulties, but not so many that Haldur can't keep his finger on the general pulse. I want you to take a few moments, now that you know what I've decided, and tell me who you think the other five should be. I'd be interested to see whether your choice matches mine.'

There was silence for a while, as Maesmorur stared into the fire. Eventually he sat up and turned to Carapethan.

'Well, I'd say Haldur's other cousin Asaldron, and maybe Tellapur if Morescar will let him go. What would you say to an older man in the party? If so, and again if he's willing, I'd pick Ir'rossung, he's steady as a rock. Then ... if Ardig would deputise for Cathasar, and look after things in Rihann y'm Aldron while he's away, as well as attending to his own duties here in Cotaerdon, Cathasar could go. So that leaves one place to fill, and it would do no harm to send one of your own household men. What about young Cureleth?'

'No.' Carapethan shook his head. 'Cureleth's a nice enough fellow, but he's too friendly for his own good and he can't keep his mouth shut. One hint that we've had Artorynas here among us ...' He left the sentence unfinished.

'Perhaps Aestrontor instead?' suggested Maesmorur, and Carapethan nodded in agreement.

'Yes, I think we can rely on him. But why not Ardig? I'd thought of having Cathasar deputise for him, rather than the other way round.'

Maesmorur laughed aloud. 'Ardig? Never! If you think Vorardynur would be too much of a risk, Ardig would be a real liability. It's not just his hair that's fiery, believe me. Not to mention the fact that he'd probably starve to death if you make him travel abroad. I've never met a man so attached to his home place. Apparently he actually takes his own food with him, even if he's only going as far as Rihann y'n Fram.'

'Really? Cathasar it is, then.' Pushing his chair back from the heat of the hearth, Carapethan looked across at his old friend. 'Well, I see we think along pretty much the same lines. Except that I did wonder whether you would include yourself.'

'Rather than Ir'rossung, I presume you mean. No, I don't think so. I would dearly love the chance to meet this Arval that Artorynas speaks of, but my keenness to learn from him might bring suspicion upon us, given what we've heard about the current leaders of Caradward and their denial of the Starborn.'

Maesmorur's voice, always quiet, had dropped even further as he spoke. The room, shadowy now as evening approached, seemed filled with a great silence in which Carapethan found himself wishing vainly once more that his beloved, familiar world need not have been so disrupted and beset.

Haldur could scarcely believe it when his father proposed the plan to the council. He was proud to be chosen, to be thought worthy of such a responsibility, but at the same time his stomach churned with apprehension. It took no great leap of the imagination to foresee just how difficult, how fraught with risk, his errand would be. At first he was so busy with his own thoughts that he barely listened as the idea was chewed over in council, but gradually it dawned on him how astute his father's decision had been. Those who had clamoured loudest for action were appeased, and those who had been against intervention were, while not exactly happy at the prospect of establishing contact with an aggressive regime, at least in agreement that it would be better to know, if it did turn out that the Nine Dales themselves were under threat. Then Carapethan said something to make Haldur secretly glow with pleasure and fire up with resolve to make a success of his journey.

'If I might just remind you all,' said Carapethan, 'of a suggestion which my son put to you last autumn, when we discussed the news which the refugees from Gwent y'm Aryframan brought to us. His feeling was that we could not simply close our eyes and ears to events outside the Nine Dales, but instead of using force, he proposed reconnaissance. Then, thinking this through, he realised that secrecy would harm us if it was detected. An apparently open approach will avoid this risk, while still giving us the chance of gathering the information we need.

'Haldur will present himself as who he is, the heir to the lordship of Rihannad Ennar. Asaldron and Tellapur will go with him as friends and companions, as will Ir'rossung as his counsellor. Cathasar and Aestrontor will seem as if they travel as outriders, to help with the tasks of the journey; but if trouble should come, there are none better able to deal with it. All six who go will say nothing at any time that will reveal our knowledge of events in Gwent y'm Aryframan or Caradward.' Carapethan's eyes flicked briefly to Haldur. 'The name of Artorynas, or of Maesrhon, will not be mentioned; and it is essential also that no man realises that fugitives have reached us.'

There was a muttering of comment on all this among his listeners and then Poenellald spoke up. 'What reason is Haldur to give for his visit? Don't you think it likely that the Caradwardans will be highly mistrustful of a party that suddenly turns up out of the unknown far beyond their borders?'

'Isn't there a first time for everything, in this world?' said Carapethan. 'But yes, you're right; I'm sure they will indeed be suspicious. Therefore I believe our best shield against this is our seeming innocence. Haldur will say that he and his friends were moved to curiosity by such tales as we have of the long-ago emigration of our people to the south; if necessary he will add that he took his only chance of travel before his fate confines him to duty in a small and isolated land. That way, the very existence of Caradward can seem a complete surprise to him and his companions. What do we care if those in Caradriggan smirk at our naievety? Let them show us their marvels, let them boast of what they have done. Their condescension will make them play into our hands by revealing what we have come to discover. But if they still show signs of disbelieving our tale, then Haldur will propose a trading deal to them.'

'What can we offer that will interest the Caradwardans?' objected Morescar. 'We know the only commodity they seem to lack is a reliable grain supply, and we have no surplus to sell them.'

'How can we know, here in the north, what they lack – until and unless they speak of it to Haldur and his companions?'

'Oh, of course.' Morescar drew a sharp breath, biting his lip with worry at the thought of his son Tellapur being involved in this risky enterprise, maybe facing danger far away there in Caradriggan. 'By my right hand, it is going to be difficult to sustain this deception!'

'Yes, it is; but if Lord Carapethan thinks we can do it, we will do it.' This was Tellapur himself, a shy young man who blushed as he spoke but doggedly continued. 'We're his chosen men. We'll find out what he needs to know, and we won't fail either him, or Rihannad Ennar, by making any mistake of word or deed.'

'Well said!' Asaldron aimed a friendly punch at Tellapur who blushed even brighter, but grinned back at him. Looking round at those gathered in discussion, Asaldron turned now to Carapethan. 'So, if necessary we distract their attention with an offer of trade. Finish the tale for us, uncle. What is the offer you authorise us to make?'

'We have two advantages, so we must use them. Firstly, we are in possession of information that those we go to treat with do not know we have. And secondly, we have this.'

Carapethan picked up a small box that had lain unnoticed beside his seat and lifted out the contents. In his left hand he held a large chunk of raw amber almost the size of a child's fist; in his right was a finished piece of similar size, worked into a perfect sphere, burnished and gleaming. There was a general gasp from his audience, followed by a moment or two of complete silence, and then Vorardynur spoke.

'Surely, the gold they mine in the forest, of which Artorynas told us, means they will not value amber enough to trade for it?'

'Again, you forget that Haldur and his companions are to know nothing of Artorynas, or of the gold mine either.'

The fiery heart of the amber woke as the lord of the Nine Dales turned it, glowing through his fingers. 'From what we have heard, it appears that one of the greatest weaknesses of those who rule in Caradriggan is greed. I judge that when once they set eyes on this, no matter what their other wealth, they will be unable to resist the desire for it. As to what we ask for in exchange, we cannot plan this in advance. Haldur must make this decision, based on the circumstances you find.'

'But father, do you really mean' – it was barely a whisper, and Haldur cleared his throat and tried again, ' – you will offer them embers from the sea's hearth?'

They shifted in their seats when they heard Haldur use this old, traditional name, looking from him to his father. Carapethan held his son's eyes; his voice rumbled deep in his chest.

'If you need to propose this trade, it will mean that your errand and maybe even the Nine Dales too are at risk. The firestones of the north will be a small price to pay then, to bring you home again with the warning that may keep Rihannad Ennar safe from danger.'

Getting ready

Once the course of action was at last decided upon, matters moved quickly. Stores and equipment had to be gathered, horses and pack animals selected, timing and routes debated and agreed. Cathasar was put in charge of assembling all the gear for the party, and Aestrontor busied himself in procuring suitable riding horses with spare mounts and mules for the baggage. Haldur and Ir'rossung rode off down the valley to seek out the men who had crossed the wilderness from Gwent y'm Aryframan and to learn from them everything they could tell about their journey. By the time they returned, much of the preparations were already complete. Twelve animals were stabled in readiness: six horses plus three spares, all of them smallish and sturdy, chosen for their endurance rather than looks; and three mules. These last would carry the heaviest items of baggage, with other gear shared among the horses not being ridden. Each man would have responsibility for two animals. Haldur looked them over and was pleased with Aestrontor's choice. In a barn next to the stable, Asaldron and Tellapur had stockpiled the stores, cooking gear, tents and other equipment they had thought necessary. The arms each man would carry had been selected with some care by Cathasar. It would not do for them to appear too warlike, but they needed to be able to defend themselves if it came to it. He settled upon items that could if necessary be passed off as hunting tack: knives and bows, rather than swords or spears. But all except Ir'rossung also carried wooden staves: the younger folk had been fascinated by the specialist gear Artorynas had brought to the Nine Dales with him, and he had been responsible for starting several trends. Asaldron had not been the only one to ask for instruction in the sparring-stave, nor was he the only member of the party wearing boots with holders into which throwing-knives were slipped. And every man carried a full quiver of arrows, with many more, plus spare bowstrings, carefully stowed among the other baggage.

Haldur called his companions together to discuss their journey. 'This is how I see it,' he said, looking round at them and producing a roll of parchment which he spread out to reveal a rough sketch map. 'Obviously, we can't know how accurate this is; but Ir'rossung and I have done our best after putting our heads together with the fellows who fled to us last year. We think the river they spoke of, the one that enters a ravine, must be the Lissad nan'Ethan, so let's say we set off this way, down Two Riversdale, then over Na Caarst as quick and straight as we can: I make it almost a south-westerly course. That should bring us to the northernmost parts of Gwent y'm Aryframan, and from all we've heard, I'll be surprised if we're not intercepted pretty quickly once we get there. But anyway, if we make it that far, the only possible danger will come from the Caradwardans. It's the earlier part of the journey we've got to worry about.'

'And on the way back, remember,' said Ir'rossung.

'Yes, I know, but at least by then we'll know exactly what to expect. Now, there's something I want to ask Aestrontor. I've seen the animals you've bought. They look ideal to me, but do you think twelve is going to be enough?'

Aestrontor had been peering at the map, his eyes moving from the Nine Dales southward and back again. Now he looked up. 'I'd say it will have to be. While we're still in Rihann y'n Devo Lissadan, we don't need to worry about fodder for them. But we've got to get across the wilderness and by all accounts there's precious little grazing there, let alone water. The fewer mouths we have to feed, the better.'

'Maybe there'll still be plenty of grass right down the valley as far as where the river goes underground,' suggested Tellapur.

'Do you have any idea how far that is?' asked Cathasar.

'Not really.' Haldur frowned, looking at the map. 'A lot of this is guesswork. But I think we should allow, say, four weeks to reach the ravine, based on how long we know it takes to travel to the lower ferry crossing. Then we've been told we can get over Na Caarst in a month. So that gives us an estimate of two months from here to the borders of Gwent y'm Aryframan: let's say ten weeks, to allow for unforeseen delays.'

A short silence fell in which each man attended to his own thoughts. Then Asaldron voiced what was in all their minds. 'Do we all trust what we've been told about crossing Na Caarst?'

'You mean about the risk of blindworms and dangers like that?'

There was no mistaking the fear lurking in Tellapur's voice, and Haldur moved swiftly to counter it.

'Of course he doesn't mean that. For all we know, blindworms are just an old wives' tale. The fugitives never saw any, and neither did Artorynas when he crossed the wilderness. Asaldron means can we do it in the time, can we do it without either man or beast dying from hunger or thirst or other mishap. In other words, are we going to come out of Na Caarst alive? Well, I'd say yes. Remember that the refugees, and Artorynas as well, ran into difficulties because they wasted time in the foothills of the mountains. We've been told we can risk the straight road. Artorynas told me he thinks the folk from Salfgard who're holding out in secret away up in the north of Gwent y'm Aryframan might have a man called Torald with them to show them the ways of the wild. That's who he learnt his fieldcraft from, and he says if this Torald taught the man who said the wilderness can be crossed in a month, that's good enough for him. But he also told me how dry conditions are in Na Caarst: he had to dig for water, as often as not, and even then there was barely enough just for him. We've got animals to consider, so that brings me to another point I wanted to make. The spring melt is already beginning. Soon the snows will retreat up to the higher slopes, and we should aim to be crossing the wilderness when the rivers are in flood. I know that the fugitives who arrived last year lost a comrade, and a horse, but they were trying to pass a ford in the hills where the torrent was swollen and too powerful. We'll be in the plain, but if we time our departure carefully, we may hope that the waters will pour down in spate far enough to help us.'

'Yes, we should leave sooner rather than later.' Ever the man of few words, Aestrontor spoke now of his own accord for the first time. 'I've heard enough from Artorynas about his journey to trust his advice, even if I doubted what others had to say. I could wish his path went south with ours.'

A murmur of agreement greeted this, but Haldur could only nod assent; his imminent parting with Artorynas was a subject too painful for him to talk about to others.

Lorekeeper of the Nine Dales

Meanwhile, Artorynas himself was sitting, deep in thought, in the porch that was built on to the south side of Astell's dwelling at the edge of Cotaerdon, waiting for the lorekeeper to return home. He had discovered that this was how the man thought of himself, rather than simply bard or storyteller; and once he had overcome the shock and embarrassment of hearing what had been revealed to him at Carapethan's behest, he had on several occasions sought Astell out in order to question him further and learn what he could from this new teacher. Another brisk spring gale was sweeping through the open sky, but he scarcely noticed it here in the sheltered garden. Not a man who was easy to get to know, Astell lived alone, in a small house that was sparely and indeed rather austerely furnished although his status and renown within the Nine Dales were generously rewarded. But Astell was full of contradictions. He made it clear that he valued his own worth highly, yet Artorynas had heard it said that he had sworn never to marry because in his youth his heart was set on Ellaaro, who was already wife to Carapethan. Whether there was truth in this or not, he could be forbidding in both manner and speech; and yet he had created this small haven of peace and beauty where a riot of flowering plants flourished well beyond their natural seasons. The garden faced south and was enclosed to hold as much sunshine as possible, with sheltering hedges and windbreaks carefully sited; and the walls of the porch, like the sides of the raised beds, were hollow-built to hold warm air from an enclosed and efficient heating system which Astell kept burning all year round except in high summer. He used slightly warmed water on his plants, too, and fed them with a concoction he made himself from comfrey leaves. The Spring Feast was still a month away, but in the warm porch where Artorynas sat there were flowers blooming in pots, and even one or two bees buzzing drowsily among them.

Rubbing his eyes, Artorynas stood up and stretched. It said something for the serenity of the garden where he sat that he had almost fallen asleep, despite what was in his mind. Those who had been chosen to go south to Caradriggan might take heart at Haldur's reassurances about the wilderness, but it would be a different matter for him. Astell had been insistent that he did not take lightly the hazards of his forthcoming onward journey.

'If you look for Asward donn'Ur, then once you have scaled the Somllichan nan'Esylt you will have to pass the northernmost expanse of the wilderness. And legend has it that a horror born from the evil deeds of long ago still lurks there, even after the ages that have passed. I know men whisper of blindworms and children invent monsters to haunt their siblings' dreams, but the names are not important; what matters is to tease out the truth that lies within these tales. For myself, I believe that some creature makes its home in Aestron na Caarst, some perversion of nature that has somehow clung on where all else is so ruined that no wholesome thing could thrive. What it could be, what form it might take, I do not know: but I suspect it will be drawn to warmth and life. Be on your guard, even of the sky above; and beware especially of using fire.'

Automatically glancing up, Artorynas saw only the small white clouds racing across the blue; but then he heard the click of the latch lifting on the garden gate and a moment later Astell came into view, stooping to pass under an arch of jasmine. He was carrying some packages and with a nod to his visitor he went through the porch and into the house. Artorynas could hear him moving about in the little kitchen and after a few moments he reappeared with a tray bearing dark rye bread, cheese and meat. Setting this down he returned with a small burner on which was a pan of steaming mulled ale. He poured two beakers for them and they settled to their meal. It suddenly occurred to Artorynas how interested Fosseiro would have been in what they were eating. Generally speaking, the food in Rihannad Ennar, although plentiful and wholesome, was plainer than what he had enjoyed in Salfgard, and completely without the spices and other elaborations that were usual in Caradriggan. However, the Nine Dales had specialities of their own, and by chance they were eating three of them now. Artorynas was particularly fond of the ewesmilk cheese, which was flavoured with herbs and nettles; but today he looked with a new eye on the meat. This was almost like a kind of large sausage or pudding, made from pork air-cured by being hung to dry and mature in special stone-built structures that dotted the hillsides in each of the dales. The hard, resilient rind that developed was in turn encased in wax; the finished product was eaten raw, very thinly sliced.

'How long does this keep fresh?' he asked, taking another piece to eat with bread.

'More or less indefinitely, if it's properly wrapped,' said Astell. 'Thinking of taking some with you, when you go? Good idea. Go to the shop on the west side of the market square, get them to pack it for you in one of their own boxes. They store it straw-wrapped in birch bark containers, so it will be fairly light to carry. This bread, too: it won't go mouldy or stale like loaves made with wheat-flour. Might as well put off relying on the meal-pot as long as you can.'

Artorynas looked across at Astell, but he was replenishing his beaker from the pan and made no sign that he had seen the glance. Sometimes Artorynas almost wondered if the other man, even though he had been courteous and helpful, deliberately worked little barbs into his conversation. Certainly, the remark about eating meal had done nothing to raise his spirits; but he had another question to ask, so he kept his thoughts to himself.

'I'll do that. You know, when I came north to the Nine Dales, I carried a supply of beans with me, and each autumn I stopped when there was still enough warmth in the ground to germinate them. When the spring came, I could gather an early harvest and have time to dry them before I travelled on again, so I kept my supply replenished. "The poor man's meat", that's what the man who showed me what to do used to call them.' He smiled at the memory. 'But they wouldn't grow, the last time I halted, and I was left with nothing but the dwindling remains of the previous year's store; that's why I nearly starved when I took the risk of crossing the wilderness. I assumed I had passed the northern limit of their range, yet I see them in every garden, here in Rihannad Ennar.'

'Shelter from the wind and a good deep soil are all you need, even this far north,' said Astell, nodding towards his own garden. 'You'll not grow anything in Aestron na Caarst. But if you can get across it, if you can reach Asward donn'Ur before the year turns to winter again... Who can say what may flourish on Porthesc nan'Esylt?'

Porthesc nan' Esylt, thought Artorynas: the Golden Strand that Cunor y'n Temennis told me of. A little flicker of hope started up in him, but then he remembered words from another conversation.

'He has not said so to my face, but I can see that to Carapethan, Asward donn'Ur belongs to the world of legend and is not a place to which a man may walk across the face of this earth. He thinks I am going to my death.'

'And do you believe him, or do you trust the Hound of the Vow?'

'I trust Cunor y'n Temennis,' answered Artorynas slowly, 'but I would hesitate to say I disbelieved Carapethan in anything. There are times when I see Ardeth of Salfgard in him: he seems bluff and hearty, but I think he is more complex than his outward bearing shows. For some reason, he and I have never been easy with one another, which I regret: he is an able leader whose decisions I respect. I was moved by his desire to avoid strife and impressed by the integrity of his resolve never to make the same mistakes as our forebears. To me he seems an honest man who deals only in truth.'

'The truth as he sees it. He wants no truck with the Hidden People. Part of his purpose in sending Haldur on this mission to the south is to wean him from his love of the As-Geg'rastigan. But there is another reason why he will even risk his only surviving son, who is dearer to him than all others. Carapethan has had two wives, but the real love of his life is Rihannad Ennar.'

For a moment they looked at each other. Into Artorynas' mind came what he had heard of the old disappointment over Ellaaro. He had been taken by surprise at what Astell had said, but maybe it was no more than this that lay behind his words. And then again, maybe not; he was struck once more by the slightly predatory cast to the lorekeeper's features, the deep-set eyes boring into him, the prominent nose like a beak.

'To carry the hopes and fears of one's people is a heavy burden, but to Carapethan it is a solemn trust,' he said eventually, 'and I think Haldur too will be wedded to the Nine Dales when his time comes. I have ridden up and down the valleys with them and I have never seen Carapethan fail to acknowledge a *numiras*.'

'Of course not. We agree, he is a worthy leader who takes his public duties seriously. Who knows, though, how many *numirasan* he honours when he travels alone, or whether he has himself ever discovered a hallowed place? Carapethan has no wish that the paths which the Starborn and the Earthborn tread should ever cross.'

A sudden flutter of wings caught Astell's attention and he turned to see a robin swaying in a shrub just outside the porch, looking in at them with a beady eye. Astell's features softened as the little bird flung down its sudden, wistful scatter of bright notes; and sweeping up the crumbs from their meal into his hand he scattered them on the ground. 'There you are, little winter-warbler!'

He turned to Artorynas with a smile. 'Look how spruce and red his feathers are. It won't be long now before it is time for nesting once again.'

Artorynas smiled in his turn; here was yet another side of this enigmatic man. He sat lost in thought: memories of Arval feeding the robin on the sill of the tower window in Tellgard, memories of the tiny wooden carving he had made as a boy and given to Ardeth. He wondered what had become of it, in the ruin of Salfgard. The silence lengthened and he looked up to find the lorekeeper watching him.

'Allow a man old enough to be your father to give you some words of advice,' said Astell. 'If something is worthy of love or honour, then give it for its own sake, rather than for others that may come to your mind. Cunor y'n Temennis reminds you of Arval; you see Ardeth of Salfgard in Carapethan. I read in your face that these are not the only examples I could give. It is a mistake that the Earthborn are prone to make, and it leads to sorrow and regret.'

A wave of sadness, a bitterness he could not have explained, washed over Artorynas. The scar on his lip twisted as he spoke, hearing himself utter words that came unbidden and unexpected. 'I will remember what you have said, but now I ask you to tell me something more. Who are the Starborn, what are they?'

Astell looked at the young-old face before him, the dark locks springing back from the forehead, the high cheekbones, the stern nose and mouth. He saw the ageless beauty of the As-Geg'rastigan in the golden eyes fixed on things faraway, unseen; and the stamp of the Earthborn in the marks of injury, the lines etched between the brows, the bitter set of the lips.

'*You* ask *me* this? Surely, it should be the other way about.'

Artorynas shook his head. 'Earthborn, Starborn: these words are no more than sounds. Men think that naming brings understanding, but they delude themselves. The Earthborn we know all too well, but what are the As-Geg'rastigan?'

There was a long silence. Astell stared into the distance, chin on hand, and then walked out into his garden, looking at the new spring growth, already far advanced. Turning back towards the house, he stood for a moment beside the climbing plant that overhung the porch. Where its tendrils clung closest to the warmth of the wall, several flowers had opened. Astell put his hand up and touched one. Its petals were cream-coloured, with a dusting of dark pink spots near the throat of the flower where yellow stamens nestled and a faint perfume, almost almond-scented, drifted out. Gently, delicately, he stroked the petals; and Artorynas sat waiting, watching as Astell looked up at the flower against the blue sky, turning it in his fingers. Letting it spring back into place, the lorekeeper returned to his seat.

'For myself,' he said, 'myself, I think the As-Geg'rastigan are the Earthborn as they should be; maybe, even as they could be. This might explain why every legend tells that though they may appear like the Ur-Geg'rastigan, their loveliness is without blemish, as their integrity is also complete. And if this is truly the nature of their being, then it follows also that they may dwell only upon the earth as it should be. We ruined this world, and the As-Geg'rastigan left it.' As he spoke, Astell's face filled with an inner life and his voice slipped unconsciously into the rolling cadences of his training.

'Little wonder that we yearn for them so, that we lift our eyes to the remotest, most beautiful thing we see and borrow its name, calling them the Starborn! But maybe, as the earth renews herself, so they will indeed return. Let them walk in this world once more, let the Hidden People show themselves!'

'You mean that the As-Geg'rastigan are simply hidden from us in a world that is perfect, as they are perfect? Is this what is meant when men say the Starborn may walk unseen? Their world is the earth as it should be, and they can pass from it to ours, if they will? But how? Where is this dwelling place? Can it be found?'

Astell raised an eyebrow. 'You turn the eyes of the As-Geg'rastigan upon me, and ask questions like these? There is nothing more that I can tell you: these things are mysteries.' But after a moment he leaned forward. 'In a month we shall be celebrating the great feast, when fire springs from the seed in life returning, as day becomes longer than night once more. But here in the Nine Dales, we also mark the beginning of the new season. That will be within a week of now, and a more informal occasion. You missed the merrymaking last year because you were sick, but be there this time and I will recite *Numir y'm Aestronnasan donn Porthesc nan Esylt*. You have not heard this before? I thought not; well, between the two of us, it will be for you.'

Taking his leave of Astell, Artorynas walked through the town to the shop in the market place that had been recommended to him, and arranged for a quantity of perishable supplies to be specially packed and stored until he was ready to collect them. As he headed back towards Carapethan's hall, he smiled a little to himself. *Who can say what the future may bring*, Arythalt had said to him on that long-ago day in the *Sword and Stars*. Who indeed; but how surprised his grandfather would have been to know where and how the last of his silver was being spent. Very little was left, now, and most of that was earmarked for the hire of a horse. Artorynas had decided to ride from Cotaerdon as far as the Golden Valley to save time; he would turn the animal in at the livery stable there and go on to the mountains on foot. I will stay for the lesser feast Astell told me of, he thought, and then gather all my gear together; within two weeks at most, I will be away. But he said nothing to Haldur of his decision, when they met that evening. This would not be the first sad parting he had endured, but it was likely to be the most painful. It could not be prevented, so why speak of it? Words would only cause the hurt to ache even more. At least Haldur would have the Spring Feast to look forward to, and his errand to Caradriggan to occupy his mind.

Maesell y'm As-Urad

The day came on which the new season's arrival was celebrated and men gathered to eat in the large hall that was used for such occasions. After the meal was over, the tables were cleared away and all who were present settled to enjoy conversation, drink and the entertainment of the evening. Down each side of the hall there was a series of hearths around which many people were seated, while others strolled from group to group exchanging news and greetings. Haldur had wandered away from where the top table had been and was sitting with a large group of his young friends; but Ir'rossung and Maesmorur were also with him, noticed Carapethan, as was Aldiro. The lord of the Nine Dales moved among his people as was his habit on these occasions, talking and laughing, but with one ear always tuned to the general tone of the hall. And then, returning to the warmth after slipping out to the privies, he stepped through the door just in time to hear what Haldur was saying.

'Well if you won't stay until the rest of us leave, at least stay until the Spring Feast! But it won't be long afterwards that those of us going south will have to be on our way, so why not wait until then, and we'll all leave at the same time? Say you will!'

'Oh yes, please stay till then, Artorynas,' said Tellapur, and as Carapethan moved past the group, he heard many other voices break in, all urging the same thing.

Carapethan walked away and retrieved his drink, standing for a moment with his back to the hall, trying to fight down his annoyance. Suddenly an outburst of cheering and stamping made him turn round: one of Astell's junior colleagues had moved to the speaking-stool and was about to launch into some comic tale that had been requested. Sitting down again in the heavy carved chair that had been left in position for him at the head of the hall, Carapethan settled to listen. He enjoyed the performance, like everyone else; the man acquitted himself well and had his audience laughing with a more discerning appreciation than they had shown for some of the rough-hewn efforts offered by one or two of the revellers themselves, though these had been greeted with good-natured enthusiasm also. But as the applause died away, he was not the only person present who was surprised to see Astell himself step forward. The lorekeeper waited a moment, and then, his resonant voice tuned to a carrying pitch, he announced his intention to give them *Numir y'm Aestronnasan donn Porthesc nan Esylt.*

One or two people exchanged glances; it was unusual enough that Astell should participate in the merriment at this celebration, but in addition he had chosen to give them a very rarely-heard tale. Soon however all were held, lost in the story as it unfolded, spellbound by the beauty of the words and the skill with which Astell delivered them. Artorynas remembered how Astell had said the recitation would be for him. As he listened, he understood why, for the words renewed hope in him that he would find what he sought. His heart warmed once more with a glow of affection towards the Nine Dales and their people, with gratitude for the way they had welcomed him, helped him, made him feel at home. Those gathered there seemed like one big extended family to him, with Carapethan at its head. There sat the lord of Rihannad Ennar in his chair, the golden circlet on his thick fair hair, the colour up in his face, his blue eyes matched by so many others around the hall: strong and sturdy, the father of his people. But Carapethan had seen Astell and Artorynas exchange glances as the tale began; as it progressed, he noticed that many in the hall turned their eyes upon the stranger in their midst. He saw how Aldiro and Lethesco smiled at him while Torello sat silent and sad, how those about to leave on the embassy to the south looked back and forth between Artorynas and Astell, hanging on every word; he sensed the bond between Haldur and Artorynas, sitting side by side as always. Unease grew in him so that he scarcely registered that the performance was over, but as he applauded automatically with the others, he came to a sudden, unpremeditated decision.

'Astell!'

The man had almost reached the far side of the hall, rejoining the audience after leaving the cleared central space. He turned to see the lord of the Nine Dales leaning forward, his hands gripping the arms of his chair.

'Lorekeeper of Rihannad Ennar,' said Carapethan, as all broke off their conversations to heed him, 'do not deprive us of your art so soon. I would have you tell us another tale now. Give us *Maesell y'm As-Urad*.'

Astell walked slowly forward for a few paces and stopped short of the speaking-stool; every eye in the place was on him. 'A strange choice, for a feast-day, lord Carapethan,' he said. 'Is this a request, or a requirement?'

The eyes swivelled back to Carapethan, still leaning forward in his chair. The high colour had ebbed from his cheeks slightly, but his brows were drawn down in a fierce glare.

'I wish you to instruct the company, lorekeeper. Take it that you are bidden to do so. You may name your fee.' He sat back with a sweeping gesture of the hand. 'Begin.'

'Very well.' Astell advanced and placed his foot upon the stool as every head turned again.

Whenever Artorynas afterwards recalled this scene, it was the eyes that stayed in his memory most clearly: eyes, turning back and forth, from Astell to Carapethan and then to himself. He saw how uneasy the people were at the tale Carapethan had asked for, at the evident tension between lord and lorekeeper, at his own presence among them for such a recitation. Men and women shifted in their seats uncomfortably; although no-one actually moved, he felt as though a space had opened up, leaving him isolated and conspicuous. Eyes, the hall seemed full of eyes, the light flickering on a multitude of sidelong glances.

Some part of Artorynas' mind was automatically registering Astell's performance, the resonant voice, the authoritative delivery; he noted that here in Rihannad Ennar the tale was cast in long, elegiac lines with an end-rhyme, unlike the alliterative prose he was used to, although the story was the same. From earliest childhood he had been familiar with it, but he realised now that he had never heard the tale spoken aloud before, neither in Caradward nor in Gwent y'm Aryframan, unless he counted Arval's exposition of it in class when he was a boy at his studies in Tellgard. Small wonder at that, he thought, considering the sorrow carried in the words. He looked up and immediately countless covert stares were switched guiltily aside. Haldur though was watching him, his face flushed, his eyes bright; but Torello, he noticed, was sitting half turned away; there were tears on her pale cheeks as the story unfolded. He remembered, with a stab of pain, Astirano's face on the day he left Salfgard. Involuntarily, Artorynas moved abruptly, looking up the hall towards Carapethan. The lord of the Nine Dales was gazing about him almost defiantly. The piercing blue stare held every eye in turn: his counsellors, his people, his lorekeeper, his son, as if willing them all to attend closely. Listen, he seemed to urge them, listen to the fate of the As-Urad, who find no place among either Earthborn or Starborn! Mark the misfortune that dogs their steps, heed what befalls those who love them!

At last Artorynas understood Carapethan's thought. Their eyes met. There was no need for you to distrust me so, thought Artorynas bitterly, looking into the shrewd face. Within days at most, I would have been gone from you, but now I will delay no longer. You need fear no more for Haldur or Torello or any other of your folk. He was scarcely listening now, but gradually it dawned on him that the tale had drawn to its close; Astell had taken his foot from the stool and was standing with arms folded, watching Carapethan. No-one applauded, but a strange sound, almost a sigh, ran round the hall. Carapethan got to his feet.

'Well told, lorekeeper! You do justice to a tale we should hear more often.'

He moved over towards the serving-table and after a moment's awkward silence, people followed suit with an almost palpable air of relief. Astell returned no answer, heading towards the far door. As he went, his eye fell on Artorynas and an odd, mirthless smile briefly touched his lips; then he was gone.

Haldur was seething with anger and embarrassment at what Carapethan had done. He shouldered his way through the throng, determined to avoid his father until he was calmer, looking everywhere for Artorynas; but it seemed that his friend had already left the hall.

VI DANGERS

CHAPTER 41

Partings and promises

It was past midnight before Haldur realised what had happened. He waited for a while, but realising that Artorynas was not going to come back into the merrymaking, went in search of him. Since he was not already in bed, or anywhere else within the lord's family rooms at the high hall, Haldur returned to the feast. The crowd had thinned out somewhat by then, but wherever he sought, and he even called on Maesmorur, thinking that Artorynas might have taken refuge there from all the staring eyes, there was no sign of him. Eventually he trailed home again, fighting down the apprehension that was rising in him with every step. The darkness was bitterly cold and he shivered as he dropped the latch behind him. Artorynas' room was as dark and cold as the night outside. Candle held high, Haldur opened the door to the adjoining closet: it was empty. Haldur stared blankly at the bare floor where a heap of equipment had been piled. He had stood beside Artorynas as he stowed all his gear in here, everything except the perishable items he had ordered; but now it was all gone. Artorynas was gone. Gone without a word, without a leave-taking. Gone in the night, gone who knew where.

Haldur sank onto the untouched bed, head in hands. How often had he watched as Artorynas overhauled his travelling gear, looking it over for signs of wear and tear that might need repairing. Fascinated by the thought and planning that had gone into the design and selection of the equipment, he had handled the items with a keen interest, asked

Artorynas to tell him about Staran y'n Forgarad and Heranwark, listened avidly to his tales of where and how he had bought his throwing-knives, devised his climbing spikes, learnt how to make the waterproof material of his pack. But valiantly though he had tried to divert his mind in this way, he realised now that nothing had really shifted the shadow on his heart, the gloom that had never been far away once the blackthorn brought the first signs of spring; and now Artorynas was gone. They might never see each other again. Time crawled by and Haldur's candle, burning low, began to sputter and smoke. He raised his head. His fingers and toes were numb and chilled, the feast-day food and drink lay cold in his stomach; but his brain was starting to work once more. Artorynas must be on foot, he would never simply take a horse from its stable. Tomorrow he would catch up with him.

The remainder of the night seemed endless to Haldur, who dozed uneasily, waiting for the dawn, afraid to let himself sleep deeply. But when dawn came, he realised he would have to wait until men were up and about their business. He kept to his room until he was sure Carapethan had left the hall; there was no sense in spoiling his plans by rowing with his father. In the market-place he discovered that the provisions which Artorynas had paid for were still in store. Retrieving them, he set off for the town's main livery stable. Yes, said the ostler, this is the horse Artorynas asked for; no, he'd not seen him for two or three days. Hastily, Haldur paid the hire fee and had the animal saddled up, then cantered off on his own horse with the other on a lead rein. He rode for some miles, looking around him all the time. How far would Artorynas have walked by now? What if, being on foot, he had not kept to the road but headed across country? Maybe he should check the side roads too? Haldur turned off for a mile or two on the next few lanes he passed, but his search was fruitless and he returned to the main route. He rode without stopping for rest or food as the morning wore away and noon came and went. So far it had not occurred to him that he would fail to find Artorynas, but the possibility began to nag at him now, together with the thought that he could not search indefinitely; his errand to the south would not wait. *You are not free to go, as I am not free to stay.* He set his teeth as he remembered these words of Artorynas. And then, just as whispers of panic were starting up in him, Haldur saw a familiar figure emerge from a tumbledown roadside barn a few hundred yards ahead. With a yell, he dug his heels into his horse, galloping wildly in pursuit as relief coursed through him.

Artorynas turned and stood waiting. His face gave little away, but Haldur was so glad to have found him at last that he was almost laughing as he slid from the saddle, gathering both sets of reins into his hands as the animals tossed their heads and backed up, sending a drift of dust blowing away downwind.

'You shouldn't have come after me,' said Artorynas. 'It will only make things worse.'

'How could it? If you've got to go now, that's bad enough, but to go off without a word like that… Why did you do it? I suppose it was because of what happened last night.'

'I was surely not intended to ignore such a public reminder that there is no place among men for the As-Urad.' Artorynas smiled, but without much mirth. 'Who knows whether it will be different with the Starborn, if ever I find them.'

Haldur winced at the words, turning his head away. His thick, heavy hair had blown back with the speed of his ride but now it flopped down again, sticking to the sweat on his forehead. Artorynas saw the colour come up into his face.

'I'm ashamed of what my father did. I don't know why he asked for *Maesell y'm As-Urad*. I'm sure Astell wasn't expecting it and I hope you could see he wasn't happy about being made to recite it, nor the rest of us to hear it. I want to apologise; I want things to be right between us before you go.'

'There's no need to be concerned. I think Astell is right, to say the greatest love of Carapethan's life is the Nine Dales. Your father isn't hostile to me personally, as he is not uncaring of others who may be hurt, but his heart is given to Rihannad Ennar. He would have the Nine Dales and their people undisturbed and undivided, therefore he wants me away. I would have been gone soon in any case, but maybe not soon enough for him.'

'Did Astell really say that?'

'Yes, and with reason. If I were lord of Rihannad Ennar, I think I should feel as Carapethan does. In spite of how I leave them, the Nine Dales have felt like home to me, as no other place has ever done. And Haldur, there could never be anything wrong between us two.' This time, Artorynas' smile was genuine. He reached out and took hold of Haldur's sleeve, giving his arm a little shake. 'Don't let's stand in the road like this. Come in here for a moment.'

Leading the two horses, Haldur followed his friend back into the old stone barn. It had fallen into disrepair, with slates missing from the roof and part of the wall in the corner opposite the door tumbled down, but the few bales of straw stacked inside were still fairly dry. Haldur hitched the horses to a rusty iron ring hanging from one of the massive cross-timbers and turned to join Artorynas where he sat on a bale.

'What were you doing in here? Have you had anything to eat?'

'No, I was just resting for a while. I've been walking since last night.'

'Well look, I've got some bread and cheese. We'll share it. And I collected all the stores you ordered and brought them along too, as well as the horse.'

They ate the food, not saying much, both of them all too conscious that the moment of parting could not be long delayed. Eventually Artorynas stood up.

'Well,' he said, 'there's no help for it. I'd better just go, and you need to get back to Cotaerdon. Say goodbye to Aldiro for me. Here's the money for the hire of the horse. Go on, take it, there's no reason why you should pay that for me.'

He pushed the coins into Haldur's hand and went over to put the stores he had brought into the saddlebags. After a moment he spoke again without looking round.

'I want to ask you if you'll do something for me when you're in Caradriggan. I know you've all sworn never to mention me, and anyway, I don't know now who you could still trust... but Haldur, would you tell Arval I got as far as Rihannad Ennar? I realise I'm asking you to break a promise to your father, but Arval has been like a father to me. You can trust him absolutely... Of course, only tell him if you're alone with him and sure no-one else can hear... but if you get the chance...'

'Yes, I'll tell him.'

Artorynas turned round. 'Take care on your journey to the south.'

'I want you to do something for me, as well.' Haldur blurted it out, his eyes very bright. 'I want you to promise me something.'

'What is it?'

'No, I want you to promise me.' When Artorynas seemed to hesitate, Haldur took a step forward. 'You said I was the brother of your heart.'

'I know. I meant it. Yes, I promise.'

'Swear that whether you find what you seek or not, you'll come back to Rihannad Ennar before you return to Caradward. Whatever happens, say you'll come back here first.'

They looked at each other, and Artorynas nodded. 'You have my promise. I swear I will return to the Nine Dales first.'

Haldur grinned rather shakily, but when he spoke, he sounded almost angry.

'You know, I realise there's no point saying this, but I wish Heredcar was still alive. I wish I wasn't destined to be lord after my father, I wish I didn't have to lead this embassy to the south, I wish we could go north together! And most of all, I wish there was some way I could help you.'

'I know, I wish you could come with me, too. But who knows, maybe there will be something you can do to help me, one day.'

'Oh? What's that?'

Artorynas shook his head. 'I don't know, it just came to me without my thinking about it. We should go now, Haldur. You go by the door, and I'll leave that way there, where the wall's fallen down, and we'll neither of us look back. It'll be easier like that.'

'Well, we'll see each other at least once more then, one of these days!' Haldur tried for a light tone, but bit his lip. Suddenly they stepped forward into a tight, silent embrace and then without another word turned away.

As the afternoon passed towards evening, the breeze strengthened a little; it blew chilly from the mountains, into Haldur's face as he rode back to Cotaerdon. He was glad of this, that it carried the sound of Artorynas' horse away from him so that he did not have to hear hoofbeats and the jingle of harness gradually fading into silence; but Artorynas would be able to hear him. Somehow, knowing this, and knowing too that his friend's heart ached like his own with the pain of parting, steadied Haldur when he would have given in to weakness and looked back. The temptation to pause, to draw rein for only a moment, was almost overwhelming; to turn for one last time just in case Artorynas too had turned, to raise a hand in a final farewell; but Haldur had known Artorynas for long enough now to know that when his resolve was set, nothing would break it. He had said he would not look back, so therefore this was something he would not do. The long journey south, and the difficult task at its end, would be far worse if Haldur had to carry the memory of watching Artorynas ride away, dwindling into the distance with his face turned from him. So he set his horse to the trot and speeded up, and not until several miles and many bends of the road were behind him did he slow to a walk and turn in the saddle. The shadows of early evening had fallen now, swallowing up all but the fields and buildings near at hand. Beyond them all was lost in the gathering dusk, and there was nothing to see but the lamplight in a window here and there. The cold began to strike at Haldur and he rode on once more, a weight of despondency bearing down upon him. When he thought of what Artorynas and he were facing, he could not force away the fear that, in spite of his cheerful words, they had parted for the last time and would never meet again.

The lorekeeeeper's fee

Back in Cotaerdon, when Carapethan returned to the hall for his usual mid-morning meal he was greeted with the news that Artorynas was gone, together with all his gear. His informant was Aldiro, who added that the servant who told her had said that Artorynas' bed had not been slept in.

'His guess was that Artorynas left during the night,' said Aldiro, 'and I think he's probably right.'

Carapethan made a non-committal noise and continued with his meal. It seemed, then, as though his moment of inspiration the previous evening had done the trick, and dislodged the wanderer from under his roof. But with Aldiro sitting by him as he ate, in what Carapethan sensed was a rather disapproving silence, he thought it best not to show the satisfaction he felt. And to give Carapethan his due, he was always honest with himself: so now, in his heart of hearts, he could not avoid the uneasy admission that what he had done was in some way unworthy of his standing. Yet, he thought, pausing to take a drink, I am prepared to shoulder the blame if it was for the good of Rihannad Ennar, and now let us hope that things can settle back into their old pattern in the Nine Dales. He turned his attention to the food again, smiling across at his wife, beginning almost visibly to relax.

'What's Haldur up to this morning?' he asked.

'I don't know, I've not seen him yet,' replied Aldiro.

'What, not at all? Didn't he eat breakfast with you?' A curious sensation griped briefly at Carapethan's stomach, which he only much later identified as the first, scarcely-noticed, twinge of alarm. 'He'd better not be still sleeping off the effects of last night's feast.'

He laughed briefly, calling a young lad of the household into the room with instructions to find Haldur and tell him his father wanted to see him. Within a fairly short time, the boy was back, bringing not Haldur, but Cureleth.

'Sir, I can't find Haldur anywhere around the hall, but Cureleth here says he thinks he's gone with Artorynas.'

With difficulty, Carapethan swallowed his last mouthful of meat, feeling it stick in his throat and then slide down to join the rest of his meal which now sat queasily within him. He pushed his plate from him, staring at Cureleth. 'Explain yourself.'

Cureleth fidgeted with the cap he held in his hands, clearly uncomfortable. 'Well, sir, I had business in town and I called at the livery stables – I've a friend who works there – and I saw that the horse reserved for Artorynas had gone; I knew which one it was, you see, because this friend of mine had pointed it out to me. And the word is that he made up his mind to go, in a bit of a hurry, you know, after last night… Well anyway, seeing the horse had gone, I asked my friend, was Artorynas away on it. And he said he thought so, because although he'd not seen Artorynas, Haldur had been in and paid the hire fee and ridden off with the horse on a lead rein.'

A very awkward silence followed this, in which Cureleth studied the floor. Eventually Carapethan got to his feet. Cureleth looked up, alarmed at what he saw in his leader's face, but Carapethan spoke quietly.

'You will find Vorardynur as quickly as you can, and the two of you will ride after Haldur and bring him back to me. You will not return without him. And you will do this discreetly, without asking any more questions than you have to.'

Cureleth gulped. 'Yes, sir. Shall I go now, then, my lord?'

'Of course!' barked Carapethan, his voice rising. 'Why would I want you to hang about? Get on with it, man!' His eye fell on the boy, whose eyes were popping with excitement. 'You as well, get yourself back to your duties.'

The lad scrambled to remove the soiled crockery and utensils from the table and scuttled off with them to the kitchen in Cureleth's wake, closing the door smartly behind him. Carapethan remained standing for a moment and then sat down heavily. He turned to Aldiro, but before he had the chance to say anything to his wife, he heard footsteps approaching and there was a tap at the door.

'What *now*?' exclaimed Carapethan.

The door swung wide, the servant who had opened it standing back respectfully. There was a moment's pause, and then Astell walked across the threshold into the room.

'Good day and good health to you, lord Carapethan. May you never know sorrow, lady Aldiro.'

Carapethan stood once more, rather than inviting Astell to sit; the last thing he wanted was to prolong this exchange. 'Astell: good day to you. No doubt you are here to claim your lorekeeper's fee.'

'On the contrary, I come to exercise the privilege you extended to me last night.'

'Oh, really?'

'Yes; if you remember, you bade me name my fee.'

'Ah, you want more than simply a token payment, is that it?'

Astell's predatory features seemed to sharpen. 'For myself I need no recompense; but a reckoning is required. I am here to name in payment the heart of your son Haldur.'

Shaking off the hand which Aldiro laid on his arm, Carapethan advanced on Astell. 'Just what is that supposed to …'

'Listen to me, lord of Rihannad Ennar.' The lorekeeper's voice rang out, resonant and carrying as if in public recitation, cutting off Carapethan in mid-sentence. 'You have set in motion a sequence of events that cannot now be called back. Artorynas is gone from you, but he journeys towards a choice. His memory of the tale you compelled me to relate last night will influence that choice; and in its turn this will shape a decision that your son will make. The payment has been named, Carapethan; in time, it will be claimed. Haldur's heart was already turned to the As-Geg'rastigan; now it will be given to them for ever.'

They stood there, Carapethan the lord of his people and Astell the keeper of their lore, gazing at one another. The colour was up in Carapethan's cheeks, his eyes shone blue in the weather-tanned face under thick, fair hair; the ashy streaks in his beard and at his temples somehow served only to emphasise his air of health and vigour. He was slightly taller than Astell, and considerably more burly in build: a big man, with a character to match; the room felt too small to contain the vitality he seemed almost to exude. Yet Astell saw what gnawed him from within: unaccustomed self-doubt about the quality of his leadership, increased frustration at his inability to grapple with the metaphysical, long-standing fears for his only surviving son now painfully renewed. Carapethan cleared his throat and swallowed, and the words seemed dragged from him.

'Haldur has gone with Artorynas... Is he to be taken by the Hidden People?'

'That is not what I said. Haldur will return; he has followed Artorynas, not gone with him: loyalty to a friend and sworn brother requires a leave-taking to ease the pain of parting. You surely cannot think that Haldur would fail you by deserting the embassy he has promised to lead? Has he ever neglected a duty, or shirked a responsibility?' Astell raised an eyebrow. 'Do not do your son an injustice in your distress, lord Carapethan.'

Receiving no immediate reply, he inclined his head and left the room with graceful formality.

For a moment there was complete silence. Aldiro watched Carapethan anxiously; he stood staring blankly as the door closed behind Astell. She hastened across when he turned to her, mute appeal in his face, and drew him down into a chair, taking his hand. She waited, but Carapethan said nothing, so she spoke herself in an attempt to comfort him.

'Don't forget that the Hound of the Vow said there was no need to fear for Haldur. Didn't he tell you his life would be long, that he would be honoured here at home and far beyond the Nine Dales?'

'Yes, he did. But I remember that wasn't all he said. There was something else, something about Haldur's search not being over. He'd told Haldur, but the boy kept it to himself.' Carapethan brooded for a moment and then spoke more forcefully. 'They are all the same, these dreamers! They deal in double meanings, they will not speak plainly... Cunor y'n Temennis, Astell, Artorynas. And Ellaaro was just such another, that's where Haldur gets it from.'

Aldiro saw a way to divert Carapethan's mind. 'Perhaps there's nothing more behind all this than the bitterness of a disappointed man. Astell has never forgotten that he was cheated of Ellaaro.'

'He wasn't cheated, that's not how it was!' exclaimed Carapethan in exasperation, and Aldiro concealed a smile. The idea had succeeded, her husband was roused from his stunned immobility.

'Look, whether Astell wanted Ellaaro or not, she was already married to me before he ever saw her!' Calming down again, Carapethan spoke more quietly. 'But you could be right. He is a man who has used his disappointment. Rather than seek a remedy for the hurt, he has nursed it and fed on it all his life. And what about the conceited way he lifted one eyebrow at me, did you see that? He is learned and astute, but it would be a lie to say I have ever liked him, and I have no doubt the feeling is mutual.'

'Well, on that subject, when Haldur comes home remember that each of you has both right and wrong on his side. Don't be too hard on him, or part with him in anger.' When Carapethan fired up again at this, Aldiro took his hand once more and gave it a little shake to emphasise her words. 'Listen to me. I know Haldur is your son – your only son, now – and there is a bond between you that cannot include me. But I have no children of my own. I know it's not the same thing, but to me Haldur is the son I never had. I love him, too.'

'I know, I know.' Carapethan stood up and drew his wife to him, caressing her hair. There were one or two strands of silver among the gold, now; he rested his cheek against them and then let her go with a sigh. 'I can't deny I'll be glad when this day's over. But in the meantime, I've plenty to do so I'd better get on with it.'

The afternoon passed and the day drew on to a chill and cloudy end; but though Carapethan's ears and eyes were alert for a sign of Haldur's return, neither he nor Vorardynur and Cureleth were anywhere to be seen. Darkness fell, and men left their tasks to seek their homes or other quarters for rest and food. Carapethan was angry with himself for loitering outside, inventing reasons for leaving the warmth indoors to stand in the deepening night listening for the sound of approaching hooves. Soon it would be time for the evening meal to be served; he wanted to eat alone, away from the whispers and speculative stares, but forced himself to sit in his hall as usual along with the other members of his household. At last all was done, and the company dispersed leaving Carapethan to his thoughts. He retired to the private family rooms, but sat near the window listening, worrying, waiting. What if Haldur did fail to return? In spite of what Astell had said earlier, Carapethan could not quite banish the fear that Haldur was not coming back, and in addition he now began to regret his decision to send Voryardynur after him with perhaps over-hasty orders. Time dragged past, and then suddenly Carapethan's ears picked up the sound he had been straining to catch. Horses, ridden at speed, rapidly approaching: they hurtled into the open court before the hall, one leading the other two. He heard trampling, shouting, doors banging, neighing from the stables, angry voices raised and then footsteps pounding on the steps of the porch.

The fury that had erupted in Haldur when he was met on the road by Vorardynur and Cureleth and told their errand was still boiling in him as he leapt from his horse and stormed into the hall in search of his father. Shame at what Carapethan had done the previous evening, shock at Artorynas' sudden departure, rage at this attempt to bring him to heel like some badly-behaved child, grief at the sorrow of the parting he had just endured, all these combined in a poisonous mixture, coursing like venom through Haldur's veins. He had galloped back to Cotaerdon as a man possessed and now strode down the corridor, bursting into the room where his father waited for him. Carapethan had got to his feet when he heard the commotion outside and stood facing the door. He too was feeling the effects of an exhausting succession of anger, fear, worry, embarrassment, foreboding. Now, sudden relief turned his anxiety once more to a surge of anger. Haldur flung the door open; it crashed back against the wall and he slammed it behind him. Father and son confronted each other, glaring, for a moment of silence; then both drew a breath to begin a tirade of recrimination. But strangely, the angry words remained unspoken. In that last tiny instant, each had had time to see the pain in the other's face, and to regret being the cause of it. Carapethan's shoulders slumped, the aggression melted from Haldur's stance; this time, words came: the same words from both of them.

'I'm sorry,' each said simply into the other's shoulder, as they wrapped their arms around one another.

Yet later, though Carapethan, wearied by the day's turmoil, slept deeply beside Aldiro, it was Ellaaro that he saw in his dreams: Ellaaro whose eyes lived again in her son's face. Haldur too was tired out, but being younger, his thoughts kept him wakeful far into the night. He hated the recent differences that had arisen between himself and Carapethan, when all his life previously there had been no dissention between father and son. Unwilling though he was to acknowledge it, he recognised that Artorynas and Carapethan had understood one another's minds, and he realised that now he could appreciate his father's fears: he saw why Carapethan wanted none from among the As-Urad to find a home in Rihnnnad Ennar. But as sleep finally took him, one last, vehement protest rose within his heart. I don't agree though, he thought; I don't think like that. If I was the lord of the Nine Dales, I'd want nothing better than to have the companionship and counsel of one of the As-Urad. Yet when he woke, the words of *Maesell y'm As-Urad* were still running in his mind, the sorrowful tale of those who had no dwelling-place among either the Earthborn or the Starborn even though they were kin to both; and he trailed over to the wash-house in the grey dawn light with a heavy heart, relying on cold water to refresh weary limbs and an aching head. Maybe it was for the best that he would soon be gone on his errand to Caradriggan; it would give him plenty to occupy his mind. He threw himself into the final preparations for departure, and neither he nor Carapethan mentioned Artorynas again. But times without number as the busy days went by, Haldur's thoughts turned to Artorynas. How did it go with him, where was he now?

Last lodgings

Mile by mile, Artorynas was pushing on with his journey, allowing the horse to pick its own pace but making sure he started early each day and kept going until sunset. As the days passed, the raw hurt caused by the circumstances of his leaving Cotaerdon and parting with Haldur settled down into a dull ache that he scarcely noticed: his mind learnt to accommodate it, as his foot might have developed a callus in response to a creased boot-sole. He found himself looking forward to what each day's dawn might bring. This was a setting-out very different from fleeing Caradriggan with the hunt on his trail; different, too, from the earlier years of his wandering, when the returning season had brought with it renewed uncertainty. Now he felt a new urgency, which was not due only to the knowledge that his time was beginning to run out. This spring, a stronger hope was born within him, a more certain sense that at last he might be nearing his goal. Occasionally he would encounter someone who recognised him, who knew him from having met him during his travels with Carapethan's entourage; and people everywhere were friendly in the frank, open way he had come to love in the Nine Dales. Yet the long-ingrained habit of caution prompted him to say little about his purpose, naming only the next settlement or valley as his destination if asked. Down from Cotaerdon through Rihann y'n Devo Lissadan he went, before turning to climb by the low road into Rihann y'n Fram where the Lissa'mor flowed wide in its lazy curves; for in one thing at least his route was similar to his first year of journeying, in that at the start, the trail he followed took him away from his northerly course. But as the season advanced he turned his face to the mountains once more and climbed up to the pass that led over into the Golden Valley.

Here he stayed for a night at the *Beehive* in Garstannad, the small town that served as the main market for the dale, and the following morning he left his horse at the livery stables and set out on foot once more. Now each day as he walked the sun cast his shadow before him and poured golden into the narrowing dale as it wound further into the hills. Eventually Artorynas was too near the head of the valley to be able to see the Golden Mountains; the peaks of the Somllichan na'Haldan rose overhead, shutting out any glimpse of the heights beyond. Late one afternoon clouds thickened as he trudged along, and looking over his shoulder he saw the sky dark and threatening behind him where a spring storm was gathering. It was still some miles to the last hamlet of the vale, where he had hoped to spend the night. By the look of the purple clouds massing in the west, he would be soaked through long before he reached its shelter; but away up the hillside he saw the buildings of a small farmstead. His mind made up, he left the main road and made his way quickly down to the river. This high up the dale it flowed swiftly and deep in its rocky course, but was no longer very wide. Artorynas took his stave from its holder at the side of his pack, hefted it in his hands and then, planting it firmly at the end of a measured approach run, used it to lever himself in a flying leap over the torrent. Landing lightly on the far bank, he set off up the slope with long strides and as the first heavy raindrops began to fall, he was crossing a small cobbled yard and knocking at a door in the corner between house and barn.

The top half of the door opened in response, revealing an elderly man who peered out with short-sighted eyes in a face rimed with a couple of days of grizzled stubble. Behind him in the dusky interior

Artorynas glimpsed a white-haired old woman who sat beside the fire.

'Good day and good health to you, master,' he said. 'The storm has caught up with me before I can reach the village: may I shelter with you tonight? I offer you my service with any task that needs help, in payment for my lodging.'

'Come on in.' The old man swung back the lower part of the door and Artorynas stepped inside. 'I can't see your face too clearly, but by your voice I'd say you're a stranger in the valley. Have you travelled far?'

Artorynas hesitated. 'I've come from Cotaerdon,' he said; and then, turning to the woman, 'Thank you for your hospitality, mistress. May you never know sorrow.'

She stood up, smiling. 'It's a pleasure to have company, young man. Sit you down with dad now and I'll see about some food.'

The two men settled on either side of the hearth as she busied herself preparing a meal. Outside, the storm broke in earnest, lashing against the shutters and tearing at the heather thatch. Artorynas listened to the wind howling in the chimney and the rain that hissed onto the glowing embers in the intervals between savage gusts and breathed a sigh of relief that he had managed to reach this warm, homely sanctuary in time.

'Bring out the damson wine, mother!' the man of the house called out to his wife. 'We've three trees, you know,' he said, turning back to Artorynas, 'just the three, under the shelter of the hill. Most of the fruit goes into damson cheese, some for ourselves and some for the market, but we always make wine with part of the crop. From Cotaerdon, you say? I've not been there myself these seven years, not since...' He broke off as his wife called them over to eat.

The meal was as simple as its setting: a bowl of mutton broth with turnip and kale, thickened with barley; and a small salty ewe's milk cheese each to go with the savoury bread. Artorynas sipped at the cold spring water to hide his smile when he broke open the loaf. It was chewy with leeks baked into it and took him straight back in memory to his ten-year-old self, turning down the chance of cheesebread at the *Sword and Stars* in a bid to toughen himself up. No need to worry on that score now, he thought wryly. When the old woman hung a griddle over the fire and made him a pancake with honey and apple he accepted it gratefully, knowing there was no longer any risk that such indulgence might weaken him.

'That was a supper fit for a lord's table,' he said. 'I'm in your debt for food and shelter, so tell me now what I may do tomorrow to repay you.'

'Well…' The man scratched his chin. 'I'll tell you what I could do with some help on. I've a wall in the top field that needs repairing; every year in the lambing season, the ewes kick it down trying to find a spot to themselves when their time comes. But I don't know, a young fellow from Cotaerdon, you'll likely not know much about dry-stone walling. Still, you could maybe pass the stones up to me, save me bending.'

He peered hopefully at Artorynas, who burst out laughing.

'I promise you, I've built a few yards of wall in my time,' he said, 'but if I don't come up to your standard, then certainly, I'll be pleased to do the lifting and carrying for you. Now, you look like a man who rises with the dawn. Maybe you'd show me a corner of your hay-loft where I could sleep, so I'll be ready for you in the morning?'

The old woman had been watching him closely and now she spoke before her husband had time to say anything. 'You'll sleep in no hay-loft. Come over here.'

She opened a door that Artorynas had assumed was a cupboard or larder, and revealed a box-bed set into the thickness of the wall and raised over several carved wooden drawers. 'You lie there. You'll be warm and snug; it was where our son used to sleep. We always keep it ready just in case.'

The old couple bade him goodnight and banked the fire, then climbed slowly up a ladder to their own chamber which extended over half the living-room below. Artorynas heard them whispering for a while and wondered whether he was the subject of their conversation. He had seen that the old fellow was taken aback to hear him offered the box-bed and sensed some unspoken sorrow to do with their son.

Next morning he stood on the hillside, gazing back across the valley. The storm had blown itself out in the night and the world was refreshed and renewed, bedecked in a million dancing drops that swung and sparkled in the sunlight. Artorynas took a deep breath and then turned back to the job in hand. The repairs to the wall were almost finished: his expertise having passed muster, he and his host had worked together.

'You're a fortunate man, to be able to look out on a prospect such as this when you go about your daily work,' he said.

'You think so? Well, maybe. But the view doesn't put bread in your belly. It's hard work to make a living from a hill farm like this, even in Rihann nan'Esylt.'

Artorynas nodded in agreement; by now he had seen the wind-bitten damson trees, the vegetable plot painstakingly tended in raised beds to deepen the soil, the squat-built byres and barns, the small flock of wild-eyed little sheep. He bent and straightened, fitting the last few stones into place; then suddenly, as if coming to a decision, the old man spoke again.

'No, don't misunderstand me, young master. It's right, what you say. I'll tell you something now. My eyes aren't what they were: I can't see much up close, these days. But that's no matter while I can still see the land drop away down to the river there and sweep up the far side of the valley.'

'May you long have the happiness of that sight.'

'They say my family's farmed these slopes ever since folk came into the valley from Rihann y'n Car, but I doubt now whether any will come after me. My daughter's got three children, but her husband keeps a shop in Cotaerdon. The two girls are all for town life and it doesn't seem as though the boy wants to work the farm: we've not seen them in the Golden Valley these three summers, now. And my son...' He paused, and when he continued, Artorynas heard the pain and pride in his voice. 'My son went to ride with the Cunorad, but he never came back. The Hidden People took him. He lies now in Rihann y'n Temenellan; but I was born here, and I'll die here, and here they'll lay me, to sleep with all my fathers that went before me.'

'At the least then, you and your land will lie together in love,' said Artorynas, his heart moved by what he had just heard.

'Aye, it'll be a long embrace.'

'I am truly sorry about your son,' said Artorynas. 'If it were not that I must go, on an errand I have sworn to complete, I would gladly stay here: not to take his place, but to work at your side.'

The old man pushed his cap back and tilted his face at Artorynas, screwing up his eyes as if to see better. 'You're a strange traveller... The wife and I talked about you last night when we were all abed, and she reckons you're the young fellow who was in the valley a couple of times with lord Carapethan, the one they say is *as-ur*?'

Artorynas bowed his head. 'Your wife is a shrewd woman as well as an excellent cook and a kindly host.'

'If only my boy could have lived to see this day.' Tears wandered down the wrinkled old cheeks unheeded as the man passed a gnarled hand almost gently over the stones of the wall. 'To think one of the As-Urad should have worked in my fields like any other man,' he said quietly, and then looked up, practical once more. 'Sir, no matter who built it, the ewes will have the wall down again next spring; but there's a *numiras* beside the spring above the house. Will you take a stone, and put it there for remembrance? And then you'll want to be gone, but mother will cook you a fresh egg to set you on your way.'

That night, Artorynas slept in the village at the head of the dale and the following morning began the long climb that would take him out of the Golden Valley, up to the pass and beyond, away from Rihannad Ennar. It was four days past the Spring Feast now; he wondered whether Haldur had started out yet on his journey to Caradriggan.

Had he known it, on that very morning, far away in Cotaerdon the six who were to go south were indeed preparing to ride. Friends and family gathered to speed Haldur and his companions on their way in a bustle of departure; many voices called farewell. Artorynas though walked alone through the narrow streets of the little hamlet and up the lane that led to the fields, and gradually the sounds of morning faded behind him. Soon the laughter of children, the slam of a door or window, the rumble of cartwheels were the only noises that carried to him; little by little these too were lost until there was nothing but a barking dog or the distant shout of a man calling to a fellow-worker to speak to him of the daily life he was leaving behind; and then even these were heard no more. He walked away from the world of men, and the quiet fell softly on his ears, while the peace of empty places filled his heart as he went.

Chapter 42

Haldur's first test

'Surely even Ir'rossung will be able to hear it now.'

Cathasar's whisper reached Haldur as he lay awake before sunrise one morning.

'I think I can feel a kind of tremble in the ground, too. If you put your hand on it flat like this – go on, you do it, see whether you can feel it too. It must be something to do with the noise. What do think it means?'

The answering whisper came from Tellapur as they sat together over the fire, the last two of the night's watchers. Haldur heard the apprehension in Tellapur's voice and recognised the first test of his leadership. He remembered that the young man had shown signs of being afraid of passing through the wilderness before they ever left Cotaerdon. If he proved unable to master his fears, it would surely be most unwise to let him continue as a member of the party: such unease might spread to the others all too easily. Haldur had no wish to shame him, but if he was to be left behind, now was the time to do it, before they struck out into the unknown in earnest. His own misgivings concerned the passage of time. They were still travelling down what he thought of as Rihann y'n Devo Lissadan, although they had ridden far beyond the last settled lands. If he had realised the extent of the valley, he would not have delayed; but it had been a wrench to tear themselves away from the hospitality that Sallic had provided when they reached the ferry village. It was obvious that

Sallic himself would have liked to have been included in the embassy – and indeed probably would have been, had he not now become the father of a young child. Haldur firmly put aside the thought that he would rather have taken Sallic with them than Tellapur, and crawled from his tent with a yawn.

'Morning, you two. Nothing to report from your watch? Right, well if you can start to get the food ready Cathasar, I'll take Tellapur to give me a hand with the horses.'

He kept a surreptitious eye on Tellapur as they worked. The lad was rather pale, but that might simply be from keeping the last watch of the night. Haldur stopped for a moment and stretched, warming up the muscles of his back.

'I reckon we'll be fairly on our way proper, by this time tomorrow. I'll be glad: we're a bit behind schedule.'

There was a short silence. 'You mean you think we've nearly reached the wilderness, then?'

'I hope so. We need to press on. If we can hear the noise of the falls in the river so clearly, we surely must be near the ravine we've been told of.'

'Oh, you think that's what the noise is?' Tellapur tried, without much success, to inject a nonchalant tone into the question.

'What else could it be?' When he received no reply, Haldur took hold of Tellapur's arm and turned him round. 'Look, if you'd rather not go on, we're still in Rihann y'n Devo Lissadan. To get home again, all you'd have to do is follow the river; but if you're going to turn back, do it now before we get out into Na Caarst.'

Too embarrassed to admit he was afraid of seeing some horror from the stories he had been brought up on, Tellapur kept his eyes fixed on the ground.

'It's just … all of us except Ir'rossung have been able to hear it since yesterday,' he said eventually. 'If it's only the water, how huge must the falls be, to make that much noise?' He looked up. 'Don't send me back home. I would be ashamed.'

'Listen, I'm not sending you anywhere. Yes, we're taking a

calculated risk, going into the wilderness, but I think there'll be more reason to fear what we find when we arrive at the far side, rather than anything we're likely to encounter during the crossing. And when we do get there, we all need to be able to rely on each other completely. We're going to need the strength that will come from having been tested together on our journey, and having passed that test. I've got to know I can have confidence in all of you. So it's now or never, Tellapur; but if you do go back, I'll think of some reason that will cover it. That's why we're talking here, away from the others. You don't need to worry that anybody will know.'

Tellapur studied his feet again. How could he return home: what would his parents think? They had enough to worry about with Torello, now that Artorynas was gone. And he had overcome his shyness to stand up to his father in the council; what was the point of speaking out like that in front of Carapethan, if he was going to give in to his fears now? Haldur had been really decent to speak to him privately, he owed him for that. Squaring his shoulders, Tellapur took a deep breath and looked Haldur in the eye.

'I'm sorry, I shouldn't have given in to weakness like that. I feel really stupid about it. It won't happen again, I swear it. I'm going on, and I promise I won't fail you or any of the others.'

'Good man, I knew I could rely on you!' Haldur grinned at him. 'That's settled then. Come on, let's finish with these horses and get some breakfast.'

But by evening, they were still following the river, and even Haldur was secretly shaken at the thought that they were approaching a cataract so enormous that for two full days already its voice had been audible. The distant roar was loud enough now to make them raise their voices when speaking to one another, and the horses were uneasy. All day as they rode the valley floor sank lower and became more barren, and by nightfall they were shut within a kind of canyon. Its sides were almost vertical and between them was a wide, stony landscape littered with broken rock and gravel banks. The river was now flowing much faster, racing along at a tremendous pace in dark, surging waves. They were careful to keep well back from its margins, drawing their water from the many streams that rushed down, because it was all too obvious that a man who slipped into that merciless, roiling current would be instantly swept away. During the morning of the next day they began to feel a fine mist that settled in beads on their clothing and wetted their faces and hands; ahead of them it rose and billowed in a huge cloud, occasionally glinting with rainbows as the breeze shifted it under the sun. The noise increased to an unremitting bellow that numbed their ears and shook the ground underfoot as if with thunder. Then at last they saw what caused it: right across its width, the river plunged suddenly down. The floor of the valley, and with it the river-bed, simply vanished where a rift had opened up in the ground, and into it the water disappeared. Haldur and his companions gazed appalled, speechless in the face of the mighty force that confronted them. It was as if the earth had gaped open in some monstrous mouth and swallowed the river whole. The shattering volume of sound, the endless motion of the water as it poured over the last edge and dropped to some horrifying, unfathomable depth, had an insidiously hypnotic effect. They all felt it: a seductive, dizzying compulsion to creep nearer, nearer to that fatal brink, to yield to that terrible power.

Something was tugging at Haldur's sleeve as he stood, the will to resist draining from him, and he turned almost reluctantly to see Tellapur shouting at him, yelling words that were drowned in the tumult. He stared vaguely at the young man for a moment but his eyes were drawn ineluctably back to the dark water. Tellapur grabbed him, shook him violently, as if he could forcibly dislodge the slack, vacant expression from his leader's face. Gesturing with his free hand, he jerked his head urgently, willing him to understand.

'Get them away! We've got to move back, come on, move!'

The ability to think, to take action, suddenly returned to Haldur. Aghast at their precarious position, he seized the bridle of Cathasar's horse, dragging him past the chasm. Ahead of him, Tellapur was guiding Ir'rossung and encouraging Asaldron to move. Looking back, he saw Aestrontor bringing up the rear and went to help him with the mules and spare horses. It was difficult going over slippery, rocky ground seamed and dissected by deep cracks. If any of the animals steps in one of these crevices, thought Haldur grimly, it will break a leg for sure. Slowly they struggled on, grateful in a way for the need to take such care on the treacherous pavement. When all their concentration was focused on keeping a sure footing, the temptation to stare into the sinister, beckoning abyss was removed. Eventually the ground became drier as they moved beyond the range of the drifting mist from the falls, and they were able to go a little more quickly. Haldur felt himself trembling in reaction as the danger receded; but though numbed with shock, he was keen to press on and could see that the others were of similar mind. Noon came and passed unnoticed, but as evening approached the valley became shallower again as its floor rose once more and its sides diminished, and the noise of the torrent faded to no more than a distant threat.

They settled the animals and then saw to their own camping place. For some time they ate without speaking, drawn together in wordless companionship by their experience. Eventually Asaldron broke the silence.

'If any man had described to me what I have seen today, I would not have believed him. Who would ever have thought that the waters that flow so peacefully through Cotaerdon should come to such a violent end?'

'Who indeed,' said Ir'rossung, 'and for myself, I've no wish ever to see that awful yawning void again. I hope when we return home we can find a different route! But surely, the river can't simply vanish into the earth and be lost. The water must flow out again above ground at some other place. I wonder where.'

'I don't.' Cathasar shuddered as he spoke. 'I don't even want to think about what we saw, or it will haunt my dreams. If ever a sight was the stuff of nightmares, that was.'

'Well, if I have a nightmare, I'll not be best pleased.' They all looked at Tellapur in some surprise, hearing the amusement in his voice. The lad seemed almost buoyant, smiling as he continued. 'Well, wouldn't it just add insult to injury? Being there in real life was bad enough, without going there all over again in my sleep; yet the strange thing is, I feel better for it. I don't mind telling you all now, I was afraid of what might be in front of us. But after today, I'm not afraid any more of anything we may have to face.'

Haldur smiled. 'You're an honest man, Tellapur,' he said, 'and I'm sure there's truth in what you say, that you'll be all right from now on. But there's something you haven't said, that needs telling. All of you should know that Tellapur was the only one of us who kept a clear head, back there. It was his quick thinking that got us away while we still had the will to move. Who knows what might have happened if he'd not brought me to my senses in time.'

Tellapur hung his head bashfully but his heart lit up at this praise from Haldur; and when they turned in for the night he found that now he had conquered his fears, he could indeed sleep peacefully, untroubled by dreams.

In the wilderness

During the following day they began to strike out into the barren lands of Na Caarst. At first, although the land was fairly level, the going was slow because the flat rocks underfoot were still split and weathered into deep, treacherous grykes; but once this terrain was behind them they made better speed across an arid landscape relieved here and there with scrubby bushes and small trees. Far away to their left, they could see mountains in the distance and Haldur, anxious though he was to push on and make up for lost time, aimed their course in a curve towards them, reckoning that this would give them a better chance of finding water than if they kept too rigidly to the straight path south. He was glad of his decision to set off as early in the year as possible, while streams were still finding their way down in spate from the high lands, because they could see from the traces carved into the gritty dust of many a shallow valley that later in the season the waters wandered only so far before they were thirstily soaked away. Occasionally a bird of prey would wheel gracefully high overhead, but it was difficult to see what hope of food they had unless it was the burrowing rodents that colonised the low, sandy banks in many of these dry valleys. They took care to be watchful at all times, two of the party being detailed to ride slightly apart from the others and to look all around them as they went. Haldur made sure that these stints of vigilance were short, and changed frequently to avoid complacency or fatigue; but he insisted that they were maintained, and a guard kept through the nights.

However, time passed without them seeing or hearing anything that seemed dangerous or threatening, apart from the inhospitable nature of the hostile land they travelled through, until one day they came across a scattering of bones. Any doubts as to what creature they might have belonged to were dispelled by the discovery first of the remains of a fireplace and then two human skulls lying broken beside the torn remnants of what might have been boots and a pack. Some of the long bones were cracked open and showed the marks of gnawing teeth; ribs and smaller fragments were tossed about over a wide area. They stared down, sickened, and then began to look around them anxiously. Haldur pulled himself together and took charge.

'Aestrontor, Ir'rossung: lead the animals over there and keep a look-out. We've got to give this a decent burial before we go on. Cathasar, bring us whatever you can find from our packs that we can use to dig with. I know we haven't got anything very suitable, but we'll do the best we can. While Asaldron and Cathasar are digging, Tellapur and I will bring up as many rocks and large stones as we can manage, and then we'll take our turn at the digging.'

When the grave was as deep as they could make it, not much more than a shallow scrape in the hard ground, they laid the bones in it.

Haldur insisted that all of them must help with the gathering up, reluctant though some of them were to handle the remains, and then they piled up rocks on top until the cairn was big enough to be proof against disturbance. They used some of their precious water to clean their hands before standing for a moment in remembrance to honour those whose end had been so desperate, and then rode off again, putting as much distance behind them as they could before stopping for the night. Their meal that evening was a subdued occasion; somehow none of them felt as hungry as usual. Deciding at last that it would be better to discuss what they had seen, rather than let it fester unspoken in their minds, Haldur glanced round at his companions.

'Well, what we came across today was a timely lesson for us. We've done well so far, but if we want to stay alive, it's all too obvious we've got to stay alert.'

'Who do you think they were?' said Asaldron.

'We'll never know, will we?'

'Whoever they were, they must have had a pressing reason to find themselves in the middle of Na Caarst. We know ourselves that no-one would be here by choice.' Cathasar lowered his voice. 'I reckon they were some from Gwent y'm Aryframan who tried to reach the Nine Dales but never made it that far.'

'Yes, but what can have happened to them?' Ir'rossung's eyes showed white for a moment in the glow of their small fire as he leaned forward a little.

Haldur shrugged, trying to be as matter-of-factly blunt as he could. 'Plenty of choice, there. Starvation, illness, attack…'

'Attack!' This was Cathasar again, nervously interrupting.

'For all we know, they could have killed each other in an argument.' Heads turned to Tellapur. He caught Haldur's gaze and smiled slightly, spreading his hands. 'Look, we all knew before we started out that we were taking a risk. The only difference now is that we know the dangers are real, after what we've seen today.'

'I'll tell you something else.' Aestrontor, who hardly ever contributed to the conversation, now joined in the discussion from his place on the edge of the group, but kept his eyes fixed on the darkness beyond the firelight as he spoke. 'Did none of you notice the marks on the bones? Whether they were gnawed by whatever did the killing, or found by carrion-eaters, they were chewed up by something with teeth that needed to feed. Something alive, in other words, and not a ghost or other bogey of the imagination. So it's like Tellapur says, we've seen the evidence of the danger; and as Haldur says, we'd best keep our wits about us if we plan to see tomorrow morning.'

'Yes, come on, let's turn in and set the watch.'

Ir'rossung and Asaldron stood up and the rest of them settled down to sleep. Haldur lay awake for a while. It occurred to him that what they had found could stand them in good stead if they were questioned too closely by the Caradwardans about fugitives. Now that they had all seen those pitiful, scattered bones, they would surely sound convincing if it proved necessary to speculate that anyone attempting to flee to Rihannad Ennar must without doubt have perished likewise. He stored the thought away, along with an idea that had come to him when he realised that Ir'rossung had been unable to hear the noise of the falls while it was still a distant, threatening rumble. Ir'rossung was much older than the rest of them, maybe he was becoming slightly deaf. Would he be willing to play along if they pretended he was much harder of hearing than was really the case? It could be a useful ploy, if it meant that men spoke more carelessly in front of him than they would otherwise have done… Haldur turned over and drew his blanket around him. Night is for sleeping, he told himself firmly; if you use the time in thinking rather than resting, you'll regret it tomorrow.

Journey's end

Some days later, circumstances brought his idea back into mind. He and Ir'rossung happened to be riding together slightly ahead of the others, exchanging the occasional word but mainly occupied in looking about them, keeping a keen eye on their surroundings. The mountains were nearer now, and Haldur noticed that the character of the landscape was changing again. There was something about the rock formations that reminded him of the ravine into which the waters of Lissad nan'Ethan had disappeared. Here too were bare grey outcrops split and weathered, and some of the fissures were dark, as if they penetrated deep below ground. The previous evening, Cathasar had suddenly raised a hand for silence as they sat round their small fire, and asked if anyone besides himself could hear running water. With the exception of Ir'rossung, they had all thought they could: it seemed quite close by, yet the sound was curiously distant in some indefinable way. They had found no spring near their camping-place, and the noise was not made by the little stream that meandered past; but now Haldur caught the sound once more. He checked his horse and sat listening, tilting his head.

'I'm sure I can hear water again,' he said, looking all around, 'but where is it?'

Ir'rossung smiled ruefully. 'It's no good asking me. I couldn't hear it last night, and I don't hear anything now. Get one of the young ones to ride along with you, they'll be more use to you than I am.'

'Don't undervalue yourself, Ir'rossung, I'm relying on your wisdom and experience to get us safely through this venture and home again. Come on, the others are catching us up.'

They moved off, but now Haldur listened constantly for that elusive sound. He edged away to his left, dismounting as soon as he heard it again. Hitching the reins to a thorny shrub that grew out of a crack in the rock, he moved slowly forward on foot, following his ears. He could have sworn he heard a sizeable river, hurrying along with a swift current; yet no such watercourse was anywhere to be seen and the sound, although it seemed close, was somewhat muffled in tone. Suddenly Haldur caught his toe in a crevice and stumbled to a fall. As he sat on a flat slab of stone, rubbing the palms of his hands where he had grazed them, the noise of water came to him much more clearly. He knelt and peered into the fissure where he had tripped. From far below, hollow-sounding as if it echoed in some vast cavern, rose the rushing, swirling voice. Haldur stood up again, this time calling Aestrontor over to him.

'Listen to that!'

Aestrontor looked down at the split in the rock. It was no more than a handspan in width, yet by what he could hear, it must go down to a tremendous depth. He frowned at Haldur.

'We're getting too far out of our way,' he said. 'We should be bearing more south-west now, not going nearer to the mountains.'

'You're probably right.' Yet as Haldur gazed around, the urge to explore a little further was irresistible. 'Could you take my horse on for me on a lead rein? I want to go on foot for a while.'

'I don't think you should, but if you're set on it, then I'm coming too and Cathasar can take both horses.'

The two of them moved slowly on, Haldur in the lead, trying to follow the sound of the water, gradually veering away further to the left of the main party. The going became progressively more difficult. Every so often there would be a sudden hollow, littered with the same kind of rock that was everywhere about them, worn and carved into slabs and clefts, sometimes even weathered into smooth holes. Several times more they heard the noise of water rising from fractures in the ground and then, clambering over a tumbled heap of great square boulders, they were confronted by something new. Below them was a kind of depression, as if the surface of the ground had been sucked down from underneath; and in the middle, it had caved in completely. Bare, stony earth and patchy grass clung to the edge of a round, ragged hole as if frozen there even as it slid into the depths beneath. And from those depths, out of the dark cavern with which the pothole connected, came the unmistakeable noise of a powerful watercourse that surged along somewhere far below their feet.

Haldur stared in amazement and then turned to Aestrontor. 'You know, this could be the Lissad nan'Ethan itself! What do you think?'

'By the Starborn, Haldur! Who cares what it is!' Aestrontor wrenched his eyes away from the black gape. A peculiar smell came from it, a rank, raw tang that was earthy but alien at the same time.

'I'll tell you what I think. We need to get out of this before anything else gives way. How do we know what we're standing on? It could go any time like it has done there, and take us with it. Let's get back to the others! It's just stupid to go looking for danger like this and I don't care if you tell your father I told you so.'

They scrambled out of the hollow and picked their way back to less treacherous ground. When they rejoined their companions it was Aestrontor, usually so silent, who described what they had seen while Haldur rode without speaking, looking away towards the mountains thoughtfully. When they halted briefly to rest the horses, he voiced his theory.

'I think the water we heard is the Lissad nan'Ethan. I think it must flow underground from where we saw it plunge downwards in the ravine.' He pointed to his left. 'It's continuing more or less southeast, and I wonder whether it might emerge above ground again somewhere in the mountains.'

They discussed the idea briefly, but like Aestrontor, most of them were not particularly curious about it. Asaldron was staring into the distance, screwing up his eyes in an attempt to see better.

'I think the mountains are taller, away there. It looks to me as though they'll block our path, if we stick to our present course.'

Cathasar, the keenest-sighted of them all, turned to look over his shoulder. 'I'd say you're right. And I'm sure I can see a sort of greenish tinge to their lower slopes, as if they were forested. But we've been told that the mountains to the north of Gwent y'm Aryframan sweep straight down into the bare wilderness; so if that's where we're heading, we're definitely out of our way.'

'How many days have we been travelling now?' Haldur did some mental calculations while rummaging in his saddlebag. 'Here we are.' He spread out the rough map they had all pored over back in

Cotaerdon. 'As soon as we're sure we can see the range Cathasar's talking about, I'm going to put this on the fire, but meanwhile…'

They put their heads together over the sketch, looking up from time to time to compare it with what they saw around them. Haldur scribbled in some notes about time and distance, and then sat back scratching his head, muttering to himself. At last he came to a conclusion.

'Right,' he said, putting his finger on the map, 'I reckon we're about here. In which case, I agree we need to change direction now and turn south-east, away from these higher mountains. And if I'm right, in about a week or ten days more, we should see the pass that leads into Gwent y'm Aryframan.'

They looked at each other without speaking. Then Tellapur got to his feet and brought over Haldur's horse with his own. One by one they climbed to the saddle and set out again on their new course, where so far they could see nothing away before them except mile upon mile of featureless wilderness. But a morning came when, as they went yawning about the first tasks of the day, Aestrontor once more startled them by breaking his silence.

'Look there, away in the south!'

The first rays of the sun were spilling over the land and they turned to see – what? Was it simply a pattern of clouds that the sun picked out, or was it shining on mountains whose peaks pierced the morning mist? Haldur looked eagerly at Cathasar, who was standing staring out, his eyes shaded by his hand.

'I'm almost sure it is mountains,' said Cathasar at last, 'and if it is, we should definitely know today, as we get nearer.'

Frustratingly, as the air warmed it became hazy and all distant prospects were hidden from them. It was not until evening that they were certain, when as the sun went down the sky cleared and there was no mistaking the rugged outline that stood out against it. There was a noticeable dip at one point in the silhouette and they wondered whether this was a trick of perspective or the place where their road would take them over the pass into the lands beyond. They ate their frugal meal that nightfall in an atmosphere of heightened awareness. Every man was busy with his own thoughts, but when their eyes met in the firelight, they could see that each of them was gripped by his own, private apprehension. Haldur leaned forward.

'Tomorrow or the next day should see us arrive, then. Give me your hands. We've made it this far, we're going to get through what's in front of us and we'll be coming home safely too. We can do this, for Rihannad Ennar.'

Fort commander

In a rather drab little office within the fort that watched over the pass, a man sat signing documents while another man stood by. When the paperwork was completed and sealed into its container, the seated man handed it to the waiting dispatch rider.

'Here you are then: that's all last week's reports finished.'

'Sir.'

The courier left the room and his footsteps faded as he crossed the small paved courtyard around which the fort was built. After a moment or two there was the noise of hooves, an exchange of passwords, the creak of the gate opening followed by a crash as it was slammed to again. The sounds were so familiar to the man still sitting at his desk that he scarcely heard them. He stared into space, absently drumming his fingers on the arm of his chair, putting off his next duty, a round of the wall walks. In theory an inspection should alleviate the day's tedium a little; but the truth was he found mingling with his troops slightly intimidating and, what was worse, had the feeling that they knew it. And in any case, any interest there might once have been in looking out from the walls of the fort had long since drained away. There was never anything to see, nothing to report: in fact secretly he saw very little point in the whole exercise. But, he thought as he stood up with a sigh, he knew the reasons for their presence and the duties they performed, and he supposed they were necessary; and, of course, all the boredom in the world was nothing compared with the happiness that his posting to this remote region had unexpectedly brought him. He was smiling a little as he left his office and headed for the stair leading to the wall.

Without even stopping to think about it, he knew that all was well within the fort. It ran smoothly thanks to the efficiency of its commanding officer, a hard-bitten type who was permanently quartered there along with the small garrison of twenty men. He himself, as the governor of the district, lived as a civilian with his family a few miles away down the valley but came up to the fort on a regular basis, switching to a night shift once a month. The fort itself was a functional, bleak little establishment. Living accommodation for the men ran down the inner side of one wall, stores and administration buildings down another, stables along the third side, and the fourth housed the workshops, wash-rooms and latrines. A stone stair in the corner led up on to the wall, which was about the height of three men with a parapet above and a turret at each angle. There were five men on wall duty this morning: one patrolling each section of the wall-walk and another stationed in the turret that housed the signal beacon. Five more, who would take the night watch, slept in the barracks below, and the rest were deployed on various other duties.

So, round the walls then, stick to the routine of question and answer: anything to report, no sir; seen anything unusual, no sir; all well then, yes sir. He paused for a moment to look out. When he had first arrived, he had gazed with reluctant fascination on the prospect of Na Caarst which the north wall afforded, but familiarity had dulled its impact. Yet today for some reason it drew his eye, that vast, barren sweep of land fading endlessly into the distance. After a moment or two he turned, sensing that he was being watched, and caught the north guard instantly swivelling his eyes away and blanking out the expression on his face. He walked on through the turret and on to the east wall, furious at the way he knew his own face was burning.

With his sandy, gingery hair and pink cheeks, he had blushed easily as a child but had always hoped that this would cease as he grew older. He knew the men thought he was just some armchair soldier foisted on them from Caradriggan. Damn that fellow, he'd find him some unpleasant duty that would wipe the smirk off his face! By now he was standing over the gate in the south wall, looking down the valley. These days there was very little to see there either, as the gloom settled and thickened over Gwent y'm Aryframan.

He returned to the sanctuary of his office where more paperwork awaited: requisitions for stores and equipment, leave passes, report sheets. After a couple of hours there was a scratch at the door and his mid-day meal was brought in. His mind drifted this way and that as he ate. For some time now there had been no further reports of fugitives slipping away and in any case they were hardly likely to attempt escape under the gaze of the fort. How desperate would you need to be, to run off into the wilderness? He felt a twinge of unwilling sympathy and sat up straighter as if to suppress such weakness, his thoughts turning to the persistent rumours that survivors from the sack of Salfgard were lurking in some secret hideout in the hills. He was supposed to be hunting them down; if he left it too long before he sent another scouting party out there would no doubt be a further unpleasant interview with Valestron in prospect. Since this was a less than welcome line of reflection, he concentrated instead on his food, but it scarcely merited close attention, consisting as it did of pease pudding with a kind of oatmeal bannock. He mopped out his bowl glumly. At one time the military had enjoyed the best of everything, but these days wheat flour was only used for ceremonial occasions. Or for visits from the top brass like Valestron of course. Finding thoughts of Valestron as uncomfortable as those of Salfgard had been, he wondered, as he had done many times before, whether his posting to this border area counted as promotion or demotion. Promotion, yes, if you considered that as governor he was responsible for the whole district; but demotion on the other hand in that instead of being stationed at the heart of things in Caradriggan, he'd been shunted off here.

The original reason had been to watch the border for any hint of Maesrhon making a break for it, and to start with he'd been more than keen to claim the reward Vorynaas had put up for his capture; but time had passed without so much as a sniff and he had long ago reverted to his original conviction that the runaway had come to a gruesome end in the darkness of the forest. Maesrhon, swallowed up by Maesaldron: it had a certain grim neatness to it. But years had gone by since then, so why had he not been recalled? A knock at the door as the orderly came in to remove the soiled food dishes caused him to start with surprise and jump forward from leaning back with his arms behind his head; the legs of his chair jarred sharply on the floor. Alone again, he reverted to his thoughts of recall. Supposing he was ordered to return to Caradriggan? In his heart he knew his wife would not want to be uprooted from her home place; but if he was sent for, she would have to go with him, and the children too. His spirits sank as he thought of his marriage-father's likely reaction if he heard they were moving to the city. It was difficult enough dealing with him as it was, and then there was his marriage-mother. What if she saw the chance to get away from her husband and Gwent y'm Aryframan and insisted on coming with them? His stomach lurched unpleasantly at this horrible idea; he would cheerfully have fed her to any demon of the wilderness he'd ever heard of. Every time this sequence of thoughts played itself out in his head, he arrived at the point he had now reached: whether or not to discuss the issue with his wife while his recall was still only theoretical; and to this question he had not yet found an answer.

He stood up and stretched, and suddenly an idea occurred to him. Sending for the fort's officer-in-charge, he gestured for him to sit.

'We should be thinking about another try at rounding up the Salfgard outlaws.'

'Have you any new intelligence that makes you sure they're there to round up?'

'No. But I'm sick of the whole thing. We've done three sweeps of the hills since I've been governor and you did what, at least two more immediately after the annexation, and we've found nothing. You'd think that would be proof enough that there's nothing to find, but no, a negative report doesn't seem to be what they want to hear, back there in Caradriggan. Suppose we call in the specialists? I could request the services of a unit from the auxiliaries. If they have no success, surely it will lay the rumours to rest once and for all. What do you think?'

'Whatever you say, sir.'

'You don't sound too thrilled.'

'Well to be honest, sir, I'm thinking of my men. Bringing in outsiders could be seen as reflecting badly on them, and I don't like the idea of that.'

'Yes, I know. But look at it this way, captain. If the specialists can't find anything either, and I can see you're sure they won't, then we'll all of us be vindicated, won't we? Anyway, think it over for a couple of days; we can send the request in with the next batch of reports. Now, I've business down the valley I need to attend to, so if you'd take over this afternoon's inspection for me …'

Alone once more, he rubbed his hands with satisfaction. He was going to call in a unit of auxiliaries whatever his captain thought; the little consultation was just to keep the man sweet. As for the fellow's reservations, no such worries bothered him because as he saw it, whatever the outcome, he'd be in the clear. If the patrol drew a blank, then as he'd just said, they themselves were exonerated. But if some secret hide-out *was* discovered, he would say it just proved what he'd suspected all along, that the staff and troops he had at his disposal were not up to the required standard. He began putting away his papers with a complacent smile. And that had been another brainwave, the story about having business elsewhere. It was pulling rank, but he couldn't bring himself to care. Let Captain Spit-and-Polish do the rounds for him, he was off home early. As he crossed the courtyard, he noticed that three men were standing together on the wall-walk looking out towards the north, but went into the stable where his horse waited without really thinking anything of it. He was just about to lead the animal out when he heard a shout followed by the sound of someone running at speed down the stone stairs and across the yard towards him. One of the guards dashed through the stable door.

Arrival

'Sir! There are riders approaching the pass, coming out of the wilderness!'

'What!' He felt the blood come up into his face, and clenched his fists. 'How many?'

'Six men, with six extra animals and baggage.'

'Wake the men on night shift, tell them they're to dress and arm as quickly as they can.'

He dashed across the courtyard, up the stairs two at a time onto the wall-walk. One glance was enough to confirm what he'd just been told. The approaching riders were advancing quite slowly as the gradient steepened. He turned to the man standing next to him.

'Captain, take eleven men with you, fully armed and mounted. Bar their way, and bring these newcomers into the fort under guard. Compel them if they resist. We'll be watching, we'll come out to back you up if you need it. That leaves eight of us in here, plus myself. Two will station themselves in each turret, covering the courtyard. If they come in of their own accord, so much the better, I'll deal with them. Don't show any outward aggression unless they do. If force must be used, try to leave at least one of them alive, preferably the leader; we'll need to question him. Right, move!'

By the time the twelve were mounted and ready to ride out, the five who had been sleeping had presented themselves for action. They opened the gate for the riders and then running to their stations on the wall watched as their comrades formed up at the head of the pass, awaiting the strangers. The mysterious travellers slowed still further when they saw that their way was blocked, and advanced at a walking pace. All except one appeared young, and although they had a self-reliant air they seemed to carry no weapons beyond bows and knives. They halted a few paces short of the men from the fort and one, presumably the leader, rode forward with his right hand held high. The watchers on the walls saw that he sat his horse easily; he smiled as he spoke with the captain, glancing up at the fort with interest. After more words were exchanged, the leader of the strangers turned to his companions and beckoned them onwards; they rode forward, through the ranks of the men from the fort, who closed in behind them. The captain moved alongside the leader, guiding him towards the gate. As they approached, it was opened from within by men who kept their hands near their weapons, watching warily as they closed the gate again. The riders dismounted and for a moment or two there was silence as the newcomers looked about them. Then the commanding officer of the fort handed his horse to a subordinate and stepped forward.

'I bid you name yourselves and declare your purpose.'

'My name is Haldur; I am the son of Carapethan, the lord of Rihannad Ennar. This is my cousin Asaldron, my counsellor Ir'rossung, and my companions Tellapur, Cathasar and Aestrontor. We have journeyed for many miles and days, seeking the land of Gwent y'm Aryframan.'

The men of the garrison stared at them, hearing the strange accents of Haldur's speech, seeing that the strangers were not so young as they had appeared. One was well into middle-age and several others looked mature men in their prime, although the leader himself seemed not much more than a youth.

'Why do you look for Gwent y'm Aryframan?'

Haldur turned at this new voice and saw a man in civilian clothes who had stood unnoticed in the corner of the courtyard. Something in his voice and demeanour, some imperceptible shift in the attitude of the captain and his troops, told Haldur that here was a man unsure of his authority.

'Because according to our legends, that country was founded long ago by pioneers setting out from the Nine Dales, although no word has come back to us from them for many generations now. We look to discover whether our kin live yet in the land they made their own. We have dared Na Caarst in the hope of safety and welcome at our journey's end: tell me now, have we succeeded? Have we reached the borders of Gwent y'm Aryframan at last? Do we look upon the faces of our ancestral cousins?'

'We... we have no such tales, here.'

'But do we stand within Gwent y'm Aryframan?'

Haldur had been watching his questioner closely as he spoke. He saw a man of medium height and build, only a few years older than himself, who although expensively dressed and apparently the most senior figure present seemed curiously ill at ease. His face was unremarkable, the sort that would be lost in a crowd, except for the flush that had been creeping into his cheeks and now, Haldur noticed, deepened appreciably at this enquiry.

'The land you name has been a province of Caradward for some time now. This is the northernmost district of Rossaestrethan, of which I am the governor.' He beckoned his officer over. 'One moment, captain.'

They stepped through the open door of a range of buildings, leaving the newcomers still standing under the scrutiny of the garrison. Haldur kept his face as amiably bland as he could, hoping his companions were also managing to disguise their opinions of this ill-mannered reception. The door had been firmly closed behind the two men; he wondered what was being said. When they came out again the captain drew one of his men with him into the stables and within a very short time the fellow emerged and went cantering off through the gate. The governor turned to Haldur.

'My home and the centre of my administration lie some way down the valley. I have sent orders for preparation to be made to receive you. We will be better able to house you and your companions there rather than here in the cramped accommodation of the fort. My captain will gather an escort and we will accompany you on the road.'

Haldur smiled. 'Our thanks! It will be an unaccustomed comfort to have a roof over our heads once more. But are you not going to introduce yourself? We have told you our names: what is the name of our host?'

'Oh, of course.' The man's face coloured up once more. 'I am Heranar of Caradriggan, son of Valafoss.'

CHAPTER 43

Guests or prisoners?

A detachment of eight men went with Heranar and the travellers from the Nine Dales as they set off down the valley; but if Haldur had had any thoughts that the fort was being left with its garrison depleted, these were dispelled when a troop of soldiers passed them, going at a smart trot in the opposite direction with a salute to Heranar as they went by. Ir'rossung and the others kept an eye on Haldur, making sure they followed his lead. They all noticed that he had said nothing so far about the gloom on this side of the pass, although they felt its oppression already. Haldur had decided to keep for tomorrow any observations of this kind, suspecting that this northern district was probably the least affected so far. Evening was approaching; it was just about feasible that the dimness could be mistaken for twilight of an unseasonably overcast day: maybe it would be best not to launch into expressions of surprise too quickly. So as they rode along at an easy pace he engaged Heranar in polite conversation, not finding this easy as his host seemed nervous and preoccupied; however he gathered that Heranar had been stationed in Rossaestrethan for some time, five years come the autumn in fact. Eventually they saw lights ahead and the governor's residence came into view. This was a large establishment consisting of many other buildings besides Heranar's own house, but its elegant air was somewhat compromised by the stout wall and other fortifications that surrounded and guarded it. They rode under a gateway flanked by turrets and dismounted in an outer courtyard where a man dressed in civilian clothes was waiting.

'This is my steward,' said Heranar, 'who will show you to your accommodation. I regret to say that my guest-wing is perhaps not entirely fitted to house the heir to a kingdom; however, a separate room has been prepared for you.'

Haldur laughed in what he hoped was a good-natured manner. 'My companions and I have shared the hardships of a long and dangerous journey, we'll share your hospitality now. There's no need to make anything special ready for me. We have no kings in Rihannad Ennar: my father is lord with the consent of his people, but we don't stand on ceremony in the Nine Dales.'

'As you wish.' The hint of a sneer crept into Heranar's voice as he said this, but he inclined his head.

They unloaded the baggage and then, leaving the animals to the care of Heranar's staff, carried their gear inside to where beds had been prepared for them. Haldur indicated the door to the wash-house with a nod and a lift of his brows. Under cover of the noise of water and a squeaking pump, they exchanged a few quick words.

'Don't say anything more than you must until we find out how the land lies, and whether we're prisoners as well as guests,' said Haldur. 'They've got us under surveillance here, that's obvious, but we don't know yet whether we can talk without being overheard.'

Later, he observed Heranar as they sat at table together. What would Artorynas say, if he knew that one of his childhood's tormentors was now lording it over a sizeable chunk of occupied land! Heranar had not tried too hard to hide his thoughts when he alluded earlier to Haldur's status; his eyes had travelled scornfully over his guest's plain attire and workaday horse and his lip curled when Haldur declined the offer of separate accommodation. But when it was time to eat and he saw the golden torc that Haldur wore as a mark of his rank, his face betrayed an avid surprise. My father was right to impute greed to these Caradwardans, thought Haldur, remembering the amber he secretly carried. He listened carefully to the voices he heard around him, and quickly came to the conclusion that all Heranar's servants and household staff, as well as the soldiers, were from Caradward like himself. Clearly, he felt unable to trust the local people. Haldur sensed weakness and arrogance in Heranar, mingled with a lack of self-confidence; but there was something else, something that was harder to define. There were women present in the room, but none sat beside Heranar although Haldur had formed the impression that he was married. Perhaps his morose air was connected to the absence of his wife? It was rather surprising also that he showed so little curiosity about his visitors, asking very few questions about their long journey and its purpose. Haldur told himself not to underestimate his host; it was more than possible that both of them were biding their time. As soon as they could do so politely, he and his companions retired to their own quarters with the excuse that they were weary from the weeks of travelling. Haldur gripped Ir'rossung's arm in a message of encouragement and thanks: the older man had played his part well, so that by the end of the evening those wishing to speak to him were pitching their voices well up and already some of the Caradwardans, assuming he was unable to hear them, were ignoring him to carry on with conversations of their own.

The following morning, Haldur and the others emerged from the guest-hall to take the measure of their new surroundings. As well as the outer courtyard by which they had entered the previous evening, the compound contained within it several other large open areas between the various buildings. The travellers strolled about as casually as they could, noting the armed sentries around the perimeter wall and the heavily-guarded gates. Haldur spoke quietly as they crossed a wide space dividing what looked like a range of storehouses and kitchens from the offices that clustered nearer to Heranar's own house.

'If we've anything private to say to each other, this is how we'll do it, to start with at least: by only talking out here where we can't be overheard. Asaldron, you come with me now; I'm going to see if I can't get Heranar to be more forthcoming than he was last night.

Ir'rossung, we need more of last night's performance from you! Tellapur, you go with him; if the chance arises, pretend you'd rather be with a companion your own age, you might get someone to let something slip. The other two can try and find out whether there are any Gwentarans in here. I don't think there are, but it would be worth knowing.'

They separated and moved off, and in due course Haldur and Asaldron were shown into a room where Heranar sat behind a large desk.

Heranar had been standing back from the window, watching them approach, doing mental calculations. The rider he had sent out from the fort yesterday as soon as the newcomers were safely within its walls had not simply carried instructions that headquarters staff were to prepare to receive six extra men. His more important orders had been to make sure a messenger went off at top speed down to Framstock with a report and a request. The report announced the arrival of strangers from out of Na Caarst; the request was for an escort so that they could be moved down under guard to Framstock where Valahald was in command these days. A movement caught Heranar's eye and he saw his marriage-father, dressed as always in the most authentically correct Gwentaran style right down to the pointed cap. He was heading towards the stables; Heranar hoped fervently that the old boy was preparing to go back to his own home up-country. He returned to his earlier train of thought. He wanted these newcomers off his hands as soon as possible but reckoned he was stuck with them for at least a week. The message would go through much faster than that, using the military posting system; but if he knew Valahald, his brother would send word to Caradriggan first. With his ever-present worry over recall gnawing at him, Heranar had spent much of the night wondering whether it would serve him best to turn the party over to Valahald without further ado, or to attempt to turn the prize to his own advantage by interrogating the strangers himself. Now here came their leader and the man named as his cousin, and he was no nearer a decision. Hastily Heranar composed himself, his hands clasped tightly together below the desk.

'Good morning, gentlemen. I trust you slept well? Please sit down.'

'Yes, indeed. We are grateful for your hospitality; beds are a welcome luxury after so many nights sleeping on the ground.'

'I can imagine. But to risk crossing Na Caarst, a journey you tell me has taken almost three months – that I cannot imagine. Surely you must have had a more pressing reason to do such a thing than the one you gave me yesterday.'

Haldur looked at Asaldron with a grin and then leaned forward confidentially.

'Well,' he said, smiling now at Heranar, 'look at it this way. You're a young man still, yet already you sit here, responsible for a province and its people from what you tell me. Don't you sometimes feel your duties weigh a little heavily on your shoulders? I know that's how I felt, when my elder brother died in an accident and I was chosen as heir to the lordship of Rihannad Ennar. My father is a man in his prime and with luck it will be many years yet before I take his place; but none can know what the future may bring; so now was the time, if I was to take the chance of adventure. Though I can tell you, when they heard what I and my friends proposed to do, my father and his counsellors took a lot of persuading before they let us go! And they insisted that I must take Aestrontor with me as guard, and Ir'rossung to guide me, should we succeed in our aim of finding our kin from long ago.'

'Ir'rossung... the elderly man, the one who doesn't hear too well?'

Realising how condescending this sounded, Heranar flushed with embarrassment, but Haldur simply nodded in friendly fashion. Clenching his hands on his knees, Heranar forced himself to hold his visitor's open gaze.

'But, adventure! There's not many would use such a light-hearted word for the journey you have made. Tell me,' he paused, lowering his voice, 'tell me, what did you see in the wilderness? Are there any signs of life, either of men or the demons that men say dwell there?'

Haldur saw a chance to play on Heranar's fears. 'I have to admit, Na Caarst is a place I might not have entered, if I'd known more about what it's like,' he said, going on to describe, with many a lurid flourish, a harsh and waterless landscape without shelter from wind or sky.

'And there are places where the earth is not solid underfoot, where the rock crumbles away without warning to reveal black fathomless depths. Whole armies might be swallowed up and never seen again, plunging down to whatever waits below. Yes, there's something lurking down there. We heard great noises, strange, terrifying sounds that echo far under ground. As to living things, we saw only small burrowing rodents, carrion birds overhead, sparse scrub and thorns. But there are indeed signs that hint at other, hidden, forms of life.'

He shuddered expressively, noticing how Heranar was hanging on his words with a kind of fascinated horror.

'Yes, signs written in death,' added Asaldron, taking his cue from Haldur. 'We found bones and skulls, scattered on the ground.'

Heranar stared. 'Human remains, you mean? How far from our borders was this? Was there any way of knowing what had happened?'

'Yes, two dead men, about two weeks' journey to the north,' replied Asaldron. 'As to how they died, it was impossible to be sure whether they were consumed at the finish by starvation or blindworms. As for why they died, I think they paid the price of foolhardiness. Daring the wilderness as we did is one thing: survival could depend on the support of comrades and to attempt the crossing alone or in a smaller group is to court disaster, in my opinion. We buried all that was left of them. Do have any idea who they could have been? Have you heard of anyone who might have tried to contact their kin in the Nine Dales, heading north as we came south?'

228

'No. No, I… No.'

Heranar swallowed and dropped his eyes to fidget with a pen on the desk-top. Haldur, knowing that he was lying, watched him closely for his reaction to Asaldron's probing questions. He noticed that Heranar's fingernails were badly bitten and Heranar, looking up again and seeing Haldur's eyes on his hands, hastily removed them below the desk once more. He cleared his throat.

'You, er… Have you ever heard tell of a man called Maesrhon? A stranger, I mean, not a man of your own country.'

'Maesrhon? No. It's an unusual name, almost ill-omened you could say. Are you thinking this Maesrhon might have been one of the dead men we found? Who is he?'

'Oh, just an outlaw. There's a price on him, alive or dead. You didn't find any clothes or other identifying objects with the bones, I suppose?'

Haldur's heart filled with anger, hearing Artorynas spoken of so callously. He was determined to outwit these Caradwardans, but for now he must bide his time.

'Not really,' he said, 'just bits of leather and torn scraps, as if from boots or a pack that had been ripped up.' Suddenly his attention was caught by the door, which had opened an inch or two. 'Hello, who's this?'

As Heranar followed his glance the door opened wider and three children tumbled into the room, running over to where he sat. They clung about him, the eldest leaning against his shoulder, another climbing to his knee, and the third, barely a toddler, clutching at his leg for support. Haldur burst out laughing as three pairs of huge brown eyes were turned on him.

'Are these all yours?' he asked Heranar.

'Yes, that's right.'

Haldur and Asaldron saw how he relaxed in the presence of the children, hoisting the toddler to share his lap, putting his arm around the eldest. They were as alike as it was possible for sisters to be, pale and delicate with long, dark red hair, those big brown eyes and a scattering of freckles over the nose. Heranar was by no means what could be called good-looking: had he somehow persuaded a beautiful woman to marry him, wondered Haldur.

'What lovely little girls they are! You're a lucky man,' he said. 'Surely, there must be barely a year between them?'

'Yes; three, two and nearly one,' said Heranar, sliding the two youngest from his knee and lining them up like three little matching dolls. The eldest whispered something into his ear, and he smiled.

'Yes, all right, I know you're three months past your third birthday. Now, I'm busy just at the moment, so you must be good girls. Run off and find out what mummy's doing, and I'll see you later.' He watched them as they slipped through the door and turned back to the two men who sat opposite.

'You're not married men, yourselves?'

'No, not yet.'

'To tell you the truth, it was the last thing I expected for myself, when I came up here, but...' Heranar broke off and changed the subject. 'I would be interested to hear more about your homeland.'

Asaldron and Haldur delivered a brief account of Rihannad Ennar, its people and governance. Following the plan they had agreed on back in Cotaerdon, they laid a certain amount of emphasis on the small size of their country, the severity of its northern winters, the isolation this imposed on the scattered population of the separate dales. Heranar avoided their eyes as he listened, fidgeting once more with the writing instruments that lay on his desk; Asaldron wondered whether he was thinking of making notes, but he heard them out in silence. After a moment, Haldur spoke again.

'According to the reckoning of our lorekeepers, a thousand years ago there were those from among our folk who set out southward, hoping to make a new life for themselves in a wider land. We have preserved tales of a time when word came back to us that some at least of them lived and prospered, but that is now so long ago that history has passed into legend. My companions and I are here to try the truth of the stories, and to renew old ties if we can. We'd like to ride out among the people, to ask whether any here remember their kin in the far north.'

Heranar shifted in his chair. 'Surely it's too soon to think of that. You should rest for a while yet, after your long journey.'

'We are rested and restored, by your kindness,' said Asaldron, 'but maybe there's no need to begin immediately. Shall we say tomorrow? Perhaps the weather will be brighter by then.'

'It would be too dangerous.' Heranar put his pen down and removed his hands from view once more. 'There are… There are outlaws in the hills.'

'Outlaws? You mean this Maesrhon that you spoke of?'

'No, no. But there is reputed to be a gang in hiding, somewhere in this area.'

'But surely, with all the soldiers we see who are at your disposal,' began Haldur, 'could we not…'

'I cannot allow it.' Heranar stood up abruptly, the colour rising in his face once more. 'You must excuse me now, I have business that requires my attention.'

A man slid into the room and held the door open; evidently he had been stationed immediately outside and must have been listening to all that was said. Haldur and Asaldron got to their feet, exchanging glances. When they were clear of the buildings and walking across the compound once more, Asaldron spoke quietly.

'Prisoners then, not guests. What do we do now?'

'There's nothing we can do, not just yet anyway. But if they were going to kill us, they'd have struck sooner. I think Heranar's waiting for something, maybe further orders or instructions; you can see he's unsure of himself. Meanwhile I think we'll go back to keeping a watch at night like we did on the way here.'

Sleepless worries

The next few days passed slowly, time seeming to hang heavily upon them. No-one prevented them from wandering at will within the confines of their quarters, but any attempt to pass beyond the outer wall of the compound was blocked if they approached the gates. Trying to talk to Heranar's people met with little encouragement, although it was obvious that they themselves were the subject of much speculation and many a conversation. When they saw no sign of Heranar, they assumed that he must have gone back up to the fort, but in this they were wrong. The governor of Rossaestrethan was closeted within his offices by day, though the administration of his province scarcely held his attention. At evening he ate in private with his family, but had to force himself to a show of interest even into their affairs. And at night he slept badly, his sleep disturbed by unsettling and most unwelcome dreams.

'Heranar! *Heranar*. Wake up!' Startled, he opened his eyes to darkness; his wife was gripping his arms.

'What's the matter?' she whispered. 'You were groaning and shouting out in your sleep.'

'It's nothing, I must have been dreaming.'

'Again? But why are you having these nightmares, what is it you're dreaming about?'

'I don't remember – maybe I just ate too much, or too late in the evening.'

'That's what you said last night. Is there a problem? You would tell me, wouldn't you?'

'Of course I would. There's nothing to worry about, I'm sorry to have wakened you. Let's go back to sleep now.'

They settled down once more and soon Heranar felt his wife relax against him as she slept again, but he lay wakeful, knowing that if he slept too, the dreams would return: the same nightmares that always came to haunt him when he felt himself under any kind of stress.

He had lied to his wife: the images he had seen were all too vivid in his mind. They flickered across his memory again now: Maesrhon standing hand to lip while he and Ghentar fled across the river into the early morning mist; Heretellar smiling, giving the amber-studded cup to Ardeth who smiled back in turn; the sweat beading on his father's brow as he offered him and Valahald to Vorynaas in Tell'Ethronad; the day of Ghentar's funeral; the faces in the crowd when the captives were paraded in Caradriggan; blood in the streets of Framstock. Some of these scenes had preyed on his mind more often, recently, but it was the arrival of the unlooked-for visitors from out of the north that had caused them to crowd from the shadows, invading his times of sleep as well as his waking hours. Take Maesrhon, for example. For the hundredth time, Heranar wondered whether it was his bones the men from the Nine Dales had found. He and Valahald had tracked him to the forest, there could be no doubt at all about that. But although he had been sure that was the end of the story, Valahald had always insisted that he might have escaped. And yet, though they had watched the northern borders ever since, he had never been seen.

Heranar turned from speculation on what terrible end Maesrhon might have met to thoughts of his brother. When they were children, he had looked up to his elder sibling, trying to emulate him, wanting to match his achievements; but if truth were told, these days he was slightly afraid of him, uneasy at the cruel streak he now displayed. Maybe it was the result of his association with Valestron. Both were ruthless in their ambition and their closeness was turning to rivalry as Valahald rose to challenge the older man's status and power. It was their orders and actions that had destroyed Salfgard... Heranar turned his head on the pillow, not wanting to think about Salfgard but unable to stop himself. I'm glad I wasn't part of what happened at Salfgard, he thought; but then immediately the horrors he had witnessed in Framstock flashed into his mind. You were part of that, said the voice he wanted so much not to hear. He clenched his hands. Yes, I was in favour of our taking of Gwent y'm Aryframan he said to himself, as firmly as he could. We were right to take revenge for what happened to Ghentar; it was my duty to march with our army in memory of my friend. Ghentar, murdered between one word and the next, cut down with his life before him, consigned to death with no warning, with no time to prepare for what he faced. But the man who killed him paid with his own life, said the unwelcome voice; you know that Vorynaas was just looking for an excuse. Without warning another scene reappeared vividly before his mind's eye: Maesrhon taking up Ghentar's challenge to fight him, sword to stave; he heard again the vile sound of the stave striking Maesrhon's head. It wouldn't make me throw up now, he thought gloomily. I've a stronger stomach these days, after all the things I've seen since then.

He closed his eyes, trying to empty his mind for sleep, but there was a dog barking incessantly somewhere outside. Listening to its deep, baying voice, Heranar was almost sure it was one of his marriage-father's animals. He always brought a couple of his huge hunting hounds with him when he visited and they never seemed to settle. Heranar pulled the covers over his ears in an attempt to block out the noise. You would think *somebody* would go and quiet the animal down! In fact was it too much to ask that Gillavar could do it himself, or even leave the damned things at home next time he came down from the uplands. How much longer was he going to foist himself upon them? Heranar could sympathise, if he was reluctant to return to that wife of his, but at the same time was willing to bet that he'd have been gone by now if it had not been for the arrival of the men from Rihannad Ennar. It was just absolutely typical that Gillavar should have to be around to see that. Heranar might have been lying low, but he had informants among his staff and he knew that his marriage-father had been talking to the strangers; so in spite of all his care to keep them from wandering about at will among the local people, word of their errand was going to leak out anyway. There was no point at all in trying to persuade Gillavar to say nothing, because any attempt of that sort would only make him do the exact opposite. Cantankerous, awkward, stubborn, cussed old mountain-man!

There was a rustle of blankets as Ilmarynvoro moved in her sleep with a soft sigh. Heranar felt his wife turn towards him and marvelled, as he had done so many times before, that she could be the child of such parents: an uncompromising Gwentaran of the old school, and a discontented woman who never stopped bewailing her exile from Caradriggan. He could remember as if it was yesterday the moment when they had met. It was not long after he had been posted to the new province of Rossaestrethan; the fort was only half-finished, and he was riding through the district, getting to know the territory for which he was responsible. Parts of it were vaguely familiar to him from his time in Salfgard, but now he was ranging more widely afield, and one day the road had climbed through a gap in the hills and below him he had seen a small level area where four valleys met. The settlement was perched on a terrace out of reach of flooding from the turbulent rivers that rushed down and mingled in the valley-bottom, and around it there was just room for enough arable land to support those who lived there, with their flocks on the high pastures above. And Gillavar was the local lordling, chief man by virtue of the fact that his own land, all half-dozen fields of it, was the best. Heranar soon discovered that his reluctant host had acquired a wife from Caradriggan, a girl whom he had met during his distant foster-years and who no doubt had been attracted by the idea of marrying into what she probably thought of as the squirearchy. Later he found out that the marriage had soured very quickly, the city girl increasingly embittered, unsuited to rural life, and her husband regretting daily that he had not sought a wife among his own people.

The governor of Rossaestrethan

Gillavar indeed was Gwentaran through and through and made no attempt to hide what he thought about Caradward's invasion of his land or his opinion of the new governor and his entourage. Even now that Heranar was his marriage-son he had never mellowed, but always made a point of keeping to the traditional Gwentaran ways: observing local customs, dressing, eating and speaking in the old style of his own country. On the day of that first meeting, he had made it clear to Heranar that he could thank the time-honoured obligations of hill-folk to travellers for any hospitality he received, rather than the subservience of vassal to lord; and he made no bones either about the fact that he had offered no resistance to the Caradwardan army. His position on this was that military defiance was futile and so, since his first duty was to his people as their lord, he had ensured their safety by keeping them out of the conflict. It was very obvious that to him the Caradwardan occupation was almost an irrelevance, a passing phase during which he and his folk would go their own way as they always had done. Although nettled by this attitude, Heranar had also been more than a little amused. Imagine the fellow, giving himself such airs, when all he was lording it over was a couple of hundred peasants in this forsaken enclave of rush-grown fields and cloud-hung pastures! He had been about to make his derision plain, and deliver a few well-chosen words aimed at bringing the new reality home to Gillavar, when for the first time he had seen Ilmarynvoro.

Even now when he thought about it, Heranar's heart lurched at the memory. What had hit him hardest at that first moment was that he could see immediately that Ilmarynvoro was looking at him with a sort of hopeful curiosity. In his whole life, no-one had ever looked at him like that before. He knew he was not attractive to women and in any case had grown up in Ghentar's shadow. His handsome friend had taken first choice of all the girls; and Valahald had never seemed particularly interested, so there had never even been any scraps to pick up from his brother's table. In more recent years, as a man with status and money of his own, some parents had considered him as a possible marriage-son but nothing had ever come of these situations: clearly the daughters in question had not been impressed. But now here was this young woman, quiet and shy, whose enormous dark eyes spoke straight to him. Heranar was not to know that Ilmarynvoro was all too used to being overlooked in favour of the sisters who were the beauties of the family. Though younger, they were already married while she still lingered at home, the goose among the swans. She saw Heranar's face change as his attention was caught and her own expression lit up in response: Heranar lost his heart on the spot before he even heard Ilmarynvoro's name.

Gillavar, sensing an opportunity, had pressed his advantage and his wife, ever-hopeful of some means of returning to Caradriggan, had been overjoyed at the idea of such a prestigious match. Heranar and Ilmarynvoro were married very quickly, setting up home in the governor's residence, and now they had the three little girls too. Girls clearly ran in the family: Ilmarynvoro was actually one of four sisters, one of whom had died as a child. Wanting boys to indoctrinate with his Gwentaran ways, Gillavar had been progressively more morose as each of his grand-daughters had been born, but Heranar didn't care. By some alchemy of genetics, the best points of both parents were somehow not just combined but intensified in the children. Ilmarynvoro's dark, heavy hair had mingled with Heranar's sandy ginger to produce that vibrant, lustrous red and her wide brown eyes looked out from three little faces that took just enough width from Heranar's to give them a stronger bone-structure than their mother. They were pale-skinned like her, with none of Heranar's propensity for patchy blushing, but a few of his freckles were sprinkled in a golden scatter over their noses. Heranar lay in bed, a man who had been ambushed by happiness and who, now that he was in its thrall, realised belatedly that he had never truly been contented in his younger life, trailing about after Ghentar, tagging along behind Valahald, always somehow failing to impress.

Sounds from outside broke into his reverie as a door opened and closed again and the dog stopped barking at last. Lost in contemplation of his children, Heranar had finally become oblivious to the noise but its sudden cessation broke his thought. In the silence of his heart he could admit to himself that he was out of his depth as governor of Rossaestrethan. He was not a natural leader and the mantle of authority sat awkwardly upon him; his orders were only obeyed because, in the case of the Gwentarans, they were backed up by the troops at his disposal, and in the case of his own men, because of the prestige of his status with Vorynaas. But precisely what was that status? Wearily, Heranar noticed that his thoughts had finally circled back into their familiar pattern. Surely, he would never have been given such a prestigious posting if it had not been for their father thrusting him and Valahald forward after Ghentar was murdered. Poor Ghentar, thought Heranar with an unaccustomed flash of insight, in spite of everything he never knew much happiness; and if it was not for the fact that being here gave me Ilmarynvoro, I would have been happier myself to stay in Caradriggan, where I was doing well in the barbican garrison, enjoying my work in the armouries there because I was good at it. It came to him now that it had been Ardeth who first noticed his aptitude for metalwork and encouraged him to develop his skill, and this turned his thoughts unwillingly to Salfgard once more.

Last time he and his brother had met, Valahald had taunted him about his lack of success in rounding up those who were said to have fled. He wondered whether it was his brother's influence that was keeping him away from the centre of things, marooned up here on the northern borders. Perhaps it suited Valahald that things should stay as they were. He had the more important and influential command, being based at Framstock in the southern province, where he was nearer to the old border with Caradward and therefore closer to the heart of power in Caradriggan. While Heranar stayed where he was, he also had the confidence of knowing that Rossaestrethan was secure behind him, not to mention the luxury of laughing in his sleeve at his brother's predicament while no doubt publicly preening himself because they both held high office. Valahald had changed a lot since they were boys together. Much the keener of the two of them to be placed at Vorynaas' disposal, he had become secretive and obsessive; these days Heranar found him uncomfortable to be with and difficult to talk to. Heranar's thoughts wandered back over the years until he drifted off at last. This time he was visited in sleep by a gentle dream of long ago that vanished upon waking.

When morning came, Heranar felt anything but rested. After such a disturbed night, with far too few hours of sleep, his head ached and his eyes were sore and puffy. However, before mid-day the expected message came. A courier rode in to say that an escort would be arriving in a couple of days' time to take the strangers from Rihannad Ennar down to Framstock. Much relieved by this news, Heranar went about his business with a lighter step but his enthusiasm was dampened when, venturing out and about once more, he rounded the corner of a building and walked straight into Haldur and Aestrontor.

'Heranar! We've not seen you for a few days, and I've been wanting to talk to you. Been busy up at the fort, have you?'

'I… I… There have been matters that needed my attention, yes. What was it you wanted to see me about?'

'I want to know why we are being confined here, why we are not permitted to leave the compound,' said Haldur.

'I explained before, it's for reasons of security. I cannot guarantee your safety,' said Heranar, feeling the tell-tale blush beginning to creep up his cheeks.

'That's nonsense, and you know it. We're prisoners here, in fact if not in name. Why are you holding us?'

Heranar stood there, wishing this encounter was taking place anywhere else but right underneath the lantern fixed at the corner of the building, its light falling full on his face.

'Look, I'm in authority here in Rossaestrethan, but there are men more senior than myself. You must see that I had no choice but to hold you here while I sent word of your arrival to those in higher command: no-one has ever come to us out of Na Caarst before, I needed to take advice. And as it happens, a message has come through just this morning, to say that you're to go on in a few days, down south to Framstock.' He forced a smile. 'So you'll see a lot more of the country, at any rate; and if it's old tales you're after, who knows what you may pick up.'

Aestrontor grunted, jerking a thumb at the lamp above them. 'According to Gillavar, we'll not see much. He says it's like this or even darker down there, is that right?'

Inwardly seething, Heranar fought to keep his voice level. 'I cannot say, it is some time since I journeyed down to Framstock myself. As for Gillavar, he has never been a widely-travelled man and knows little of the world beyond his mountain territory.'

'I wouldn't be so sure about that,' said Aestrontor bluntly. 'Your marriage-father's had plenty to say, even if you've been avoiding us, and he seems shrewd enough to me. The way things are around here these days, he wonders why you feel so insecure that you think six men pose some kind of threat, and I might ask the same thing myself.'

If I could do it without Ilmarynvoro knowing, I would feed that leathery old goat to the blindworms along with his vulture of a wife, thought Heranar. He took a deep breath. 'We've just been waiting for clearance, that's all. Framstock is several days' journey from here: you'll be travelling right through the heart of the country, so you can see there's no question of any kind of threat, and no need for that sort of talk, either.'

'We can set off in the morning, then?' asked Haldur.

'Well, no, not tomorrow.' The blotchy flush deepened on Heranar's face. 'You'll have to wait for the escort to arrive. They should be here within two or three days to take you down to my brother in Framstock.'

'Ah. So, we're still not to come and go freely.'

'I can't answer for my brother,' muttered Heranar through gritted teeth. 'Valahald is senior to myself, his decisions are his business.' He turned abruptly and walked off.

On the evening before their departure, Haldur and his companions were shown to places at Heranar's high table along with his captains and the two officers in charge of the escort which had now arrived.

Ilmarynvoro was at Haldur's side, though Gillavar was as far removed from his marriage-son as politeness would allow and sat between Tellapur and a man who had come up from Framstock. Haldur looked at this newcomer with interest, wondering if he could be one of the Outlanders he had heard about from Artorynas. His facial cast tallied with the descriptions he had been given, but his eyes, instead of being dark, were a surprisingly bright, greenish-grey. Suddenly the man turned towards Haldur before he himself had the chance to look away. Slightly embarrassed to be caught apparently staring, he smiled across and the other raised a hand in acknowledgement. For a moment Haldur seemed to detect a hint of speculation in his face, but when he looked more closely, the man's expression was impenetrable. Haldur wondered what his errand was, since he was clearly not a member of the visiting party, who were a good deal more flamboyant in dress and manner than those stationed up here in the north and their speech and bearing showed a rather brash, careless confidence. One thing however was beyond doubt, and that was Heranar's efforts to impress the delegation from his brother. To his own surprise, Haldur found himself feeling a little sorry for Heranar as food and drink far more lavish than any they had been served hitherto was offered. He could see the man's unease, but was not in a position to spare too much sympathy with so many problems of his own to concern him. If they were always going to be watched and guarded as closely as this, how were they ever going to find out anything worth knowing? And more to the point, would they be allowed to leave again when they wanted to? Well, that time had not arrived yet; and meanwhile the only thing to do was keep up the ingenuous front they were presenting. He got on with his meal, exchanging pleasantries with those around him.

This was the first time he had been able to speak with Ilmarynvoro at any length, or to observe her at close quarters; most likely the only time, too, thought Haldur, if we're to go on tomorrow. She was not the most talkative of dinner companions and Haldur, casting about for something to say, expressed his admiration of the three silver lamps that hung over the table, intricate in design and crafted with exquisite skill.

'Yes, they are lovely, and so light and delicate,' said Ilmarynvoro. She glanced at her husband. 'They were a wedding-gift to me from Heranar.'

'Really? That was generous – or maybe he wanted to make a lavish demonstration of his affection?'

Heranar blushed, but Haldur saw that this time he seemed unconcerned, exchanging smiles with Ilmarynvoro as if they sat alone together. Evidently this was a love-match on which the bloom had not faded. Haldur hid his private amusement, remembering how he had thought Heranar's wife must be a beauty when he saw the three little girls. It was true that the lamplight brought out the lustre in her thick, dark hair and lit the deep brown of her eyes, but although these were her best features they scarcely made up for the plain, rather anxious face, the thin-lipped mouth, the pallid, slightly downtrodden air that seemed to hang about her; and when he looked at Heranar's small eyes with their sandy lashes, his florid complexion and widely-spaced little teeth, he was reminded irresistibly of a piglet. But clearly Ilmarynvoro and Heranar were fair in each other's eyes, so maybe this was how they had made such unexpectedly lovely children. Once more Haldur was caught out by a stab of compassion for Heranar and barely listened to his account of where and how he had acquired the lamps. Feeling that he must make amends for his inattention, he lifted his cup in a kind of informal toast to Ilmarynvoro.

'I am sure there is no more beautiful sight than the silver lamplight falling upon your daughters and waking the red gold in their hair.'

Ilmarynvoro smiled with pleasure at this compliment and a faint colour rose in her pale cheeks; but by contrast Heranar seemed uncomfortable. Haldur wondered why, when he seemed so fond of his children; but changed the subject and established instead conversational flow with the man on his left. He now found himself involved in a discussion of the armour and accoutrements borne by the contingent from Framstock, and to his surprise discovered that much of the credit for their innovatory design and make was due to Heranar. He looked across the table with a smile.

'You have a real talent,' he said.

'Thank you. I was based in the armouries in Caradriggan, before I was posted here.'

A change of heart

Heranar looked down at his plate, breaking eye contact. He had not mentioned the encouragement he had received from Ardeth, but those days had come into his mind with painful clarity as suddenly he realised that there was something in Haldur that reminded him of Ardeth, something in his description of Rihannad Ennar that brought back boyhood memories of Salfgard. And now from nowhere another memory surfaced, as it were a picture from his earliest days. His mind's eye saw the garden of the family home in Caradriggan, before they had moved to occupy Arythalt's more spacious dwelling. He remembered how as toddlers he and Valahald had loved to play in the tumbledown summerhouse that leaned against the wall at the very end of the garden; how disappointed they had been when their father had converted it for his own use.

'Don't bother me and make noise, I'm busy in my office,' Valafoss used to say; but his mother would whisper, 'Daddy's in his den, so you'll have to pretend to be little boys of the Starborn, who can play unseen!'

Then she would put her finger to her lips and smile at the brothers conspiratorially. Heranar sat, oblivious to his surroundings, amazed at the intensity of this recollection from so long ago; it came to him that he had recently dreamed of it also. He had not thought much about his mother for years; she was long dead and now, as an adult and a father himself, he regretted her sorrow. She had been a timid, rather shy woman whose whole life was bound up in her husband and family and now he realised how unhappy she had been as Valafoss ignored her in pursuit of his ambition, how hurt as her sons grew away from her, how lonely, drifting from room to room in Arythalt's grand mansion. She would have so loved her three granddaughters, and now it was too late. He glanced at Ilmarynvoro and it was as if an icy fist gripped his heart. His children looked out at him from his wife's face, he saw the three little girls running about in play in the garden of his old home under the glow of a summer's day. That summerhouse in Caradriggan, the workroom at Salfgard: it was only his memory that showed them golden with sunlight. The best they could hope for here was lamplight, however beautiful the silver lanterns from which it came, as Haldur's earlier remark had brought home to him.

Ilmarynvoro squeezed his wrist, a question in her face at his prolonged silence; but as he shook his head, sitting up straighter, his attention was distracted. One of the officers from Framstock was sitting on Haldur's right. He had partaken freely of the drink as it went round and had shed an inhibition or two too many. His voice, slightly louder than necessary, now cut through the general buzz of conversation.

'I gather I'm sitting next to the heir to a throne,' he said, looking round with an aggressive grin as if inviting others to join him in baiting Haldur. 'Shouldn't you be wearing a crown or something, to give us a bit of a hint?'

Heranar saw Tellapur flush with anger, saw Cathasar and Asaldron look to Haldur for a lead, saw Aestrontor's knuckles whiten as he gripped his cup. Haldur's face set, but he spoke quietly.

'I think you've been listening to too many tales of olden times, captain. This is what the heirs to Rihannad Ennar wear, once they have been named.' He touched the gold torc at his neck.

'Oh yes?' The man peered at it, lips pursed. 'Bit plain, isn't it? You want to give it an extra twist, to make the ends match.'

Haldur smiled. 'Take another look tomorrow when the wine fumes have cleared. Each finial is an eye: this one looks inwards and

244

sees my heart; but this one…' he held Heranar's gaze, '…this one looks outwards; and whether in darkness or in light, it sees into the hearts of other men.'

The fellow subsided with an ugly frown, then Gillavar laughed, ending an awkward little silence, and shortly afterwards, the gathering began to break up; but Haldur noticed as he left the room that the *sigitsar*-seeming man had stayed behind when the others left the table. He caught a final glimpse of Heranar, flushed and uncomfortable-looking under the inscrutable gaze of the Outlander, and then the door closed behind him.

Alone together now, the governor of Rossaestrethan and his guest sat without speaking for several moments. Heranar could guess what he was about to be asked and his mind darted this way and that, seeking an answer that would be acceptably plausible. Eventually the other man spoke.

'You have put in a request for aid from the auxiliaries, but when I come up here to discuss this with you, it seems you have nothing to say to me. We're due to leave in the morning, so what am I to report?'

Heranar glanced towards him, but without meeting his eyes. As soon as the escort had arrived, he had noticed the small badge, dull pewter with a small leaf worked in green enamel, which was the only sign of rank or profession the man bore, and realised immediately what had brought him north from Framstock. Leaving aside any other considerations, such a man, the second in a troop of irregulars, as tough as they came with the exception only of whatever hard man held command, would never understand the change of heart that had come to Heranar as he sat, pushing the food about on his plate with no appetite, his children's faces clear before him, Haldur's words and Gillavar's laughter ringing in his ears. No, he was not going to send for men to smoke out the fugitives from Salfgard. He realised now that he hoped they had indeed escaped as it was rumoured they had; and what was more, he hoped they stayed free.

'Ah, well.' He cleared his throat. 'Well yes, I did think of calling in the specialists. But I've changed my mind. Yes, I've decided against the idea. Not good for the morale of my own troops, you know. Once these fellows who've blown in from the wilderness are off my hands, I'll organise another sweep of the hills. Not that I myself think there's anything to find; you'll know we've combed through the north country several times already. If anyone was hiding up there, I'm confident my lads would have routed them out by now. So, my thanks to your commanding officer for his swift response, and you can travel back south with the others tomorrow.'

'Oh, I don't think so.'

Heranar looked up anxiously and saw that the fellow was almost laughing. Some faint recollection, some long-buried memory, stirred in his mind and was gone before he could hold on to it.

'What do you mean?' he asked.

'I can't come all this way and go back with nothing to report but your change of mind. You can spare your troops for the present, governor. I'll go on a little solo reconnaissance myself, I think, and see what I can find.'

'What – alone, you mean?'

'That's right. I'm quite used to living off the land, you know.'

Again a flash of mirth passed across the Outlander's face, and as it lit his strange bright eyes, it broke Heranar's memory.

'Haven't I seen you somewhere before?' he said, frowning. 'What was the name, did you say?'

'I didn't, you'd never be able to pronounce it. I'm known as Sigitsinen and yes, we've met before. You were introduced to me by Maesrhon, the day Ghentar tried to kill him. As I recall, you threw up all over my feet. But anyway, as I was saying, we make it a point of honour in the patrols, always to have something to report for our efforts. And if I might give you a little piece of advice, governor: if I were you, I'd practise sounding confident, even if you can't be confident. It should stand you in good stead, when you make your report to Lord Valahald. Your brother will be expecting to hear from you, won't he?'

Chapter 44

Under surveillance in Framstock

Haldur stood on the old bridge at Framstock, looking down at the river without really seeing it, blowing at his hair from time to time in a fruitless attempt to stop it sticking to his forehead. The day was warm and close, but this was not summer as he was used to it in the Nine Dales. Here the heat was sullen, oppressive, the air lifeless under the gloom that spread above, seeming to shut him in with his thoughts as it blanketed all else with dejection. Indeed Haldur was anything but cheerful as he contemplated the course of his errand so far, and wondered what to do for the best. He turned round with a sigh and leaned his back against the stone parapet. The only thing he really wanted to do was to get away as quickly as possible, to make all speed back north to Rihannad Ennar, back to his home with its bright sun and bracing wind, its straightforward, honest folk. Surely he and his companions had seen and heard enough now to be able to verify what they had been told, first by Artorynas and then by those who had fled from Gwent y'm Aryframan. But they were still far away from Caradriggan; and going by all the signs, this was the place where the real power lay and the important decisions were taken. It was also the place where Arval was to be found. Haldur ran his hands through his hair, which fell heavily back again, and turned to stare down at the flowing water once more. If at all possible, they must make contact with Arval, the one person whose truth and advice they knew could be trusted. If he was still in Tellgard, it would be safe to talk to him.

And I must go to Caradriggan if I am to keep my promise to Artorynas, thought Haldur. Hearing someone call his name, he looked over his shoulder to see Ir'rossung, Cathasar and Tellapur approaching.

The four of them moved aside. Where the wall followed the outline of one of the massive bridge piers, there was a small area to the side of the thoroughfare with a stone seat, but Haldur got the impression that passers-by were eyeing them suspiciously as they stood here. Perhaps the fact that they were crammed into a confined space gave them a slightly conspiratorial air. He pointed towards the river bank.

'Come on, let's go down there, it'll be easier to talk freely.'

There was a broad water-meadow where the river made a wide curve in its course, and here a path ran along near the water's edge. They strolled along this and then sat down near a stand of chestnut trees whose leaves were sparse and shrivelled. Some had already fallen, even though mid-summer was only just over, and lay brown on the ground below.

'Where are Aestrontor and Asaldron?' asked Haldur.

Cathasar jerked his head. 'They've gone up into the town. Asaldron said he was going to wander round the mart and Aestrontor's in the *Fly* to see what he can pick up.'

They looked over the river, where the *Salmon Fly* was almost directly opposite.

'Good idea,' said Haldur. 'He might have more success on his own, especially being such a quiet fellow. It was pretty clear none of the locals were going to risk getting too friendly with us, that time we all went in together.'

'It must have been a really nice little inn, once. In fact,' said Ir'rossung, 'in fact the more I see of Framstock, the more it strikes me that before these Caradwardans ruined it, it must have been a bit like Cotaerdon. Bigger, of course.'

'Yes, that struck me, too. It's strange how Valahald doesn't seem bothered about where we go or what we see. I wonder why that is,' said Cathasar thoughtfully.

'It's a way of showing us that the power is his,' said Haldur. 'You can be sure if we crossed whatever boundaries he has set, we'd know about it soon enough. He's very arrogant, but there's more to it than that. There's a kind of gloating to his authority. It's as if demonstrating that he has it gives him almost as much pleasure as wielding it.'

'I can't stand him,' said Tellapur, loathing in his every syllable. 'He makes my flesh creep. And you're right, there's something about him... I can't put my finger on quite what it is: cruel isn't really the word I'm searching for, although I'm sure he could be absolutely merciless without losing sleep over it. I think he relishes seeing the unhappiness he and his people have caused.'

'Yes,' said Haldur slowly, 'yes, that's a shrewd judgement. I can't say I exactly warmed to Heranar, but he seems almost pleasant compared with Valahald. Now I've met them both, I can see why Heranar was so keen not to step out of line in his dealings with us. It's not just that he's a much less confident character than his brother, I wouldn't be at all surprised if he's rather afraid of him.'

'And if he is, I'd say he's got reason to be. I've not had the chance yet to tell you what I heard from Valahald yesterday evening,' said Ir'rossung. 'Asaldron and I were talking with some of his men when he appeared out of nowhere in that way he has and took us off for a tour of the armoury; no doubt he thought it would do us good to see that they're armed to the teeth. Anyway, we put up the best show we could of looking suitably impressed, but when Asaldron made some remark about how we'd heard that Heranar had been involved in some of the technological development, it didn't go down well at all. Very condescending about his brother, was Valahald, with an eye on his men to see how they appreciated his wit. I thought I'd turn the conversation by complimenting him on his pretty little nieces, and do you know what he said to that? "They're all right, if you go for half-breeds." They all smirked at each other, but when I cupped my ear as if I'd not heard, Valahald, as cool as you like, came out with, "I said, *You're right, they are indeed,*" and then there was a real outburst of sniggering which of course we had to pretend to ignore.'

'But he has Gwentarans working for him, we've seen them about the place,' said Cathasar. 'Yet there were none with Heranar.'

'Well, Heranar's put himself in an awkward position through his marriage, hasn't he?' said Haldur. 'He's stuck in the middle now where whatever he does is going to seem suspicious to one side or the other, not to mention old Gillavar griping away, finding fault with everything he comes across.'

Ir'rossung smiled at this. As the oldest man in the party from Rihannad Ennar, he had been on the receiving end of several of Gillavar's tirades of complaint; but Tellapur was still thinking about Valahald.

'I don't know about *working*,' he said bitterly. 'If you said *slaving*, you'd be closer to the truth, I think. We've seen the kind of tasks they do, the way Valahald and his people speak to them. I feel ashamed just being here; I wish we could… oh, here comes Asaldron now.'

Glancing about him as he approached to make sure no-one was following him, Asaldron came up and sat down with the others. He shook his head.

'I've nothing much to report. The only thing I've found out is that Ardeth's family home used to stand where the new granary's been built; apparently the house was knocked down as soon as the fighting was over. The site must have been chosen deliberately, to make a point. They were wasting their time making the grain store so big, though. No doubt they were expecting the usual bumper yields from the area around Framstock. But I've heard it's nowhere near capacity now, after the harvest failed last year and was meagre enough the year before.'

'And will be scantier than ever this year.' Haldur stared moodily before him, crumbling up a dried chestnut leaf with his fingers. 'Ir'rossung was just telling us about your pleasant little exchange with our host yesterday evening.'

'By the Starborn!' Asaldron's face darkened, but he remembered to keep his voice down. 'There was a fellow working in the corner of the armoury and I could tell he'd heard what Valahald said. The blood came up in his face and when I caught his eye he put his rag and polish down and rolled his sleeve up, holding my gaze until he was sure I'd realised he was deliberately showing me the corn-sign on his arm before he went back to his task. There'll be trouble here, eventually.'

'Only too likely, if things don't improve soon; and it's the Gwentarans who stand to come off worst,' said Haldur.

'Oh, I don't know. Depends on how you look at it,' said Asaldron. His voice was hard and angry. 'If it was a choice between death in life, or life in death, there might be many who preferred the latter option. The slave I saw last night had made his decision. I could see in his eyes that he thought death was a price worth paying, if only he got the chance to take Valahald with him.'

Haldur sighed and chewed his lip, remembering what Artorynas had told him of Geraswic's attempt to kill Vorynaas. For a few moments they sat in silence, each man deep in his own thoughts, and then Tellapur spoke.

'I hate it here. If I could have one wish, it would be to wake up in my own bed tomorrow. But we knew before we set out that we'd got difficult times ahead of us, and we're not half through yet. Let's just push on for Caradriggan, see what we can learn there. The sooner we do that, the sooner we can turn for home again.'

There was a murmur of agreement and Haldur looked around at his companions.

'Are we all of the same mind? Well then, unless we hear anything from Aestrontor that holds us back, I'll tell Valahald tonight that we'll be going on south.'

'Why wait?' said Cathasar. 'Come on, let's bring Aestrontor away with us and go to Valahald now.'

They got to their feet and walked back towards the bridge, but before they reached the street where the *Salmon Fly* was situated, they saw Aestrontor hurrying towards them. One look at his face told them he had news to impart.

'I've found out where we can hear the *Temennis* this evening,' he said.

That night they slept with a serenity they had not known since leaving Rihannad Ennar: their minds refreshed; their hearts calmed, purified as their bodies were cleansed; their resolve strengthened. No matter that the rite was shorn of its majesty, performed in secret in a shabby room; no matter that the words were spoken by an ancient man who trembled with poverty and hunger. His voice retained an echo of old authority and nothing could detract from the power of the words or the sweet solace of hearing the pledge renewed and seeing the flame leap up brightly from the lamps. When Haldur woke next morning he felt light, as if a burden had been lifted from him; the day seemed full of hope once more. His thoughts ran on, imagining the journey down to Caradriggan and whatever awaited them there, the longed-for moment when they could turn towards home, the joy of seeing Cotaerdon again. Smiling to himself, he reached for his clothes and began to dress. This time tomorrow, they might be already on the road; there was no need to delay any longer. He had just passed through the door of the small building across from the guest-hall where their morning food was served when a voice spoke close behind him.

'We missed you at supper yesterday. Did you eat at the *Fly*?'

The governor of Rosmorric

Haldur started in surprise, having not yet managed to accustom himself to Valahald's habit of materialising silently when least expected. He turned to face him, suppressing the annoyance he felt. It seemed likely that this time they had crossed one of Valahald's invisible lines; and it went without saying that it was also highly probable he knew quite well where they had been.

'No,' he said, 'no, we didn't. We had a matter to attend to in the town.'

'Mm, yes. Perhaps you'd like to tell me what took you to a house in Wide Westgate.'

So, he had had them followed.

'And perhaps I wouldn't.' Haldur kept his voice level, but there was an edge to it; he and Valahald had come to a halt just inside the doorway and as Cathasar, Asaldron and the others edged past into the room they glanced at their leader curiously. 'What business is it of yours where we go or who we talk to?'

'Oh, but everything that happens here is my business,' said Valahald, smiling slightly. 'With power goes responsibility, as surely you must know even in Rihannad Ennar. As governor of Rosmorric province, I regard it as my duty to keep my finger on the pulse in this region. The man you visited was a notorious troublemaker at one time and I find it interesting that the travellers who have astonished us all by appearing suddenly out of the legendary north should seek him out.'

'Troublemaker!' Haldur forced himself to laugh. 'Surely not; but whatever may have been the case in the past, the old fellow's in no state now to cause any disturbance. No doubt you're aware of what we discovered, that once he was the most renowned storyteller of Framstock, and the man most often chosen to lead the rites. You speak of legends, yet since we passed your borders, we've seen no wayside *numirasan*, nor any sign that the old customs are still followed here. It's true that at midsummer we were still travelling down the road from your brother's headquarters, but even then, no man lit the flame to mark the day. We ourselves did the only thing we could, and spoke the words in our hearts; but that is nothing compared with hearing *Temennis y'm As-Geg'rastigan ach Ur* recited by one who has had the training for such lore. When a chance word put the opportunity in our path, we were bound to take it.'

He gave Valahald a direct stare, touching the torc at his neck as he spoke. 'And there's no need for you to remind me of the responsibilities that go with lordship. My father made sure I learnt that lesson before my head was much higher than his knee.'

Apparently choosing to ignore this, Valahald raised an eyebrow. 'Am I to assume, then, that in your homeland you still take superstitions about the Starborn for the truth?'

In spite of all he could do, Haldur's face showed something of his anger at these words, his plain features setting into an expression altogether sterner.

'I wouldn't put it like that, Valahald. But if you ask me whether we honour the Starborn and believe that once they walked in this world, then I say yes, certainly we do. I myself rode with the Cunorad y'm As-Geg'rastigan for two years and would gladly have stayed longer in Seth y'n Temenellan if my father had not called me home to his side.'

Valahald inclined his head. 'The Hounds of the Starborn, how charming. You must tell me more some time.'

There was a sudden scrape of wood on stone as Aestrontor leapt to his feet and moved swiftly from his place at the table to stand in Valahald's way as he turned towards the door. 'I'll tell you more now, friend.' He spoke very quietly, but his words came through clenched teeth. 'I rode in the Cunorad too, when I was younger. It's an oath-bound fellowship hallowed by its promises to the Starborn: to honour the Hidden People, to seek for them always, to hope for their return, to look for any trace of where they may once have walked. Every man and woman in Rihann y'n Temenellan has made solemn vows which only death can break.'

'Fascinating, *friend*.' It was as if Valahald, somehow absorbing emotion from Haldur and Aestrontor, drained it of anger and warmth and rendered it back cold, colourless and infinitely more menacing. He took a step forwards. 'Get out of my way, please.'

Aestrontor turned his back without a word and resumed his seat, ignoring his companions' astonished stares. Haldur hesitated briefly and then ducked through the door.

'Wait, Valahald. We were going to speak to you yesterday evening, but as things turned out… Anyway, this won't take long. We'd like to travel on, down to Caradriggan. We can be ready to ride by tomorrow morning, but I imagine we may need some kind of permit for the border crossing. If so, could you issue us with whatever documentation we need, or tell us who we need to see to get it?'

For a moment or two Valahald stood looking at Haldur in silence before he replied.

'Why do you want to go to Caradriggan? I understood from what my brother told me that your purpose here was to discover whether any old tales of Rihannad Ennar were still remembered.'

Haldur shrugged his shoulders as if in resignation. 'That's why we came, yes. But now, there's no point in pretending, is there? Gwent y'm Aryframan doesn't exist any more. Oh, I know, times change; but Heranar refused to let us mingle with the people at all, and down here you've had us followed so you'll know well enough that no-one's prepared to do more than pass the time of day with us. I must say it's not been the welcome we hoped for or expected, but we'll take ourselves off tomorrow if you'll let us have the paperwork.'

A hint of secret amusement crept back into Valahald's voice. 'The world moves on, as you observe. And they say that travel broadens the mind: certainly it shows that different lands have different customs and policies, which those who journey abroad do well to heed. But I'm glad to have confirmation from you of what Heranar says in his report. It seems at least he's capable of following orders, if nothing else.' As he spoke, Valahald examined one of his fastidiously clean and manicured hands, and the contrast with Heranar flashed suddenly before Haldur, who saw him in his mind's eye, trying to hide his bitten nails under the desk. He felt another unexpected stab of sympathy for the younger brother, swallowed up in a surge of renewed anger.

'You're a fine one to be lecturing me on respect for the customs of others!' Haldur shoved his own hands into his sleeves and gripped his arms tightly, inwardly willing himself to calm down, to put on a convincing act, while all the time hating himself for what he was about to say.

'Well, maybe we'll just have to agree to differ. But if you've had a report from Heranar, perhaps he told you the other reason we had for travelling: to dare the unknown, to see as much of the world as we could; in other words, for the adventure of it. Now we've got so far in safety, it seems a waste not to go on further and see more while the chance is there. Ever since we arrived, we've been hearing about Caradriggan. From what we've been told, we have nothing to compare with it, back in the Nine Dales. We want to see the marvels of the city for ourselves before we turn again for home.'

Now there could be no doubt about it, the ghost of that infuriating smile was beginning to play over Valahald's face once more.

'But how would you manage, all that time with no-one to celebrate the rites for you?' he asked.

'That's our problem,' said Haldur brusquely. 'Look, can we have the permit or not?'

'Oh, you won't need a travel pass. You'll be riding under guard, my captain will have all the necessary documents.' Valahald paused for a moment to let the implications of this sink in with Haldur. He smiled. 'Yes, I'm sending you on to Caradriggan at the end of the week, so I'm delighted to hear that you're all so keen to see it. And I've just had an idea. I'll arrange for you to be quartered in Tellgard, which I expect you've also heard about. They've plenty of spare accommodation these days, and you'll get as much lore of the As-Geg'rastigan there as you can take. Well, I interrupted your meal, so I won't keep you from it any longer.' And he strolled off, leaving Haldur completely lost for words.

Later that day, the men of the Nine Dales were having their horses and mules re-shod in preparation for the journey down to Caradward, and were taking advantage of the opportunity to talk under cover of the noise from the forge. Haldur was muttering to Aestrontor and Cathasar as they stood outside with the animals yet to take their turn, while Tellapur and Asaldron were inside and Ir'rossung was busy checking over all their gear.

'You could have knocked me down with a feather: I must have looked absolutely stunned. I just hope Valahald didn't notice or if he did, that he mistook the reason. Plenty of scope there, after all.'

'Yes.' Cathasar leaned against his horse, scowling. 'I wonder what it's all about. They're just playing cat and mouse with us. You know what's beginning to worry me, Haldur? What if they won't let us go, when the time comes? How are we going to get away, if they make difficulties then?'

'Don't think that hasn't occurred to me, too.' Aestrontor and Cathasar looked expectantly at Haldur, clearly assuming he had made some kind of plan; but his mind was blank. What *could* he say to them? 'It's just wasting energy to think about that at this stage, we'll face the problem when we see what things are like in Caradriggan. I'm more concerned about being billeted on Tellgard. It seems too easy, when the one person we want to talk to is Arval. Valahald obviously has a reason of his own, which I could see was amusing him: no doubt that will reveal itself with time, also.'

'But we've been followed and watched ever since we arrived, what if there are spies in Tellgard too?' said Cathasar.

'I know, we've got to face the fact that it's a possibility. But still,' said Haldur, brightening up slightly, 'we don't know what to expect. After all, from what we've been allowed to see here, and up north with Heranar, we'd never have guessed at what we heard last night, would we? You know – what old Morancras told us,' he finished under his breath.

'Let's hope it's all as secret as they think,' said Aestrontor grimly, and the other two nodded. 'I shouldn't have lost my temper with Valahald, earlier,' he added. 'It was the way he sneered, when you mentioned Rihann y'n Temennellan. Wouldn't I love to be the one to wipe that look off his face! It'll be my fault, though, if we find our errand even more difficult now.'

'No it won't, there's nothing to blame yourself for,' said Haldur. 'Listen, we don't have to turn the cheek to everything these Caradwardans insult us with, as long as we always remember what not to say, and what we're not supposed to know. And anyway, I had a sharp enough exchange with Valahald myself. At least going on to Caradriggan will get us away from him.'

An accident reported

A few days after this, in an auxiliary camp some miles outside Framstock, two men spoke together. It was after the time when lamps were dimmed for the night, and their exchange took place within the private quarters of the commanding officer, who sat contemplating his second as this man stood before him.

'Can't this wait until morning?'

'I don't think so, sir. My patrol has just returned to base from exercise, and I have to report a fatal accident to one of the men.'

'Who is it?'

'Staranavar, sir.'

'I see.' Clever, thought the seated man, that's brought down several birds with the one cast; but his face gave nothing away. 'Well, let's have the details.'

'We were north of here, near the river. He'd kept on baiting our newest recruit, snide stuff about him being part-Outlander, and was insolent when I warned him about it. So I told him if he thought he was so much better than us, he'd need to prove it to me; and I took him out myself with the intention of giving him a hard time of it.'

'Yes, I've heard complaints before about his offensive remarks.' They shared a moment of silent understanding: both were *sigitsaran*, the commander showing it in his speech as well as his colouring and facial cast, the other in his features only, although his eyes were pale and bright rather than black. 'And what happened?'

'Well, as we were crossing the river by the rocks above the rapids, he slipped and you know yourself what the strength of the current's like. He was away downstream and over the falls in an instant. Never even had time to cry out.'

'Most unfortunate.'

'Yes… I waited for a bit to see if an eddy would bring him to shore, but he never surfaced; must have got trapped underwater somehow.

Anyway, in the end I came away, told the others what had happened, and gave them orders to move camp and stand guard while I went back to try to retrieve the body. I'm only stating fact when I say I'm far the best swimmer, you know that, captain Naasigits, so it made sense. I might be a while, I said to the others, because I'll not give up easily. But all I found was this: it must have been ripped off as he was torn on the rocks.'

He held out his hand to show a scrap of cloth with a badge still pinned to it, a small leaf in plain unadorned pewter. 'Staranavar had no family that I ever heard of, but the lads say he'd fathered a child on some woman back in Caradriggan. I don't even know if it's a girl or a boy, but if we can find the woman, maybe she'll like to keep this for the child when it's older.'

So, no witnesses of the accident, the body apparently lost to the river, and its only form of identification removed for a good reason and in plausible circumstances, thought Naasigits. He took the proferred badge. 'And how long do you say you spent, trying to find and recover the body?'

'A full day, sir.'

On Naasigits' own orders it was forbidden for the Outlanders among the irregulars to speak together in their own language, even in private, on the grounds that this would have a detrimental effect on overall morale. But now, leaning forward and lowering his voice slightly, he switched briefly to the *sigitsaran* tongue, and received an equally brief and quiet reply; no listener would have guessed that a question and response had been exchanged. He sat back, speaking now in the language of every day again.

'Well, as we always say in the patrols, never leave a bad apple in the barrel. Staranavar was no great loss, but it costs us nothing to mark his end with the words our ancestors used.' A tiny change registered for a moment in his unreadable eyes, as if some message had passed. 'If we can find the woman as you suggest, we'll see she gets some financial help. Your concern is commendable. And by the way, Sigitsinen, you did well up in Rossaestrethan too. Yes, very well.' Again there was that imperceptible change of expression. 'Now, it's very late. I suggest we both turn in and get some rest.'

Valahald's mistake

The morning of departure came at last for Haldur and his companions and those who were to journey with them. They made an early start and the noise of their going echoed against the blank walls of the half-empty new granary as they rode down the street at an easy pace and out from the town, heading away on the long road south. Haldur found himself remembering other settings-out: those wild rides with the Cunorad under the blue stars of morning; the sweet air of quiet summer dawns as the sun rose on journeys with his father through the hills and dales of Rihannad Ennar. He had claimed to both Heranar and Valahald that part of the reason for his roving far from home was to satisfy a certain reckless daring, and smiled sadly to himself at the thought. This could have been the greatest adventure of all: to have come so far, to have proved their wits and courage by surviving the wilderness, to have encountered new peoples and strange lands even their wise men could only read about, to have gazed on a world wider than most of their fellows back home had ever dreamed existed. Could have been, and might have been – had the sun shone, had men welcomed them, had they been free to make merry with new friends, to renew old ties. Might have been, and should have been – but there was no thrill in a dour daybreak such as this, which served only to remind them that they were being moved under surveillance from one confinement to another.

The street was curved, and as they rounded the bend they saw the old boundary posts ahead of them. Not many people were about and few of these took much notice of them as they passed. On the near side of the gate there was a fellow with a brush, sweeping the road. At the sound of hooves he looked up, withdrawing onto the pavement where a small water hand-cart was parked. Though he leaned casually on his broom, his eyes were intent as he scanned the faces before him. When his gaze met Haldur's, he held it deliberately, pushing up his sleeve; but suddenly there was a yell from the rear of the column.

'Hey you! Don't stand there gawping, get back to your work!'

Taking up his brush again, the man turned away and began sweeping at the accumulation of dust and dirt where the wall met the pavement. Haldur looked back as they neared the gate, but the man was bent to his task and made no further sign. They clattered past the stone columns with their weathered carvings and Haldur glanced at Asaldron: yes, he'd noticed too. His mind raced. Twice now, a Gwentaran had pointedly drawn their attention to the corn-mark: surely they were to understand that some message was intended, but how were they to know what it meant? Deep in thought, he scarcely noticed their progress away from the last of the houses and down a gentle slope as the road descended into a shallow valley. His mind had gone back to what they had heard from Morancras during the evening they had spent with him. It was to be hoped the old fellow would not be made to pay for their visit, now that they had left Framstock, but maybe there was no need to fear. After all, Valahald had made it plain that Morancras had been under observation before ever they arrived, and it would have likely been more in his style, if he was going to interrogate him, to do it while they were still present to see him exercise his power. It was not until very much later that Haldur was to discover that both his fears and his assumptions were incorrect.

Valahald had delayed purposely, reasoning that this would dupe Morancras and any associates he might have among the native population into thinking that no move was to be made against him; but he had every intention of bringing him in to wring from him everything he could tell about his evening with the men from Rihannad Ennar. He passed the morning of their departure in attending to various items of paperwork, enjoyed a light mid-day meal, and then sent two men from his household troop over to Wide Westgate. Within the hour they were back. Valahald heard the exchange of passwords outside and settled back in his chair with pleasant anticipation, but the door opened to admit only the two fellows he had sent out. He leaned forwards, frowning. What was the matter with them? Both men were pale and sweaty and seemed curiously reluctant to look at him.

'Well?' he enquired sharply, when neither spoke. 'Where is he?'

The older of the two took a deep breath and swallowed hard. 'Sir, he's dead. There was no answer when we knocked, so we broke the door and went in. And there he was, on the floor – well, what was left of him, anyway.'

'What do you mean, what was left of him? What had happened?'

'Well sir, who's to know how it happened. Perhaps he left the back door open, and the dogs got in and attacked him; or maybe he was taken ill and they sniffed him out and got in before he could get help… He was old, after all, and he lived alone. But from what we, er, found in there, him and these dogs had been shut up together for some days now…'

'Oh? The dogs shut the door again behind them, did they?'

'There'd been a struggle, sir.' The younger fellow took up the tale. 'Either he'd tried to fend them off, or they'd fought among themselves – there were three dogs in there, all filthy strays. The furniture was smashed up, and a heavy chair had fallen against the door and jammed it shut. When we forced our way in through the front they pelted out like mad things, they'd be desperate for water. It was that dark in there we didn't realise at first what we'd stood in, then we saw. We, well, we gathered it together as best we could and tied it up in an old curtain and took it to the lime pit. There was nothing left of him but rags and gnawed bones, only the soles of his feet and part of one hand was still lying there, even his face had been chewed off and eaten…'

'All right, all right! There's no need to describe every gruesome detail.' Valahald was nearly as green as they by now, his mouth stretched in a grimace of disgust. 'You've brought the stink in here with you, I suppose it never occurred to you to leave your boots outside after stepping in dog shit and rotting meat. You'd better get moving quickly: I want all three dogs destroyed before the day's out, we can't have strays with a taste for human flesh roaming round the town. Don't come back until you've cut their throats.'

The men left rapidly and Valahald paced the corridor, shouting for his secretary and others from his administrative staff.

'Take the rugs up out of there and burn them; dock the wages of those two troopers to pay for their replacements. Empty the desk, put the paperwork in separate labelled boxes and take it away before that picks up the stench too, then replace the drawer-liners. Clear another room somewhere and put all the furniture in it temporarily, then have this room fumigated. Oh, and have someone bring me a fresh set of clothes, I can even smell the whiff on these. I'll be in the bath-house in the meantime; what I'm wearing now can be burned with the rugs. Let me know as soon as my new office is ready, I'll need to sign an order for the demolition of the old charlatan's hovel in Wide Westgate. And I'm expecting that fellow Naasigits from the auxiliaries, so if necessary show him where to find me.'

Some time later, he looked up as the secretary ushered his visitor into the room.

'You're late,' said Valahald. 'I've got more to do than wait around all day for you to show up whenever it suits you.'

'On the contrary, sir. I arrived at the agreed time but was told you were detained in the bath-house; so to save delay later, I went over to arrange for a horse to be ready for me after our meeting.'

Valahald sat back and contemplated the newcomer. He noted the slight accent in his speech; evidently the man hailed from a true Outland family. Certainly he had the looks for it: the black hair, the dark hooded eyes that gave nothing away. The man's cool self-possession annoyed him: who did he think he was, to put his own convenience before that of the governor? He opened a file on his desk and glanced at its contents.

'What's happening up in Rossaestrethan? That fellow who went up there at my brother's request – how much longer is he going to be away?'

'Oh, he's been back for some time now. Returned to normal patrol duties.'

'What? I've had no report from him.'

'He reported to me.'

'Now look here.' As his anger increased, so Valahald spoke more quietly. 'You need to remember that as governor of Rosmorric, I am also your commander-in-chief. I find your attitude very close to insubordination.'

'With respect sir, I must disagree. May I remind you that no governor has authority over the irregular troops. We take our orders from Lord Valestron and report directly to him. By all means raise the matter with him if you have a formal complaint. However if you wish me to summarise my second's findings after his mission to the north, I can do so for you now.'

'Perhaps you'd condescend so far, if you're sure it won't *delay* you unduly.' The mention of Valestron's name had checked Valahald; he waited, watching his visitor closely.

Naasigits spoke as levelly as ever, ignoring the sarcasm. 'Lord Heranar had apparently changed his mind. He said he no longer wished to call in a specialist team; he felt this might adversely affect the morale of his own men, who had themselves conducted several previous searches of the territory under his command and found nothing. He is satisfied that these tales of outlaws have no truth in them.'

'He is, is he? And what about your man? Came tamely back just to report that my brother doesn't know his own mind, did he? That's not the kind of death-or-glory stuff I've been led to expect from you fellows.'

'No sir, he went out on reconnaissance himself, to form his own opinion.'

When Valahald laughed sceptically, Naasigits permitted the merest suggestion of a smile to crease the corners of his black eyes, although his amusement was of a very different kind. 'I can assure you that we speak of a most competent, reliable and resourceful man, one who has consistently achieved the highest standards in both training and service, and has been decorated by Atranaar himself. It's only a matter of time before Sigitsinen has a command of his own and if he too found nothing in the hill country, we may all of us be sure there's nothing there to find.'

'Well, let's all hope he's right,' said Valahald. 'I wouldn't care to be in this Sigitsinen's shoes, nor indeed in Heranar's, if events prove otherwise. Right, that's all the time I can spare on this.' The man rose from his seat, but Valahald thought he would add a parting shot. 'As I'm sure you're aware, neither Atranaar nor myself suffer fools gladly.'

With his hand on the door, Naasigits turned. 'Absolutely, sir. Nor does Valestron.'

For a moment they stared at each other in silence, then with the merest suggestion of a salute Valahald's visitor was gone.

The governor of Rosmorric province jumped up from his desk and took a pace towards the door, then sat down again, breathing hard. Had that been a veiled threat? The Outland dog! Valahald's eyes narrowed. There were too many *sigitsaran* for his liking enlisted among the irregulars, and he'd always been uneasy that the auxiliaries had been split off from central command and put under Valestron's personal control. And what did Heranar think he was doing, dithering about up there in the north? Could the fool not make any kind of decision and stick to it? Valahald's lip curled. Imagine tying himself to that pale, dreary woman and then producing all those children! He smiled unpleasantly to himself: you've gone native in a big way, little brother. As his anger receded, his clenched fists gradually relaxed. He examined his hands, comparing them in his mind's eye with Heranar's chewed and bitten fingers, and then suddenly recoiled. Had he caught a faint hint of decomposing flesh, even after his prolonged soak in the bath-house? How was it that the smell still clung about him? His face twisted with revulsion as he wrenched the door open, shouting for hot water. He scrubbed desperately at his nails, his thoughts darting this way and that.

What damned bad luck that the mumbling old fool should have gone for dogs' meat before he'd had the chance to question him. Instinctively, Valahald was sure there was more than met the eye to the strangers from Rihannad Ennar, but was unable to pin down what he thought it might be. Suppose Valestron got the secret out of them? He realised he was no longer so pleased as he had been with his position as governor of Rosmorric. What was the good of having the status of a son with Vorynaas if he was out of sight and out of mind, stuck up here in Framstock, when Valestron was free to do as he pleased, to be on hand in Caradriggan if he so chose, worming his way into the ascendancy? With that, his error seemed clear to Valahald. I should have gone with Haldur and the others, he realised. I should have taken them to Caradriggan myself, not just packed them off for Valestron to claim any credit he can from dealing with them. He threw the brush back into the bowl with a splash and sat down again, snatching up pen and paper. Scribbling out orders for Heranar to come down to Framstock and assume temporary charge of the southern province in addition to his own, he did rapid mental calculations. Yes, if he commandeered a fresh horse from every posting station, he should still be able to overtake the travellers in time. They would be taking it easily, he would catch up with them before they got anywhere near the old border. He smiled. So they expected to be impressed with Caradriggan, did they? They'd have plenty to make them stare long before they arrived in the city.

Naasigits rode at a leisurely pace, heading eastwards out of the town. Suddenly he heard a commotion of yelling and snarling from around a sharp bend in the road, then all went quiet. He rounded the corner to see two soldiers and three dead dogs. The men were covered in dust and sweat, breathing heavily; one of them was bleeding from a bite on his forearm. A bloody knife lay on the ground, and more blood was pooling from the slit throats of the animals. The horse tossed its head and shied a little at the smell, and instinctively the men scrambled back, looking up to see who the rider was. For a moment a smile lit up Naasigits' dark eyes; the teeth flashed white in his sallow face. He brought the horse under quick control and lifted a hand in greeting.

'Good day and good health, friends.'

The men stared after him as he rode on, and then looked at each other. 'I don't think I've ever seen one of the *sigitsaran* smile before,' said one. 'What's to grin about in three dead dogs?'

'Probably fancied them for his dinner,' said the other, scowling. 'I've heard they eat worse than dogs. Outland bastard!' He spat into the dust, nursing his bleeding arm. 'All right for him, sitting up there on his horse, laughing because I'm hurt. Come on, let's get this lot back to show Valahald – another prize bastard – and then I can get this arm seen to.'

CHAPTER 45

The lonely quest continues

The sun of mid-day was warm on his back as Artorynas plodded on, climbing slowly but steadily. Surely he must be close now to the head of the pass leading out of the Golden Valley. He glanced up, but the gradient meant that the horizon was too near for him to see anything other than the rocks and slopes close by. Meltwater poured down, splashing and gurgling in narrow channels as it found its way down to the valley below. It was greenish-blue, milky with sediment from glacial run-off. Somewhere up here there must be snow still lying and indeed Artorynas could smell it, clean and cold on the wind; but underneath there was a hint of green, a promise of spring growth beginning. Fixing his eyes on the ground before his feet he toiled on, resolving not to stop or rest until he reached the crown of the road. Another hour went by and then, raising his head, he got a first glimpse of what awaited him. Now he was near enough to the gap in the hills to see the summits of mountains far beyond. He stopped, hands on hips, straightening his back and looking about him. The sun had moved round and the slopes to his left were now all in shadow. Snow lay deep there in hollows beside the path, the chill reaching out to him, laying cold fingers against the warmth of his face and hands. Far below, green and golden, Rihann nan' Esylt held out its arms like a lover to the embrace of the sun. Artorynas saw silver threads here and there where mountain torrents caught the light, saw where the purple of the moorland above changed to the bright emerald of fields, but was too far away now to be able to see any other signs of the handiwork of men. He stood there, a few steps below the crest of the trail, looking back: back to where he knew there were farms and villages, markets and little towns; back to where the old couple had made him welcome, back to the inns where he had slept, back to the stable where he had left his horse; back to where the Golden Valley broadened out into Rihann y'n Cathtor. After a few moments he took off his pack, propping it up on rocks off the wet ground, and sat down on a boulder where the sun fell and warmed it. He would rest here, gazing for maybe the last time on the world of men; and after he had eaten, he would go on, leaving behind the things of the Earthborn.

Two ravens were soaring overhead; there must be a nest on a ledge somewhere close by. Their harsh cries echoed in the crags, the only sound in all that wide emptiness except the whisper of the wind in his ears, the wind that brought with it a faint breath of the new season's life. Artorynas finished his meal and stepped over a silty torrent of meltwater, kneeling to drink instead at a spring that issued, cold and peaty, from under a rock. Putting on his pack once more he paused for a moment, taking a final look at Rihannad Ennar spread out below him; then he turned away. Up to the summit of the pass he strode, and over it. As he began to descend, the westering sun shone into the corner of his left eye and he put up his hand, looking out under it at the new lands that lay before him. It could not be long before he knew whether success or failure waited ahead; whichever it was to be, time was running short. There was not much more than two years left to him now: two years in which either to achieve his quest, fulfil his promise to Haldur and then return to Arval; or to return defeated, loyal but empty-handed. Or to die in the attempt, alone here in the vastness of the north, friendless and bereft of help. But thoughts of death, and the sight of the Somllichan nan'Esylt towering far off, yet another daunting barrier that must be overcome in due course, could not cast down Artorynas' heart. His gaze was drawn, not so much by the mountains ahead, but by the land below them, green and fresh under the bright sun. This was where the scent of new life growing came from, drifting up to him where he stood, still high up on the downward path.

Artorynas soon found that even reaching the low ground, leaving aside the matter of crossing it to tackle the next climb, would take much longer than he had at first realised. The air was so clear that distances were deceptive: the mountains beyond had seemed quite close, but now he saw that in fact they were still many miles away, though their folded slopes and snowy peaks stood out against the blue sky in crystalline detail. At their feet lay a wide green valley through which a broad river flowed in easy winding curves. Out of the west it came, and meandered gently away eastward. While Artorynas was still high enough up to be able to survey the whole sweep of this new land, he noticed the gleam of water reflecting the sky here and there and saw how the course of the river must have changed from time to time, so that some of its wider bends were now cut off from the main channel and formed separate lakes and meres. Probably the waters spilled out when the autumn rains swelled the flow and maybe then much of the valley lay under water. There were wide stands of willow trees and huge reed banks, all swaying in the soft breeze. One morning before he set out for the day, Artorynas spared time to stand, studying the lie of the land. Unless he was much mistaken, before evening he would be deep within the cover of the broad-leaved forest that clothed the lower slopes, so this might be his last chance for detailed observation of the valley floor. He devoted an hour or more to a slow, painstaking scrutiny. Small clouds floated overhead and shadows inched slowly round, and still he stood, knowing time so used was time well spent.

It was likely that the river, free to wander with the seasons to and fro between the two mountain ranges, would be shallow, and it was not fast-flowing; crossing it should not present too much difficulty therefore. The problems might lie in approaching the water, where the low ground would be wet underfoot at best, and swampy at worst. The willows he saw, and the alders and birches, were all trees of the marsh. His eyes moved over an area of reedbed and suddenly a flock of birds leapt from it, wheeling and turning as one, wings flashing in the early sun, and then, as if at a signal, sinking back out of sight again into the safety of cover. Well, food would not be a problem. The whole place was alive with birds, and it was nesting-time: there would be eggs, and the water must be teeming with fish. Artorynas looked again at the reeds and the willows. There was plenty of raw material there for one who knew, as he did, how best to use it. He had seen how the *sigitsaran* of the far south, living in the wetlands of the Haarnouten, made marsh-boots from withies plaited into wide flat discs. He could make some for himself, if he had to, and maybe also a raft on which to punt or float his gear over the river. Time to go, then. He bent to lift his pack, and a robin that had hopped close in its foraging took flight at the movement. It perched now on a thorn bush only feet away, watching him with bright, knowing gaze, and as Artorynas smiled at the little bird his eye was drawn to a detail far beyond that suddenly caught his attention. The Somllichan nan'Esylt had seemed to bar his path in one continuous sweep, but now he looked again and wondered whether he was right. Old Torald had taught him many a lesson in how to read the hills; could it be that in fact there was a break, where the range divided and its two ends overlapped? If so, maybe he could find an easier way between them to what lay beyond, rather than labouring up to some high and perilous pass. Artorynas stared hard, committing to memory every formation of rock and pinnacle he could see in the blue air, making sure he would know the place again from a different angle. He glanced back at the thorn bush, but the robin had gone, and so now must he. Shouldering his burden he walked on, down into the trees.

Getting across the low lands of the broad valley, negotiating its many lakes and meres and crossing its wide river, did indeed take longer than Artorynas had bargained for. But though the going was slow, it was easy compared with other obstacles he had overcome. The days lengthened and warmed, and the reflected sunlight sparkled on a thousand dazzling ripples as he waded cautiously through shallow backwaters or swam across slow-flowing channels, pushing his gear before him on a woven willow raft. He kept back his stores for harsher days ahead, eating well on the abundance that was readily available; and indeed it often occurred to him as strange that the people of the Nine Dales had not also taken this valley to live in when they abandoned their ancient homes away in Valward. Maybe the mountains that sheltered Rihannad Ennar from the north ran on into the forbidding promontory that Carapethan had described to him; the barrier that, extending far out into the northern seas, had caused them to turn for land rather than attempt to sail around it. Resting in the warm evening at the end of a tiring day, waiting for the fish he had caught to bake in the embers of his fire, Artorynas looked back at the Somllichan na'Haldan. Their higher slopes glowed in the late sunlight and he turned to his left, where the mountains receded away north-east until he could see them no more. Yes, perhaps that was it. And then when the people reached Rihann y'n Car, and spread thence eventually into the other valleys, they would instinctively move southwards, turning away so that the mountains were at their back.

Artorynas raked his supper away from the heat, picking open the package of fleshy leaves in which the fish was wrapped; a little cloud of savoury steam curled up and wisped away. He smiled to himself, remembering Torald's warning that the smell of cooking could betray a camp. No need to worry about that here: he had seen nothing bigger than deer or more alarming than beavers, although he had not forgotten what Astell had said about the dangers in Aestron na Caarst. He would be more cautious there, that was certain. As he ate, he considered his course so far. In finding a path through all the waters of the valley floor, he had gone out of his way downstream where the crossings, though wider, were shallower; and now he would need to turn west. He reckoned it could take him many days before he reached the place where he had thought there might be an overlap in the Golden Mountains, because in order to be sure he would know again the landmarks he had memorised, he needed to keep distance between them and himself and that meant staying in the low country for a while yet. It was fortunate that little rain had fallen to increase the difficulty of the terrain he was struggling through, and the weather was becoming hotter as the summer advanced, so that the shallow waters were reasonably warm; but he was certainly facing a lot more wading and swimming before he began to climb again. I shall be growing webbed feet like a frog or a duck before all is over, he thought, as he banked the fire for the night and settled to rest under the first of the summer stars.

Before many days of his journey upstream had passed, a new and strange idea began to form in Artorynas' mind. Earlier, during his crossing from one side of the valley to the other, he had occasionally come across places where the going was easier than expected because a low ridge of higher ground divided one marshy area from another, or the waters were held back by what almost looked like ancient embankments. He had simply taken these for lucky paths and picked his way across by using them, but now he was not so sure. As he walked further west the banks and ridges became more numerous and noticeable; and though it was hard to be certain, where so much was a tangle of alder-carr and reeds or hidden under shallow water, he almost thought he could detect a pattern to these earthworks. Surely there were too many of them, arranged too symmetrically at right-angles to each other, to be a natural formation; and if this were so, then only one conclusion followed: they were the handiwork of men. But what men could they be, when had they laboured here, where were they now? Not folk of Rihannad Ennar, at any rate, or he would have heard tell of it. Maybe I am just imagining things, thought Artorynas as he pushed slowly on. Every so often he scanned the mountains to his left, trying to recognise the place where he had come down from the pass. There was an unusual rock-formation which he hoped to recognise, but now that he guessed the place must be near, the good weather had broken and the crags were wreathed in low cloud. Then one afternoon the sky began to clear again and he looked up hopefully.

Yes! Up there, that might be the place; if he could just press on for a few more miles, he might be sure of it before he stopped to sleep. Here in the north, the summer nights were short and evenings lingered in a late twilight. The sun blazed out again, shining into his face as it sank; there would be some hours of daylight yet. Artorynas hit on another of those strange ridges of drier ground and hurried forward eagerly, making the best speed he could, concentrating now rather upon the ground before his feet. Then he felt the change as the sun slid behind the Somllichan nan'Esylt. Shadows fell, down in the valley bottom, prompting him to look up once more. What he saw brought him to a halt. He had been right about the shape of the crags away up there, and tomorrow would search for the corresponding signs that would show him where to try for the passage through the Golden Mountains. But a distinctive pattern of rocks was not all there was to see. The level rays of the setting sun fell across the green slopes westward of where his downward path had lain. And there, picked out in a sharp contrast of shadow and light was the unmistakeable outline of fields and terraces upon the hillside, the rig and furrow of bygone farms, the mounds and ridges of buildings, boundaries, dwellings all now abandoned and lost to time. Artorynas stood, staring. So it was true: there beyond doubt was the proof that men had once lived here. The terrible history that had unfolded before him with Astell's words came into his mind. Had the fires of death upon earth that Carapethan had told him of swept through here also? Perhaps not: the valley seemed peaceful and untouched, not blighted like the wilderness; and yet it lay deserted now. Artorynas thought of the sword Sleccenal that had come down to the present day from time beyond memory, and the set of silver arm-rings that Haldur had shown him. He had realised when he tested the metal between fingers and thumb that even the smallest ring was thin with use, though only babies could have worn it.

'How many tiny children must have worn this, and each for such a short time,' he had said. 'Generations beyond count.'

And Haldur had been sorry to see him sad, saying he wished he had not shown the rings to him.

But for now, strangely, elation rather than sorrow was in his heart. He hurried to his rest, even though there was still light in the sky overhead, meaning to rise before dawn and hasten on his way. That so much about the past should be unknown to Arval had come as almost as great a shock to him as the knowledge itself, but suddenly he thought how wonderful it would be when, reunited at last, they were able to study together all the new tidings he would bring back with him to share with his beloved counsellor and guide. *A man is never too young to begin learning, and never too old to stop.* How often had he heard those words! Artorynas laughed aloud for joy of remembered happiness and pleasure to come. I must walk more swiftly tomorrow, he thought; I must press on, I must, I *will*, find the arrow that Arymaldur took away with him. Let the mystery that surrounds it and him, that entangles me also in its web, work itself out as it pleases! Let follow what may, when I return to Caradriggan with my errand accomplished! I have made two promises only, to Haldur and to Arval: I will keep them both. And I *will* succeed in my quest. Time passed as he lay, unable to sleep for the thoughts that chased each other through his mind, and over him the summer night gradually darkened to deepest blue. Suddenly a shooting star left a momentary golden streak across the silent heavens. Could he take this as an omen? If there could be some hint, however small, thought Artorynas as his eyes began to close at last, if there could be something to show me my feet are on the right path, if I could just see some sign to hearten me…

Delayed by bad weather

It was still early morning, two days later, when he rounded the last low slopes of the nearer spur of the Somllichan nan' Esylt and saw that his fieldcraft had not deceived him. Rising before him, at a gentle but steady gradient, was a rock-strewn, rather bare dale. Its general lie was parallel with the broad valley he had crossed, so that initially at any rate it seemed he must back-track in an easterly direction again; but it was to be hoped that once he had climbed high enough he would see a way either through or around the other side of this split in the mountain range. He scanned what he could see of this new terrain carefully. The dale was grass-grown with a scattering of small trees here and there, thorn and birch for the most part, and a small river came splashing swiftly down to lose itself in the meandering channels of the lower lands. It looked likely country for rabbits and maybe ptarmigan higher up, and there would be trout in the river. Artorynas had no need to check whether his snares and sling were in order; he never lay down to sleep at night before overhauling all his gear. But an hour's patience would be well rewarded if he paused here, in spite of his eagerness to begin the new trail. He cut an armful of withies from the nearest stand of willows and then sat down in the sun to weave them into a couple of fish traps, one fitting inside the other. Then, tying them onto the outside of his pack, he set out. By his calculations it was almost mid-summer, and the less time he used on finding food the more time he would have for walking. Snares and traps could be set and left to do their work overnight and would mean he could still hold back his preserved stores for use in Aestron na Caarst. Artorynas shivered slightly in spite of the warmth of the day. The sun might shine here, beaming down on this tranquil and generous land, but it would not do to forget what lay waiting for him beyond the mountains.

After he had climbed steadily for some days, Artorynas was forced to a halt by a turn in the weather. Low cloud rolled down the mountainsides, hiding the heights above, and thick mist blanketed from view anything further than a few paces away. There was nothing to do but sit it out and wait. Forming his pack into the tiny emergency shelter into which it converted, Artorynas crawled inside and tried to school himself to patience. The little tent kept him and his gear dry, but could not repel the dank chill that crept into his bones. Hour after hour he lay, listening to the endless chatter of the stream nearby in its rocky channel and the wild, bubbling cries of curlew. High and lonely they called to him, the voice of desolate, empty places. For two long days and on into a third Artorynas waited, fretting at the delay and forcing down the whispers of fear that drifted with the fog. Then a new sound came to him, a sigh as if the hills breathed deeply in their sleep, and he felt the air stirring. Untying the flaps of his tent, he peered out hopefully. The mist was gleaming and opalescent, lit by a ghostly sun that had at last appeared again overhead; and a breeze was starting up, rolling great banks of cloud along at ground level across the soaking grass. Artorynas ducked back inside, lacing the soles to his boots and putting them on. Within the hour he was able to set out once more. He went cautiously, for the weather had not yet completely cleared and visibility was still limited. But the wind was strengthening, and clouds raced along high above, streaming across the face of the sun.

It was mid-afternoon when Artorynas sensed a levelling-off in the slope he had been climbing and paused to take stock. The view was clearing all the time: he could see back over the way he had come, and the summits above him were now only partially obscured by scudding clouds, but nearer at hand the mist still lingered. He frowned, considering the possibilities. It could be that this was just some hollow in the hills where the ground dipped and formed a pocket where fog was slow to clear, or maybe at last he had reached the place at which the way through to what lay beyond would be revealed. But it could also be that, concealed within the mist, a cliff-edge or hidden corrie awaited the incautious wayfarer. It would be better to wait for a while in the hope that the freshening breeze would sweep his path completely clear. Artorynas took off his pack and sat down, but the wind was cold and he stood again, moving about to keep warm and flapping his arms. He glanced back and got a distant glimpse of the valley he had left behind. Far, far away now, the river and other waters shone here and there amid the green, reflecting the sunlight; and Artorynas, chafing his fingers, thought longingly of the days he had journeyed there in warmth and plenty. Then suddenly a stronger, keener gust whistled through, carrying away with it the clouds and fog; and when Artorynas saw what was revealed to him as the last shreds of mist wisped away he stood in amazement, cold fingers forgotten.

As silent as standing stones

He had reached the edge of an extensive, roughly level area of upland. Behind him was the dale leading back to the broad river valley; to his right were the peaks that rose above the nearer spur of the Somllichan nan'Esylt. Ahead, eastward, where he had thought maybe there was a gap between the two parts of the range, his way was in fact blocked by more rising ground. He had scaled greater heights, but even so there was something so forbidding about these bare, bleak hills that he turned automatically to his left, to the north. Here, the flat upland he had reached seemed to rise gradually until it blended with the sky in a wide, undulating horizon: here the sharp summits of the further range descended and thereafter rose only a little into those frowning eastern foothills. Artorynas stood just within a kind of saddle of land that was entirely enclosed except where it looked back down-dale to the river and where, turning at an angle and rising slightly, it apparently showed him the way beyond the mountains. Wide and gale-swept, dotted with an occasional thorn-bush crouched away from the prevailing winds, it lay green and bare under a grey, hurrying sky; but it was not empty. At its centre was a huge circle of massive stones, standing indifferent to time and weather with only the deserted hills around and the birds sweeping overhead to heed it. *As silent as standing stones.* With a shock that set his heart racing, Artorynas realised he had looked upon this sight before. Once again he was ten years old, sitting in Arval's study as the old man turned the pages of Numirantoro's book. Here was the very picture his mother had made, which she had seen only as an image in the mind, but which he saw now in reality, spread out before his living eyes. This is the sign I wished for, thought Artorynas; the sign that tells me I am in the right path, the sign that points my way and gives me hope.

Time went by and still he stood there staring, as silent and unmoving as a stone himself. He was unsure, even now, whether he fully understood what Arval had tried to show him concerning Numirantoro and Arymaldur; but here in this long-abandoned place where even the rocks and trees seemed hung about with loneliness a new insight came to him. If Numirantoro could walk in thought where her feet had never trod, if she could see an imagined landscape corresponding in every detail with a reality unknown to her; if she was able, even though of the Earthborn, to achieve such things, then maybe this was why she so yearned for the As-Geg'rastigan; perhaps this was how she could pass the hidden door in Tellgard; perhaps this was why she willingly embraced the life of the Starborn even though she knew it would consume her own. Artorynas drew a deep breath, returning to himself. He was chilled through: it had been foolish to stand so long in this biting wind. He strode off across the plain towards the stone circle, walking briskly to set his blood moving again, and at nightfall he set up his small tent, telling himself it would not be warm enough to sleep without its protection. But in truth, Artorynas wanted shelter from more than the cold. Although he had walked for many hours before stopping, the stones were still distant and he realised that once more the clarity of the mountain air had deceived him. Yet far-off though they were, they dominated the landscape in which they were set: Artorynas felt their eyes upon him, and his dreams were full of their brooding presence.

By the time he approached the circle next day, the sun was almost at the bright noon and he was glad of its warmth and light. The stones loomed above him, grey, lichen-crusted, veined here and there with a thread of some mineral. Some had shifted in the passing of untold ages, and were leaning at perilous angles, but none had fallen; and they had lost nothing of their wordless power. Not for anything would Artorynas have touched them or walked among them. And yet, though stern and silent, though mighty and enduring, their poignant majesty was freighted with sorrow and loss. Their very triumph over time was eloquent of the futile strivings of those who had placed them there, of the impotence of men in the face of their own mortality. For Artorynas had no doubt that it was men who had raised these gigantic stones. Only the Earthborn would have expended the enormous effort which must have been necessary for such a task, straining and struggling to prise them from their rocky beds, move them to this wild upland setting, heave them upright to stand in the earth pointing skywards. The old scar showed white as these bleak reflections twisted at his mouth, and he tramped on, a tiny figure dwarfed by the immensity of the plain.

The days passed and now the ground was rising once again as he climbed up the northward slopes he had seen. These were not steep, but what had seemed from far away to be one upward sweep was in reality a tract of broken ground, strewn with boulders and clothed in thin, wiry turf. The land undulated in many ridges and unexpected hollows, but it never dropped away altogether; and steadily, though laboriously, Artorynas was gaining height. Now when he looked back, the plain was below him and the standing stones seemed no more than a grey detail on that great bare expanse. But from this elevated vantage point, a new thought came to him with the new perspective. He saw now more clearly how the saddle of land he had crossed was enclosed all around by the mountains, all except the one place by which he had climbed to it, the dale that led down to the river valley. And there seemed no way out of it, unless it were by scrambling up the slopes where he now stood, the slopes which, if he was right in his guess, would lead him to Aestron na Caarst. If this was so, then the level ground where the stones stood formed the final boundary between the wilderness and the lands of men. Was this the significance of the stones? He looked again at how they had been set to stand alone in the middle of that huge empty space with the hills looking on, almost as a storyteller would stand surrounded by his audience. Maybe this was the message that those who had raised them intended. We mark the edge of the world: pass us at your peril. Another long summer day was almost over and the glow of evening lay golden and benign as

Artorynas gazed out, but apprehension griped at his stomach when he glanced over his shoulder at the slopes behind him. Midsummer must be two weeks past by now. He had not even reached the northern wilderness yet, and there was still Asward donn'Ur to find. Renewed doubt gnawed at him. The stone circle was likely to be the last handiwork of men he saw, if he never returned; and with that his thoughts turned to Haldur, wondering how the companions from Rihannad Ennar were faring on their errand.

A new young friend

Far, far away in the south, there was a bustle of activity at a rather dingy *gradstedd* where a party of travellers intended to pass the night. Those who worked at the inn were well used to catering for military customers and the occasional civilian administrator passing on business, but a flurry of interest and excitement had broken out when they discovered that this time there were six men from Rihannad Ennar to be accommodated as well. Rumour of these strangers had run ahead of them down the road, and there was so much gawping from windows and peeping around doors that in the end the owner of the *gradstedd* had been forced to clip several ears in the kitchen and do a certain amount of shouting at the rest of his staff to make sure that they concentrated on their tasks. As Haldur went into the tack-room, a member of the escort who was already in there glanced round at him.

'Only another three days.'

Haldur paused in what he was doing and looked across at the other man. 'What, are we so near Caradriggan already?'

'No, no. I meant that's when we should be arriving at the border.'

During the course of their journey down the road, the men of their escort had become more relaxed about chatting with their charges; and as the days went by Haldur's present companion, a very young man, had become quite friendly with Tellapur in particular, being apparently of an age with him.

'You seem pleased about it,' said Haldur.

'Oh, well. It's going back home, isn't it? The thing is, if I get some time off when we're in the city, I'll be able to visit my family. See, I'm only doing military service for a year, like all younger sons have to. It's not been too bad, but I don't want to stay in the army permanently.'

Later, when they went to eat in the common room of the inn, Haldur waved the young fellow over to the bench where he sat with Tellapur and Aestrontor. They moved up to make room for him and soon he and Tellapur were laughing together while Haldur put in a word or two here and there and Aestrontor, as usual, ate in silence. The room was small, hot and noisy and the food nothing to get enthusiastic about. After a while, their companion from Caradriggan pushed his bowl away and leaned towards Haldur.

'This isn't much of a place, I know, but it'll be different in the city. Will you be staying at the *Sword and Stars* while you're there?'

'No, not according to what Valahald told me,' said Haldur. 'Apparently he's sent word on that we're to be quartered in Tellgard.'

'Oh! Oh, right. I didn't know that.'

Obviously embarrassed; he looked down at the table, blushing uncomfortably. The other three exchanged a swift glance and Aestrontor, without saying anything, quietly topped up the young fellow's drink to the full mark again. Tellapur covered the awkward moment.

'You'd recommend this *Sword and Stars* then, would you?'

'Well, most of us soldiers drink in the *Golden Leopard*, but everyone says the *Sword* is the best place – its reputation goes way back. I've never stayed there myself, it's very expensive. I'll tell you what, though!' He grinned at Tellapur, grateful to him for turning the conversation. 'If I get leave, I'll show you round the city, if you like. And I could take you to the *Sword*, I've a friend who works there – well actually he's a sort of second cousin. But anyway, Isteddar would see us right: the food's really good.'

Tellapur raised his cup. 'Thanks, I'll take you up on that. Where will we find you?'

The young man drank deeply in response; now he put down his own cup, shaking his head, and again Aestrontor plied the wine jug.

'No, I'll come to Tellgard for you. They'll not let you in to the barbican barracks to come calling on me.'

Haldur saw a chance to draw him out. 'In the Nine Dales our chief town is Cotaerdon, but I can tell from what I've heard that it's not to be compared with Caradriggan. We're all looking forward to seeing your city. Can you give us some idea of how big it is? How many people would you say it held?'

'Caradriggan?' The young fellow frowned in concentration, swallowing down more wine. 'Well, numbers-wise, I don't know. But say you walked round the walls, if you were to go all round the wall-walk on foot, including the battlement round the barbican and right round the south circuit as well where it looks down on Seth y'n Carad, if you went right round, it would take you all day.'

'What, you mean from dawn to dusk?'

They could see the drink beginning to slow their young companion down; he was taking longer to react to what was said to him, but something in this phrase of Haldur's seemed to catch his attention. He looked up.

'All day,' he mumbled, slurring slightly. 'That's what I'm saying, all day.' His voice fell away. 'I don't know why they've put you in Tellgard; I never thought I'd be going there again. I've not been inside for years, not since I was a boy at my lessons…' His head drooped onto his chest; then he spoke again, almost as if talking to himself.

'I don't want to stay in military service but I might have to. I don't see how I can support myself otherwise: the family business won't be able to feed another mouth. I thought, when we started farming the fields in Gwent y'm Aryframan… I asked to be stationed up here after I'd done my training… but the things I've seen… it's all gone wrong… my parents are frightened but it's all very well for old folk who'll be dead anyway before, before… there's something wrong. It's us young ones who should be afraid…'

With a sudden jerk of the head he sat upright again, staring round. 'What?'

'You were just saying how you might be able to show us around Caradriggan,' said Haldur.

'Yes... Yes, I'd be pleased to do that.' He wiped his forehead, looking faintly puzzled. 'It's hot in here. You fellows can certainly get through the drink. Maybe I'll just go outside for a bit and get some air.'

He lurched to his feet and Tellapur shoved a shoulder under his arm, easing him through the throng. Best to get him out of the door before the other members of the escort realised he was drunk.

Later, after the lamps were extinguished for the night they talked things over among themselves. Their beds were in a sleeping-barn at the side of the wagon-park, but although the soldiers were accommodated within the *gradstedd* itself, one of their number was out there, sitting with his back to the brazier, watching. Well, two could play at that game. Cathasar was keeping first guard for them, staying well back from the window, his eye on the wakeful soldier as the others lay down to rest.

'So the doubts are beginning to creep in,' said Asaldron thoughtfully. 'I'm glad to know some of them can feel remorse, even if they have to be drunk before they let it show.'

'One thing I wonder about is how much loyalty they'd show, if it came to it. Would they always obey orders without question, or have some of them started to think for themselves? These troops with us look to be decent enough, now they're away from Framstock. Maybe Valahald wouldn't be so smug if he knew his hold over them's not so tight once he's not around in person to enforce it.' This was Aestrontor, making by far his longest observation of the day.

'Valahald, huh! You don't know the half of it.' Ir'rossung laughed quietly in the darkness. 'They've got so used to assuming I can't hear them, that what I do hear can be pretty loose talk. They've come out with some choice stuff about Governor Valahald. Even the captain seems to hate him, and that time in the armoury when Valahald was so unpleasant about his brother's marriage, he was one of the fellows sniggering away at the joke. So either he's playing a double game with Valahald, or at the least his men believe he is, because they wouldn't speak as they do if they didn't trust him.'

Across the border

These words were to come vividly back into all their minds a couple of days later. They were riding along fairly slowly, Haldur and his companions staring before them in increasing wonder at the huge array of lights that had come into view, marking the distant border. Tellapur was listening to his young friend's description of the permanent encampments and patrol bases, the checkpoints and earthworks, when an urgent, almost panicky shout from behind them where one of the soldiers was riding, ostensibly as rearguard, alerted them to the news that Valahald himself had appeared on the southward road and was rapidly catching them up. The officer in charge swung round with an oath, barking at his men to get back into formation. In an instant the travellers from Rihannad Ennar found themselves within a hollow column of troops, backed off to the side of the road. As Valahald approached they drew themselves up to the salute. Acknowledging this, he sat for a moment in silence, looking them over. He's not ridden far today, thought Haldur, noting Valahald's smart, unstained turn-out, the fresh state of his horse, the comparative absence of dust and sweat. And he might be alone now, but he hasn't journeyed alone: where's all his gear? He's got no saddlebags or luggage.

'Not exactly pushing on at your best speed, are you, captain?' said Valahald.

'Just giving the horses a bit of a breather, sir. Didn't expect to see you here, sir. Don't like to see you taking the risk of riding alone.'

'I'm not alone, I've six men following from the last *gradstedd*. They'll be here shortly. But you surely don't think I feel threatened by any stray peasants left wandering about down here?'

Valahald glanced ahead to where the bulk of the Somllichan Ghent reared up, a dark mass against the dark sky. 'If they don't know by now what would happen to them if they raised their hands to me, they're even more stupid than I take them for. Well Haldur, we meet again sooner than I expected. I hope you've had a pleasant journey so far?'

'It's been agreeable enough; your men have been most courteous.'

'Really. Now, no doubt you're wondering what brings me here.' No-one made any response and Valahald smiled. 'I've things that need my attention in Caradriggan, so we might as well all travel forward together. Captain, I'll lead on now, so if you'd take three of the men and ride at the rear.'

'Sir.'

The column re-formed and the four men changed places. Under cover of the noise of hooves and harness Ir'rossung distinctly heard a savage mutter: *May the Waste take him.* Then Valahald gave the word and they all began to move again, but as the officer swung into his place at the rear Haldur saw him turn his head and spit with great accuracy into the dust where Valahald had reined in to speak to them.

Down to the border they rode, and through its intricate system of checks. The men of the Nine Dales gazed in disbelief at the vast banks and ditches gouged into the land, snaking away across the dim landscape as far as the eye could see and discernible beyond this by the lights that burned above them. They spent their first night within Caradward in the guest-wing of a large fort. It was comfortable, even luxurious compared with some of the inns they had recently patronised, spotlessly clean and with better food than they had been served for many days, but as they looked in one another's eyes they could read the thought that was in every man's mind. They would never be able to pass this fortified frontier without permission. How were they ever to get away and return to Rihannad Ennar if the Caradwardans chose to prevent them? But meanwhile, they had their onward road to think about. They discovered that business began very early in their new surroundings. While they were still finishing their morning meal next day, there was much shouting to be heard on the fort's parade-ground and from where they sat they could see many men hurrying back and forth across the courtyard.

'Come on, let's get moving. There's Valahald,' said Haldur. 'If we've got to put up with him all the way to Caradriggan, we don't want to start by giving him the chance to taunt us with sitting about over our bread.'

They made haste to get everything packed up and ready. When Cathasar and Aestrontor emerged from the stable block with their mounts and baggage animals, the rest of them were waiting in a corner of the yard with their gear piled up for loading. As they busied themselves with this, the captain of their escort from Framstock came up to them.

'We're ready now,' Haldur assured him, buckling down a loose strap.

'That's all right, they'll not be setting off for a moment or two yet,' said the man. 'I just came to wish you a smooth onward journey.' He held out his hand.

Haldur pushed his hair back, taken by surprise. 'You're not coming any further?'

'No, myself and six others are to go back to Framstock. Lord Valahald's replacing us with the men he brought down with him.'

'I see.' Haldur took the proferred hand. 'Well, thanks for your good wishes. Maybe we'll meet again when we go back north on our homeward journey.'

'Maybe.' The man hesitated, glancing about, and then seemed to come to a sudden decision. He turned back to Haldur. 'You'll likely run into a man called Heretellar in Caradriggan, especially if it's true what we hear, that you'll be staying in Tellgard. If you do, say Tirathalt was asking after him. We did our lessons together, when we were young boys, he might remember me. Tell him I often think about what we learnt then, these days.' With a nod of farewell, he turned and walked quickly away.

Soon they were passing through the main gate of the fort, riding more swiftly now on the main road to Caradriggan, leaving the lights and activity of the frontier zone behind. Valahald had increased the size of the party by a further detachment of troops requisitioned from the garrison of the fort, in addition to those who had accompanied him from Framstock. Watching him, Haldur wondered what had caused him to change his mind and come with them to Caradriggan. One thing at any rate was obvious: clearly Valahald intended to cut something of a dash when they arrived at the city. There was much traffic passing to and fro on the road and Valahald missed no chance either of forcing civilians and subordinates off the highway or of acknowledging the salutes of others. Towards the day's end a large open wagon passed them, heavily guarded. In it were a slumped a dozen or so people, including a white-haired old man, two or three women and a few youths barely out of boyhood. Most stared before them, their eyes dead in ashen faces, although one of the women was weeping quietly. Haldur turned in the saddle to look again. The Somllichan Ghent stood behind them now; in days when the light of evening filled the sky, their ruddy slopes would have glowed red in the sunset. As it was, Haldur saw only a black, crouching mass barely distinguishable from the dark clouds banked behind and above. But not far from the end of the mountain range, a deeper, more impenetrable blackness seemed to yawn from earth to sky, as if a vast door had opened in the night itself to reveal only the terror of the void beyond. He appealed to the soldier riding beside him.

'What in the name of the Starborn is that?'

'That? That's Assynt y'm Atrannaas.' The man kept his eyes on the road, but he jerked his head to indicate the wagon they had passed. 'That's where they'll be going.'

Haldur turned round again, but already the wagon was almost swallowed up in the dreadful darkness. And as Haldur stared in horror at Assynt y'm Atrannaas, so, far away in the pale twilight of the north, Artorynas scrambled to the top of the final ridge of his long climb and gazed at last on the endless expanse of Aestron na Caarst.

Chapter 46

Caradriggan at last

Now at last the city walls rose before them. On the final day of their journey they had turned off from the main thoroughfare and travelled for some distance out of their direct way on a minor road. Valahald had scheduled an extended halt in their progress at mid-day, during which his men had been ordered to spruce up their horses and turn out for inspection in dress uniform. Shortly thereafter they had climbed the embankment onto the great highway that ran north from Caradriggan to the gold mine in the forest, turning now towards the city. Valahald rode at the head of their small column, setting a smart pace and looking about him haughtily as other travellers scrambled to get out of his way. Behind him came his personal escort in close formation; the other troops formed a rearguard, with two men detailed to patrol up and down at each side, and between them were the wayfarers from Rihannad Ennar. As evening approached they drew near the north gate of the city. This opened into the great barbican, whose mighty battlemented walls were hung with torches and guarded by armed sentries. Haldur could see that though these men were staring down as openly as the gawping bystanders, all eyes slid blankly over themselves to linger on Valahald and his soldiers. They think we're just another gang of prisoners, thought Haldur; then suddenly it struck him that surely this lack of curiosity must mean it was not generally known that they had come all the way from Rihannad Ennar.

Once within the walls, it was the turn of Haldur and his companions to stare. The streets of the barbican were thronged with armed men, clamorous with all the sounds of a military establishment: marching feet, shouted orders, hammering and banging from workshops where armourers and smiths worked on into the evening. So far as they could see, these premises were the only signs of civilian life or commerce and even then, some artisans were clearly attached to the garrison if the badges above their doors were anything to go by. Occasionally an off-duty man passing them on foot would call out a greeting to a friend among the mounted party; Haldur heard the name of the *Golden Leopard* more than once as arrangements for later meetings were hastily agreed. Eventually they saw the inner gate in the distance, beyond which the city proper awaited. Haldur felt his heartbeat quicken in anticipation of his meeting with Arval, but no sooner had this thought crossed his mind than matters took an unexpected turn. The soldiers at the gate moved to bar their way and out from the guardroom strolled a man who, although bare-headed and only lightly-armed, was uniformed and had an air of authority about him. A perceptible frisson of surprise ran through their company at the sight of this man and Valahald's horse tossed its head with a snort as if his hand had jerked at the reins. Recovering himself instantly, Valahald saluted the newcomer as the gate guards also stood to attention. The man raised a hand in rather languid acknowledgement and told the guards to stand at ease, all the while looking over Haldur and his companions.

'Our visitors from the north, I assume,' he said, his head slightly tilted. 'And Valahald too! This is a pleasant surprise.'

He had a light, rather knowing voice and Haldur guessed immediately that, on the contrary, he had been expecting Valahald and was waiting in the barbican purposely to intercept him. 'You are Haldur, son of Carapethan? Welcome to Caradriggan. I am Valestron of Heranwark. Please, do proceed: they are waiting to receive you, up in Seth y'n Carad.'

So this was Valestron! Haldur had suspected it the moment he appeared.

'Good day and good health to you,' he replied, 'and our thanks for your welcome. But we understood that we were to be accommodated in Tellgard; has there been some change of plan?'

Somewhere behind him Haldur could hear a low mutter of voices but his attention was fixed on the two men before him. Valahald was clearly furious, although doing his best to conceal it. He jumped from his horse, throwing the reins to the trooper beside him, and stepped up to Valestron.

'I have already made all the necessary arrangements,' he began, sounding as though he spoke through gritted teeth, but Valestron cut across him.

'Lord Vorynaas insisted that men who had journeyed so far to reach Caradriggan must be his personal guests.' Valestron's voice seemed to hold some hint of private amusement, but everyone could see that part of the joke at least was obviously on Valahald.

'Wouldn't hear of anything else,' added Valestron blandly, telling the soldier nearest to him to move the party on. Again Valahald attempted to intervene, but Valestron put out a hand.

'Governor, just come into the guardroom here with me a moment. We've new passwords, you need to know what they are.' This was all the rest of them heard before the inner gates of the barbican were thrown wide to admit them to the streets of Caradriggan.

As they rode, Haldur was still thinking about the exchange they had just witnessed. He was glad now of a decision that he and his father had made. After Carapethan had made up his mind to send an embassy to the south, the two of them had discussed at some length the question of how much information about Caradward it would be wise for those travelling to have. With a certain amount of reluctance, Carapethan had agreed that it would be well for Haldur to learn as much as his friendship with Artorynas would permit; but for the others, he felt that within reason, the less each man knew, the better. Remembering to be constantly on guard against revealing that they knew more than they should was going to be difficult and dangerous and Carapethan was painfully conscious that this was a weak point in his plan. So it was, that while the others had all heard the fugitives' tales and were broadly familiar with what Artorynas had told the council, sometimes it was Haldur alone who needed to conceal his true thoughts as events unfolded, or to whom a new name meant more than simply a new face. He remembered what Artorynas had heard from the Outlanders who helped him, that a rivalry was brewing between Valahald and Valestron. Haldur sensed a likeness between the two. Had Valahald learnt his cruelty and coldness from Valestron, but strove now to make it a case of pupil outstripping the master? Maybe Valestron felt this too, and was determined to prevent it? It was apparent that though one or two of their escort had smirked covertly at Valahald's discomfiture, they all seemed afraid of Valestron. But now a man was tapping his arm, pointing. Seth y'n Carad lay ahead of them at the end of the street.

Festering resentment

Thaltor flicked a small silver coin to the young man clearing the supper dishes and settled back comfortably into his seat, cradling his drink and contemplating his dinner companion. Unlike Thaltor, Valahald had eaten his food without any sign that he even noticed what was on his plate, and was now glaring before him, throwing his drink down in angry silence. Thaltor could almost feel the waves of fury emanating from him. When he showed no sign of speaking, Thaltor broke the silence himself.

'Relax, man! Don't let Valestron get to you like this, it's exactly what he'd want.'

Valahald shot a contemptuous glance at Thaltor. 'It's all very well for you to talk. If you're happy with your place in life, that's up to you; some of us are more ambitious. How can you tolerate him anywhere near you? I know perfectly well you can't stand him, either.' He stood up. 'I'm going to tell them to keep me a room here.'

'No, you're not.' Thaltor pulled his companion back to his seat. 'That really would play right into his hands.'

'It's the only option. The *Leopard* is out of the question for me these days, so it'll have to be here at the *Sword*.'

'If you feel that strongly about it, why don't you stay at home while you're in the city? There'd be no loss of face that way.'

Valahald grimaced in distaste. 'Have sense, Thaltor! I'll not stay under my father's roof while that little tart shares his bed. How long has he been making a fool of himself with her?'

'Oh, not that long… Three, four months maybe.' Thaltor laughed. They had all derived a tremendous amount of malicious amusement at Valafoss' expense, ever since he'd begun trailing about after that girl of his. Or maybe waddling would be nearer the mark. Valafoss was so obese these days that whatever it was he did behind closed doors, and there had been much lewd speculation on that subject, Thaltor was expecting to hear at any moment that his exertions had caused him to drop dead. But to install the girl in his house! She looked to be younger even than Heranar: Valafoss must be really besotted. He laughed again, landing a friendly punch on Valahald's arm.

'You want to hope he doesn't marry her, eh?'

'By my right hand!' Valahald's head jerked round. 'That's it, that's what she'll be after. It's got to be his money, it can't be for any other reason. Well, at least coming down to Caradriggan means I've found out in time to do something about it. Heranar's nearly as bad, marrying the daughter of that peasant from the hill country and producing all those children. Do you know he's got three now? Barely a year between them, and all girls. He and my father reflect badly on me, they're an embarrassment.'

'Well, if you're so concerned about the family honour, you want to think again about flouncing off to the *Sword and Stars*. You're going to come back up to Seth y'n Carad tonight, you can have my guest-room. You won't have to see Valestron except at this reception tomorrow evening and if you don't want to talk to him then, it'll be easy enough to avoid him. He'll be off again to Rigg'ymvala before long, you'll get your chance to impress Vorynaas. But meanwhile, we've the evening before us, yet. Let's order up some more drink and then you can put me in the picture about these birds of passage who've blown in on the north wind.'

Much later, as Valahald made to enter his bedroom in the officer-in-command's guest suite, up in Seth y'n Carad, he turned to bid Thaltor good night.

'You know, I have things how I want them within the governor's residence in Framstock, true; but once out of its doors, there's nowhere to compare with Caradriggan. Where else would you get service like we had in the *Sword* tonight? That young fellow who looked after us, very attentive… That's civilisation for you. You're lucky to be based here in the city, Thaltor; I could almost envy you your contentment.'

'Valahald, please! You've had one too many, that's all. Don't get sentimental, it doesn't suit you.'

With a grin, Thaltor closed the door of his room. He was still smiling as he lay down to sleep. Valahald certainly had a very high opinion of himself; imagine making that conceited crack about the *Leopard*! But for all that, thought Thaltor, I'd still rather have him than Valestron. Although who could say which of them would climb highest, in the end? Perhaps Vorynaas would play them off one against the other. Thaltor turned over, yawning, and a final drowsy thought drifted through his mind. It would be best for himself to keep in with both his younger colleagues, for the time being at any rate.

In spite of Thaltor's joke at his expense, Valahald was far from drunk. Loss of control was not his style and while it was true that he could feel the effects of what he'd consumed, his head cleared very quickly. In the quiet of the night he sat on his bed, fully dressed, thinking over the events of the day and considering his next move. He was still seething with rage at the way Valestron had pulled rank on him, appearing at the inner gate of the barbican like that to send the travellers from Rihannad Ennar up to Seth y'n Carad. I should never have dismounted, thought Valahald. If I'd stayed on the horse, I could have just ridden off with them; he wouldn't have been able to stop me. As it was, he made me trail after him to learn new passwords like some raw recruit; and then he enjoyed himself at my expense over my father's ludicrous behaviour! Getting to his feet, Valahald went over and drew the curtain aside, breathing quickly with renewed anger. For a few moments he stood at the window, looking down on the compound where lights burned and sentries paced to and fro across the gate and armed men guarded the doors to the granaries and store-vaults. Memories flitted through his mind. It was not so very long ago since he himself had been officer-in-charge here, and occupied this suite of rooms; it was within these living-quarters that Ghentar and he had quarrelled, and he had first begun to tighten his grip on Vorynaas' heir. So much had happened since, that these episodes now seemed like scenes from another life. If Ghentar had succeeded in eliminating Maesrhon and had not himself been killed, Valahald thought bitterly, his position would have been unchallenged, and my hold over him unassailable. And then where would Valestron be today? Letting the curtain fall again, Valahald threw his clothes onto the stand and climbed into bed. Get some rest, he told himself. You're going to need all your wits about you during this visit to Caradriggan.

A cold mind at work

By mid-morning next day he was making for the barbican gate as fast as he could walk through the crowded city streets. Running into Valestron again was a risk he would just have to take: he needed to send out a courier to Heranar as soon as possible, so it made sense to make use of the barbican garrison's office facilities too. Clerks scrambled to supply him with desk-space and writing materials and then, exchanging curious glances among themselves, settled back to their own work as quietly as possible. They knew only too well what could follow if an already irritated officer was provoked further, and as Valahald scribbled furiously, frequently crossing out words and starting again, they could see his temper was on the edge. Suddenly ripping up what he had written so far, Valahald sat back, drumming his fingers on the arm of his chair, staring into space with narrowed eyes. How could he convey what he had seen at their father's house? Valafoss had been already seriously overweight the last time Valahald had seen him, but now he was grotesquely fat, a sweating, panting mass of lard. What a monument to massive self-indulgence! How could a man inflict such indignity on himself? And the girl was scarcely into her third ten years and maybe even younger – Valafoss was old enough to be her grandfather! Valahald's mind shied away from imagining what they did together: he felt his own body shrivel at the thought. He bent to his writing again. It was essential that Heranar realised the implications of the situation, that the brothers united in their opposition to any idea of their father making a second marriage. Yes, Heranar had children of his own, he wouldn't want to lose the chance of his shared inheritance. Valahald signed off his message with an insincere appeal along those lines, and sealing it up hurried away to despatch it by the speediest military post.

Having concluded his business, he found himself at something of a loss as to how to spend his day. Going back to his father's house was unthinkable, and returning to Seth y'n Carad held no appeal either; but he would have to be there at evening for the formal reception, so that ruled out a large meal in the *Sword* at mid-day. A mental image of Valafoss floated before his mind's eye. Would his father be there tonight, his snout in the trough? He shuddered with disgust at the thought. For some moments Valahald stood staring into a shop, seeing nothing of the goods on display. He might have passed the time in strolling through the city's markets or walking around the walls, but it was likely that this was exactly what the party from Rihannad Ennar would be doing and the last thing he wanted was for any chance encounter to remind them of the humiliation he had endured in their presence. A fresh tide of fury washed over Valahald, but its waves were colder now and retreated more quickly. Thaltor had been right, he would get his chance with Vorynaas;

it was just a question of being patient and, more importantly, being prepared. Maybe he would go to the *Sword* after all. He would have a session in the steam-room and a massage, and then instead of a meal, he would… Rounding a corner as he set off again, Valahald walked straight into Forgard. Each man automatically put out a hand to the other with an apology and then stepping back, saw with whom he had collided. Forgard was the first to recover, with a nod and smile of unusual warmth before going swiftly on his way. Valahald watched him for a moment, a frown deepening between his eyes. What did Forgard have to be so cheerful about?

He had always thought of Forgard as being older than his own father, probably because of his prematurely silver hair; but they were actually more or less of an age and now, white hair or no, he looked years younger and unquestionably fitter. Valahald turned back into his own path, smirking slightly to himself as he remembered the stories he had heard in his childhood. No wonder Forgard was so lean: what a fool, to have turned down the chance of buying into all the new developments when he had the opportunity! These days his estates could be producing very little in the way of either food or money. I wonder if the worthy Heretellar is in town, thought Valahald, or still stuck down there in the Ellanwic breeding mules for the pack-trains. Suddenly he recalled something he had not thought of in years, that Forgard had lost a child to the spring sickness people still spoke of with fear and sorrow. If the boy had lived, Heretellar as the second son would have been compelled to do military service. Valahald acknowledged the salute of a passing group of half a dozen soldiers, imagining the pleasure he would have derived from being able to make Heretellar obey him. But all this daydreaming had interrupted his thoughts. At the *Sword* there was an old crone whose speciality was secret Outland herbal recipes and remedies. He would lay in a supply of one of her concoctions, one to depress his appetite but sharpen and clear his mind, so that when his chance came with Vorynaas, he would be ready to seize the moment of opportunity.

Arval hears the news

Meanwhile Forgard had arrived at Tellgard, only to discover that Arval, usually free at this time of day, was teaching. He was covering for a colleague who was unwell; this instructor in turn was being treated in the medical wing as students looked on, taking notes and occasionally assisting. Knowing that he would have been watched, even though he spent time in Tellgard almost every day, Forgard withdrew into the communal study room next to the library so that anyone looking through the colonnade from the street would not see him obviously waiting to speak with Arval. Forgard turned the pages of a book, attempting to distract himself from impatience at the delay, but time seemed to crawl by. At last he saw movement outside as people passed to and fro across the exercise court and Arval himself approached the entrance to the tower. Forgard ran softly up the stair after him and tapped at his study door. Dispensing with any kind of greeting, he came straight to the point.

'Arval! There are men here in the city from Rihannad Ennar!'

The deep, dark eyes widened in Arval's thin face. 'The Nine Dales! Quick, Forgard, tell me all you know!'

Forgard sat down but had hardly begun his tale before he was on his feet again, pacing the room. In him alone had Arval confided, sharing the secret that when Artorynas left Caradriggan he had gone north in search of the Nine Dales; and Forgard had held this trust in the highest honour, keeping his knowledge from all, even from Ancrascaro and Rhostellat, even from Heretellar his own son. It meant more to him than he could say that now, when after the years of waiting there were tidings at last, it had fallen to him to bring the news to Arval.

'I have it from Isteddar. He called to see his family, he's not on duty at the *Sword* this morning because he was working there until late last night. He was saying that Thaltor was there with Valahald; they had supper and then sat drinking together. He served their table, he heard parts of what they said to each other. Apparently Valahald escorted them down to the city himself, they arrived yesterday evening and…'

'Where are they now?'

'They were taken up to Seth y'n Carad, but…'

'How many of them are there? Where are they today? I must speak with them. Somehow, I must speak with them!'

'It's a party of six, apparently. No, wait, Arval, let me finish what I'm trying to tell you! While Isteddar was at my place chatting to his mother in the kitchen, a young fellow arrived, an acquaintance of his, asking to speak to him. They'd sent him over from the *Sword*, when he turned up there expecting to see Isteddar. He'd come from the barbican garrison, but he's only there for the time being; he was one of those in the escort who rode down from Framstock. He's not much more than a boy, he's just doing his year of service; but it seems he's made friends with the youngest of those from the Nine Dales as they got talking along the way, and he'd offered to show them round the city. He wanted to explain to Isteddar that they might come down to the *Sword* to ask him to get a message passed on, so he would know where and when to meet them.'

'Why all this complication?' asked Arval who, though listening intently, seemed a little puzzled.

'Oh, Arval.' Forgard sat down, laughing. 'The lad's only a conscript, he's not going to go anywhere near Seth y'n Carad unless somebody sends him under orders, and any stranger who went knocking on the barbican gate asking for him would get sent packing without much ceremony. But all that's of no consequence. The interesting thing is what I found out from the boy: which was that originally, the men from the Nine Dales were to be quartered here, here in Tellgard, and on Valahald's orders! He sent them off from Framstock with these instructions, and then I gather that for some reason he came after them, caught them up and took over the escort himself; but no sooner had they arrived in the city than Valestron intercepted them and diverted the party off up to Seth y'n Carad. Hence, of course, all this rigmarole about leaving messages, when the young fellow realised he couldn't just come here and meet his new friend.'

Arval smiled slightly. 'I imagine it would not go down too well with Valahald, finding his orders countermanded by Valestron.'

'That's right. I got a fairly graphic description in my own kitchen this morning, but I'd already heard from Isteddar that Valahald was raging about it to Thaltor yesterday evening. Incidentally, I bumped into him on my way here.'

'Mm.' Arval sat in silence for a moment, staring before him, his fingers massaging his temples. 'Let me make sure I've got all this right. Six men from Rihannad Ennar turn up in Framstock. Valahald sends them to Tellgard. Valestron blocks this and sweeps them off to Seth y'n Carad. Do you know anything about how they got to Framstock and why?'

'Only what Isteddar's young friend had heard, that Heranar intercepted them on the northern border and sent them down under escort. They said they'd come to renew ties of old kinship in Gwent y'm Aryframan, but no doubt they found out fairly quickly there was no hope of that. Now it seems they're keen to see Caradriggan before they go back home.'

Forgard and Arval looked at each other. After a moment, Arval got to his feet and began moving about the room, touching the books on the shelves gently in passing as if this helped him to think.

'Valestron and Valahald scoring points off one another is nothing new: we've all seen them striving to obtain the upper hand. This business of Valahald taking over the escort himself is rather odd, though. It looks as though initially he had no intention of coming to Caradriggan and then changed his mind. Maybe it was something to do with the situation involving his father.'

'Possibly. I forgot to mention it, but Isteddar said he was fuming about that too, in the last night with Thaltor.'

'Yes… Anyway, two things about all this stand out in my mind. The first is that these men from the Nine Dales have been under guard from the moment they encountered Heranar. Whether they wanted to see Caradriggan or not, it's obvious they were going to be brought here. This suggests to me that, for whatever reason, they are being viewed with distrust. But the second thing is the strangest of all: that Valahald should send them to Tellgard. We know what he thinks of our work here, and his opinion of me. And he knows perfectly well how difficult it would have been for us to feed six extra mouths, to accommodate guests adequately. So therefore his intention must have been to embarrass and discredit Tellgard, and insult the travellers from the Nine Dales. Why would he want to do that? The only reason I can think of is that they must have annoyed him in some way: belittled him, perhaps, or made him look foolish in public.'

'Well, think how Vorynaas judges everyone by his own standards. He's untrustworthy himself, therefore he in turn trusts no-one; and you may be sure his subordinates have learnt to follow his lead in this. But there is one good thing, though.' Arval turned at the eager note in Forgard's voice.

'If Valahald was going to put the men from Rihannad Ennar in Tellgard to satisfy his malice, clearly he had no reason to suspect that speaking with them was the one thing you would have most wished for. So I can't see him stopping them, if they come to Tellgard of their own accord. The opportunity to meet them might arise quite naturally.'

'Valestron might prevent them, though, or Vorynaas.' Arval sat down again with a snap of laughter. 'I never thought I'd be taking sides in the power struggle between Valahald and Valestron, but on this occasion at least I have to hope that Valahald will win the day.'

Sightseeing

As Arval and Forgard spoke together in Tellgard, and Valahald lay on the massage table in the bath-house of the *Sword and Stars*, Haldur and his companions were being shepherded along a section of the wall walk by Thaltor. Looking down from up there, they saw that Escanic, their young friend from Framstock, had not exaggerated the size of Caradriggan. A bewildering maze of streets and buildings spread out below them: houses, shops, halls, towers, with here and there a courtyard, a market or an open square; all was hung with lamps and lights, and a smog spread out over all, its reek drifting up to them where they stood, along with the never-ceasing undertone of thousands of people going about their daily business.

'It's like a beehive, or an anthill,' said Cathasar, and Thaltor smiled indulgently. Really, these northerners were like children, overawed by their first sight of a city!

Asaldron had turned away and was leaning against the battlements. 'Are there are other cities like this in Caradward?' he asked.

'Caradriggan is the biggest,' replied Thaltor, 'but there's Staran y'n Forgarad as well, away in the south, and Heranwark to the west. And of course there are many smaller towns throughout the country.'

'And what lies beyond Caradward?'

Thaltor eyed Tellapur, beginning to wish the travellers had been left to make the best of it in Tellgard: they could have had as many geography lessons as they wanted there.

'Nothing worth bothering about,' he said rather shortly. 'There's a few Sigitsaran down in the south, in the Outlands; nomads mostly, wandering through the scrub. And to the north there's Maesaldron, and beyond that the wilderness.'

He had tried to suppress it, but fear of the forest was bred into the bones of all Caradwardans and they had heard it in his voice.

'Is that what the walls are for, to protect you from whatever lurks in the forest? Or do you expect some threat from elsewhere?'

Thaltor was already aware of a faint dislike for Aestrontor, and at these words he felt it intensify. 'Of course not,' he said with an aggressive stare. 'Who do you think would dare attack Caradward?'

He fiddled with one of the many gold rings he was wearing, allowing his eyes to travel over the plain attire of his companions, and then pointed to the north. 'The gold mine is in the forest; the bullion comes in to the city down the road there, in through the barbican gate.'

At these words all of them except Ir'rossung turned to look out towards the north road. Thaltor ran his hands through his hair, fighting boredom and irritation. Look at them, he thought, staring like cows at a gate – all except the old boy, of course, so deaf he hasn't even heard what we've been talking about. How much more of this am I going to have to put up with? His gloom deepened further when Haldur spoke.

'You know, Thaltor, we might have to spend quite a while here so as to wait for the right time to cross Na Caarst again on our way home. Do you think we'll be able to visit the other parts of your land, maybe see the other cities too?'

Thaltor's heart sank. Showing them round Caradriggan was bad enough, escorting them the length and breadth of the country was too dire to even contemplate.

'Maybe, I don't know. That would be for Lord Vorynaas to say.'

'Why haven't we seen Vorynaas yet? In Rihannad Ennar, Carapethan always greets his guests in person.'

'Is that so, young man?' Thaltor looked Tellapur up and down. 'Well, you're not in the Nine Dales now. Lord Vorynaas is an extremely busy man, he delegates less pressing tasks. He'll greet you formally this evening at the reception to welcome you to the city. Shall we go down from the wall now? You might want to take a look at the horse-market, and you should see the review ground, and of course the Open Hall.'

After an hour or so of wandering to and fro in the mart, Thaltor's patience finally ran out. Why was it that he always got the really tedious jobs that nobody else wanted? If his charges were set on examining every beast on offer, then as far as he was concerned they could get on with it. He was off to the *Golden Leopard* for a much-needed drink in more congenial company, and Vorynaas could say whatever he liked: Thaltor was sick of being taken for granted. He muttered a perfunctory comment or two about meeting up at supper time and then strode off. They watched him disappear into the crowd and then Ir'rossung turned to Haldur.

'What about it, then? Shall we ask someone to direct us to Tellgard?'

'No, I don't think so, we don't want to attract too much attention by going straight there. Let's get this evening over with first, find out what we're up against in Vorynaas, and see if we can't get some idea of why he blocked Valahald's orders.'

Cathasar snorted with laughter. 'The look on his face when that fellow Valestron appeared and flattened his crest for him! It cheers me up every time I think about it.'

They grinned at each other as they strolled along, sharing the joke. Suddenly Tellapur pointed up the street.

'Look! That must be the *Sword and Stars* that Escanic told us about. Why don't I go in and leave a message for him, like he asked me to?'

'Yes, all right. We'll go back to that little square with the seats that we passed, and wait for you there. Oh, and there's something else,' added Haldur. 'We've got that message to pass on from Tirathalt, if we can. Find out whether Isteddar knows Heretellar, or can tell us where to find him.'

Tellapur was gone for much longer than they expected, but just as they were beginning to get anxious he reappeared.

'I've had a real piece of luck,' he announced. 'I've met someone who knows Arval, who spends time in Tellgard every day! Isteddar wasn't in the *Sword*: they said he was off duty this morning, but they directed me to a house where his mother's the cook, and when I asked there for him, they showed me through to the kitchen where he was talking to her. I introduced myself and he said Escanic had called earlier, so he knew all about putting us in touch if we want to meet him. I told him that Thaltor had shown us round a bit already, then I mentioned the message for Heretellar; and not only did Isteddar know who he was, but didn't it turn out that he's the son of Forgard, whose house we were actually sitting in! And when I asked if I could see Forgard to give him the message, because it seems Heretellar doesn't live in the city but away south on the family estates, Isteddar told me that he'd gone over to Tellgard and offered to take me there. Just as we approached, Forgard came out, and I gave him Tirathalt's message for his son.'

'What's Tellgard like? Did you go in?' asked Asaldron eagerly.

'No, I talked to Forgard in the street. Tellgard... Well, I was surprised. You can see what it must have been like, once, but now it's quite dilapidated and I'd say it could do with some urgent maintenance work. But there's something else.' Tellapur looked at Aestrontor and Haldur.

'The whole place is one vast *numiras*. You can't mistake it: I've never recognised the sign so strongly, not even up in the mountains or the woods. When I told him I sensed a place that had known the footsteps of the As-Geg'rastigan, Forgard wanted me to go in with him, but I explained that you were waiting and I'd already been gone much longer than I expected. Then he said that Arval would want to talk with us, giving me a brief explanation of who Arval is, and told me that they'd have a message sent over to Seth y'n Carad. I hope I've done the right thing – I know we decided we wouldn't go to Tellgard today.'

'Don't worry, you couldn't have done better.' Haldur smiled, feeling a lot more cheerful. 'Maybe things are running in our favour after all: look how quickly we've been led to Arval without having to contrive it, in spite of all that Valestron and the others could do. Come on, let's walk on again and see what there is to see. It will help when we have to make conversation this evening; I'm sure I don't need to remind you all to be very careful in what you say.'

'And don't let's forget that even though Thaltor may have lost interest in us, it's likely we're being watched,' said Aestrontor. 'I'm certain we were under observation this morning, in that room where we ate, up in Seth y'n Carad.'

In Seth y'n Carad

Eventually the hour of their much-heralded meeting with Vorynaas arrived. This took place in an audience chamber which, like much else in Seth y'n Carad, was too ostentatious to be truly impressive. The same could not, however, be said of Vorynaas. He was in his late sixties now, but could have passed for ten years younger. Although slightly heavier than in his youth, he carried the extra weight easily with his powerful, stocky build. His hair and beard were brindled where grey had invaded the glossy chestnut tones, but his thick eyebrows were still dark, arching sardonically over the dark, dangerous eyes. Like his associates and supporters, he was richly dressed and adorned. His robes were of a heavy green brocaded fabric, elaborately pleated in the sleeves and skirt; there was gold woven into the collar and fastenings, and gold gleamed at his wrists and neck; but he had known when to stop, unlike Thaltor, whose fingers and arms were loaded with more rings than good taste indicated. Valestron was in uniform, and Valahald, who was wearing his governor's chain of office, had rendered his lack of colour curiously sinister by dressing in plain, darkest blue from head to foot. Haldur saw immediately that whatever tensions might simmer between Vorynaas' subordinates, none of them thought to rival the man himself, at least not yet: it was his presence that dominated the room.

As he introduced his companions, Haldur looked them over with pride and affection. Plain and drab though they might seem amidst all this finery, he knew their true worth. Suddenly conscious of the weight of the gold torc on his own neck, he thought of his father, far away in Rihannad Ennar. He and Vorynaas were of comparable height and build and wore their authority with the same easy strength. Yet whereas men looked for Carapethan's approval out of love and loyalty, Haldur saw that in Caradward fear was the driving force in any attempt to impress Vorynaas and win his favour. He looked again at Vorynaas, unable to decide whether it was the similarity or the difference between him and Carapethan that struck him most. It was as if Vorynaas and he were two aspects of the same person, but Vorynaas was the dark twin who stood in the shadow cast by the warm sun of Carapethan. Haldur's heart went out to his father, who would be counting the hours until his return; and then, unwillingly, he was aware of a tiny stirring of pity within him for Vorynaas. Powerful, unassailable, wealthy beyond counting he might be, but he was alone: he had no wife to love him, no son to come after him, no friend to stand beside him. Then Haldur felt the touch of Vorynaas' black, probing gaze, and memories passed through his mind: all that he had heard from Artorynas of the deeds and actions that lay to Vorynaas' account. Dealing with this menacing man would bring them into the greatest jeopardy of their mission. They must never lower their guard.

The folding doors were now pushed back to admit servants who scurried through from the kitchens to set out the food on tables placed around the room. There was a mixture of hot and cold dishes, arranged so that the guests could serve themselves as they wished. In addition to the visitors from the Nine Dales and Vorynaas' immediate entourage, about twenty other people were present. Most of them ate standing, moving about and drifting from one group to another as the conversation flowed; but there was a grossly overweight man who loaded his plate and then sat in a corner eating voraciously, largely ignored by the rest of the company. Haldur was astonished to learn that this was Valahald's father but realised before long that some estrangement divided them. The younger man kept well away, occasionally talking to Thaltor but mostly standing alone, slightly withdrawn from the rest of the company. How unbearable it would have been, thought Valahald, if his father had shamed him further by bringing that girl with him; but fortunately, with the exception of some of the servants, this was an all-male gathering. Asaldron now walked over to him, remarking on this very fact.

'Well, Lord Vorynaas is a widower,' said Valahald with a shrug, 'so it would be discourteous on an occasion such as this for other men to bring their wives. Thaltor is unmarried, as I am myself. Presumably the custom is different in your homeland? But in any case, I understand from my brother that you too are all single men.'

'Yes, though Heranar seemed keen to impress upon us the delights of family life,' smiled Asaldron. 'What about Valestron? Does he have sons who will follow him into military life?'

Asaldron saw Valahald's eyes flick briefly in Valestron's direction but his voice was expressionless.

'My brother has rushed into marriage unusually young, especially for a man with a career to think of: I myself do not intend to select a wife until the end of my fourth ten years. Excuse me please, I see a colleague with whom I must speak.'

He moved off, but Asaldron saw that he sought no-one out for conversation. Haldur was talking to Vorynaas, so Asaldron joined Cathasar at a side table to replenish his plate.

'There's certainly no love lost between Valahald and Valestron, is there?' he began, but feeling Cathasar's elbow in his ribs he changed tack as Thaltor approached them.

'I was just wondering what it is that flavours this particular dish?'

'Lemons,' said Thaltor, helping himself. 'Preserved lemons. Imported from the Outlands in the south, they're a very expensive delicacy. I take it they're new to you?'

'They are, but then many of the dishes we've been served tonight are unusual to us. The flavours are more pungent than we're used to at home, and certainly the style of cooking is more complex and elaborate than anything we've seen as we've journeyed down through Gwent y'm Aryframan, or even here in Caradward until now.'

'Remember it's Lord Vorynaas who's your host, he won't compromise on standards. You'll get only the best of everything in Seth y'n Carad.'

'One thing I've observed, and that's the amount and variety of bread on offer tonight.' Aestrontor spoke from behind them, where he had been standing unnoticed. 'If bread's a luxury, you've got a problem here. I suppose that's why Vorynaas has armed guards on his granaries, to protect what he's got stored if the wheat won't grow.'

For a moment or two Thaltor stood speechless. He had been enjoying a comfortable feeling of superiority at what he saw as these bumpkins' ignorance and was temporarily taken aback by Aestrontor's bluntness. Now his simmering dislike of the man boiled over. He thrust his head forward.

'Who says it won't grow? And how do you know what the men are guarding? Don't you be so sure of yourself, fellow.'

Aestrontor laughed. He leaned forward to pick up a small loaf and broke it open. The smell of new-baked bread curled into their senses and Aestrontor felt his mouth water, even though his appetite had been satisfied.

'It's easy enough to work out. Only a precious commodity would be kept so secure, and you've already told us all about the gold mine and showed us the bullion vaults. What else could there be that's so valuable here? We've ridden a long road, down from the far north to this city. Do you think we heard nothing along the way, that we didn't see the empty new granary in Framstock and the barren fields of Gwent y'm Aryframan?'

'Gwent y'm Aryframan is a name of history only: you have travelled through our provinces of Rossaestrethan and Rosmorric. You need to remember that, and there's something else I might remind you of.' Thaltor's arm rings rang together as he placed his hands on his hips. 'You are guests here, you should take care that your comments do not cause offence. Wait until you see the growing-houses in the Cottan na Salf before you start making assumptions about our grain supplies.'

'In Rihannad Ennar men speak their minds plainly, whether in conversation with neighbours or standing before Lord Carapethan. Perhaps you should remember the courtesy expected from a host, and not address me as *fellow* when you've been introduced to me by name.' Hearing the faint chime from Thaltor's rings, Aestrontor laughed again. 'Gold is beautiful and endures for ever once it is won from the ground, unlike grain; but men cannot eat it. I would wager that these growing-houses are not producing much wheat and that what there is comes straight here. It's not only beyond, in your – provinces – that men mutter about the poor fare set before them.'

'You'd not have eaten this well in Tellgard, that's certain,' snarled Thaltor, losing his temper completely.

Cathasar and Asaldron, initially surprised and alarmed at this exchange, realised that Aestrontor, usually so silent, had lifted a huge burden from them. It would be safe now for all of them to know about the grain shortage, after he had managed to bring the subject out into the open. Asaldron spoke up.

'We thought that's where we would be staying. Do you know why Valahald was so put out, when Valestron brought us here instead?'

Mention of this name brought Thaltor up short. He remembered past occasions when he had been taunted by Valestron for being unable to keep a grip on his emotions and sure enough, when he glanced across the room, there was Valestron, watching them with that knowing look on his face. Thaltor knew where his loyalties lay: first to himself, and then to Vorynaas. He had risen to a position of wealth and comfort by backing Vorynaas, and he wanted to hold on to what he had. Vorynaas had told him to mingle with the guests, picking up what information he could. Tomorrow there was to be a meeting where they would all compare their impressions and it was not going to go down well if he had to report that he had rowed with one of the newcomers. He glanced in Valestron's direction again and saw him beginning to head towards them. Instant evasive action was clearly called for. Thaltor forced himself to relax and smile.

'Ah, he's young for the responsible position he holds, I suppose it's not surprising if he's touchy about his dignity. Aestrontor, you're right. Plain talking never hurt anyone, we're all friends here. Enjoy the rest of the evening. Now, Cathasar, there's something over here you should try…'

With an affable nod to the other two, Thaltor took Cathasar by the elbow and steered him away as Valestron came up; and Vorynaas, now standing alone for a moment in thought, one hand to his beard, read the patterns that formed before him as men grouped and re-grouped in their talk.

Chapter 47

The hidden watcher

Forgard's point about Vorynaas' lack of trust, even in his own associates, had been shrewdly made. He was spying on them now, while they waited for him to join them, watching them through the squint whose existence still remained a secret: the masons who had been ordered to insert this unofficial addition to the building plans had long since been disposed of, despatched to the mine, eliminated and forgotten. Vorynaas kept the knowledge of it to himself alone, never shared or revealed. He looked down to where his closest supporters awaited him. Valafoss was not present, having indeed not been sent for. His behaviour the previous evening had been the last straw, as far as Vorynaas was concerned. If his appetites had mastered him to the extent it appeared, then let him dig his grave with his teeth if his breath was not stopped first in some bout of rutting. No, he had served his purpose; it was his sons with whom Vorynaas would deal in future. A brief snort of laughter escaped him as his eye fell on Valahald, sitting half turned away from Valestron. Theirs was a rivalry that he must watch carefully; he was not prepared to tolerate either of them becoming powerful enough to challenge himself. He knew that he could still inspire fear in both of them if he needed to, and it was his intention to maintain this hold. Vorynaas glanced now at Thaltor, lounging casually in his seat; and his mind turned back to the previous morning, when he had spied also on his guests from the north, after they were shown into the same small room and invited to help themselves from the food set out for them.

Having carefully read and re-read the reports which had come to him from Heranar and Valahald, Vorynaas had matched their accounts to the men before him, observing, assessing. Watching covertly, he saw how they looked to Haldur for a lead, but showed him no apparent deference, and his mouth set scornfully. This homespun fellow was in line for the lordship of his land, was he? Then something had happened to put a seed of doubt in Vorynaas' easy contempt. He found himself watching another man, who ate his breakfast without speaking. This fellow had a self-sufficient air and carried himself as though he might have spent time under arms, but what attracted Vorynaas' attention was the way his eyes roved around the room. After a while he stood up and went over to look out of the window; then he actually opened the door and put his head round it briefly. Returning to his seat, he spoke to Haldur and it seemed he posed a question, for Haldur broke off his own conversation, cocking his head as if listening. He turned to the other man, nodding slowly; then as they both began to look about them keenly, their gaze locked directly with Vorynaas' watching eyes. Though he knew he was hidden from them, in spite of himself Vorynaas had moved back a little.

He saw then that he might have underestimated Haldur. Laughing with his fellows, eating with them companionably, he had seemed ordinary and of little account; but now that his face was alert it held a strength and some other, indefinable quality that he shared only with the man who had spoken to him. There was some bond between them that the others had no part in. Vorynaas switched his attention to what were clearly the oldest and the youngest men in the group. The older man seemed to be offering comfort of some kind as the other, really scarcely more than a youth, sat picking at his food. Suddenly the boy's face brightened as if at some shared joke and they laughed together; but then Vorynaas saw the young man sigh deeply and sit back from the table. He pointed here and there as if indicating items in the room and then made a dismissive gesture; the other man shook his head with a shrug and patted him on the shoulder. Vorynaas had wished he could hear what was being said. Unless he was much mistaken, these fellows enjoying his food and drink were finding fault of some kind with his hospitality. His brows drew down as the anger smouldered in his hot, dark eyes. Then Thaltor had come into the room below, and after a few moments of greeting and introduction, the visitors and he all left together.

Vorynaas lingered for a few more moments in his private chamber, reviewing this scene in his mind, setting it against the impressions he had formed at first-hand during the reception the previous evening. That fellow Aestrontor, now... Vorynaas smiled to himself. It had certainly not taken long for Thaltor to cross swords with him. Then suddenly his face changed. For some reason, contemplation of Thaltor had triggered the memory of a long-ago conversation in which his old friend had suggested that Vorynaas should marry again. At the time this had seemed preposterous, but, thought Vorynaas now, if I had known then what would happen to Ghentar, maybe I should not have dismissed the idea so quickly. I could have had other sons scarcely five years younger than he, who would have been coming to manhood by now. Abruptly, Vorynaas got to his feet. The unaccustomed bleakness that had shown in his eyes was gone. Why should I care who or what comes after me, he said in his heart. After I am dead, will it matter to me whether it is my son or another man's who takes my place? The past is over, the future cannot be known: the present is all, and it is mine. Slamming the door behind him, he descended the stair, invigorated by this ruthless exercise of his will, and smiled knowingly to see the men who sat waiting for him start with surprise and fright as he appeared without warning among them. But though Vorynaas might tell himself the years gone by were finished and done with, there were parts of his own past that had never been brought to a full conclusion and he carried them within him still, like a sickness in remission that could wake again to malignant life. There were faces that lurked in the shadows of his memory, voices that called from its darkest corners: ignore them though he might, they were never entirely banished. But long practice had enabled him to divert his thought if ever it strayed near these danger areas and it was the ingrained habit of years that now automatically blanked the names of Numirantoro, Arymaldur and Maesrhon from his mind. Vorynaas sat down at the head of the table and called the meeting to order.

A weary vigil

In Aestron na Caarst, Artorynas peered out from a tiny cave at the foot of a low cliff, trying to force down his fear and tackle the new day's journey. He wondered whether it would be better or worse for him, if he were to get a sight of whatever it was that had made the terrible sound he had heard now for a second time. He swallowed convulsively, sick and appalled but thankful for the meagre shelter that the rocks provided. On the first occasion, he had been caught in the open. What had begun as a distant, indefinable yet somehow ominous drone, had increased in intensity with terrifying speed and volume until the noise was almost intolerable, so loud that the ground had actually shaken with its unbearable power. A wild, primal panic had seized Artorynas. With frantic haste he had pulled his pack apart and huddled trembling beneath the flimsy cover of its fabric, his hands over his ears, his eyes squeezed tightly shut, unable to stop himself from crying out in terror. And then, when the sound had reached such a pitch as to render all rational thought impossible, it had abruptly ceased completely, leaving his hearing stunned and deadened. Shivering again, Artorynas took a cautious step outside the cave. As far as his view stretched the land seemed as empty as ever, withered and barren under an empty blue sky; but during that day's anxious walking he found the same signs as he had seen before. Very few animals made their homes here, just rabbits, rodents, small burrowing creatures. And those that had been caught too far from their holes and warrens lay here and there, or all that was left of them: the fur still smooth and supple, but limp and empty, even the eyes gone, as if everything had been sucked out, leaving only a husk; and each pelt unmarked except for a neat round hole with barely a trace of blood around it.

Artorynas was sure now that Astell had been correct in his warning that some unknown horror made its home here in the northern wilderness, and that it struck from above. Was this what men meant by blindworms? He had no mental picture to go with the name and could not help constantly turning to look about him and above, slowing his slow progress still further. For days on end now he had been heading across Aestron na Caarst, the mountains receding gradually behind him, an empty horizon before him. When he had first gazed out over this northern wilderness, he had been surprised by what met his eyes. The land, rather than dropping down again from the crest to which he had climbed, stretched before him at the same elevation, a high plateau whose nearer edge formed the slope down to the upland plain where the circle of stones stood. However there were two things he had noticed. He had quickly discovered that, while the ground was level overall, the plateau undulated in many empty valleys and low ridges; but as he walked on and on, it struck him that the land was tending to slope gently, almost imperceptibly downwards before him towards the north; and furthermore, in that same direction, there was a subtle change in the quality of the light, especially where earth met sky. He was considering the possible significance of these observations when, during the day after he heard the second blindworm, if such it was, he crested a rise and began to drop down into a wide grey valley whose further side rose without feature in the far distance. Suddenly he halted, staring in disbelief. If it had been a shock to look upon the circle of stones after seeing the picture of them that Numirantoro had made, here surely was an even greater portent.

Standing on the bleak slope as it swept away down before him, he gazed at the emptiness and realised he had seen it before. He was now standing exactly at the point where he had stood in his childhood dream, long ago: the unsettling dream that he had shared with Arval and had never forgotten. He remembered describing the desolate scene, and Arval telling him he had looked in sleep upon the wilderness; and then Arval had shown him the book with the picture of the stones in it. Slowly Artorynas began to descend into the barren valley, his feet brushing through the harsh, wiry grasses; and by evening he was climbing the far slope. The light was fading now, and Artorynas looked about him for a camping-place. He stopped among some rocks, manhandling those he could manage into new positions, hollowing out a shallow depression in the ground to improve his refuge. As he worked he felt the temperature dropping, the chill creeping from the ground into his feet. Here in the wilderness, when the sun shone unclouded it burned down without mercy but the nights were bitterly cold. Suddenly his heart rebelled against the loneliness and fear in a hungry craving for the comfort of fire. Artorynas could not resist, but took great care for safety nonetheless. He had no means of knowing whether the thing that made the noise hunted by night, so his firepit was small, dug deep and shielded by his firescreen and yet more rocks and stones. The tiny glow warmed his meal pot as, cold and pale, the full moon rose and cast its wan light down upon him.

Alert and watchful though he sat, his back to the fire, his golden eyes, wide with night-sight, fixed upon the surrounding darkness, Artorynas' thoughts ran restlessly to and fro. His heart ached with memories and doubts: scenes from long ago played out before him, the mystery of his errand weighed upon him, the constant fear that time was running out gnawed at him. At last he crawled into his den like some creature of the wild and lay down to sleep, oppressed by the vast silence of that huge, empty darkness.

Vorynaas calls a meeting

'So, gentlemen: to business. Naturally I've formed my own opinions about these strangers from the north, and doubtless those of you who have spent time with them' – here Vorynaas nodded towards Valahald – 'have done so as well; but first impressions can be useful whether right or wrong, so let's hear what the rest of you have to say after yesterday evening. Valestron?'

'Well, they're pleasant enough in small doses, although I myself would tire of their company very quickly. Some of us here had the misfortune to waste their young years in Gwent y'm Aryframan, as it was then, and I was strongly reminded of those days when talking to them, especially to Haldur: but then I suppose that's natural enough, if it's true that there was a southerly migration from Rihannad Ennar in the distant past.'

'Yes, you've put your finger on something there,' said Thaltor. 'They've got that same "I'm a plain-speaking fellow and proud of it" air about them. In fact I was informed in no uncertain terms last night that they don't hesitate to speak their minds, in the Nine Dales, and they'd do the same here whether I liked it or not.'

Vorynaas laughed. Thaltor was growing lazy in his middle-aged security but his hold over his short temper was as uncertain as ever. Maybe a jolt to your comfort would do you good, my old friend, thought Vorynaas... but let's see how the meeting goes, first.

'What about you?' he asked, turning to a younger man.

This was Temenghent, Thaltor's second-in-command at Seth y'n Carad, and keen to make a good impression. 'I notice that they're always asking things, especially that young fellow Tellapur and Asaldron as well. Why all the questions? Maybe they've come to spy on us.'

Now it was Thaltor's turn to laugh. 'No, no, they wouldn't have the wit for it. You should have seen them yesterday morning when I took them round the city. Mouths open wider than their eyes, gaping at all the wonders on show. It was one question after another then too, but they were like children at school who are still ignorant of the world.'

'Well, I gather their journey home will have to be timed for early next year, so we're stuck with them at least until then. Better get used to your new tutorial role in case you find yourself their guide again.'

The sly amusement was easy to hear in Valestron's voice, and Thaltor swung round on him angrily. 'By my right hand! I'm not trailing hither and yon across Caradward showing them the sights, so don't think I am!'

'You'll do it if I say you will. And the same applies to the rest of you, make no mistake about that.' Vorynaas paused to let this sink in and let the silence continue until even Valahald, who had been scowling down at the floor in silence, had been forced to look up. Then he sat back, glancing round the table. 'There's something between Haldur and that Aestrontor fellow: anybody got any theories on what it might be?'

'Oh, there's no need to waste time on speculation. If anyone had asked me earlier, I could have told them exactly what they've got in common. They were both members of some company, back in the Nine Dales; young people, who ride about calling themselves the Hounds of the Starborn. Apparently they keep up these old superstitions in Rihannad Ennar.'

Valahald spoke in a careless, almost bored tone. He was determined to wait until Valestron was out of the way and he could get Vorynaas on his own before he tried to insinuate some of the ideas that were forming in his mind. Vorynaas contemplated his son-before-the-law. Obviously something had happened between him and the strangers that had touched him on the raw; equally clearly, Vorynaas saw that the younger man was concealing something. Valahald could be extremely devious, he knew; and probably that business of sending Haldur and his companions to Tellgard was part of some maliciously-convoluted response to an insult. He would get to the bottom of it in due course, but meanwhile he was not prepared to let Valahald's manner go unchecked.

'Perhaps you'd also like to enlighten us as to why you thought it necessary to leave your province in order to personally escort half a dozen old-fashioned types all the way down to Caradriggan.'

Valahald saw Valestron smirk at this piece of sarcasm, but having swallowed a precautionary measure of the potion from the *Sword and Stars* before the meeting he was able to master his anger, and his response was cold and calculated.

'Let me assure you that the administration of Rosmorric is under complete control. But the provision of an escort surely speaks for itself. These men have been monitored from the moment they appeared out of the wilderness, right down through my brother's jurisdiction and into mine. Would it have made any sense to permit them to wander off on their own wherever their fancy took them once they left Framstock? They maintained they wanted to see Caradriggan: I felt it would be salutary for them to realise that they would be seeing Caradriggan whether they had a wish to or not.'

'Yet you did not travel with them from the first?'

'There were certain duties I had to attend to, and the necessary arrangements to make for Heranar to take over in my absence.'

Valahald felt uneasy at the way Vorynaas was probing at his motives and actions, remembering how he had once accused him of over-complicating an assignment. What if it came out that he had delayed questioning Morancras until it was too late? Valahald much regretted now that he had not hauled the fairytale-peddling old fool in sooner. He decided to take a calculated risk.

'I was under the impression that this meeting was called to discuss the travellers from the Nine Dales, not my own reasons for coming down to Caradriggan.'

A little snigger from Valestron made them all look round at him. 'You can get off your high horse, Valahald. Your father's goings-on aren't on the agenda.'

Staring back at his hated rival, Valahald congratulated himself for his foresight in obtaining the calming concoction. The day will come, he thought; but his face betrayed no emotion and his voice was level.

'My family's business is no-one's concern except my own. But with regard to these men from Rihannad Ennar: I don't like them and more to the point, I don't trust them. Nor do I see any reason why Lord Vorynaas should take on the burden of supporting them at his own expense. If they must stay among us for the next few months, let them pay their own way at the *Sword and Stars* or some other inn; or failing that, why not let them stay in Tellgard as I originally arranged? That would show them soon enough what happens here to those too stubborn to turn away from the old superstitions, and teach them to be less forward in boasting about their own customs.'

Valestron, thinking this was the end of it, shrugged off-handedly but froze in his seat as Valahald added a venomous little tailpiece.

'And as to my father, I will deal with Valafoss as I see fit; but everyone here knows that my paternal duties as well as my loyalties have been owed to Lord Vorynaas alone these five years now.'

Well, well, thought Vorynaas. I see the day coming when I may be left with just one of these two, or neither; clearly the ranks of those who hold office below me are not wide enough to accommodate them both. His dark eyes slid from one rival to the other, and the two younger men, noting that sardonic gaze, sat back with a show of indifference. The discussion now shifted this way and that as each man had his say; and then Vorynaas, while seeming to summarise proceedings, revealed what he had intended from the start should be done. The meeting broke up, those who had attended either returning to their regular duties or hurrying off to ensure that Vorynaas' instructions were carried out. By nightfall the word was all over the city that the strangers would be included by invitation at the next assembly of Tell'Ethronad, to which every eligible delegate was bidden to come; and messengers were already far away, hastening along the main highways the length and breadth of Caradward with orders that all distant members of the council who could were to be present when it next gathered.

Unexpected information

When the day came, the council chamber was thronged as it had not been in years. Attendance had fallen off as Vorynaas' hold on power gradually tightened: those opposed to him had learnt the hard way that at best they were wasting their time in being there, and at worst could incur the risk of reprisal; while for those who backed him the novelty of carrying every vote had long since faded when in their hearts they knew Vorynaas would have his own way regardless. But today curiosity combined with orders had produced a crowded chamber. Even Valafoss was there, sweating uneasily in his seat. Vorynaas watched as men came in and sought their places, turning their heads for a better look at the strangers who sat together facing the entrance. Now a stir by the door heralded the appearance of Arval and his friends. The men from Rihannad Ennar had been gazing about them and Vorynaas smiled behind his hand as he saw Haldur and his companions notice the contrast between the Tellgard party and those who were already seated. Obedient to his instructions, the majority of delegates were dressed in their richest clothes and adorned with jewellery and expensive accoutrements; but not so Arval and his followers. There they were, Forgard, Heretellar, Rhostellat and the others, plainly attired as usual: indeed in this company seeming not so much sober as almost shabby. Yes: look well, Haldur, thought Vorynaas, moving smoothly on to the public demonstration of his power that he had planned. Welcoming the travellers from the Nine Dales to Tell'Ethronad, he proceeded to the business of the day, speaker after speaker endorsing his will, belittling and drowning out the voices of Arval and his small band of adherents. Vorynaas noticed however that Valahald, although apparently composed enough, sat silent and detached; and reflected that it would do the young man no harm to see how much more effective this handling of the situation was than his own idea of shutting up all birds of the same feather in the one coop at Tellgard.

At last the formal agenda was concluded and now Vorynaas invited Haldur to address the assembly. Naming and introducing his companions, Haldur spoke briefly, responding to the welcome they had received and expressing the hope of seeing more of Caradward before it was time to travel back home. Some of his audience had questions to put, the younger men interested in details of their adventurous journey while the elders probed for information about the Nine Dales. Haldur let Asaldron deal with much of this: he sat by, wishing Arval would ask something so that they could establish contact. Vorynaas, watchful in his high seat, saw Haldur's eyes rove about the room, lingering on the tracery of the high windows and the delicate lamps. He assumed the young man to be overawed by his elegant surroundings, to which, no doubt, he was unaccustomed. How could he know that Haldur was imagining scenes from the past that had been enacted here, that his mind's eye was seeing Artorynas defying Vorynaas in this very chamber? He noted with approval the way his own men patronised the northerners with condescending tones and smiles, but his satisfaction with proceedings received a sudden setback. A stolid-looking man who fingered his broad gold belt as he spoke had been enquiring about the possibilities of trade, but found himself interrupted.

'Oh really, Morstann! Trade is a two-way process, surely? But it sounds to me as though any exchange with the Nine Dales would be heavily weighted in their favour rather than of mutual benefit.'

Asaldron rounded on this speaker, stung by his supercilious tone. 'Are you not going to introduce yourself, before you jump to conclusions about Rihannad Ennar?'

'Yes, certainly.' The man was still comparatively young, with a lazily arrogant manner. 'I am Haartell of Staran y'n Forgarad.' He sat forward as if for emphasis. 'I am in charge of the gold mine.'

Immediately, Vorynaas' dark brows drew down. Men exchanged glances as he fixed Haartell with his black gaze. 'In charge of running operations at the mine,' he said with pointed emphasis.

There was a brief, awkward silence and then the man called Morstann, looking doubtfully from Vorynaas to Haartell and back, began to mutter something about corn supplies. Vorynaas cut him off in mid-sentence with a forceful gesture. Curse the man, he thought; I'll have no money-grubbing merchant spoiling the impression I want to make on these fellows from the Nine Dales. He turned to Asaldron.

'There is no commodity we are looking to purchase. If you wish to take items of our goldsmiths' art home with you, these are available to buy, though I should warn you the price is high.' He stroked his beard, considering. 'Are we to assume that you do in fact have a trade exchange in mind? If so, why did you not say so from the start?'

The colour had come up in Asaldron's face; his blue eyes, bright under the fair hair, locked proudly with Vorynaas' brooding stare. Before he could stop himself, the words were spoken.

'We have not come to trade.'

Haldur's mind began to race. He looked at his cousin and was reminded painfully of his father, although he knew Carapethan would never have allowed himself to be so carried away by anger as to abandon without warning one of the carefully thought-out pretexts for their journey. And to think it was Vorardynur who had been left at home as being too hot-headed! But a quiet voice spoke.

'Tell us then why you are here.'

Asaldron's blood was still up: since he could not take back what he had said, he would give these Caradwardans something more.

'We are in this city under duress. We came in friendship, seeking Gwent y'm Aryframan and our kin from long ago, but found that you have taken that land and its people into bondage. So then we thought to see Caradriggan before we returned homeward, to make our long journey worth the while; but when we spoke of this, Valahald there brought us south under guard whether we wanted it or not.'

Men murmured to each other and shifted in their seats, but silence fell as Vorynaas spoke. 'Lord Valahald is one of my governors and it is a duty of his high office to safeguard the security of his people.'

Haldur stood up, indicating to a furious Asaldron that he should resume his seat. The quiet voice had belonged to Forgard: here, at last, was the opportunity they needed, if he could only dissemble convincingly enough. Haldur's hair turned with a silvery sheen as he ran his hand through it, and fell down heavily again on to his forehead. He forced himself to smile around the chamber.

'Valahald and I have already agreed that many things may change over the course of time. Though I and my companions find it strange that you are so wary of us, I acknowledge the hospitality of Lord Vorynaas.' With the tail of his eye Haldur saw Forgard and Arval watching and a sudden inspiration came to him.

'Let us all join in ensuring that though we may have differences, we do not make these into difficulties. It seems that many of you regard the Nine Dales as backward and old-fashioned and think that away in the north there we cling to the past in a wilful adherence to outdated values and beliefs. It is true that we look for the As-Geg'rastigan to return; but you are wrong to believe that we reject the new and yearn for the past: rather, we have vowed to remember the errors of old in order to move forward and never repeat them. Surely all of us owe it to our children to extend our hands in friendship in order that *Vala na Naasan* is never repeated, that we never bring the fires of death upon earth again.'

As he neared the end of this speech, Haldur became aware of the effect his words were having upon his audience. By the time he sat down, men were staring at him in a breathless silence, and an instant later, heads were together in a gabble of talk. Vorynaas slapped his hand onto the board before him.

'Order!' he called, and with perfect timing, Arval took advantage of the sudden quiet. Thin-faced and frail-seeming in his plain dark robe he stood, but Haldur heard the power in his voice.

'Answer me, Haldur. Do you speak figuratively, when you talk of battle accursed; or do you mean what we refer to as the bad time, when men's evil deeds drove the Starborn from the earth?' As he spoke, he and several others near him made the sign.

'No, I speak of historical fact, of which I see that you too have knowledge.'

An indefinable expression passed across Arval's face. 'With regret, I must contradict you. This is lore which we have allowed to slip from memory in Caradward and it is not preserved in our records. I call upon you now to remedy our ignorance by revealing to Tell'Ethronad what you know.'

'This is a council meeting, not some damned poetry class,' barked Vorynaas. 'You can spare us the ancient history. If Arval's so keen to hear it, let him ask you down to Tellgard tomorrow.'

All around the room, eyes swivelled back to Haldur, whose own gaze was fixed on Arval. 'I will be honoured to stand within a *numiras* which has known the presence of the Starborn,' he said.

This time, even though Vorynaas glowered darkly down, even though Haartell and Valestron and others affected indifference, at Haldur's reference to Tellgard it was not just Arval and those around him who made the sign.

Vorynaas sensed the focus of the meeting slipping away from him and moved swiftly to limit any damage to his prestige. Sooner than he had intended, he wound up business for the day and swept off with his entourage; but at a nod from him, Temenghent and two or three others stepped forward, separating Haldur and his companions from the throng that pressed towards them as neatly as dogs cutting ewes from a flock. Elated in spite of all at the thought of talking with Arval so soon now, Haldur smiled to himself as this image came into his mind, and the smile broadened as he caught Temenghent's eye and saw how the young man was puzzled by his amusement. By evening, even within Seth y'n Carad it was obvious that word of what had happened was spreading like wildfire. The servants who brought in the food stared with open curiosity, loitering over their duties as if hoping they too might hear something of which rumour spoke; and in the street outside the compound a crowd had gathered, peering in hopefully. But the men from the Nine Dales, though left to their own devices, kept themselves to themselves. They had seen the heavy guard at the gates and had no wish to compromise their chances of being allowed to proceed unhindered next day.

326

Haldur keeps his promise

In the morning they were awake in the dark before Caradriggan's murky dawn. As he emerged from the bath-house, Cathasar encountered Temenghent who appeared to be off duty. Receiving what seemed a rather embarrassed response to his cheerful greeting, on impulse Cathasar stopped.

'Coming down to Tellgard with us, if you're free this morning?' he suggested.

'No, no.' Temenghent half turned away. 'I'm a soldier. I don't hold with all that kind of thing,' he muttered.

Cathasar laughed. 'All the more reason to learn how men slid into wars they could have prevented. After all, as I'm sure you've heard said here, knowledge is power.' He indicated the open-sided shed into which Temenghent was apparently staring and which contained wood for bow-staves, stacked for seasoning. 'I'm an archer myself, in fact I'm the champion of Rihann y'm Aldron, back home.'

Temenghent had looked round when Cathasar laughed, but saw that his amusement held none of the edge he was used to from Thaltor. Cathasar smiled again.

'Well, it's up to you. I must be off, I can't keep them waiting.'

He walked away, leaving Temenghent standing staring after him, baffled and irresolute.

At last then, the travellers from Rihannad Ennar passed the doors of Tellgard and were greeted by Arval. If Haldur, in spite of all he had heard, was surprised at the extent to which this ancient seat of learning was crumbling into disrepair, he was even more amazed when he entered the great hall. It was packed to the doors: not only all those who taught and studied in Tellgard, but men and women of all ages, some with children, stood waiting expectantly. Haldur drew Arval aside.

'I thought we would speak with you alone! None of us has the skill to hold an audience such as this. Who are all these people?'

'They are those who look for the light, all those in Caradriggan who could be here today, be they lords or lowly. None who come to Tellgard are ever turned away: will you deny them?'

Haldur looked around him. He saw some faces he recognised from yesterday's proceedings in Tell'Ethronad, and many others who seemed to have left their work to be there: men with the tools of their trade, women whose clothes carried the smell of food and cooking. Here and there was some care-worn unfortunate whose arms showed the corn-sign or whose ears bore only a piercing where an amber drop should have swung; there were even some among the throng who seemed to have come from the garrison. They had taken a risk to be present: could he send them away without telling them what they had come to hear?

Ir'rossung pulled at his sleeve. 'You're the man for this, Haldur. Remember, I was there when we tested you in Cotaerdon. You might not be able to recite like Astell, but you've a natural feeling for words. It comes from your mother, and though it passed Heredcar by, you have it. Give them the learning they've lost, so their children won't lack the knowledge every youngster in the Nine Dales knows by heart.'

So Haldur stood up before them all to repeat both *Stirfellaedon donn'Ur* and *Vala na Naasan*, warning beforehand that this would not be easy listening; and indeed they heard him out in a shocked silence that continued long after he had finished. Clear before his eyes came the memory of how horrified Artorynas too had been, and his heart leapt when Arval asked him to come up to his study in order that both tales could be set down on paper. When all was done and he had copied down the words Haldur recited to him, Arval closed his book and sat in silence for a moment.

'You tell me a token payment is required,' he said eventually, 'so what shall this be?'

'I would have you renew the pledge, you and I alone,' said Haldur.

'Come with me then.' Arval led the way to the secret room behind the sanctuary, but catching sight of Haldur's face as he lit the lamp, he paused.

'What is it?' he asked.

'Arval the Earth-wise.' Haldur heard his own voice tremble and steadied himself. 'Lord Arval, I have a vow to keep. I promised Artorynas that if you and I ever met, I would tell you that he reached the Nine Dales.'

For a long moment, Arval stood motionless and silent. Then he spoke. 'Where is he now?'

'I cannot say; all I know is that he set out again early this year to continue his northward quest, seeking Asward donn'Ur.'

Arval put his hands to his face, brushing away the tears that brimmed in his eyes. 'We will celebrate the rite together first, and afterwards you shall tell me what I have waited so long to hear.'

Much later, they went down together to the old wooden bench seat in the shadowy court. Arval had made Haldur repeat his story over and over, as if he would never tire of hearing it, but now they were quiet. Lamps burned in the hot, breathless evening and each man sat silent with his thoughts; but then Arval turned to his companion.

'He will succeed, I know it. He will return, he will bring us hope. Do you not feel this also?'

Haldur looked at Arval. 'He will return at least, for he told me he had sworn to do so. Didn't he promise you that he would stand beside you once more before seven years had passed?'

'He did.' Arval sighed. 'And long ago I promised his mother I would guard and guide him, but for five years now he has been gone, gone far beyond my protection.'

'Well, then at least there's a much shorter time left to wait,' said Haldur, not knowing quite how to respond. 'Within two years more at most, you will see him again.' He bit off his final phrase as ill-omened, not adding the words that came into his mind: *if he lives*. Instead, he glanced up into the heavy darkness above.

'Far in the north, even at this late hour the sun will not yet have gone down. Maybe at the very moment that we sit here, Artorynas is achieving his quest.'

'Yes, maybe so. Haldur, you have brought light back into an old man's dark dreams. May it shine on Artorynas, may he walk with the Starborn! Let us sit here just a little longer, before we go in to our rest.'

'Of course.' Hearing the smile in Arval's voice, Haldur smiled back and they sat on for a while listening to the robin warbling from the tree beside the lamp; but the darkness oppressed him and he could not prevent the unspoken words from echoing in his heart.

The As-Geg'rastigan

In Aestron na Caarst, Artorynas walked on and on far into the evening. Somehow he felt wearier than usual. Even after so many years of wandering, today his legs ached and his back was bent under the load he carried. Perhaps it was simply that he had slept badly during the previous night, on that bleak grey valley-side, and was not sufficiently rested. Grim thoughts, the bitter sense of having no place where he truly belonged, had disturbed his dreams; again and again he had waked to see faces from the past vanish as he opened his eyes. And all day as he trudged along, the fear that time was running out, that only failure awaited, grew in him until its weight was heavier to bear than the pack on his shoulders. He stopped for a moment, stretching his protesting muscles. After climbing over the shallow crest of the valley-side where he had slept, he had walked all day across fairly level terrain; but now as he looked about him, he sensed more strongly than before that the ground was imperceptibly sloping away. He was more certain than ever, too, that there was some different quality to the light, something which baffled his attempts to define it. The declining sun burned on his left cheekbone as he stared ahead into the distance. It would be some time yet before actual sunset and the light would last long after that; but there was no escaping the fact that it must be two months after midsummer and far in the north though he now was, the days were beginning to shorten again. Artorynas felt his stomach tighten as once more a feather of panic brushed lightly at him. There was no time to stand staring, he must move on.

The sun was shining right into the corner of his eye now as he walked. Suddenly he checked, listening. There had been scarcely a sound all day, except the brushing of his feet through vegetation. Low-growing, shrubby willow and tough heather stems scraped against his boots as he walked, and when he paused there was nothing but the sigh of air moving over the land. Fear rose in his throat again. If a blindworm or other unknown creature of dread should come, there was no cover anywhere, nowhere to hide. But this was not the visceral terror he had experienced before: rather, it was a tremor as of awe before some long-awaited, scarce hoped-for revelation. No, what he had heard – thought he had heard – was a sound unlike anything he had ever heard before: a hint, the merest hint, of something at once so sweet, yet so powerful… but it was gone. Strain his ears though he might, it had faded beyond recall. Artorynas raised his head and found himself trembling slightly. Now he noticed how the sunlight seemed to pick out a shining path before him, a broad straight way where grass divided the scrub. He began walking again, the sward soft and green beneath his feet. His new course had turned a little west of north so that the sun was now directly before him.

And now he heard that tantalising thread of sound again, but where did it come from? Artorynas began to walk faster as his heart started to race. The sound grew: it was beneath him, above him, around him. He wanted it to stop, and yet was desperate for it to go on for ever. Was it the sunlight, that blazed as if with a crash of brazen gold; was it the sky that seemed to speak in tones of unbearable purity; did the very earth have a mighty voice of thunder? Artorynas could not have said, for the sound was an irresistible force that welled around him, bearing him upon its flow even as it crushed him from above, filling his ears, tearing his heart, stopping his power of thought. Without being aware of it, he was running now, running as he had never done before, covering the ground in weightless, leaping strides straight into the sun; and as he ran, the tormenting loveliness of what he heard shimmered into substance before him and was made visible to his eyes. A mighty company of the As-Geg'rastigan passed before him, so that he saw their faces and heard their voices: now he recognised that unearthly quality he had noticed in the light, now he felt an energy that woke and danced in the very air.

In his heart he cried out to the Starborn, imploring them to wait, wait! Surely he had stepped through some veil from his own world into theirs, and if he could only run a little faster he would come up with them; but they were hastening into the distance too swiftly for him, strive to overtake them though he might. His breath sobbed in his throat; he ran and ran, the ground flew beneath his feet; and then suddenly he saw where his headlong course was leading. Before him the earth ended, and beyond it stretched the northern sea, its waves kindled to molten gold as the sun sank towards the water. A wild despair seized Artorynas: the As-Geg'rastigan, who could walk unseen, would tread this golden sunset path; in the very moment of his finding them, they would pass into their own world once more and leave him bereft. Again he called out in anguish, and though far away now, he saw their faces turn to him. With a speed beyond his strength, as if in a dream he ran on, faster and faster. Too late he realised that the ground fell away in a sheer cliff with the sea spread out far below at its feet; there was no way down. But the Starborn did not check, they swept on, straight into the sunset; and as they disappeared into its glory Artorynas caught a final glimpse of hands stretched out to him, bidding him follow. Consumed, like Numirantoro before him, by an overwhelming yearning for the As-Geg'rastigan whatever the cost, Artorynas followed without hesitation where they had gone, leaping after them: but their way was not his. For his feet there was no path beyond the cliff's edge. Through the golden air he plunged, and the golden sea rushed up to meet him as he fell.